Ellen Wiles is a writer, sound artist, and anthropologist, and teaches creative writing at the University of Exeter. She previously worked as a barrister and as a musician. This is her second novel. She lives in Devon with her family.

Also by Ellen Wiles

The Invisible Crowd

The Unexpected

Ellen Wiles

ONE PLACE. MANY STORIES

HQ
An imprint of HarperCollins*Publishers* Ltd
1 London Bridge Street
London SE1 9GF

www.harpercollins.co.uk

HarperCollins*Publishers*
Macken House, 39/40 Mayor Street Upper,
Dublin 1, D01 C9W8, Ireland

This edition 2024

1
First published in Great Britain by
HQ, an imprint of HarperCollins*Publishers* Ltd 2024

Copyright © Ellen Wiles 2024

Ellen Wiles asserts the moral right to be identified as the author of this work.
A catalogue record for this book is available from the British Library.

ISBN: 9780008267889

This book contains FSC™ certified paper and other controlled
sources to ensure responsible forest management.

For more information visit: www.harpercollins.co.uk/green

This book is set in 11.4/16 pt. Adobe Garamond by Type-it AS, Norway

Printed and Bound in the UK using 100% Renewable Electricity at
CPI Group (UK) Ltd, Croydon, CR0 4YY

A mother's canopy
and a baby's shoots –
in both of them the fingerprint
of ancient woods.
– Penny Boxall

> Bluntly put, motherhood has become a minefield,
> and we are walking through it
> without so much as a map to guide us
> – Sarah Blaffer Hrdy

Anything is more endurable than to change
our established formulae about women.
– George Eliot

> A friend may well be reckoned a masterpiece of nature.
> – Ralph Waldo Emerson

For my (allo)mother friends

Prologue

It was obviously a bad idea, in retrospect, to run away, age ten, in the middle of the night, in the middle of nowhere, in the middle of a different country – and yet it came to seem inevitable.

How that neon moon hung over the black trees like an overripe peach as they stood in the car park, dithering: Robin hanging back, Kessie urging on.

How, after they'd continued into the forest, following a frail torch beam, and found themselves lost, strange sounds began to close in on them – branches creaking like bad cellists, owl whoops and bat skitters, the moaning of distant planes, and the scuttle of giant, furry spiders – so very possible after that sleepover screening of *Arachnophobia* the week before.

How, as they stumbled on in the dark, over tree roots and potholes, fatigue entangled their fear. How, finally, once they could go on no longer and found a glade to lie down in, it seemed impossible that they would ever be able to get to sleep on that damp, knobbly earth, burrowed in blankets, shivering up against each other.

How ecstatic their delight when they woke, with aching

bodies, to find themselves in the epicentre of a vast orchestra of birdsong, surrounded by iridescent green! How they celebrated by leaping around like sprites and then binging on a glut of stolen custard creams from their backpacks. How visceral the sense of freedom, away from all the bitchy girls on the school trip, away from everyone except each other, protected beneath the canopy of a gnarled old oak which had quietly watched over them all night like a fairy godmother. How they vowed to stay besties forever, and to never take off their half-of-a-heart necklaces.

How delight ceded to panic when they realized that they had no idea how to get back to the outdoor pursuits centre and would be in a shiteload of trouble if they did. How that distant siren wail could be the police out looking for them already. How it might lead to prison or, worse, to enforced separation. How Kessie began to wail about what the news that they were missing might do to her mum, who was already turning translucent in her final months of illness.

How finally, late that afternoon, after they managed to find their way back, they were not in fact met with shouts and dire punishments, but instead by faces creased with worry. How they learned, then, what had happened – not to Kessie's mum, after all – but to Robin's dad during the night.

PART I

Chapter 1

Robin

The bus shunts forward in the traffic, then stops. Grinding her teeth, Robin asks herself why oh why she didn't just get a taxi. But it's just a small slice of time. She needs to be more like Berlioz, her bristlenose catfish, who spends his days contentedly inching along the glass of her tank while the prettier fish flicker about.

A shaggy man gets on at the next stop and tries to persuade the driver to let him ride even though his card isn't working, and a snake of impatient passengers lengthens outside with glowering faces like scales in the rain. She texts Kessie to say she'll be late.

Kessie will be powering along on her bike right now, regardless of the weather, perhaps turning into Brick Lane already, with that enormous waterproof Eighties purple cape billowing behind her. Robin has long envied Kessie's talent for finding distinctive vintage clothes bargains and her confidence in flaunting them – but then Kessie doesn't have to wear corporate attire five days a week. Robin usually ends up buying most of her own clothes at the Jigsaw by the office during snatched lunch breaks, and mostly sticking to black or navy.

She pulls her book out of her bag: Margaret Mead's *Coming of*

5

Age in Samoa. She's meant to present on this text to her anthropology seminar group next week, but it's proving so hard to fit in all the reading and writing she needs to do to keep up with the master's degree alongside her job. It still stings that Sanjay has refused to let her go part-time, even though she's worked her guts out for the company for a decade. He clearly thinks it's ridiculous for her to be doing another degree that's not an MBA. And maybe it is. But the truth is she couldn't care less about increasing corporate profit margins, and this job was only ever meant to be a means to an end, namely not feeling anxious about money all the time.

As the only woman in the senior management team, it often feels like the others are constantly on the lookout for new ways to undermine her, despite the fact that she brings in more money than most of them. Or perhaps because of it. Anyway, she's pretty sure they've already put their neatly cropped heads together and agreed she's likely to take maternity leave before too long, just because she's in her thirties and has ovaries, and that they should therefore wring her out before that day comes. Which seems like another reason to put off having a baby, just to prove them wrong . . . But the fact is that her 35th birthday is coming up next month, and that's a fertility tipping point.

She's going to have to talk about this seriously with Max. It's not as if she hasn't tried. But he always brushes her off, says he's not ready – that he wants the stability of a permanent academic job before committing. Which is sort of fair enough. But then he's two years younger than her, and as Sally pointed out to Harry in the movie, it's not the same for men: Charlie Chaplin had babies when he was seventy-three. Even though, as Harry retorted, he couldn't pick them up.

To be fair, she hasn't exactly sprinted to retrieve the topic from the long grass. Partly because, although she definitely wants to have a family one day, she's always been secretly grossed-out by the whole idea of growing an alien protohuman among her internal organs – a creature that could cause extreme nausea for nine months and rip her vagina upon exit. Her phobia of injections and tendency to faint at the sight of blood don't bode well either. She's not sure why more women don't seem to fear pregnancy. As for breastfeeding – well, it's just too weird to imagine doing that herself.

But most women just get on with it and take the risk. Multiple times. And she does love kids. Definitely when they've got past the baby phase, which seems like a lot of work. She loves their imaginations, their hilarious comments, and their ability to live in the moment, which she finds herself struggling to do more and more these days. She'd love to read her own child the books she'd loved when she was little, like the Little House on the Prairie series . . . though that would probably be completely different upon rereading. The whole concept of the white settlers making their way across indigenous territory and setting up towns at whatever human cost is awful to contemplate. But there must be plenty of great new children's books to discover . . .

She finds herself staring into the window of a new burger bar with hospital-bright lighting and red and white decor that's somehow already packed with diners – then blinks hard and returns to her book. Apparently, when a Samoan baby is born, the whole village community gathers in support, and there's a big celebration when the umbilical cord is buried, but after that, the child's birthdays go unmarked until after puberty, and precise ages get forgotten. This, Mead explains, reflects the emphasis on relative age over individual age in Samoan society, and indicates the value of the collective over the self. Robin underlines this part. It's hard to conceive of a life not punctuated by annual birthday celebrations. She loves that about anthropology – the way it blows your mind in tiny ways.

Outside her window, a cyclist seems about to be squashed between the bus and the pavement. Robin jerks her head away, unable to avoid replaying the moment that supermarket lorry crushed her dad on his ride home from work, the night that she and Kessie were busy losing themselves in the forest. It had invaded her sleep for so long, this imaginary movie clip, that she'd had to see a therapist. She'll never ride a bike in a city as an adult – never. Max didn't even manage to persuade her to do it in Amsterdam. But what would she regret a few years from now if she were to be killed in a freak accident? Not quitting her job? Probably. Not having a child? Almost certainly. If only her dad were still here to cook her his special cassoulet and talk through all these things over dinner in his calm bass voice. If only her mum hadn't emigrated to live with a bunch of sheep.

She reads a few more pages, then leans her head against the window, allowing the engine vibration to make her brain buzz in her skull. She loves the sheer sass of Margaret Mead's decision to head off solo to Polynesia back in the 1920s – when women had only just won the battle for suffrage – and then to return to the US a year later and knock off an anthropology classic, defying expectations of what anthropology could and should do. And what women could and should do, for that matter. Part of her is so ready to quit consultancy, to fly away and spend time researching what it's like to exist in a completely different culture. To spend time walking around in sunshine instead of sitting around in office air con, wearing flip-flops instead of polished shoes, and learning from people with craft skills instead of managers with balance sheets. But she has a mortgage to pay. And Mead went off to Polynesia when she was still in her twenties – young enough to live out there, return home, write a book, and then have a child.

The bus grinds to a halt. The rain has intensified, and the pavement is alive with colourful umbrellas ducking and dodging each other like fish in a reef. How did she come to be tiptoeing around Max on the topic of kids? When they first met, she'd thought the age gap was too big; she was two years ahead of him at university when they'd kissed at a party. He'd asked her out, and her refusal didn't seem to bother him; he was dating plenty of prettier girls. But when they bumped into each other in a coffee shop on Holloway Road years later, he was doing his PhD in archaeological anthropology and was just back from a year in Sicily, while she was climbing the consultancy ladder and was about to buy her first flat – and the age gap felt meaningless.

At the next stop, a woman with a buggy gets on, manoeuvres it into the space in front of Robin, and plonks herself on the seat next to her. She's wearing an oversized olive raincoat, and pulls the hood down to reveal a frizzy halo of hair and mascara smears. After a futile attempt to smooth her hair down, she closes her eyes. A long white slug trail extends down one thigh of her jeans. Dried milk vomit? High-pitched shrieks emerge from the buggy, and the woman opens one eye, then gets up again to go and crouch down beside it.

9

Robin pulls out her headphones, plugs them into her phone, and searches for *Blue*. 'California' rolls into her ears and through her veins, its melodic waves glinting with Joni's mermaid voice. Closing her eyes and smiling a little, she imagines driving down the West Coast with Darsha, who keeps trying to persuade her to visit her in San Francisco again. She really should do it soon. Darsha is living the good life out there, and clearly doesn't regret leaving the UK one iota. It's always sunny, her design business is going great, she has all kinds of cool clients with exciting briefs, and she's living in this intellectual commune and constantly going to amazing events and on trips to Burning Man and Lake Tahoe. She has absolutely *no* intention of tying herself down with kids any time soon. Robin pictures the two of them, reunited, borrowing the commune's car – which is probably open-top like the one in *Thelma and Louise* – and heading off on a road trip . . . playing Nineties tunes and reminiscing about their gap year travels . . . pulling up at Big Sur and running towards the turquoise waves . . .

Sensing that she's being watched, she opens her eyes again. The raincoated woman has returned to the seat next to her with her baby, who is now sitting on her lap, inches away from Robin, and staring unflinchingly at her with mauve-grey eyes. A forgotten tear hovers on one silken cheek. On its head, a tuft of coppery hair swirls up in an absurd Tintin quiff that reminds her of the baby orangutan on the David Attenborough doc she watched the other night. She gives the baby a small smile – and to her surprise, it grins back, revealing a single gleaming tooth.

'Hi!' she finds herself saying, in that squeaky baby-talk voice that often irritates her when other people use it. She wants to return to her reading, but can't quite tear her eyes away. Remembering a childhood picture book that she'd salvaged before her mum sold up, she covers her eyes with her palms, then uncovers them. 'Peepo!'

The baby's smile expands, and it emits a gurgle like a woodland spring. 'She likes you!' the mother says.

Robin's heart cracks open a little, and she tries the trick again. The second eruption of tinkly laughter from the baby triggers a rush inside her, not unlike the effect of the shrooms Kessie made her try that time in Berlin – as if all her veins have filled with light. She feels like taking this baby in her arms and rubbing her cheek in its bright hair.

Face burning, she turns and looks back out of the window, at the rain puckering the tarmac. She does crave that, after all. Not just a family, but a child who can find delight in small gestures, who can make her feel that tenderness. She wants to experience that depth of love that seems unique to mothers. It's palpable now in this woman next to her, despite her fatigue.

There are so many stressed commuters on the pavement, some bent low behind umbrella shields against the wind and wet, most probably worrying, like her, about client satisfaction and urgent deliverables. It's ridiculous to be getting so emotional about this random bus baby. Is she about to get her period? Or is she finally allowing herself to acknowledge the urgency of this desire, now that it's fizzing on the surface of her consciousness like a soluble vitamin?

She needs to talk to Max, and this time insist that he listens.

Chapter 2

Kessie

Masala, turmeric, sizzling chicken – bitter smoke and ripped tees – colour-shot saris and faded jeans – cigarette butts floating in puddles – a polystyrene box perched on a post – tie-dye tops and coal-smudged eyelids – turquoise locks and prune-dark lips – two stubbly men at each other's throats – backpacks, hunchbacks – boxes loaded with yellow dates, rice sacks that could feed five thousand – *Lady, are you hungry, special deal, take leaflet, wait* – new pop-up juice bars – tattooed arms – art sale posters, grunge-night flyers – slow-brewing fist fights and easy-care lovers . . . Kessie pauses outside the blue front door to the flat she once shared with Robin and Timmo. Good times. Even in the rain she loves this place.

She locks her bike up round the corner from the Truman Brewery and wipes her dripping face. Every Saturday late afternoon, she and Robin used to wander up Brick Lane and come here for a warm-up drink.

It's busy inside already, and she nabs the only free table. Robin's running late, so she pulls out her notebook to scribble some phrases, just in case they materialize into lyrics. It would be fun to recapture how she once felt about this area in song form. She wouldn't want to live back in its colourful anarchy now – she already feels too old, and if her baby plan comes off it's no place to be a new mum – but she misses it all the same. Misses who she was when she lived here, with Robin, happily broke. Not that it was all hunky-dory. Timmo was a friendly enough guy, but never saw the need to clear up after making himself a late-night bacon butty and leaving crumbs all over the place, and appeared never to have heard of a toilet brush.

It was the beginning of the end when the two of them moved to Holloway Road in order to extricate themselves from him. Weeks later, Robin bumped into Max while queuing for flat whites in the local hipster café. Their relationship evolved quickly enough that he soon started making noises about moving in if Robin bought her own place. Which was highly convenient, seeing as she'd saved up enough for a mortgage deposit and he could only afford to live in a scummy studio near Seven Sisters at the time.

It wasn't that Kessie was jealous of Robin exactly; she was delighted for her that she'd finally found a relationship that seemed to make her happy after a long desert of singledom. It was just that the impact on their friendship sucked. Before Max came along, Kessie had felt guilty about being constantly in a relationship when Robin never was. She'd basically been a serial monogamist (with occasional overlaps) from her late teens through her twenties. Most of her exes were fine, and some were lovely, but none felt like The One. Right now she would be much more willing to compromise on her ideals for a guy who was kind and sane and keen to start a family – but there seem to be no decent fish left in the sea. Meanwhile, Robin and Max are still going strong. Outwardly. Though she's not sure they're all that happy these days.

A tall guy walks up to the bar rocking an African print jacket in orange, black and green. He's light-brown-skinned with a neat 'fro, and Kessie wonders for a moment whether he's single, until a woman with pink hair slips her arm around him.

It was just up the road from here, in a tiny art gallery with a late night show, that she'd met that delicious Swedish architect who was exhibiting. What was his name again? Lars, that's it. She'd downed a vodka tonic and gone up to him to ask him what he would build and where if he had a blank cheque, and the evening melted into her first, and probably last, one-night stand. She can't remember much else about it – until the morning after. He looked beautiful in her bed, his lean arms glazed with golden hair. But over breakfast, he just talked lazily about himself and how great he was at everything. They never called each other again. At that point she was interested in someone else anyway: Jez, an African-American jazz trumpeter from Baltimore with perfect cheekbones and basketballer biceps. They'd kissed, but then he moved back across the ocean and she'd found someone else. So many wasted intimacies.

She taps on the Acorn app, newly downloaded. Her conventional online dating days are done – that guy with hair plugs who had the gall to suggest she straighten her 'fro was the final straw – but co-parent matching seems more promising. At least it theoretically removes from the table all the guys who are only out to get laid. It also seems like her best and most affordable chance of having a baby before her late thirties. It is a bit of an odd concept though. On one hand it seems radical; on the other, it's not unlike an arranged marriage.

A new message pops up and she taps on it. A cute Greek guy who favourited her earlier, and who she favourited back, has got in touch.

Hey Kessie, you look beautiful. I love that you're
a musician. Want to chat sometime?

His name is Angelo, which makes him sound like a renaissance artist or someone out of *The Wire*. He has a chiselled chin and shinier-than-natural hair, and neat brows framing dark eyes. His profile description says he 'values family more than anything' – a dull enough cliché, but also, in fairness, what she's looking for. He says he loves kids and works in finance, is into endurance sports, music, wine, and film, and enjoys exploring Greek islands on a Vespa. So far, so generic, apart from the last thing, which sounds pretty great.

She tries to picture their future baby. Tight curls, caramel skin, a dimply smile. Family holidays in the Greek islands could be glorious. They could hike between jewelled beaches, carrying the baby in a backpack, bounce him in shallow waves, then put him to bed, and sip rough red wine watching the sunset.

Hey Angelo, nice to hear from you! I've never ridden
on a Vespa but I'd like to try. So, Pinot Noir or Merlot?
Almodóvar or Spielberg? And which sports do you enjoy
enduring, if that's not a contradiction?

Another message pops up from Auntie Elmi in Nepal. A photo of a woman with a clarinet posing on the nunnery steps with children clustered around her, some striking kung fu poses.

Kessie, dearest! An Italian visitor produced his clarinet and played for us today – unexpected treat. Children adored it! If only you'd been here to make it a duet. XOXOXO

Kessie was eleven the first time she went to Nepal, to visit the foundation Auntie Elmi had set up to support girls' education at the orphanage where she and Kessie's mum used to volunteer. The scale of the mountains made her feel like Gulliver arriving in Brobdingnag, and the sky was so luminous it seemed as if the edge of the Earth was dissolving. It was strange but soothing to be taken around to visit her mum's favourite haunts for tea and dumplings, to meet the children being supported by the foundation, and to realize how absurdly lucky she was to have *had* a mother for ten whole years. A couple of grown-up nuns with shaved heads and bright smiles used the English words that her mother had once taught them to tell her how kind she had been.

She stares at Auntie Elmi's photo again, at one little girl reaching out for the man's clarinet. If she hadn't had this woman in her life as a kind of surrogate mother for so long she might well have gone off the rails in her teens, back in the days when her dad was consumed by his training for the ministry and often seemed to forget he had a daughter at home. It would be nice if Auntie Elmi didn't live so far away now – but their daily photo and message exchange is a huge comfort. Kessie holds up her drink to the light in one hand and her phone up in the other, smiles for a selfie, and types a few words to accompany it:

> Amazing! I'd so love to fly over and play a duet. I've started listening to Benny Goodman again lately – even improvising a bit. Miss our jazz days. Let's go to Ronnie Scott's again when you're next back in London? XOXO

A hand squeezes her shoulder. 'Hey hon, sorry I'm so late!'

Robin, finally. Kessie gets up for a hug. There seems to be even less flesh than usual on her friend's bones under the sleek suit. She steps back. Robin's face is chalky, and there are craters under her eyes. 'You look whacked.'

'Well thanks very much.' Robin cocks an eyebrow then sighs. 'You're right, but I'm happy to be out. I *love* your shirt – is that silk?'

Kessie rubs her sleeve. It is a lush emerald colour, and feels sumptuous on her skin. 'Shouldn't have splashed out, really. It's from this cute little vintage shop in Notting Hill, near where I teach.'

Robin heads to the bar for another round, and Kessie's phone pings. Not Auntie Elmi, this time, but a notification from the Acorn app: Angelo has replied.

> Hey Kessie. I'd love to give you your first Vespa experience. I guess I'd go for Merlot. I admit I've never watched an Almodóvar film, so I guess Spielberg. How about you? I enjoy ultramarathons, that kind of thing. Keeps me fit ;) Do you like running?

So he clearly hasn't seen *Sideways*. Which seems quite a feat for someone who claims to be into wine and film. And not a single Almodóvar movie either. As for ultramarathons, Kessie has never understood why anyone would want to run even a standard marathon. Isn't someone who runs multiple ultramarathons likely to be . . . *intense*? Whizzing on a Vespa around a Greek island, though: that could still work.

A couple are walking by her table. The woman, wearing dungarees, is shouting to her partner that it's too hectic in here. He is carrying a baby in a patchwork carrier strapped to his chest, and nods, smiling easily – as if nothing could make him happier than carrying his child around, following her lead.

Kessie types a reply, recommending *Sideways*, explaining that there's a Merlot vs Pinot joke in it, and asking him to explain what an ultramarathon is and why any sane person would want to do one. She deletes that last bit.

'Here you go!' Robin puts the drinks down on the table, takes her coat off, and glugs most of her G & T in one go. 'So, what do you think about a joint birthday party again this year?'

'Oh! Old school. I like it.' Their old joint party tradition had fizzled out when Max instituted an annual romantic city break for Robin's birthday weekend. They clink glasses.

'Maybe our last joint hoorah before one of us has a baby,' Robin muses.

Kessie leans forward. 'Something you need to tell me?'

Robin tips her head from side to side. 'Not what you're thinking. But I did just have a moment on the bus. This mum with a baby sat next to me, and the baby was super cute. I was just watching how they were together and something inside me just – *broke open*.'

'Welcome to the broody club,' Kessie grins.

Robin rolls her eyes. 'How's the donor hunt going?'

'Well – I reserved some jizz.'

'You did?'

'Yup. "Donor 2052" – I'm calling him Obamarama. He's half-Kenyan, a green energy advisor, plays the trombone, and likes paddle boarding and travelling . . . he's not cheap though.'

'How much?'

'Two grand. Including insemination. Just one round. And that's not even guaranteed to result in a pregnancy.' Saying it out loud makes it seem even more extortionate.

'Oof. Weren't you, I mean, struggling to pay your rent last month?'

This is a sensible point, obviously made with the best of intentions, but coming from Robin, with her mortgage on a lovely two-bed flat and her enormous income, it irks. 'Yeah, yeah, I know. I was thinking I could get some kind of admin job in the City or something – a friend of Jo's works as a receptionist at an investment bank . . . or maybe take a loan . . .'

Robin looks horrified. 'Er, please don't do that? And *definitely* don't go to a shark. I can lend you money if you need it. But the job thing sounds sensible too.'

'That's so sweet, but I wouldn't want to . . .'

'Honestly, Kess. I have savings – and of course I want to help you have a baby if I can! So, how much would you get in statutory maternity pay, do you know? '

Kessie's stomach tightens. It's another sensible question – but why should they have to be so unequal financially when they were always parallel growing up? It's never mattered much in their friendship until now. She has looked into the economics of single motherhood, and frankly childcare seems totally unaffordable, but there must be a way. She can't not become a mother just because she can't figure out the budget in advance. She sighs. 'Not much. But I'll manage. Other women do, right? Women who are single too, and working class, and who've had way more difficult lives than me.' She's starting to tear up – pathetic.

Robin, stricken, reaches over for her hand. 'Oh gosh, I'm so sorry – I didn't mean to suggest – that came out all wrong – you'll be fine. You'll be an amazing mum!'

Kessie blinks. 'Thanks. No, it's cool. You're totally right to raise it. You've always been a lot savvier about money. Anyway, I'm still not *completely* sure I'll have to go down the donor route.' She pulls up Angelo's profile picture on her phone and offers it over.

*

A week later, she's emerging from the Tube at Hyde Park Corner and following her phone map to Angelo's favourite pub. The route takes her down a tucked-away mews where all the little terraced houses have gaudy flower-box moustaches, must cost several million, and are probably all owned by the same oligarch. The pub is at the end of the road, and a llama-shaped cloud is hovering over it. A sign? Of what?

She heads in and looks around. No sign of him. On a whim, she orders herself a cherry brandy – her favourite drink in her early teens, ever since reading that scene in *I Capture the Castle* when sisters Rose and Cassandra go on their first double date. Rose vainly chooses a crème de menthe to complement her coppery hair, while Cassandra, the dark-haired clever one, goes for a cherry brandy, and it all works out for her in the end. Kind of.

She'd forgotten how sweet the drink is – like a medicine lollipop. *Cherry brandy, cotton candy, way to snag yourself a dandy . . .*

A couple of women come in wearing heels and leather jackets. It strikes Kessie that she's underdressed for this date in her leopard print cardigan, vintage Eighties Jaeger though it is. Her outfit might as well have SHOEBOX COUNCIL TENANT stitched in hot pink on the back. If Angelo's truly at home here in Knightsbridge, he surely wouldn't want his future child being brought up in the East London slums, would he? Maybe this whole co-parenting app experiment was a big mistake . . . But then she can't afford Obamarama's wares. Nor can she really afford to bring up a child on her own. She'll sign up with employment agencies this weekend. Send speculative covering letters to a clutch of investment banks and consultancy firms like Robin's . . .

'You must be Kessie?' Angelo is as chiselled as his picture, but a bit shorter than she'd expected, and architecturally gelled on top. He kisses her firmly on each cheek, and her first thought is to wonder whether his dense eyelashes translate into a hairy back. 'Wow, your hair's amazing!' he says, and pats it. She tries not to flinch. 'You look great. Even better than your profile. So, where are you from originally?'

'Bicester,' she says, with a tight smile. 'Or are you getting at my ethnicity?'

'Either? Both? Tell me all about you.'

'Okay.' She laughs. At least he's not easily riled. 'Well, I'm mostly British. But I'm also a quarter Nepali on my mum's side, and half Ghanaian on my dad's.'

He nods, eyebrows raised. 'Woah. That's cool. That where your name comes from?'

'Uh huh. It means cassia tree. They grow in Nepal as well as Ghana. How about you – your profile says you're Greek, but do I detect an American twang?'

He grins. 'I've spent some time over there. New York. D.C. Can I get you a drink?'

She says she's just had one, but if he's going for a Merlot, she might join him. He orders the wine for her, then orders a soda water for himself, which seems oddly virtuous for a wine lover on a first date. Turns out he has a 20k run in the morning.

They find a table, and he launches into quizzing her about her work, where she lives, her music, her hobbies . . . It feels a bit like a questionnaire, but it's nice that he's curious, and he does seem genuinely eager to listen. She takes on the respondent role with as much coquettish energy as she can muster, trying to sound as bubbly as possible about life as a musician, despite how erratic her gigs are these days, and how fed up she is with trekking around London to teach – and then she tries to turn the tables. A few times. But somehow he always manages to flip it back to her. Perhaps he's nervous, though he doesn't seem it.

When their glasses are empty, they head to Hyde Park. Out in the fresh air, walking among the gaggles of pigeons and tourists, chat flows more easily. Kessie finds herself splurging all kinds of things she hadn't planned to. About her mum's death, and what a wonderful singer and pianist and parent she had been. About how her dad had grieved for a while, but then 'found Jesus' who told him to quit being a plumber and start preaching, but failed to advise him against his second marriage to Cara, which involved taking on her three spoilt boys, her penchant for designer clothes, and her determination to erase all evidence of his former family. She tells him about Auntie Elmi – how she'd looked after her right through her teens, and then moved into a commune of Buddhist women until the 2015 earthquake in Nepal prompted her to move over there full-time, to help the kung fu nuns with food deliveries and education.

Angelo makes all the right noises, and guffaws at the idea of kung fu nuns. He looks them up on his phone to check the veracity of her story, as if she'd have made up something like that just to impress him. She can't help wondering what it would be like to do that – to go on a date, having pre-invented an absurd life story about your past as a trapeze artist with a pet anaconda. Aside from his scepticism, though, he really is a good listener.

She tells him about Robin too – how they've been besties since they were eight, when they randomly stood next to each other at their first junior choir practice one Saturday morning, and how, when they each lost a parent the same year, they started to rely on each other like sisters. Eventually, she clears her throat. 'Come onnn, Angelo,' she goads. 'I've told you so much about me, I'm getting hoarse – I need to hear about you!'

'You're getting a horse? Exciting.'

'Ha ha. Tell me about your family!'

He grins, shrugs. His dad is in banking, he says, and his mum is a homemaker. His brother's gone into accountancy too, over in the US, which sounds dull but pays for a nice lifestyle . . . but he's not done hearing about her yet. 'I want to know more about what it's *really* like to be a musician. It must be competitive, but such a fun job, right? Do you ever get nervous?'

'Well, sometimes . . .' Never crippling nerves, thankfully, like Robin used to get before she gave up the oboe. Kessie often wonders if non-musicians have the slightest idea of how much practice is needed to get to the 'fun' bits, not to mention how competitive and precarious it is to play professionally. She cherry-picks some more details about her work, somewhat exaggerating the ratio of her professional gigs over teaching. He admits he's never been to a classical concert, and couldn't tell the difference between Bach and Beethoven, but says he would like to go one day if she'd invite him. Although his reticence in talking about himself is a bit weird, it does feel kind of liberating to air the story of her life in some detail to the person who might, just *might*, become her baby's father – like flinging all her laundry out from her tiny concrete balcony, sheets, bras and all. If he doesn't like the difficult bits, he can call it off, and they can both move on, right?

But he seems to be into it. As they walk along the Serpentine, the sky turns a garish pink, and she laughingly insists that he tells her a *little* more about himself or she'll have to conclude he's a spy. He laughs loudly. 'Well, I guess if the spooks were to invite me, I might be interested.' He grins. 'But I quite like the predictability of working in finance. It means I can plan for my training, my races, you know?' He launches into a long account of an ultramarathon he did across the desert last year, down to the level of what freeze-dried meals they ate, what brand of sleeping bag and self-inflating mat he took, and who overtook who in what terrain in what temperatures.

Kessie murmurs words of admiration, and then, to lighten the tone, asks what animal he was in his most recent past life – presumably some hardy desert lizard?

After a pout, he says he's pretty sure he was a leopard, and that her cardigan print proves that she was too, and therefore they were meant for each other. A swan gliding by in the other direction seems to give her a dubious look, but she can't help smiling. He swings an arm around her shoulders, then pats her hair again as they walk on. 'I love big cats,' he muses. 'Seeing lions and leopards on safari was one of the best moments of my life. I'll take you sometime!'

'That would be fun,' she says. 'I've never been anywhere in Africa except Ghana when I was little.'

'I'd love to go to Ghana!' he beams. 'Tell me what it's like.'

As dusk is setting in, he tugs her gently to a stop, and looks into her eyes. 'I've been having such a great time with you, Kessie. *Such* a great time. And I just want to say something. I mean, I figure you have to pounce on an opportunity when it comes along, you know? Leopard-style . . .'

She scrunches her toes. What the hell is he suggesting – sex in the park?

'I can already tell that you would be an incredible mother,' he continues. 'And I just feel, in my gut, like there's a real spark between us. A deep connection.' He's looking at her as intently as if he were tossing darts into her pupils: *bam, bam, bullseye.*

Kessie feels her eyebrows tilt. It's all a bit full-on; but then there's no established protocol for a first co-parent date, is there? He's really quite handsome, especially in this light. Nerves probably account for some of his awkwardness. She has to be stricter with herself about being too fussy. And his genes seem decent enough. 'I know what you mean.' She smiles. 'I guess the question is whether that spark is strong enough to sustain a flame.' *Jesus*, she thinks – I sound cheesier than him.

But he grins, his teeth film-star straight. 'Well this wick is waiting to be lit, baby. So . . . can I taste that gorgeous smile of yours now?' He pulls her close, and tilts her head until their lips meet. He tastes of popcorn, and his scent is even more metallic up close. *Cinema seats, heartbeats syncing – tinned sweetcorn, swans honking – hands on bodies, hot Greek beaches – ticking clocks, ready or not . . .*

Chapter 3

Robin

Party time! Perching on a stool, Robin taps her maroon nails on the bar. She always forgets, until the day of hosting, the inevitable anxiety that no guests will show up. But so long as Kessie comes, it doesn't really matter. She orders two negronis from a bartender who has a delicate chain of olive branches tattooed up one brown, sinewy arm, and wants to ask where she got her grey jeans – such a flattering cut.

She checks her watch. This place was a good choice, with its stripped wood floors and fringed lampshades, and the soundtrack is spot on. She has no idea who the artist is. There's a bit of soul in there, a smidgen of hip hop . . . Kessie would probably know. She must remember to ask how the songwriting's going – Kessie's been uncharacteristically shy about sharing any songs since she started experimenting. The few that Robin has cajoled her into playing were great – not unexpected, given that she's a professional musician, but she's a good lyricist too, with a knack for splicing images together. And her singing voice is distinctive: mellowish yet spicy, like a nutmeg hot chocolate. Kessie doesn't often complain about her career, but Robin knows how tough it's been for her to find her dream of being a full-time clarinettist ebbing away, with peripatetic teaching dominating her time and barely paying the bills.

The bartender returns bearing two blood-red negronis, each with a vivid lemon slice. She looks very like Darsha, actually, with her petite physique, shiny black hair, narrow, slightly upturned nose, and similarly rich skin tone . . . Wanting to start a conversation, Robin opens her mouth, but can't work out what to say in time, and the bartender gives her a half-smile then walks off to serve someone else.

She and Darsha met for their mini book club last night on video chat after a three-month lapse. It was Robin's turn to choose this time, and she'd picked Zora Neale Hurston's classic, *Their Eyes Were Watching God* – partly because her seminar tutor had recommended reading Hurston's anthropological work. The title had made Darsha groan at the prospect, but she ended up loving it. She said she felt like she understood the legacy of slavery in a whole new way now. As for toxic masculinity: having to experience Janie's three husbands in succession treating her like crap – even Tea Cake, whom she actually loved – it was as infuriating as it was compelling. In Darsha's opinion, Janie should just have got together with Phoeby, and in a more permissive era, she bet they would have done.

The idea hadn't occurred to Robin before, but she agreed.

'How did it make you feel about marriage?' Darsha had asked. 'I mean, it's always been an institutional vehicle for misogyny and abuse of women, right? And I like how that's welded into this story. I mean, I know you've said before that you're not that bothered about getting married, but if Max asked, would you say yes?'

Robin went quiet. 'Well . . . I wouldn't want to take his surname, that's for sure,' she said, cautiously. 'I guess if we were to have a kid, then being married might make for a more secure parenting unit? Oh, I don't know. He's still ambivalent about kids anyway.' She hasn't yet told Darsha about her bus baby revelation – how her maternal desire switch had flicked to urgent. Or about how Max had laughed off her feelings about it, leading to an almighty row.

They managed to focus on the book for longer than usual, batting ideas, quotes, questions and musings back and forth, between other things, until after midnight. Before they hung up, Darsha coaxed her again to book a flight to California. It is extremely tempting.

She checks her watch again. Max is going to be late – he had asked her if she'd mind him fitting in a squash match before the party, so as not to let the team down, and she'd lied that it was fine with her. There's always a squash match, or a meeting, or a grant application, these days. She pulls her book out of her bag: another from his anthropology shelves, this time promisingly titled *A World of Babies*. Her heart had flickered to see it there, but when she showed him the cover, he'd shrugged it off as a populist experiment in 'accessible' academic writing that he didn't think much of.

It's written as a set of imaginary childcare guides for a range of different societies, based on ethnographic evidence. She's finding it really interesting so far, and doesn't get what's meant to be so wrong with accessible writing – but some of the contents are disturbing.

She's just finished a chapter about Guinean Muslim women living in Portugal, for whom circumcision is normal, and who believe that you only fully become an adult when you become a parent, and that you'd better not be jealous when you're pregnant or bad spirits might hack your belly open with giant machetes. As if she wasn't scared of pregnancy enough already. Her mind turns to her dissertation topic. Maybe she could focus it on women's experiences of childlessness across a selection of different cultures . . .

'Happy birthday, dearest!' Kessie has appeared next to her in a red maxi dress, her mass of curls loose for once.

'Likewise! You look fabulous.' Robin springs off her stool for a hug – and notices a stocky guy standing nearby, grinning creepily at them. She pulls back a little. 'Can I help you?'

Kessie wheels around. 'Oh gosh, sorry. I should have introduced you! Robs, Angelo; Angelo, Robin.'

Robin struggles to conceal her surprise. Angelo grasps her hand like he might a cricket bat, then tugs her in and kisses her firmly on each cheek. He's about a head shorter than her, not much taller than Kessie, and he's pretty good-looking, but smells oddly metallic. His hair is so thoroughly gelled he could fit in at Madame Tussaud's.

'We actually have some news to share, but it's a secret for now . . .' Kessie squeezes Angelo's arm and leans towards Robin. 'Robs, I can't not tell *you*: I'm *pregnant*!' Something in Robin's stomach collapses like a failed cake. It takes her a few seconds to remember to say congratulations. Kessie beams, biting her lip. 'We just found out this afternoon, so we're only a few weeks in. I mean, it's crazy right? After all that worrying, and then just one roll of the dice!'

After some small talk with Angelo, Robin heads to the bathroom.

Sitting on a toilet lid, she pushes her fingertips hard into her forehead. *Pregnant.* She feels like Kessie's made a huge, impulsive mistake – but she can't possibly say so now. On the other hand, whatever happens with Angelo as a partner, this does at least save her the cost of a donor, and Robin from loaning her the money. It's stupid to feel offended that Kessie didn't tell her that she and Angelo were already trying – it's not as if she had a right to know – plus the two of them met on a co-parent dating app, so it should have been bloomin' obvious what would happen if they hit it off. Kessie has always been so much better at going with her instincts. At not over-thinking.

Robin ponders the blue bubble writing on the toilet door. *PEACE AND LOVE FUCKERS.* Yes, of course Kessie should take the plunge if she's found someone she likes who actively wants to have a baby with her. Eight years into their relationship, Max doesn't seem any closer to wanting to have a baby with *her* than he did on day one.

A sticker further down the door recommends Mooncups. She probably should try them, for environmental reasons, but the name seems deceptively cute.

Washing her hands, she looks in the mirror. Mascara on one cheek and a shiny pink nose. She digs out her make-up bag – which always makes her think of her mum, who she has never witnessed wearing any make-up whatsoever. While she didn't ban Robin from wearing it as a teenager, she tutted whenever she saw her putting it on, saying she looked much better *au naturel.* She hasn't called to say happy birthday this year, but she did post a small package from France. Inside was a postcard of a ram with the sun illuminating its horns against a backdrop of snowy peaks, and a pair of wool socks that she'd knitted herself from the sheep she's helping with at the farm down the mountain.

Scrubbing at her mascara smear, and reapplying powder and lipstick, Robin pictures Kessie's face just now when she told her the news. Eyes bright as a fox's under their smoky shadow. She absolutely deserves this.

By the time Robin spots Max arriving, she has sunk three negronis and ordered another. Her frustration with him melts as she thinks how good he looks from across the room with his messy brown curls and teal cord shirt. She struggles to unhook her bag from under the table – and when she looks up again, Edith Lint, a cellist friend of Kessie's, has made a beeline for him. Edith has always flirted like crazy with Max, whether she's single or not. Robin has to battle her way through the crowd – and is stopped on the way by Paolo, Kessie's best mate from music college days, who is enthusiastically wishing her a happy birthday. As she's extricating herself, she notices Benjy waving excitedly at her – he's brought Dom, his new fiancé, and he's barrelling through people to get to her.

Benjy always makes her feel better. He's wearing a fabulous cerise velvet jacket and matching nail varnish, and he has news: their wedding's going to be in Mykonos next year and she absolutely *has* to be there, and would she please do a reading? Thrilled, she assures him that nothing will keep her away.

Darsha's question pops back into her mind. If Max were to propose, and if she were to say yes, and if they were to get married – many ifs – she would like it to be in London, somewhere like the Hackney Round Chapel, in the midst of their life together. Perhaps their honeymoon could be in Barcelona, where he first took her for a city break. When she finally makes it over to Max, she leans in for a kiss which, fortunately, prompts Edith to bid him a cutesy 'toodle-oo'.

'Hey there, birthday girl!' he grins. 'You look beautiful. Sorry I'm so late. Good turnout, right? Can I get you another drink?'

'Why thank you,' she says, though she's swaying in her heels. She is so over wearing heels: nevermore after tonight. Maybe she should just have a Diet Coke. 'So I have some news,' she says. 'Two bits, actually. One: Benjy and Dom are getting married in Mykonos next year!'

'Fancy.'

'I know. They've asked me to do a reading. Shall we plan a holiday around it? We could finally go island hopping.'

'Sure! I actually need to go to Greece for some research anyway.'

She looks around. Angelo and Kessie are in a corner. She whispers the secret second bit of news in his ear, then draws back.

His face tightens. 'Hasty,' he remarks, then takes her hand and leads her to the bar.

She feels like retorting that at least Angelo understands the concept of the biological clock – but her birthday party is not the place to start another row. Moving across the floor feels oddly strenuous, like driving with a punctured tyre.

Waiting for their drinks, Max starts telling her about the squash match, and various things going on with the league.

'Great,' she says, trying to take it in. Then, suddenly: 'Listen, Max.' She really wasn't going to do this now. 'About the baby thing. I know you've said you're not ready yet, but I'm 35 now.

33

I've objectively hit the fertility tipping point. So although it might seem like Kessie's being "hasty" with Angelo, by biological standards we've both left it late. It can take at least a year to get pregnant when you're mid-thirties . . . So can we please try soon?'

He considers. 'That's quite the birthday request. You didn't think much of the trainers I got you then?'

'Max! You know I love them. I actually wish I was wearing them right now. But you're changing the subject. Again.'

He rolls his eyes. 'Okay, Birdie. I do get that you're worried about fertility. But just because Kessie's suddenly got knocked up, it's a bit much to expect me to suddenly change my position.' He strokes her cheek. 'Come on – you do realize you sound like Sally crying to Harry – *I'm going to be forty* – o*ne day!* In five years. And fertility treatments have come on a million miles since that film.'

She looks away and clenches her teeth. How dare he quote her favourite movie at her, now of all moments? She watches the bartender with the tattoos, how gracefully she moves.

He takes her hand. 'Loads of women these days have kids when they're older,' he adds. 'My mum had me when she was 39. Didn't Geena Davis have kids at, like, 47?'

'Well all power to her,' she says, 'but not every woman can, and fertility treatment costs a bomb, and can have awful side effects, and often doesn't even work, and I just don't want to take the risk unless I have to.'

He sighs audibly, as if she's nagging him about the laundry. 'Can we talk about this another time?'

Before long she has to stagger off the mini dance floor to

a toilet cubicle, kneel down, and vomit into the bowl, like it's her and Kessie's joint 18th all over again.

When she wakes in the morning, gravel-eyed, Max's side of the bed is empty. Kessie's news jolts back, and her head starts to thud like timpani. She tries to remember how she got home, and vaguely remembers the argument, and the vomiting, but can't recall exactly what was said. Hopefully not yelled. Did anyone overhear? She pulls on a dressing gown, splashes her face at the sink, glugs down a glass of water, and goes through to the living room.

Max is sleeping open-mouthed on the sofa, in the same teal shirt, his head resting on the old sage cushion that her dad used to use for lumbar support. After watching him for a moment, she treads softly over to her fish tank and observes the quiet flit and drift of her fiery little tetras, her blousy angelfish and fan-tailed guppies, her danios like minute zebras, her electric blue acara, and good old Berlioz, sucking his way meditatively along a lacy trail of algae.

When her parents first gave her the tank, the year she'd started pleading with them for a puppy, her dad bought her a book about tropical fish to go with it. He used to test her on her knowledge over breakfast. She had been flabbergasted to find out all the different ways that fish go about reproducing – and that was before she'd even fully realized how humans did it. Tetras do some kind of elaborate bird-like mating dance, and she'd spent hours by the tank waiting for this to happen, until her dad explained that all their tetras were male. As for danios, when they pair up and are ready to go, the female just scatters a load of eggs around the ground, and the male swims around to fertilize as many as he can.

She watches Berlioz steadily munching. Male catfish are meant to be super caring parents. Each one finds himself a cave-like space to make into a nest, and cleans the walls until it's spick and span in the hope that a wandering female likes the look of it. If one ventures in and finds it to her satisfaction, she'll plaster her eggs around the walls, then swim off to enjoy the rest of her life – while he stays put, and patiently nurtures all the eggs until they hatch. Robin wonders for the first time if it's a bit mean that she's effectively denied Berlioz the experience of fatherhood. But he does at least have a comfortable, clean, predator-free life in the tank, with nice plants, regular food, and a ready-made cave.

She decides to get dressed into sports gear and head out for a run. Ace of Base gets her around the park, despite the blood moshing in her skull. Her knees begin to ache, as if making a point that they're supporting an ageing body whose womb is already starting to deteriorate. Parents with babies and small children are parading the paths, and dogs scampering to and fro. Robin has always liked the idea of having a dog, but since gaining the financial independence to have one, she's balked at the realities, not least picking up poo on a daily basis. If she lets motherhood slip through her fingers, though, perhaps she'll have to adopt a dog. She would never want to replace her fish, but they're hardly the most affectionate of creatures.

A smell of pancakes from the café at the corner inspires her: yes, the way to a man's heart . . . and if there's one thing she can cook, besides a boiled egg, it's this. She diverts to the shop and buys blueberries, maple syrup and eggs.

By the time she gets home, Max is up and in the shower. Robin gets in after him, then puts on her new maroon silk shirt, inspired by Kessie's green one, brews a pot of coffee, and prepares a pancake batter. Cracking two eggs into the mixing bowl, she imagines the eggs in her belly shrivelling like raisins.

Max emerges, and halts in the kitchen doorway. 'Woah, Birdie – is that pancake prep I see before me?' He comes over to her and pecks her on the lips. 'Look, don't worry about last night, okay? Birthdays can be emotional. I'm glad we got to a solution. Jesus I'm parched!' He pours himself a pint of water.

'Right,' she says, slowly. *Solution?*

She serves him a stack, drizzled with syrup and arrayed with berries and mint leaves from the window box – perhaps the most professional-looking meal she's ever produced. He makes appreciative noises and tucks in. She sits opposite, watching him chew, swallow, shovel more in and chew some more. She loads up a small forkful for herself and lifts it from the plate, but somehow can't face ingesting it, so rolls a blueberry around the navy patterns of the plate with the tip of her knife instead.

'Delish,' he says, then looks up at her. 'Wait, how come you're not eating?'

'Oh, I'm just . . . Can we talk?'

'Again? Okay.' He sounds guarded.

'I can't honestly remember a lot of last night – you said something about a solution?'

He raises one eyebrow, then smiles. 'Well, I guess I'm glad it's all a bit hazy.' He pops in another mouthful. 'All right, to recap, in a nutshell, you ranted at me about how feckless I was, and how your womb was the Sahara desert, then threw up again over my shoes, and eventually calmed down, listened to what I was saying, and offered to freeze your eggs and to get your company to pay for it.'

Her jaw drops. Good thing she hadn't put any pancake in her mouth. She didn't think Max even knew that her company had announced they were going to offer to fund egg freezing.

'Are you – messing with me?'

'What? No! It seemed like a sensible idea. And in two years, if you still want to, I agreed we can start trying naturally. Fingers crossed I'll have a permanent job by then. Ringing bells now?' He checks his phone. 'Ah, I'm running late – said I'd meet Giles at the gym and then I'm off to that coding workshop – but listen, thanks so much for that breakfast. Delish. I'll cook supper later, and wash up too. Have a good one!' With a scrape of his chair, he's gone.

Chapter 4

Kessie

Kessie plods home from the concert with cement-filled legs. She hadn't anticipated how tiring pregnancy would be before she'd even started to show. But Angelo will be waiting, and might just give her one of his orgasmic foot massages. It's such a shame he had to work late tonight and couldn't come. He did at least come to see her play at St John's Smith Square a couple of weeks ago – his first classical concert – and said he enjoyed it, though she could tell he was partly being polite. He admitted to being a bit bored by the Bruch violin concerto, but that's fair enough; she can't stand it, though didn't tell him that until afterwards .

Tonight was Shostakovich Symphony No. 5 at the Queen Elizabeth Hall – much more exciting. She'd persuaded Angelo to listen to a recording of it over dinner the other night, and he pronounced it pretty intense but said he liked the drama, and he was interested in the politics around it in the context of Soviet censorship under Stalin – how Shostakovich had previously been threatened by the regime after writing an opera that officials disapproved of, and how they applauded this symphony as an appropriately triumphal return to form; but how the public read it as another secret critique, with the first ostensibly upbeat movement working parodically to represent the people being ordered to rejoice . . . Still, he clearly wasn't interested enough to change his work plans. Or maybe he genuinely couldn't. She still doesn't get exactly what his job entails.

At least Robin came, and brought Max, Benjy and Dom along too. Benjy rocked up in a zebra print coat, which meant Kessie was able to spot them all from the stage. Her solo went well, and the fixer promised she'd call her to book her again. Which was great – but typical, just as she's contemplating quitting music for a while. Still, this baby will be worth it, a thousand times over.

Turning the corner into the estate, she spots the hunched elderly guy walking his bow-legged bulldog. It's true what they say about people growing to look like their hounds – these two have such sketchable jowls. She says hello, and he nods back.

Only a few flights of stairs until she can lie down – and just one sleep until the scan! The moment when this constant fatigue and boob ache will suddenly feel worth it. She and Angelo have planned to go out for a celebration dinner at a secret restaurant he's booked, all being well. The only clue he's given her is that the food is European. If her instincts are right, he might be planning to invite her to move in with him. She doesn't have any desire to leave Hackney for Knightsbridge – and moving in together does feel a bit soon still – but his flat is at least triple the square footage of her shoebox, plus it has a huge lift which is much more practical for getting a buggy in and out. He's still only got one picture up on the walls, and it's a purple Pollock imitation that looks like a Blue Peter creation, but she has lots of better prints that she could contribute. She would bring some house plants in, too.

After the first flight of steps, she has to pause for breath. A couple of silver bullets are scattered at her feet, remnants of legal highs. She found out just the other day that they contain the same chemical as laughing gas, so she might finally get to partake herself in a few months.

Up the next flight. Each foot seems to be trying to glue itself to each step. She considers calling Angelo to come and ask him to help her up, but that would be ridiculous – she's nearly there. She supposes she does still feel a tiny bit shy around him. But their relationship has been intense, and unlike any she's had before. They've become really close in some ways, but in others, she barely knows him still – she's never met his family, or spoken to them, and hasn't met any of his friends either, come to think about it. But it's only been three months and there's time for that. And everything feels different once you agree to have a child together.

The sex has been good – surprisingly so. His body evidences his obsession with extreme fitness, and he's somehow both passionate and efficient, always in control while not quite dominating. He invariably attends to her pleasure, as well as his own, which is a rarer quality than it should be in her experience – she's never once had to fake it. Despite his thick head of hair and dense eyebrows, his body is almost hairless, which pleases her.

They've fallen into a sort of pattern. He calls her every day, and often sends her flowers on days he doesn't see her, which feels extravagant but flattering. She stays at his place two nights a week, while he stays at hers once a week – and that's felt like enough, so far. He takes her out for dinner regularly, and always takes care of the bill. He's got her back into going to the theatre and cinema, after she'd got out of the habit to save money – he's bought them tickets to plays at the National and at the Arcola in the past month. They've had good low-down chats afterwards, from which it's become clear that he favours a strong and twisty plot, while she's more interested in compelling characters.

They've discussed things like the cost of childcare, and the terms of a formal signed agreement. He was super amenable to most of her suggestions, and even offered to contribute 80% of the cost of the baby's upbringing for six months while she's on mat leave, when she'd only asked for 50%, and to contribute at least 50% thereafter. He's also agreed that, in the awkward-to-contemplate scenario that they were to break up, he wouldn't seek custody; only visiting rights every other weekend or less, and for a week every summer in August. Which all seems fair. They just need to get a draft in writing now, and book an appointment with a lawyer.

Until being pregnant, she had never noticed how many steps she had to climb to get to her flat: 73, it turns out. Pausing at 46, she sees Leona come out of her flat to put the bin out, and waves. Leona grins, revealing her missing tooth. 'All right, love?'

Kessie says she's great thanks, even though she feels like she's halfway up Kilimanjaro. Leona must be in her eighties, and often grumbles in the cheeriest way. She has a marvellous voice – a growly baritone like Frank Sinatra – and has lived on the estate in the same flat since it was built in the early Seventies. Kessie first got to know her when she saw her struggling on crutches a couple of years ago and offered to do her grocery shopping until she was better. She wonders now whether being in your eighties is more or less tiring than the first trimester.

'How are you getting on, Leona? Do you need anything?'
'Oh, yeah, surviving – don't you worry your curly head.'

At the fourth floor she pauses again and looks at the green graffiti signature on the wall, and at the various bits of rubbish strewn on the concrete. Chewing gum globs, crisp packets, polystyrene fried chicken boxes . . . *Wild nights out keeping time with the foxes . . .* How many other people go around thinking up silly rhyming lyrics in their heads? Will she still be here, like Leona, in fifty years' time?

Finally, the fifth floor, and home. Odd that the windows are dark.

She opens the front door. Dark in the bedroom, too. Angelo usually gets home much earlier than this when he stays over, even when he's working late, and it's nearly 11 p.m. now. She goes over to the bed – still made. He didn't message her to say he'd be back this late. She puts the light on and calls out his name. As if he could be hiding in the dark in a flat this small.

Silence. She perches on the sofa, closing her eyes for a second at the relief of being off her feet, then gets out her phone. No messages. She calls him.

This number is not in use.

She dials again. Same autoreply.

On the shoe rack, his towelling slippers are missing – her heart accelerates. In the bathroom, his toothbrush is gone – in the bedroom, his spare PJs are gone. *Fuck fuck fuck.* Her finger hovers over the number 9 – but if it was an emergency, why did he come here and take his stuff? She flops into a seat at the table.

His key is lying on a saucer in the middle. Under it is a folded piece of paper.

She slides the key away and picks up the paper with shaking fingers. It's been ripped from a bigger sheet – from her scrap paper pile, probably.

Dear Kessie,

I am very sorry to tell you this, but I need to leave the UK, for work, for reasons I cannot explain. Please do not try to find me. You will not succeed. I am sorry that I will not have the chance to meet our baby. But you will be a brilliant mother, I am sure of it. A fierce mama leopard. I knew that from the first day I met you. Thanks for all the good times. Best of luck. Goodbye.

Angelo

Best of luck?

She looks wildly around the kitchen. Her laptop is on the side – he hasn't nicked that, so he's not a thief – of objects at least . . .

She opens the laptop. No sign that he's tried to log in. She chews her fist. What's going on? Did he change his mind, just like that? Decide she wasn't good enough for him? Or was this whole relationship an elaborate fraud from the start? *Don't try to find me?*

She searches on her phone for things she'd vaguely thought about but perhaps never properly asked about.

His claimed job: non-existent.

His Acorn profile: deleted.

He'd never had social media beyond that – told her he didn't agree with it, that his work didn't require it, that it was the cause of so much hate and distrust in society today – a position she'd naively accepted, even admired a little. How bloody convenient. It's too late to call Acorn's customer support line, and what could they do anyway? She should never have signed up.

She thinks back to their conversation on that first date in Hyde Park. How much he'd held back about his life. How she'd jokingly hypothesized that he must be a spy. Could that be it? Or was he just a commitment-phobic alpha trickster, out to spread his seed through hoodwinking women into unprotected sex followed by a vanishing act? Why take things so far, though? Why talk legal agreements? Come to concerts? Buy flowers? Her mind is a kaleidoscope.

Why didn't she go for Obamarama?

Because his genes were too bloody expensive: that's why.

She wants to throw her phone across the room but can't afford a new one.

Maybe Angelo – is that even his real *name*? – just saw this as another kind of adventure, another way to test himself in another extreme 'endurance experience' . . . is *that* how he saw their relationship? If it can be called a relationship. Maybe she'll never know. What an *idiot* she was for thinking he was about to invite her to move in with him after the scan. Which he was supposed to come to. He didn't even want to hang around long enough to see a moving image of their baby for the first time? Guttural sounds fall out of her.

After a while, she blows her nose. It's too late at night to call anyone, really, except Robin . . . But Robin's phone rings and rings. She leaves a message, just asking her to please call back, then hangs up and howls like a wolf at the moon.

She contemplates going down to Leona's, but it feels like too much to descend on her at this hour. They might see each other most days, but they really don't know each other all that well.

She reads the note aloud to herself once, just to externalize it, convince herself it's real – then runs to the drawer and scrabbles around until she finds the box of matches at the back.

Out on her balcony, she lights a match, and holds the flame to the bottom corner, so that his name – or pseudonym? – burns first and then, one by one, the rest of his rotten words follow. Ashes float like fairies into the night.

*

The next morning she cancels all her clarinet lessons. Time passes in a fog.

Finally she gets up, makes herself a coffee, goes back out onto the balcony, and calls Robin again. No answer. Unlike her not to call back. A pigeon shits on the metal rail right next to her. It might as well have shat on her head; this is her life now. She calls her dad, but just gets his cheery voicemail, telling his parishioners that he blesses them. He's probably busy running an errand for Cara, or taxiing one of her snarky boys around.

After hesitating for a moment, she goes downstairs and knocks on Leona's door. As soon as the old woman sees her face, she invites her in and offers her a cuppa. When she hears what's happened, she sloshes the milk over the counter. 'You're bloody well jokin', ent ya?' she splutters. 'Oh duck. What a bastard. Never liked the look of 'im if I'm honest with you. You were too good for 'im.'

It's so exactly what she needed to hear that Kessie can't help laughing, and Leona joins in with a cackle so brilliantly raucous that life seems to flick from black and white back into colour again, like the land of Oz.

After listening to the whole story, Leona says she hasn't heard the like in all her days. 'You know what, love, you're best off bein' shot of a man like that,' she says. 'You'll do all right. I managed. Not easy, mind, bein' a single mum. But I see you, girl. You're strong.'

Kessie frowns. Is that true? She wants to hug Leona, but isn't sure how that would go down. 'Where are your kids now?'

'Oh, all grown up. One in Beckenham. Disabled, can't get up here much. One in Florida. Don't call very often. That's boys for ya. Know what you're having?'

'Not yet. We think – I think it's a boy. No reason, really.' She floats the idea to Leona that she should maybe call the police, to report Angelo for fraud – or misrepresentation at least . . . but Leona sticks her bottom lip out and shakes her head.

'Waste of time if you ask me. I mean, it's not really a crime 'e's done, duck, is it? He's just messed you up.' But she concedes that it just might be worth going over to his flat one more time to see if she can track him down and get him to sign the agreement. 'Want company?' she asks.

Kessie tells her not to worry – but then Robin still isn't answering, and it would be nice not to be alone.

'I've got me bus pass,' Leona adds, looking almost eager.

The idea of Leona shaking a stick in Angelo's face is kind of appealing, and it's so kind of her to offer that Kessie agrees.

As they approach his iced Christmas cake of a building, she wonders whether she should feel scared, whether they should just turn around. But the injustice has begun to solidify around her like armour, and having Leona huffing along next to her feels a bit like having a fire-breathing dragon as a sidekick.

The doorman recognizes her and nods like usual. *If he knew.* They go up in the gleaming lift, where she'd imagined taking her baby in its buggy, and even though she has a key, she knocks on the door – five loud raps.

No sound.

She opens up and walks in, Leona behind her. The place is empty. She knew it would be, really. But still, it's just so weird to see with her own eyes that there's nothing here any more, except furniture. No mess. No personal items.

'Yup, buggered off,' Leona sighs. 'This place is fancy.'

Kessie walks through the kitchen, living room, bathroom and both bedrooms, pausing by the main bed to remember the first time she climbed onto it. The garish purple Pollock imitation is still on the living room wall. She gives it a long look, then gets out her pen, and writes BASTARD over it diagonally from corner to corner in giant capital letters. It feels deliciously bad to deface an artwork, even a rubbish one. Only as she finishes does it strike her that, according to the original meaning of that word, her child will be one. Leona comes in and claps her gnarled hands delightedly.

As they're walking slowly back to the bus stop, her phone rings. It's Robin, finally calling back. Kessie excuses herself to Leona and presses answer, but doesn't get a chance to say anything before Robin blurts out that she's been arguing with Max, who's dug his heels in about having a baby, and she thinks their relationship might have reached the end of the line, and she's got tons of work for a client so her head's been all over the place . . .

'Oh hon, I'm so sorry,' Kessie says. She really had hoped she was wrong about Max.

'I meant to call earlier . . .' Robin says. 'Isn't it your scan today?'

Kessie looks over at Leona, who winks. 'It's this afternoon,' she says. 'I wanted to ask a huge favour, actually – can you come with me? Angelo's left.'

'What – what do you mean, left?'

'Vanished. Erased himself. False identity. Turns out I have no fucking idea who the father of my unborn child actually is, and now he's gone. Taken all his stuff. Left a note telling me not to look for him, but I decided to try his flat just in case . . . My lovely neighbour Leona came with me. But he's cleared everything out. No sign. He's ghosted me, Robs.'

For once, Robin appears to be speechless.

*

Later that afternoon, on the way to the hospital, Kessie diverts down a street to the police station. Hovering outside it, she tries to think about what she could possibly allege and prove, and whether it would be worth it just to report him and see what they could do about it. Angelo definitely lied to her about his identity. He almost certainly misrepresented his intentions. But how could she prove that he didn't just legitimately change his mind?

He took it so far, though: telling her he'd contribute financially, agreeing plans for the first year . . . but they never wrote anything down. Even in an email. He certainly never signed on a dotted line.

She scrolls through her message thread with him: the story of their relationship. All of it trivial – plans to get together, expressions of affection. Whenever they discussed longer-term family-related plans, it was face-to-face. How could she have been so *naive*? She always thought of herself as perceptive when it came to other people, a good judge of character. Turns out she's a dupe.

Inside the police station, there's a long queue of people waiting to be seen, and more sitting around in the waiting room, all with haunted eyes. She turns and walks out.

Pacing down the street, her legs are wobbly and slow. The thing she needs to focus on today is her scan: the closest thing to meeting her very own baby for the very first time. And before that, food. Urgently. She buys a bar of Dairy Milk at a corner shop and wolfs it just outside the door.

Pausing on a bench for a rest, she rests her hand on her belly for a few moments, and decides to call Acorn's customer support team. They should at least know about what's happened, hear how their service is being abused by fraudsters and take some responsibility.

When she finally gets through, the woman on the other end, who sounds like a teenager, says cheerily that she's sorry to hear about her situation, but 'unfortunately our terms and conditions *do* state clearly that the company is not responsible for the conduct of any of their members outside the app?' Her intonation rises, as if she were posing a question, though she's doing the opposite. 'They *do* also state that we don't run background checks on members? And that it's every member's responsibility to take *appropriate* precautions when interacting with other members? Following our safety and security guidelines? These include drawing up a legal agreement *before* beginning the conception process, so that there's some recourse if a relationship breaks down? But I assume from what you've said that you didn't do that – is that right?'

'Well, not yet – but we'd talked about it and agreed . . . we were going to meet a lawyer, and . . .'

'Yeah, yeah, I see, well in that case I'm afraid we can't help in this instance. Sorry about that. Is there anything else I can help you with?'

Kessie spends a few seconds controlling her breath. 'So, let me get this straight . . . are you saying there's *nothing* you'll do to help me in a situation that *your* company facilitated? Like, there are *no* negative consequences for a male user of your app who fakes his identity, knocks a woman up based on fake promises, and then *vanishes*?'

'Madam, if what you say happened . . .'

'Um, it definitely *did* happen.'

'I see, madam. Well, our terms and conditions *do* state that members are required to disclose accurate information when they sign up to our service? So if there *is* evidence, as you're suggesting, that another member has lied about their identity, or behaved inappropriately, then they could be banned from our app? But we *would* need proof of that. I'd have to refer you to our complaints team?'

'Well okay,' Kessie says, trying not to scream into the phone. 'I mean, I have evidence of the messages through the app when we first met up – and texts since, obviously texts you'd send to a romantic partner – which then just suddenly cut out, out of nowhere, yesterday – and I have his phone number, which is suddenly not in use – and he's not in the job he said he was – and he's not on social media and—'

'Right,' the woman cuts in, 'well, as I was saying, you'd have to speak to our complaints team to take this any further? I can give you their email address and you can write to them and attach your evidence? But without an agreement between you and the user in question, I'm afraid it's highly unlikely that this would lead—'

'But his identity – he *obviously* lied – the Angelo Panassos I thought I knew doesn't exist anywhere on the internet, and he doesn't seem to be on your app any more . . . Can you at least tell me the details about his identity that he shared when he signed up? I didn't think to keep a copy . . .'

'Unfortunately, madam, due to data protection, we can't share information about another user's account?'

'Oh, forget it.' Kessie hangs up. Then feels bad for being rude. The woman was only doing her job. But terms and conditions shouldn't be a strategic defence against basic empathy, should they?

Outside the hospital, she stands on the pavement, on the other side of the road, watching people process in and out of the revolving doors. *Birth, swivel; pain, swivel; fear, swivel; death, swivel; birth, swivel.* This moment was meant to be golden. *Dam this river.* She perches on the bus stop bench and lowers her face into her hands again, only to see Angelo's grinning face emerge from the wet dark of her palms, sprouting ears like the Donnie Darko bunny.

A boy whizzes past on a purple scooter, inches from her toes, whooping at something or other, and his little sister follows, puffing to catch up. Why weren't scooters invented when she and Robin were kids? She doesn't remember them being around anyway. They look like so much fun. Will theirs – hers – have one? Is this child really going to materialize?

Was she really such a despicable person that Angelo felt it was okay to use her like that and leave such a curt note? How many other women has he done this to? Why didn't she ask him more questions earlier, more sensible questions? Why couldn't she *be* more sensible in life generally – more cautious – more like Robin? Why couldn't she have picked a more sensible, stable career? Gone to university instead of music college. And why couldn't she have settled for a sensible, stable man too when she had the chance? Tom Dalby would have been great – he's a deputy headteacher now, and she only broke up with him because she fell for Ezekiel Temba. Ezekiel would have been good too – a software developer with a sweetly wonky grin. He now has three adorable kids and a wife with a Julia Roberts smile.

She remembers Leona's reaction to her news, and her raucous cackle. At least there is one big silver lining of this mess – the thing she's dreamed of for so long now, the thing that she'd resolved to dedicate the next few years to above all else: she's finally pregnant. Without having to fork out for Obamarama. She leapt into the deep end with Angelo, knowing it was rash, and he did at least 'give' her a baby before scarpering. They didn't even have an upsetting, acrimonious break-up. So, in a way, what does it matter if he was a hoaxer, or just a commitment-phobic arsehole? Those aren't genetic traits, are they? There's nothing fake about the life inside her. At least, she's pretty sure there isn't . . . phantom pregnancies are a thing . . . but no, she had a positive test. And before he came along, with his unwanted patting of her hair, and his hardcore endurance stories and polystyrene promises, getting pregnant had been a far higher priority for her than finding a romantic relationship. Yes, from now on, she'll just have to start thinking of Angelo as a facilitator. That's what she'll call him: *The Facilitator*. A semen-wielding human who gave her a freebie and even paid for some nice meals out along the way – and who will, when this is all less raw, make for a good story to tell at parties.

To tell her child, though?

Now he's here; now he's not. Baby mother morphs to slut. Go online and take a gamble – somewhere lies a comic angle . . .

Maybe his vanishing act was a bad omen. It would be just her luck to find out today that there's something terribly wrong with this baby. A life-changing syndrome . . .

'There you are!' It's Robin, her arms open. 'My love – I still can't believe he did this.' She enfolds Kessie in a hug. 'I'm so sorry. It's beyond shitty.' They rock from side to side. 'I'm here for you though, okay? We'll get through this. Remember that rollercoaster you made me go on in Blackpool? This is just a dip in the ride.'

Kessie grins. She had persuaded Robin to brave that ride when they were on a residential orchestra trip in their mid-teens – that summer of crop tops, of trying to sing as high as Minnie Riperton in 'Lovin' You' while knocking back Archers and lemonade . . . That summer when she had snogged the two cutest boys on the trip. As their little carriage rattled slowly up and up those long, rickety rails towards the sea, and the people in the crowd below shrank into ants, Robin had groaned and threatened to be sick – and Kessie had squeezed her hand and begun to regret making her do it. When they finally reached the top, and all they could see was the grey-blue sea, she'd screamed out '*love youuu*' just before the nosedive, when their stomachs hit their skulls.

They wait on plastic chairs in the hospital corridor. Robin starts firing off some work emails on her phone. Kessie closes her eyes, listens to the soundtrack of robotic beeps and trundling trolleys, and tells herself to be prepared for the worst. Silence instead of a heartbeat. A genetic aberration. A doomed thing floating inside her, a fragment of seaweed, a dandelion seed . . . This could prove to be an apocalyptic interlude in her life. She remembers that grey llama cloud hovering above that pub just before her first date with . . . The Facilitator. *The llama the drama the bleak panorama, the bastard who scarpered he'd better face karma . . .*

The thought of karma reminds her of Auntie Elmi. Of how she lived through the earthquake in Nepal on top of all the other grief. *That's* resilience. And she would have loved to have had a baby of her own, which Kessie is lucky to be expecting now. When this baby is old enough, she will take him on Elmi-inspired adventures, like camping and mountain climbing – and then, when he's old enough and she can afford it, they'll fly out to Nepal for a visit.

Robin puts her phone away. 'Sorry hon, just a couple of urgent things. Feeling okay?'

Kessie's name is finally called. She clambers onto the bed, pulls up her top, pushes down the waistband of her leggings, and waits. A giant, cold slug lands on her belly and slides around. She cranes her neck to see the screen, and the sonographer angles it slightly towards her. After several long seconds of silence, during which the slug's quest begins to seem hopeless – a whooshing pulse strikes up. It's unexpectedly fast, like fluttering wings.

'There we are!' the sonographer says triumphantly. 'A very healthy-sounding baby!'

Kessie has to bite down on both lips. She glances at Robin, who's excitedly waving upturned thumbs.

Back on the screen, a ghostly form has emerged, moving in a sludgy sea like a creature from the Mariana Trench. Somehow the sonographer is able to read this gritty scene, and to chat amiably through a series of precise interpretations. She turns to look at Kessie. 'So! We can't give reliable predictions of the sex at twelve weeks – but in your case, I think I *could* give you a likely determination, if you'd like me to?'

Kessie hesitates. She hadn't expected this – they normally don't tell you until the twenty-week scan. She already feels pretty sure it's a boy. Angelo – The Facilitator – had told her straight up that he'd prefer a boy, and he's such an alpha type that it had somehow seemed likely to her that he'd produce one. They had even spent most of an evening discussing boys' names, and she had finally agreed to Theodoros – Theo for short. So much for *that*. 'Yes please,' she says.

'Okay then!' The sonographer turns and points to a still image on the screen. 'See that? That's the hamburger.'

'Excuse me?'

'Those three lines – that's how we identify female genitalia. The hamburger's an affectionate shorthand.'

Kessie squints at her face to make sure she's heard correctly. 'Charming! So . . . you mean . . .'

'That's right: I'm 90 per cent certain you're carrying a little girl! But we'll be able to confirm it for sure at your next scan.'

A girl? It's a struggle to process . . . Her eyes are hot. She searches the sonographer's face for an indication that this is a joke.

'Are you disappointed?' The face has become perplexed. 'Don't be – all the signs are that she'll be a healthy and beautiful baby.'

Kessie shakes her head, vigorously. It occurs to her that her dismayed reaction is not only completely irrational, it's a betrayal of this child inside her who didn't choose to be a girl, and to all the women in the world who'd give anything for a healthy baby. 'Gosh, no, I'm sorry, I just thought . . . for some reason . . .' The fact that *he* didn't want a girl actually makes it all the better, it occurs to her. A girl won't remind her so much of him. And it'll probably be easier to bring up a girl as a single mum, because she'll be able to relate to her more, having been a girl herself. Plus her baby girl is going to be beautiful, because the sonographer said so. She starts to laugh, uncontrollably, like a crazy person.

Thankfully, Robin intervenes to ask all the questions that should be asked, like about what information they'll look for in the next scan and so forth. Kessie watches her take in the answers with grateful admiration, suddenly wondering how her friend can be so calm and supportive, when she wants to be pregnant herself, and yet Max is forcing her to freeze her eggs and wait two more years.

It actually feels totally right that Robin should be here with her for this. She wouldn't want The Facilitator here even if he were to push through the door right now, get down on his knees and apologize. Her twenty-something self wouldn't have entertained the thought of a second date with him, after his police-like inter- rogations and heroic ultramarathon memoirs and hair patting – she'd settled for him because she wanted a baby, and now she's got what she wanted. He was just a flash in the pan. Robin has always been there for her at the best of times and the worst of times – times that entangled them forever, like tree roots.

At the crossroads, just before Robin leaves to get the Tube back to the office, Kessie remembers something. 'Wait, Robs – do you think you could find out if there are any jobs going in your company for PAs, or secretaries, or anything like that? I've signed up with that agency I mentioned, but nothing's come through yet, and this is all suddenly feeling really *real*. I mean, if this baby's going to have a decent life with a single mum who's failed to even—'

'Hey! Shh.' Robin puts her finger softly over Kessie's lips. 'No talk of failure, okay?' Listen to me, you're an amazing human. And a gifted musician who just played an awesome concert in the Queen Elizabeth Hall. You wanted to be a mum, you decided to take action, and you've *already* made it happen! Your little girl's going to have the best life because she's lucky enough to have *you*. And me, as a back-up. So yes, I'll happily look into jobs for you if you're sure that's what you want – people are going to want to hire you, why wouldn't they? – but also, please don't panic about money. Okay? I can help if you need. Look, sorry, but I've really got to—'

'You're the best, go, go, go . . . Hey, no, but wait, sorry, just one second. Will you be my birth partner?'

Robin makes a heart shape with her fingers and thumbs.

Kessie finds she's still smiling as she walks down the road. Having Robin as a birth partner is a relief . . . but it will also take their friendship to a new, unexpected level. She's never even seen her own vagina from the vantage point that Robin's going to get of it. Which is pretty weird. Robin has a genuine phobia of injections . . . and a tendency to faint at the sight of blood . . . Holy moly. Is this beating being inside her truly going to barge its way out of her in a few months? Somehow it all felt like an elaborate fantasy until today.

Shudder. Smile at the sky. Circle the park. Sun on skin. Friendship like kin. Male pigeons by the path, puffed-out necks, strutting their stuff, pestering females who've seen enough, knobbly feet, missing toes – buds blast open, smell that rose – crows swoop as if they know that deep in me a child grows.

Chapter 5

Robin

Robin clambers onto the hard white bed, picturing Kessie doing the same last week, and the surprising urgency of the heartbeat that emerged, like the tapping of a woodpecker. No chance of the rhythm of life striking up to join the chorus in *her* belly any time soon. If only she'd never drunkenly agreed to having her eggs frozen. And if only she didn't have to endure this procedure while being watched by Max. She turns her gaze away from him to the picture on the wall next to her.

It's a large metal-framed image of an orchid with a baby-pink background, photoshopped into ostentatious perfection. Her dad used to love orchids, almost as much as he loved algae. He taught her about their remarkable abilities – not least how some wily species mimic the shape and scent of bees to lure them into pseudo-copulation among their petals. After the bee has scrabbled erotically about for a bit, gathering pollen and disappointment as it fails to mate, it flies off and lands on another duplicitous bloom, depositing the pollen there, and allowing the first orchid to reproduce. Pseudo-copulation, pseudo-co-parenting . . . maybe

Angelo learned his tricks from an orchid? There is a sexual quality to this flower on the wall, despite its pristineness. Did O'Keefe paint orchids?

Max coughs from across the room. He initiated sex last night, for the first time in a while, telling her how beautiful she was and how much he wanted her. It felt like he was over-compensating after effectively rejecting her as a mother. She was noisier than usual, which he seemed to think indicated pleasure; in fact she was mostly venting her fury, which felt almost as gratifying as the climax. He seemed as satisfied as ever. Didn't seem to notice that her mind was flying like a bat out of the window and over the dark treetops.

The orchid regards her coolly as the doctor says introductory things and fiddles with equipment. For a while, Robin's mum kept a violet orchid in a pot by the living room window to remember her dad by, but then it died and wasn't replaced. She wonders how her mum's doing now, up in the mountain hut. Talking to herself – to her sheep. It's madness for her to still be living that way, with no farming skills to speak of, and so remotely too, half an hour's walk from the nearest village, without even a landline and with no mobile reception . . . but it's been a year now, and she's given no indication that she wants to return to the UK. Or even to be in touch, beyond the occasional letter. The Brexit referendum is coming up, and it seems impossible that more than 50 per cent of the UK population could vote no . . . but if the worst does come to the worst, perhaps being resident in France will be no bad thing . . .

'We'll start with a few blood tests,' the doctor is saying. 'Could you roll up your sleeve for me?'

Robin obeys, fingers trembling. How pathetic to be so terrified of needles, *still*, in her mid-thirties.

If only she were a snail. Those hermaphrodites know how to make reproduction fair and equitable, and probably pleasurable. She was enraptured, as a kid, when she came across the passage in *My Family and Other Animals* where Gerald discovers how they do it: how any snail can just glide up to whichever other snail they fancy, and if the other one's up for mating too, they can each shoot white arrows into each other, winch each other in, wait for the arrows to dissolve, and glide blithely off again to each have their own babies in their own sweet time.

'Just a little scratch . . .'

But it never is . . .

'Try to relax your arm . . .'

How can I fucking relax when you're about to stab me? Her eyes scrunch, heart races. A spear is piercing through her, she's dying . . .

'Lovely! That's all done. We'll pop these off to the lab now and find out whether you're a good candidate.'

She takes in a shuddery breath and releases it. *Good candidate.* She's always been a good candidate for anything she's had to work hard for, but *this*? This is just pot luck.

'. . . levels of RSH, AMH, E2 . . .' Something about hormones. She can't seem to focus.

An ultrasound scan follows. She half expects the screen to reveal a tiny creature swimming around in her belly, like it did in Kessie's. Instead, her screen shows a spooky cave with lumpy walls, like that shell grotto that Max took her to at Margate once.

'Robin, were you aware that you have polycystic ovaries?'

'Um, sorry? No – is that . . . serious?'

'Oh, not to worry! It's a very common condition, one in ten women have it. If you haven't noticed symptoms then you don't have it badly. Do you have regular periods?'

'Not very . . . but then I'm not great at taking a note of them. I did go to the doctor about that once, but he said I was probably just too thin.' She hadn't liked that man, smugly appraising her body from his swivel chair, judging it as inadequate. How can it be that she's only just heard about a condition that affects one in ten women?

'Being too thin *can* affect your periods,' this doctor is saying. 'But irregular menstruation is also one of the symptoms of PCOS – that's polycystic ovary syndrome. I can get you a leaflet about it if you like? It can cause different symptoms for different women – some put on weight, some experience some hair loss, or excessive hair growth, some get very oily skin – and it *can* affect fertility as well. It often doesn't, but it can sometimes. You can't really know until you try.'

Robin nods, imagining her future self as fat, spotty, and hairy, as well as childless.

'You can sit up now.'

Max smiles at her from across the room, and Robin looks away again. She can tell he's grossed out by this new information about her cyst-ridden insides and erratic bodily fluids. He's probably imagining her growing a fuzzy beard.

She tries to tune back in to what the doctor is telling them – about what happens next if she passes this so-called 'good candidate' test. To have a decent chance of creating a viable embryo, they'll have to extract at least twenty high-quality eggs. *Twenty?*

'I would strongly recommend that you try naturally at this point if you want to maximize your chances of a live birth,' the doctor adds, somewhat sternly.

A live birth. Visions of bloody baby lambs and chicks. This time, Max is the one avoiding her eye.

'You're thirty-five now, aren't you Robin?' the doctor continues. 'You'll have heard the term 'geriatric' used for women over that age, I expect?' She grins, as if this were a joke. Robin reflects that she has possibly never felt less attractive. 'Of course I doubt you *feel* geriatric,' the doctor adds, 'but the point is, even at this stage, ovarian ageing can affect egg quality. Now, have you considered FET?'

Frozen Embryo Transfer is an acronym she learned recently, among many others, while researching fertility online. She'd probably be a 'good candidate' for a fertility-speak test. Anyway, Max is set against FET, since it would mean that he'd be manacled to her. Not that he put it quite that way. He had suggested they look at it the other way around: that FET could be a *dis*empowering option for her if she didn't want to commit to using his sperm in a couple of years' time.

'I think we've pretty much ruled that out,' Max tells the doctor. 'Out of interest though, do you have clear *evidence* that FET is more likely to result in a live birth? I did a bit of research and it didn't seem like the stats were showing that.'

'Well, of course statistics are variable,' the doctor says, staying remarkably calm in the face of mansplaining, 'but yes, overall the medical evidence suggests that FET is 5 to 10 per cent more successful than freezing eggs on their own. Trying naturally would increase your chances significantly more, though, as I said.'

Robin returns her gaze to Max, searching for signs that this has changed his view, but he maintains a poker face.

Walking down the road afterwards, he takes her hand and gives it a squeeze. 'Well done for being so brave, Birdie,' he says, as if she were a small child who'd just conquered a slide at the playground.

'Well, it was horrible,' she says. 'And if I go through with this whole thing I'll have to be injected multiple times a day for weeks with crazy amounts of hormones – and I just don't know if I can . . .' She pulls her hand away, emotion bubbling up.

'Oh sweetie,' he says, like he's genuinely sympathetic, like he didn't initiate this whole situation. 'It'll be tough, I know, but you'll probably find it easier each time – and it'll be worth it to get a nice crop of eggs frozen, right?'

A nice crop. A decent harvest. All this farm animal jargon is so demeaning. Robin is seething so much she can barely see the pavement ahead of her, and nearly trips over a loose paving stone. If he *still* can't see that they need to try naturally, after that clear advice from a doctor who's literally seen inside her womb – if he *still* thinks it's okay to put her through this operation and all the hormone injections leading up to it, just to buy himself a little more freedom, maybe . . . maybe it should be over? But eight years together! That's nearly a quarter of her life. She needs to give him an ultimatum. How, and when, are tricker things to decide.

That evening, he loads the dishwasher then heads out to play squash. Robin pours herself a glass of red wine and puts on

Rachmaninov's Second Symphony. It's such romantic piece, it always makes her heart swell to bursting and then release – she needs that right now. She and Kessie played it in youth orchestra once, and to her embarrassment she was so moved in the moment that she wept on stage and the whole wind section mocked her afterwards.

She opens her laptop to search her way back into fertility land, with all its mad hatters and sobbing dormice and crazy queens and croquet battles. Still, it's reassuring to return there and be reminded that you're not alone: that there are other people who've gone through similar things, worse things, and who've shared frank accounts of what it's like.

But sometimes it's just too frank, and too much. All the conflicting advice and twisted stats and anxious reams and opinion-lobbing . . . She takes another sip of wine – Merlot, in fact, Angelo's supposed favourite that Kessie never once saw him drink. What a creep. At least Max is being honest with her.

Her phone rings: the clinic. Results are already in – she wasn't expecting them until tomorrow. She glugs the rest of her wine and listens.

Her hormone stats: not great. Signs are that she is already experiencing premature ovarian ageing. Her womb walls, in other words, are shrivelling like a walnut shell.

But there's 'good news': she's on the borderline for eligibility, so they can proceed with the extraction procedure. If she still wishes to go ahead.

She takes a breath. Says she'll do it. Puts the phone down, and imagines needles stabbing her all over her body.

The second movement of the Rachmaninov expands and contracts. She goes to sit by the tank and watch the fish pootle around. If only having kids were as simple for women as it is for most female fish – basically just dropping a load of eggs in a place that seems safe, then swimming off. Is there any other animal species that spends as much time looking after their babies as humans do? Not to mention this insane amount of advance planning? Parenthood is, of course, a lot harder for some animals – even some that lay eggs. Those poor parent penguins, for instance, who have to wait in the ice for months without eating, while the other parent goes off to get food for their chick. But at least when they find a mate, most non-human species can pretty much guarantee that he or she will be suitably focused on the task of procreating.

She turns the music off, gets ready for bed, and watches an episode of *Friends* in her PJs: the one where Phoebe agrees to have triplets for her newly discovered half-brother, who she's only just met, who's only just left school, who appears to have severe learning difficulties, and who is marrying his former schoolteacher who is three times his age. But Phoebe's a generous soul, and giving birth to three babies and then handing them all over as soon as they're born to this improbable couple will be a cinch, right?

By the end of the episode, Max still isn't back, and Robin's not feeling remotely sleepy, so she opens the *World of Babies* book again, and grabs a pencil to make some notes.

Her bookmark is at the imaginary childcare guide for Palestinian women. If a woman is having trouble conceiving, an independent midwife called a *dayat* will massage her belly

67

and place a lit candle on it to warm her insides and encourage conception. Meanwhile, her husband is recommended to eat a spoonful of honey with chopped nuts.

Robin thinks about her dad again. He didn't have a particularly sweet tooth; his passion was cheese, especially blue varieties. Their mouldy veins, which revolted her as a small child, invariably prompted him to tell her more about algae, and about the magical abilities of moulds, especially slime moulds. She wishes she could share a blue cheese plate with him now that she's mature enough to appreciate it; the thought tickles her: he loved a pun almost as much as a Roquefort. He would be great to confide in – he was always so calm and good at talking things through with. Unlike her mum. And as a scientist, he would be able to help her process all the stats. How *could* her mum have chosen so well in her dad, and then have chosen Brian, with his farcical dot com start-up bucket-with-a-hole-in-the-bottom? Had she ever sought Robin's opinion on Brian, she could have told her straight away that he was a creep and not a keeper. Though she couldn't have predicted the wrecking ball he'd swing into their financial security.

At least they've still got her dad's Pyrenean hut. He would be gobsmacked if he knew her mum was living there now, full-time. The last summer that they'd all gone up there together as a family of three, it was the height of August, and they'd spent a blissful week hiking in the early mornings when it wasn't yet too hot, reading on deckchairs in the afternoons, or playing boules in the garden, then playing cards and eating out at the village bistro in the evenings – that thick garbure soup with baguette and butter, followed by *tarte aux myrtilles*, the tang of those tiny berries freshly picked from the mountain slopes.

The summer after he died, her mum took her back there, and they brought Kessie along with them. They all held a little memorial for him in the garden one night as the sun set. Robin and Kessie played some duets on their instruments, and her mum read a poem by Wendell Berry about the peace of wild things. They went through the motions of some of the same holiday activities as the year before, but her mum didn't know the hiking routes so well, and got them terribly lost one day and ran out of water – they were lucky to be rescued by some helpful hikers before collapsing with heat stroke.

One night, after Robin and Kessie were meant to be asleep, she'd finally heard her mum crying in the living room – hollow, hacking sobs. Until that moment, she'd thought her a little heart-less, wondered if she really cared that much that her dad had died. It dawned on her that her mum was not so much heartless as heartbroken – and that she not only no longer had two parents, she no longer even had *one* parent who was secure or reliable. She was going to have to fend for herself.

She wonders what her mum is doing right now, all on her own up in the mountains. Is she sitting on one of the two scuffed red armchairs, reading a paperback – Francoise Sagan perhaps – illuminated by the old gasoline lamp? For the first time, Robin feels a little envious. It might be lovely to shut off the world for a while and embrace solitude amidst the peaks, perched high above the fray, without any of this stress. Could it be that her mum is more genius than lunatic?

*

In the morning she gets up at first light, packs herself a lunch, and unearths her walking boots and waterproof. After what she's about to do, and how she's going to feel if it goes as she predicts, she'll need to get out. The forecast isn't bad, mostly cloudy. She pulls out her old OS map of the Chilterns and pores over it. Yes, she'll get the train to Tring, then walk through Dockey Wood and up to the Ivinghoe Beacon. It's not the Pyrenees, but it's still a good viewpoint.

She picks up the framed selfie of her and Max standing on a canal bridge in Amsterdam, water gleaming behind them like a halo: one of their early city breaks for her birthday. He had just been offered his first postdoc and they celebrated that too. She makes two cups of coffee, then knocks on the spare room door.

He grunts, calls for her to come in, pushes himself up on his pillow, and beckons her to come and give him a hug. She walks over to sit on the side of the bed and strokes his hair. 'Morning, beautiful,' he says. 'Sorry, I was late back – did I wake you?'

'No,' she lies. 'But I need to talk to you.'

'Oh.' His smile fades.

'I've tried really hard to understand your position, and your feelings, and all the seemingly rational points you've made about why it's not the right time for you to have a baby – but I just can't wait any longer. The medical advice is crystal clear. With the state of my fertility, and at my age, freezing my eggs and trying to use them down the line is massively more risky than trying naturally now. And I'm hoping you've been reflecting on that too since the scan and what the doctor said. But if you haven't come round yet – I just don't . . . I don't see any way forward for us. I actually can't do this any more. So I'm asking you one

70

last time to please say yes to trying naturally – *not* in two years' time, or even in six months' time, but now.' She's not quite sure how she just held that together. But she did it: she said what she'd planned to say.

Max leans forward. 'You . . . I'm sorry, *what*? Is this . . . you're telling me you need me to say yes right *now*, like, you want me to fuck you without protection right now, or you're ending our *seven-year* relationship?'

'Eight years, Max. I mean, I could wait til tonight to be fucked. But I'm ovulating today, so yeah, that's basically it.'

'Seriously, Robin?'

'Yup. Ideally I'd like to be fucked with love, and commitment to having a family together, but it just doesn't really seem like that's where you're at.'

'Well, no, but . . . Listen, I do love you. You know that. Or I thought you did.' His tone is defensive. Petulant, even.

'I know you say you do.'

Max gives her a glare, then tilts it up to the ceiling, then drops his face into his hands and groans. She waits until he looks at her again. 'You're in walking gear,' he remarks.

'I am. I'm going to get the train out to the Chilterns and climb a hill. If you say yes to what I've just asked you, I'd love for you to come with me. We could fuck when we get home. Or even in a meadow . . .'

'In a meadow!'

She smiles, wryly. 'You probably don't remember, but you once said we should do it in a meadow on a summer's day. Guess that was like the cold hard Mexican ceramic tile on the kitchen floor in *When Harry Met Sally*.'

This makes him laugh, but then he stops. For once, he seems confused.

'Look, Max,' she says. 'I expect you have plans to play squash today anyway, or work on another article.'

He frowns. 'Er, well . . . I *could* cancel my plans to come on a walk with you . . . But I . . . I can't just say *yes* right now to something as big as the thing you're asking.'

'Okay then,' she says, brightly, and gets to her feet, pulling her hands from his. 'I expected that, to be honest. I mean, you say *just like that*, but we've been discussing this for ages and you've kept on procrastinating, and I just can't trust that you'll really do it, even in two years' time. And my body doesn't have time to wait and see. So, yeah, that's that then, I think. You might need to change your morning plans anyway, because I'll need you to move all your stuff out of here while I'm out. I'll be back by 6 p.m. and I don't want to see any of it here if that's okay.' It's kind of thrilling to turn to walk away.

He springs out of bed, runs up to her and grabs her shoulder. 'Bloody hell, Robin, are you kidding me?'

She spins to face him, suddenly feeling as powerful as Aretha Franklin. 'Do I look like I'm kidding? I love you, Max, or I did love you; but if you really loved me as much as you say you do, you wouldn't have kept stringing me along when you know my body's running out of time, and you know how much this means to me – and you wouldn't have forced me into agreeing to freezing my eggs when I was drunk, and refused to make any embryos. You've never even got close to proposing, and I feel like an idiot that I've only just realized it's not actually because of the institu-tion or anything like that – it's because you don't actually want to commit to our relationship.' He starts to stutter. 'No, please don't try to deny it,' she cuts in, shaking her head and scrunching her eyes shut until he stops. She opens them to find him staring at her, with a more confused expression on his face than any she's seen before. 'We've had good times, right? I appreciate those. But I'm done now. I'm going to try not to harbour hard feelings. I wish you luck.'

All the way to Euston, her brain is a spinning top, whirling around a dark point, deep in the middle of her brain.

The overground train carriage isn't busy, and half the people in it are in walking garb too. All seem to be in groups or pairs, chattering contentedly. Several people say good morning to her, cheerily, as if it were just a lovely normal day to be going for a walk, as if she hadn't just locked the biggest drawer of her life and thrown away the key.

By the time the footpath leads her into Dockey Woods, she's alone. It feels good to be enclosed by the trees, like escaping from the glare of the real world, and she increases her pace. Fortunately there aren't any other walkers around to see her weeping as she strides. After a while, she stops for a drink of water and, perched on a stump, decides to be still for a moment. When she came here last, several years ago, with Max, it was peak bluebell time, and these woods had felt like an exquisite dream – the ground had been aglow with a purply carpet of blooms. She's too late for them this year, though there are a few mournful old flowers scattered here and there, hanging on. It's still beautiful, all the same – the ground is dappled with light from the intricate leaf canopy. She listens to the birds' pointillistic rhythms and watches the patterns shift. If only she could tell a nuthatch from a chaffinch. These are the kinds of things she can learn, now that she has her agency back.

She gets up again and walks more slowly, trying to be fully in the present. This seems like a good way to begin her next phase of life, post-Max: to navigate this route all by herself, surrounded by nature, which is always changing, always renewing. She picks up an abandoned plastic Coke bottle and stuffs it in her rucksack.

Emerging from the woods, she takes several deep breaths into the back of her lungs – the place she learned to breathe into while playing the oboe – then powers up onto the hillside.

At the top of the beacon, she sits on the grass and looks out over rolling fields etched with hedgerow squares, allowing the wind to buffet her skin. It was a misty day, though, and there wasn't much of a view. Today's is infinitely better. She takes another drink of water – a river running through her, washing away detritus. So much detritus. Overhead, a couple of kestrels glide and swerve with such energy that she finds herself getting to her feet and raising her arms like wings.

Chapter 6

Kessie

Kessie gazes unseeingly out of the train window with both palms resting on her bump, inside of which she's just begun to feel an odd fluttery sensation. Is that her girl? She imagines her bobbing about like a seahorse, exploring new sensations, and perhaps forming wordless thoughts . . . Though she can have no idea that the universe apparently contained within the walls of this womb is about to be opened up, like theatre curtains, to reveal something infinitely bigger, more wondrous, more polluted, more terrifying. Kessie looks around the carriage, as if the other passengers might have felt a tingle of the magic that's happening right here in their midst, and might be asking themselves existential questions about consciousness and perception – but they're all munching on crisps or playing Tetris on their phones.

Only thirty minutes until she's due to arrive in Bicester. She needs to be prepared to stay calm if her dad rages at her for being pregnant out of wedlock. What a term: as if being 'locked' to a husband were ever remotely acceptable. She'll just have to hope that he finds his way to forgiveness, à la Mary Magdalene.

Not that she deserves to be forgiven for doing nothing wrong. But whatever it takes for things to be okay between them again.

It's been months since she last saw him; she had been summoning up the courage to tell him about her sperm donor plan – The Facilitator wasn't even on the scene yet. He's been too busy with his congregation duties to visit her in London lately, and she's kept on pushing back a visit to Bicester because it means seeing Cara too. She can't bear discovering what her stepmother has done next to tackify the interior of the house that her mum had decorated with such love and good taste. All her Nepalese artwork and rugs replaced by 'contemporary interior design' in nasty colours. And seeing him, especially there, has just made it obvious how detached they've become from each other. He's become a completely different person these past few years – so focused on the church, and on being a good shepherd to his community, caught firmly under Cara's thumb. But if her little girl can't have a father in her life, she can at least have a grandfather.

Leaning her forehead on the vibrating window, Kessie looks out at the landscape passing like a flip book. Fields, farm buildings, scrapyards, copses, box homes, pylons, a bus station . . . *Yes, I remember Adlestrop – who wrote that? . . .* and as the train slows to a stop, a family, five of them, enfolded in a group hug on the platform. Her hand floats back to her belly.

Breathe in, one, two, three; hold it; breath out, one, two, three. Fiddle-dee-dee. Yoga classes on YouTube have helped to allay the skitters of panic about motherhood now that it's upon her. Adriene, the online yoga priestess, exudes a vibe of contentment that always makes her feel better. She has begun to feel like a friend now, and Benji, her canine muse, like a surrogate pet.

Hey there, my darling friends! Let's start by lying on our backs . . .
Find what feels good . . .

Bicester Village approaches, and the excitable shoppers pile off the train, eager to enter the white picket-fenced domain of designer outlets to root through rails of floral dresses in virulent shades, pose with studded handbags, waggle feet into stilettos . . . Kessie tells herself to stop being so snooty. She never used to loathe it until her dad met Cara here. And the irony of that first meeting is kind of hilarious.

He had been standing near the café, handing out leaflets about Jesus, doing his bit to challenge the capitalist 'moneychangers' and 'men who sold doves' by proclaiming: *ye have made this town a den of thieves!* – or something similarly embarrassing – and meanwhile Cara was dragging her three whining boys around, frantically shopping for herself without really having enough spare cash to do it, desperate to find a man to fund her habit. Their eyes met, Cara's fake lashes batted up and down, she asked him for tips on how to pray, and her dad saw an opportunity to kill two birds: religious conversion plus a hot date. At least, that's how Kessie imagines the scene playing out.

The person he used to be would never have glanced at Cara. He was a cheery, youthful dad when her mum was alive – he rocked a full 'fro, could fix any plumbing crisis with no stress, didn't judge anyone, and loved playing jazz sax, scatting in the shower, and bickering amiably over things like the relative virtues of pilau vs jollof, or the meaning of life. He was the kind of dad who took her and Robin up to London when they'd just turned ten to go to Ronnie Scott's so they could see Roy Ayers make vibraphone magic, mallets flying, euphoric jazz riffs spinning off the walls, elegant adults all around them sipping on Martinis and swaying and beating their hands together as the atmosphere intensified. Then he took them for wonton noodles in Chinatown, and back home on the night bus, letting both of them curl up on the seats and fall asleep with their heads on his old leather jacket to the sound of his humming.

After her mum died, the church offered him a sanctuary when he needed it — she gets that. And she's glad, of course, that he found comfort. But why did it have to change him quite so much? If only she could be sure he was genuinely happy in this new phase, she probably wouldn't mind him being more distant.

Or maybe she would. Maybe she's just being selfish, wishing she could be the light of his life again, like she was as his only child. Maybe she needs to accept that he's found family and illumination elsewhere now . . .

But this baby? She will surely bring a new, more sparkly light to the table. She could be the one to bring his old self out of its shell.

At the end of the front path to the house, she pauses. The ghost of her child-self skips out of the front door, followed by her mum, ready to get into the car and drive to choir or wind band. If only she could ring the doorbell now and her mum would open it, wafting out the smell of her lemon pilau. There's a new lace curtain concealing the room where she lay at the end, on the temporary bed, feather-light, like a paper doll, eyes burning.

Just before she reaches the door, Cara opens it. 'Kessie, hi! No need to hover there — come in, come in, boys are getting ready for footy, and I have a ladies' coffee meeting, your dad's just making sandwiches . . .'

Kessie makes her feet move forward, and air-kisses Cara's powdered cheek, aborting an inhale of Chanel No°5.

Her dad calls hello through the kitchen door, then charges over to give her a hug, followed by a rub on the back. He exclaims at how lovely it is to see her, but in the same breath calls up the stairs for the boys to say hi to their big sister and come to collect their sandwiches.

They clump down and grunt at Kessie before grabbing their food from the kitchen. Not a word of thanks to him for making them, even though they're all in their teens. Does he not remember that he expected Kessie to make her own sandwiches while she was still in primary school? Or maybe that was her mum's idea.

When they've left for football, he puts the kettle on for tea and she helps him tidy up the kitchen. 'So, Dad,' she says, wondering why she's feeling so cautious. 'Would you have time to come with me to visit Mum's grave?' She hasn't been for a year, and hasn't been with him for several.

'Oh, sure,' he says, sounding mildly surprised, even though she'd suggested it last time they saw each other, and not pausing in his unloading of the dishwasher. 'I do have a couple of things I need to do today, but it would be nice to go.' It's like he's humouring her – as if she'd suggested going to visit a neighbour's cat.

She waits until they're turning into the main street to tell him the news, figuring he won't want to yell at his own daughter in front of potential members of his congregation. 'Dad, there's something I wanted to tell you in person. It's kind of a significant thing, for me. I'm pregnant! And the father's left me, so I'm going solo. And

I'm fine with that. I mean, it'll be hard, I know, but I'm ready for it.' The sound of her voice seems to ring on over the traffic.

He stops walking, his face flickers – and then he laughs! The way he used to laugh after executing a ping pong smash that actually landed on the table during their summer holidays. He congratulates her, hugs her, congratulates her again, sounding so genuinely delighted, she wants to cry. But then pregnancy seems to make her want to cry at every fricking thing. The relief of it. She allowed herself to acknowledge quite how much she'd been dreading a negative reaction.

'That's just wonderful,' he says, and links his arm with hers as they continue walking. She wonders whether he's going to be able to resist mentioning wedlock, but for now he just asks to know more about it all. She explains that she had been going to go with a donor but was balking at the cost, and tells him about discovering Acorn, then meeting Angelo – The Facilitator – with all his big promises, and then about that awful night after the concert. 'Thank God for . . . I mean, I'm so lucky to have Robin.'

To her relief, he listens to it all, and doesn't criticize. When she's finally finished, he smiles tenderly, and tells her he'll pray for her. Then adds, 'We all will.'

We all? She slows her pace. Does he mean him and Cara? Or the whole congregation? Is he going to tell the whole church now? Maybe spin it into a sermon or two? Put it in the parish newsletter? Is this what happens if you have a minister for a father?

'Well, I'm just thrilled to have my first grandchild on the way,' he proclaims. 'I hope you'll allow me to baptize her?'

'Oh! Sure.' At least that's a sign that he wants to be involved. A baptism might end up being useful, too. When she told her school friend Anna that she was pregnant, Anna, an atheist, had advised booking a christening ASAP as a strategy to open up good C of E school options, and Kessie had thought she was kidding – but no; she's since discovered that this seems to be a lynchpin in the structure of London parenting.

As they approach the church – not her Dad's, which is a modern building, but the old stone one with the pretty green graveyard that her mother chose to be buried in – he starts humming 'Honeysuckle Moon'. She looks at him sideways, at his almost backward-leaning posture as he walks, hands linked behind his back, as if his forehead is connected by a thread to the sky. His toffee tones are reassuring. Cara and Jesus can't be such bad influences if he's in this mood.

Just as they're closing the churchyard gate behind them, his phone rings. He holds a hand up to Kessie apologetically, answers it, and proceeds to spend several minutes in conversation with his back to her, mm-hmming, and oh-dearing, while she picks some daisies near the entrance and starts to make a chain.

His palm lands on her back. 'Sweetheart, I'm so sorry, I have to go – family crisis in the congregation. Shouldn't be long though.'

She stares at him, beseeching. But he just says he'll be back soon, and strides away.

She walks into the graveyard alone. A few swifts squeal and wheel around the church tower, and a Monster Munch bag bounces across the path. Just in time, she stamps on it and puts it in her pocket. She used to beg for the pickled onion ones in her lunchbox, just once a week, or a month, but her mum banned crisps except on her birthday – always packed her home-baked things like seeded flapjacks and cardamom cookies. She's grateful for that now. That would be a good thing to replicate for her child – if only she weren't so bad at cooking. If only her mum had left her copies of those recipes.

Further along the path, to the rear of the graveyard, beyond the yew tree – there it is, the familiar stone. *Ehani Oduro, beloved wife and mother. She loved to sing.* Kessie pulls the tulips out of her tote bag and lays them gently down, then takes a photo of them to send to Auntie Elmi.

After looking around to check she's still alone, she sits herself down on the grave, then curls her body up into a foetal position, lying her head on the crook of her arm. 'Hi Mama. Sorry I haven't come for so long. I still miss you every day. But I've got some good news. You're going to be a grandma! How about that? I told Auntie Elmi already. She seems really happy about it.'

She closes her eyes and pictures her mum and Elmi with their arms around each other – it's really picturing a photo she has in a frame, but it's come to seem like a memory. Elmi wasn't able to have children of her own. She did get married, not long after Kessie's parents married, to a bear-like banker called Mick, and for several years they had lived in a terraced house five minutes away. She and her mum used to dream of bringing up their children together and, for a while, this had seemed likely to materialize. But after the heartbreak of multiple ectopic pregnancies, Elmi had been forced to come to terms with the fact that she wouldn't be able to have a child – and Mick took this opportunity to leave her for a woman at work who was half his age, and to get her pregnant almost instantaneously. The following year, Kessie's mum's CT scan results came through, and she died within six months. It's incredible, really, that Elmi didn't let this triple-whammy of grief destroy her. Instead, she took up meditation and yoga, and threw her energies into caring for Kessie.

Her phone vibrates – and her first thought is that it's Auntie Elmi, reading her mind from another time zone – but it's Robin. She pushes herself up to a seated position. 'Hey.'

A weird sound from the other end of the phone. 'I – I gave Max the ultimatum . . . and he . . .' Robin croaks. 'I told him if he didn't say yes he'd have to pack up and leave, today . . . and he fucking *has*! And now the flat's so empty. Did I just fuck up the rest of my life? I mean, I felt so sure, but now that he's gone . . . I feel like I barely know who I am any more – is that crazy? It's just, I've wasted eight years on him, and now I have to inject myself for this egg extraction, and I can't do it, Kess, I just can't do it!'

'Hey, shh, hon,' Kessie soothes, wishing she were there to give her a hug. 'You haven't wasted any years. You were so brave, and totally right – I'm just so sorry he ended up being gutless. Of course it's going to feel rubbish right now. But it will pass.' Still, facing a series of injections is a real kicker for Robin. She vividly remembers her friend's panic attacks on vaccination days at school, and that time when she fainted at the sight of a diabetic kid in their choir injecting herself with insulin, bashed her head on the floor, and had to be rushed to hospital – Kessie was distraught, convinced that she'd died. 'Listen, let me help with the injections at least,' she says. 'I'm actually in Bicester right now, visiting Dad, and Mum's grave, but I was just about to leave – I'll get the next train and come straight to yours, okay?'

She'll just text her dad goodbye, she decides, as she gathers her things. She hadn't promised she'd stay. 'Bye Mum,' she whispers. 'Love you.'

On the train back to London, her thoughts drift from the thick stone between her and her mother to the cold air between her and her father, and to the new barbed wire fence between Robin and Max. It's so sad, this break-up. Obviously for Robin, who's had her life dreams shattered, but for her, too, in a small, selfish way. They'd shared countless fun times together, the three of them – eating Max's delectable curries, going on trips to his parents' cottage in Norfolk, parties at their flat, camping at Latitude Festival . . . He genuinely loved to cook for people, which was a bonus – especially if you were shit at cooking but liked to eat, as she was, and Robin too – and it was also a generous trait. He was always up for an adventure – at least, in the earlier days. Objectively, he's a good-looking guy, though Kessie had never fancied him. Being Robin's boyfriend, he was forbidden fruit anyway. Still, she'd always found him a bit arrogant. The way he strode around everywhere on his long legs, sweeping his loose curls out of his eyes like a twenty-first-century Byron, confident that he could charm anyone. Worst of all, there were times, especially lately, in group situations, when he'd put Robin down, subtly but repeatedly, and she couldn't help suspecting that he was getting a kick out of it.

Three hours later, Kessie is holding a needle over Robin's bare belly as she lies like a soldier on the sofa, her long body rigid, eyes tight shut, fists clenched. Gently, Kessie places her left palm on the skin and stretches it taut, as the video instructed. The protobaby in her own belly flutters. *Here goes.* She feels like Brutus poised to stab Caesar. *No pain no gain. Seconds away and she'll be okay . . .* 'All right, Robs, we're all set. It'll be over in 3 . . . 2 . . . 1 . . .' The steel point slides into flesh like soft cheese and Robin's head jerks to one side.

'FUUUCK,' she breathes.

'We did it! Well done.' Out comes the needle, and a ruby bead of blood rolls slowly down Robin's side. Kessie wipes it off, then offers her hand and pulls Robin up to a sitting position. 'One down – not all that many more to go.'

Robin manages a small smile. 'If someone has to torture me, I'm glad it's you.'

They decide to watch a cheesy film, and land on *Dirty Dancing* as a reminiscent choice. The night of their thirteenth birthday, they'd watched it three times in a row with a couple of other girls, hugging knees inside sleeping bags on the living room sofa, munching through pick 'n' mix, and wondering at what it might be like to actually kiss a man on the lips. At the time, she had pronounced it her favourite film forever. Two decades later, though, it's actually quite troubling.

She had remembered some elements very clearly – the iconic lake lift, obviously, and Patrick Swayze's biceps. But she'd forgotten so many things, not least the centrality of Penny's backstreet abortion to the storyline. As a tween, she had experienced this as a token plot point which meant that Johnny could eventually prove that he wasn't *just* a heart throb, and Baby could shed some naivety and show that she'd come to understand the world of adults. She hadn't fully recognized the structural misogyny that underpinned the whole scenario, and what it revealed about the underbelly of the smiley white American patriarchal dreamworld. She and Robin chew over this now as they watch, wondering how it's possible that abortion remains such a touchpaper across the pond. Robin says she's worried that the extreme right in the US is inflaming to the point that the election next year might result in Obama being replaced by sinister chump Donald Trump, and maybe even Roe v. Wade being overturned, and states like South Carolina banning abortions again. Kessie reckons that's not conceivable. 'No pun intended,' she adds.

Robin laughs. 'Hope you're right. Also, after what's just happened with Max, I can't help wondering what would have happened if Baby had told Johnny he'd got *her* pregnant. I mean, he'd probably have done a runner, right?' Her face falls, comically, as soon as she's said it. 'Oh God, sorry, Kess . . .'

Kessie tells her not to be silly – that it's a good point. 'Her dad would probably have disowned her too,' she adds. 'Someone should make a sequel to see how she'd have got on as a single mum.'

Chapter 7

Robin

No eating is allowed on the day of the extraction procedure, but Robin is sure she will faint otherwise. People assume she must barely eat anything because of how thin she is, but she must have a ridiculously fast metabolism because she can't get through half a morning without breakfast. At the corner shop she buys a packet of fruit pastilles, and eats the lot on the way to the Tube, one after the other: green, orange, green, black, yellow, green, red, green. A surprisingly good ratio of lime. Kessie wouldn't agree, of course; blackcurrant is always her favourite. The sugar burst reminds her that she's empowering herself, that she's now choosing to do this, not because Max is telling her to, but despite him. Maybe she doesn't even *want* his sperm any more. It occurs to her that, after all these years, she doesn't even know his favourite fruit pastille flavour.

When she emerges from the Tube at Oxford Street, a message from Darsha pings up on her screen, wishing her lashings of luck and sending sun and heart emojis. And there's Kessie, her bump now evident, her skin glowing despite the early hour, smiling in an excessively reassuring way.

By the time they reach the reception desk, Robin is effervescing with fear and ready to turn and run – but Kessie, apparently reading her mind, grasps her hand, and she manages to confirm her name.

Another hard bed. Another needle. *Just one more . . .* A dark purple fuzz, a jangle between her ears, a double bass strumming the blues deep in her abdomen.

Kessie's voice, saying . . . *what is she saying . . .*

Her own voice, a crackle. The light – too bright.

Sometime later, information: they have extracted three eggs. *You said I needed twenty.* They are being checked for viability.

Hobbling to the taxi is a challenge. Robin has to hold on to Kessie's arm like an old woman. Kessie has begun to hobble herself, from pain in her pelvis: a pregnancy complication called PGP which is apparently quite common. 'Look at us two!' she laughs. 'Prep for when we move into a retirement home together in a few decades?'

Back at the flat, Kessie tucks her into bed and sets her up with tea, water, and snacks, books and an iPad, before she has to dash off to teach. 'Remember what the doctor said, okay? Don't try to do anything. Just relax. I'll be back tonight to check on you.'

Robin decides to watch the whole of *Pride and Prejudice* – the BBC series where Colin Firth clambers erotically out of the pond. The rest of it is excellent too – just as good as she'd remembered. By the time Kessie comes back that evening, she hasn't got out of bed except to go to the toilet. She agrees to drink a cup of soup, like a child.

That night, sleep is fitful. Every so often she comes to with shrapnel sensations in her core. Tentacles of pain.

*

Morning light. Wakefulness drifts in and out. At some point it becomes difficult to breathe. She needs water. If only Max were here – no. If only her mum were here. If only Kessie . . .

A wave of nausea. Someone is holding a candle flame to her belly, which seems to have swollen up, and is hot and hard to the touch. Not unlike a pregnant belly – irony of ironies. She checks the time: 4 p.m. It's been over twenty-four hours now. It wasn't meant to feel like this. The internet had assured her that the vast majority of women who have eggs extracted feel groggy for twenty-four hours but can go back to work the next day. Is she really so thin-skinned? Or is she one of the fraction who contract – what's it called, some acronym . . .

She phones the hospital. To her surprise, she is put straight through to the doctor, who asks cheerily how she's feeling.

'Bad. My belly's swollen up like a balloon and it hurts like hell.'

'Sorry to hear that. But some swelling and discomfort is quite normal in the first few days. 'Can you tell me how bad the pain is on a scale of one to ten?'

'Nine?'

'I see. Why don't we see how you do overnight?' the doctor says. 'If it gets worse, and you can't speak, then do call us again. How does that sound?'

Robin wants to point out the impossible conundrum of this instruction, but it hurts too much to figure out how to do so politely. She remembers the term, now: ovarian hyperstimulation syndrome, which sounds more like a hit of cocaine than prolonged agony. 'I'm just worried it could be OHSS . . .'

'Oh, that's unlikely. Even if it is, the symptoms usually pass quickly, so don't worry. As it happens, your results came through about an hour ago. I was going to call you in the morning. Would you like me to discuss them with you now?'

'Oh, yes, definitely.' As if she'd say no. Though her brain might struggle to process anything beyond this pain. She needs to concentrate.

'Right then. Well, I'm sorry to say that the news isn't great,' the doctor continues. 'As you know, we only extracted three eggs, and I'm afraid that our tests have found two of them to be flawed, with at least one chromosome missing. If they were to be fertilized, and survive to term, that would lead to some terribly serious conditions. Life-altering. So we wouldn't be able to proceed with those.'

'Mm hmm.' Robin finds she's chewing on her cheeks like bubble gum. A joke comes to mind that she read on one of the forums. *How would you like your eggs: fertilized or scrambled?*

'Alright? So I'm afraid this means that only one egg is viable, at least for this round, and as you know, since you're over 35 now, the chances of success using frozen eggs are a lot lower. We *can* still freeze this one egg for you, if you wish, but you do just need to be aware that the chances of it leading to a live birth are minimal. I know this will be difficult news.'

'Er, yeah.' She should have known this would fail. 'I still want to freeze it,' she blurts. 'Please.'

'Of course. I suggest we talk about next steps once you're feeling better, and we can discuss the possibility of further treatment then too. Does that sound okay? Sorry, I'm just being paged – I have to go, but any questions, do call again. I hope you're feeling better in the morning.'

Click.

Robin holds the coolness of her phone screen against her cheek. Five thousand quid down the drain. At least the company's paying. So, that's it then. Her womb is a malfunctioning vending machine. Empty but for one mouldy Bounty bar.

She reaches over for her cup of tea. Reaching hurts. The tea is no longer even tepid. Her heart starts racing. What if she does have OHSS, and it escalates, and she's in too much pain to call again for help, or genuinely can't speak to let anyone know what's happening, and dies alone here, with only her fish for company? And they're not even in the same room. *Berlioz – help me.* She did glimpse some horror stories about egg extraction fallouts on the various fertility forums but couldn't bring herself to read them properly at the time. *Wouldn't happen to me.*

Chewing her fist, lying on the bed, she finds herself picturing Kurt Cobain's dimple-chinned face, with the mournful, reflective expression he wore as he looked out of the giant poster she'd stuck up on her wall when she was thirteen. The news of his suicide came out of nowhere, like the pain she's in now. She and Kessie had holed up in her bedroom and wept their way through *Unplugged in New York* several times over.

She searches for the album on her phone now and puts it on, for the first time in years, then types OHSS into the search bar. Turns out it is more likely to be a side effect for women with polycystic ovaries – a fact that none of the medics had thought to tell her before she went ahead with the operation – and that vomiting is one of the symptoms. The thought triggers her to lunge to the bathroom and hang over the toilet.

After brushing her teeth, splashing her face, and avoiding looking at it in the mirror, she staggers back to bed again. After the album reaches its fatalistic end, she opens the nature sounds app. Forest rain, *yes* – the gentle rush of water on leaves, that fairy godmother oak from when she and Kessie were kids, reaching down two gnarled arms to scoop her up.

Chapter 8

Kessie

Kessie waddles towards the primary school entrance with Robin, an invisible penknife sliding up and down her groin with every step. She'd never even heard of pelvic girdle pain until she got it, but it turns out one in five pregnant women do. At least she'll get to sit down all day at this prenatal class. She had been loath to splash out on the course, but Helena and Jen, who've both done it, convinced her that it's an invaluable way to meet other local mums-to-be, so that, once your babies arrive, you have people to hang out with in the park, ask silly questions about breastfeeding, and vent to about sleep routines. It's a bit of a gamble – she can hardly claim a refund if she doesn't like any of these women. Is it too much to hope that she won't be the only single one?

At the gates, she rewinds to her infant self, dressed in clean white knee-high socks and a cotton checked dress, scared about going to school for the very first time and wanting desperately to suck her thumb. To her mum, crouching down, kissing her forehead, producing a flying saucer wrapped in tin foil from her pocket, telling her she loves her to the moon and back, the sherbet tingling on her tongue. One day, before too long, she will be walking through the gates of a primary school to drop her own daughter off.

'You okay?' Robin's asking.

'Yeah yeah, sorry! Let's go in.'

Robin gives her a contorted smile, her face still puffy from last month's nightmare. Kessie still feels haunted by that evening she came back from work to Robin's flat the day after the extraction, just to check on her, expecting them to have a drink together – to find her almost passed out, unable to utter a word from the pain, her belly inflated like a watermelon, and her face as bloated as Violet Beauregard's in *Charlie and the Chocolate Factory* when she began to transform into a blueberry. Kessie had called 999, and fortunately an ambulance came quickly. Robin spent the next twenty-four hours in intensive care, and it took a week before she was well enough to walk properly again. Of course, being Robin, she went back to work the first day she could.

They follow the signs to a classroom in which bucket chairs are arranged in a circle. Four heavily expectant women and four men glance around at them and nod or smile. Kessie sits down, inelegantly, trying not to groan. Inevitably, they will all have already assumed that she and Robin are lesbian mums-to-be, which would be fine if it were true.

The teacher arrives, bearing a large thermos decorated with 1970s brown and orange flower patterns which she sets down next to a tray full of mugs on a table. She has a long plait of greying hair extending to a thin rat's tail, and a multicoloured patchwork dress. 'Welcome, everyone!' she announces. 'I'm Yvonne, and

I'll be leading these classes. I thought we'd start off with a nice chamomile tea – please go over and help yourselves.'

'Not even any *normal* tea,' the older guy mutters loudly to the woman next to him. 'Told you.'

Once they're all seated again, Yvonne picks up her bag and pulls out a frayed woolly mammoth with a drooping trunk and a wonky ear. 'I'd like to introduce you all to Magnus!' Magnus looks mournfully into the middle distance. 'All my children *adored* this chap. For our first activity I'd like us to pass him around – when you get him, can you please tell us your name and what you're most looking forward to about parenthood.'

The woman seated on Yvonne's right takes the toy gingerly between her fingertips and rests him lightly on the corner of one knee – probably wondering, like Kessie, whether it has been washed in the last twenty-odd years. She is wearing a floaty floral dress and is petite, and Asian, with enviable hair like a black mirror. 'I'm Alice,' she says, 'and this probably seems trivial, but I'm looking forward to putting my baby girl in this super cute Stella McCartney dress that my mum has already bought her . . . and actually,' she adds, confiding, 'Stella's the name we've picked out! Hope none of you are going for that too?'

Kessie glances at Robin. Is this woman bagsying a name right now?

The man next to her, attired in an ironed shirt and deck shoes, relieves her of the toy and announces himself as Ralph, her husband – he's looking forward to introducing Stella to his rowing team.

'Well, *I'm* Alice too!' the next woman bursts out, before she's even got hold of Magnus. Alice Two has a cascade of reddish curls and is wearing baggy dungarees. 'So good to meet you all at this incredible moment in our parenting journey.' She smiles around at everyone, misty-eyed. 'We have a home birth planned,' she adds. 'I'm actually feeling *really* ready, like, I'm actually looking *forward* to it now, you know? I admit I *was* initially a little bit worried about pain, but then I realized that was mostly because of all the media depictions of women in hospitals, and it doesn't actually have to be like that, you know? So we've looked into other ways of doing it – more holistic ways. And getting more in touch with our bodies – getting spiritually ready, too. So, meditating a lot, and doing tantric yoga to connect with each other on a deeper level . . . it's been an amazing experience already, honestly.'

Alice Two's partner squeezes her knee, nodding earnestly, and takes Magnus. 'Totally. I'm Seth, and what I cannot wait for is my first skin-to-skin with our baby.' He grins and nods around the circle, as if they should all know what he's talking about. 'I admit, I've cried at the YouTube videos already,' he says, pushing out his lower lip as if this would make them all want to shed a tear too. 'And yeah, totally recommend tantric. It goes deep, at a deep time in our lives, right?'

'Excuse me, I'm just popping to the loo,' Robin croaks.

Magnus is now dangling by his trunk in Kessie's direction, so she takes him, and looks into his button eyes for a moment, as if he could give her some last-minute advice, then out to the group. 'Hi, I'm Kessie – I'm here with my best mate, Robin, and I've got to admit I'm pretty nervous about the birth. I do like yoga, but I can't do much of it at the moment . . . I'll probably be a total wuss at the birth and max out on the drugs! I'm definitely looking forward to not being pregnant any more. I've got PGP so I'm struggling to walk – I feel like a ninety-year-old.'

She had meant to be amusing, but Yvonne is glaring at her like she's just blasphemed.

The woman to her left cackles and reaches out for Magnus. 'Love it,' she says. 'I'll be asking for all the drugs too.'

Kessie grins, grateful not to be the only aspiring drug user in the room. She likes her neighbour's style: cropped hair that suits her heart-shaped face, baggy jeans, a blue checked shirt with turquoise lines in it.

'Well,' Yvonne cuts in sternly, 'drugs are, of course, available to those who choose to take them – but I hope this class will help you to make an *informed* choice once we've talked about the *very real* benefits of a *natural* birth. Now, would you like to tell everyone your name please?'

'Oh sure. I'm Sam.' Sam passes Magnus quickly on to her partner, who clears his throat.

'And I'm Al. I'm actually transitioning at the moment, in case anyone was wondering – when Sam got pregnant it really hit me I'd always wanted to be a dad, rather than a mum. It had been a long time coming, though.' He gives Sam a half-smile. 'We've both been through the mill already, in some ways, but this baby means the world to us. As for something particular I'm looking forward to – well, I'm half German, so I'm looking forward to singing her some German lullabies.'

Kessie had never thought of this before – what it would be like to dream of being a dad in a woman's body. She wonders what lullabies her mum used to sing her – she'll have to ask her dad. She's pretty sure he used to sing her jazz standards in her cradle.

As Robin comes back in from the loo, Al tosses Magnus across to her – she catches him deftly before sitting down. 'Thanks! Hi there, Magnus.' She sits down. 'Well, I'm Robin, Kessie's my oldest friend, and it's a huge privilege for me to be involved in the birth. She's going to take motherhood by *storm* and be the most amazing parent. So I'm just looking forward to being there to help if she needs me – during the birth, afterwards.'

'Aww! That's soooo cute!' Alice Two coos, hands clasped. Kessie stares at Robin, biting her cheeks. She didn't expect such a public testament, or how much it would mean.

'Well, that's very nice to hear,' Yvonne the teacher says briskly. 'And I hope this group will prove helpful for those of us who need *more positive thinking.*'

The day takes a turn for the worse after lunch when Yvonne opens a large duffle bag and produces a pair of tights, a sack of potatoes, a pack of currants, a can of beans and a bottle of water. 'Our next theme,' she announces, 'is how pregnancy affects women's bodies. Here's the baby in the uterus!' – she stuffs the potatoes into the tights – 'so you can see, the uterus expands a *lot.*' She looks around to check that they're paying attention. 'This compresses the stomach, squashes the bladder and bowels, and puts a lot of weight on the perineum. Now, here's the placenta . . .' – she pushes the currants on top – 'here's the expanded uterus . . .' – in goes the can of beans – 'and here's the amniotic fluid!' She shoves in the water bottle, and ladders the tights. 'So it's no wonder you all need the *loo* more these days!' A half-hearted ripple of laughter passes around the circle.

'We also need to be aware that the size of the baby requires women's vaginas to expand *significantly* to deliver it,' she continues. Kessie glances at Robin, who's looking fixedly at a child's painting on the wall. She's always been a bit grossed-out by this stuff – it hadn't occurred to Kessie until now that accompanying her to this class might make her feel ill. 'Now, this is Gertrude.' Yvonne pulls out a model pelvis skeleton, and a rubber baby attached by a wire to a red blob bigger than its skull. The blob, she explains, is a model of the placenta. She pushes the doll firmly through the pelvis, making the bones expand dramatically, like a book opening – then repeats the action several times. She looks around, to check that the mums-to-be have all registered the extent of the contortions their bodies are about to go through. 'Now,' she says, 'as you can see, women's bodies are very well designed to allow us to give birth naturally, with a bit of help from gravity. The problem is that *Western* medical culture has *medicalized* pregnancy and birth, obstructing women from our innate *instinct* to know and trust our own bodies. We get told by male doctors to lie on our backs and raise our legs, just so that they can get an easy view, and we're pressured to accept all *sorts* of *drugs* that *interfere* with the natural processes, and risk doing a lot more harm.'

Robin sits forward. 'I was just wondering what you thought about the reseach that says that human babies' skulls have always been proportionately bigger than other mammals' skulls in relation to birth canals, and that they seem to be getting bigger, partly because of c-sections, but also because of Western lifestyles and diets, so vaginal birth is even more difficult than it used to be,' she says. 'Is that making natural birth, as you put it, a bit riskier, too?'

Yvonne smiles at her overly sweetly. 'There are plenty of articles offering opinions on things like that, and there is of course always some risk involved in giving birth, but I'm talking about my experience from *thirty years* of working with women through childbirth. Now, to pick up from where I was: then there's the *stress* of birth, which is *exacerbated* by the soulless environment of hospitals, and that makes us even *more* likely to need interventions, like forceps, or vaginal cutting – which can take *months* to heal. It's *far* better to avoid all that, where possible, and walk around during labour, move, dance, crawl . . . embrace your animal side! We are all animals after all!'

It's quite a persuasive speech, Kessie thinks, although there's something about Yvonne's tone that grates. She sounds so certain that she's right. And all those potatoes bulging out of the tights . . . Kessie is pretty sure she still wants all the drugs on hand if she needs them. Or does she?

'When labour begins,' Yvonne continues, 'you'll find yourself wanting to express sounds – deep, guttural sounds. Embrace that! Let it all out! It will help. You might even find that you get to experience an *ecstatic* birth – anyone know about those?'

Seth's hand shoots up. 'That's when the mother orgasms on delivery, right?' Kessie and Robin look at each other, checking they heard right. 'We heard perineal massage can help to make that happen,' Seth continues, like it's totally normal, 'so . . . we've been practising.'

'Fantastic!' Yvonne beams at him as if she'd like to give him a gold star. 'Now, birth partners first: I'd like you all to make a *sound* you might expect your partner to make when giving birth. Don't hold back. I'll count to three then we'll vocalize together. One, two, three, *UUUHHHHH!*'

At the sound that comes out of her, Kessie half expects the

windows to rattle. She leans towards Robin. 'I'll feel let down if you hold back on this.'

*

That evening, they recount the funniest moments from the class while making dhal. Neither of them has ever been any good at cooking, but when Kessie told Robin she wanted to learn to do it better so that she and her daughter wouldn't have to live on tinned soup and sliced bread, Robin said she'd try to learn too, and turned up last week with a book of recipes. 'That moo-roaring was quite something,' Robin recalls. 'I channelled all my rage into it – it was kind of liberating.'

'I was impressed.'

'Made me think about laughter yoga,' Robin says. 'Heard of that? Started in India I think. It basically involves making yourself laugh, and then the laughter gets infectious, and before long everyone in the group is in stitches. Ready to add the garlic?'

Kessie tips her chopped garlic cloves into the oil and watches the pieces sizzle. She could do with a laughter yoga class – she's started to get increasingly anxious that she's really not up to the task of parenting. She thinks about Alice One who had been going on earlier about various purees that she'd already been making, so that she'd be able to avoid the supermarket versions with their high sugar content for their already-perfect unborn child. She thinks about Alice Two and her tantric yoga. 'That ecstatic birth thing – is that just a myth, do you think?' she asks. 'I mean, the *idea* of orgasming when my vagina's just had to expand to fit that bag of potatoes . . .'

Robin makes a face. 'God, yeah. I've gotta say, that part triggered all my old fears. But if anyone deserves an ecstatic birth, Kess, it's you. Hey, wouldn't it be great if someone made a film referencing the orgasm scene in *When Harry Met Sally* but set in a labour ward?'

Kessie claps her hands. 'You should write the script! You know, alongside a dissertation. And a full-on full-time job.'

Robin side-grins and consults the recipe book. 'Time for the lentils?'

Kessie pours them in. 'I mean, I know Yvonne was a bit out there, but she did make me think. Like, maybe I shouldn't take all the drugs, necessarily. Maybe I should just walk around and dance and moo a lot.'

Robin stirs the pan. 'Well . . . I guess you can give that a try and see how you feel on the day?'

Kessie nods, washing her hands. 'I guess.'

'Chopping a chilli, Robin says: 'You know, I was just reading about women giving birth in Guinea-Bissau, where most of them get no pain relief. They don't forbid screaming, but it's only allowed if it's *appropriate*.'

'Harsh. I hadn't really contemplated effing and blinding at you while screaming . . .'

'Feel free!' Robin tips in the chilli. 'Come, even better! I'm here for it. Wait, that sounded wrong.'

Chapter 9

Robin

Robin wakes to a vague feeling that she has lost something. She turns over to an empty half of the bed. Why is she still sticking to her side? *You're the love of my life,* Max had told her once, on the balcony of a B & B in Ljubljana. She pictures Kessie's hand stroking the incline of her bump in the prenatal class, the glimmer of a smile on her lips. For now, she can fill this new emptiness by focusing on making Kessie's experience of having a baby as positive as it can be. And ideally not stealing the limelight by fainting at a critical moment, cracking her head open and becoming a useless birth partner.

But what about after this child arrives? Kessie will be besotted, and surrounded by her all her new mum friends. Robin will be left alone with her malfunctioning womb.

She swings her legs out of the bed and reaches for her dressing gown.

Down in the kitchen, she makes a coffee, and stands at the counter looking out of the window. A robin flutters onto a low wall and hops lightly along. She's always felt so unlike her namesake bird, with its dinky neatness and confident colour. But she does love the song. Will this one sing? It seems to consider it for a moment, and then flies off.

She goes through to the living room to feed the fish. Berlioz is hiding out in his cave and the others look despondent, save for two of the tetras who are sniping at each other. She sprinkles in their flakes, but doesn't get the usual pleasure from seeing them scurry to the surface to gobble them up. Her brain hurts. Her heart hurts. She calls in sick for work, claiming continuing side effects from her extraction, which is true, and goes back to bed.

After skimming through friends' social media posts, including lots of smiley baby pictures, she gets up again. In the kitchen, she takes a big bar of Lindt chocolate out of the high cupboard, brings it back to bed, and eats it steadily while searching for articles on the anthropology of childless women.

She clicks on a piece about attitudes towards family formation among Danish women in their mid to late thirties. Interviewees were attending a fertility clinic and were all very conscious of their biological clock; one felt as if she were being held at gunpoint. Their adult lives had been occupied by education, careers, and travelling, and they had harboured ambiguous feelings about forming a family until recently, but now felt it would be a deep loss not to have children, especially as they got older. Robin closes the laptop. She's just a grain of sand on a very long beach.

The walls of the flat seem to be closing in. She has to get out or she might implode. Time to go and seek inspiration.

As soon as she steps into the first of the National Gallery's giant rooms she feels the glow of having made a good decision. It's what she needed, this quiet riot of colour and form, of ideas, and people. So many characters, from so many eras and places, looking out at her, silently feeling all kinds of unnamable things. For a while, she wanders around aimlessly.

She pauses at a sixteenth-century painting by Pinturicchio titled *Virgin and Child*. Mary and the baby Jesus are both balancing halos like brass plates on their heads. He looks like a savvy miniature teen aristocrat who knows full well that he's going to dominate the lives of millions for centuries to come. Does he realize he'll have to be crucified first, though? Mary is too modest to look at the painter. She's looking down at her baby with an expression that is almost serene – but her lips are slightly pursed. Is she trying to hold back her feelings? Or is she wary of more angels turning up out of the blue and making demands about how she should go about parenting God's son? It occurs to Robin that, so far as she can recall, Mary didn't even consent to her impregnation; Gabriel effectively ambushed her, in her house, and informed her of her imminent fate, with no explanation. The realities of her pregnancy are largely omitted from the story too – no hint of morning sickness, or PGP. As for labour, the babe appears to emerge painlessly from Mary's body, in a filthy stable full of defecating animals, and is immediately cleaned-up and ready for portraits. How would you go about parenting the son of God, through the toddler years? Should he be required to follow a sleep routine? Be allowed to suck his thumb? Get a telling off after a tantrum? Or did God make sure that he was always a model baby? Why does she have to be so cynical? Religion would provide exactly the spiritual reassurance she needs right now.

She walks on for a bit, until her attention is caught by a couple of small paintings that look like bronze sculptures of women, painted in the fifteenth century by an Italian court artist called Mantagena. One of the women is standing under a tree, knocking back a huge glass of wine, while looking up towards the sky. She has sturdy arms, bulbous breasts, curly locks, and drop earrings, and she looks intent and serious. According to the interpretation board, she was probably meant to be Sophonisba: a Carthaginian ruler who drank poison rather than be taken into slavery by a Roman general. Robin wonders what this woman would advise her right now, if she could put the drink down and give her one final piece of advice. *Mamma mia – you are lucky – you have women's rights! A job! You'll never have to face being enslaved! Quit worrying and enjoy your freedom.*

Walking on, she passes a gay couple holding hands and laughing about something – and an idea strikes.

*

The next day, waiting for Benjy in the pub garden in the chilly sunshine, she finds she can't sit still, and begins to pace around, rehearsing lines under her breath as if she's about to give a high-stakes client presentation – even though they've been friends since day one of university. This could be super awkward. Or it could be great. It would probably be best to wait until they've eaten and absorbed some alcohol before raising it.

Benjy would be an ideal dad, all things considered: he's fun, clever, witty, kind, and loves kids. Last year, when they were sitting next to each other at a friend's wedding, he told her that he and Dom had both decided they were ready to have a family. 'You've gotta be open-minded about kids if you're gay though,' he'd pointed out, sanguinely, as if he could take it or leave it. It could be that her offer today will turn out to be an ideal opportunity for them both at the ideal time. They're getting married next summer, and Dom's a successful actuary so money won't be an issue. Benjy's acting career has taken off too – until recently, his income was as erratic as Kessie's, but now he's getting regular gigs on stage and TV, and they've moved into a house in Dulwich. This could be the answer for all of them. Robin pauses to take a deep breath and release it, slowly. She plucks a holly leaf from the bush by the path, and runs her finger along the rim of a leaf to its point. She has already faced her phobia and endured multiple injections and surgery in this quest for a baby. What she's about to do now is easy in comparison.

'Suarez! Yoo-hoo!' Benjy appears at the gate garbed in a long purple tweed coat. 'How are you, gorgeous girl? He gives her his usual three cheek kisses, then takes her by the shoulder to look at her tenderly. 'I'm sorry you've been having such a crappy time.'

'Thanks Benj. I'm doing all right. Let's get drinks!'

Benjy effortlessly chats up a cute bartender while ordering fizz. He has always been so elegant, like a camp Fred Astaire. Robin was the second person he came out to, in their first year, after the boy he had a crush on rejected him. She'd confessed to him a year or so later that she'd fancied a few girls as well as boys, and wondered if she might be gay too – but he'd just laughed at her. He was like: 'Girl, those are crushes. Take it from me, if you're actually gay, you know it.' Was it because of that conversation that she had only kissed another girl twice in her life?

The first was Michelle, a blue-haired girl from orchestra who'd lunged at Robin on a drunken night out and inserted a pierced tongue into her mouth, so forcefully that she had feared for a moment that she might gag. Fortunately she didn't, and instead found herself reciprocating, partly out of surprise, partly self-defence, and partly curiosity, along with a smidgen of desire. The next day, nursing a hangover, she felt too confused and embarrassed even to tell Kessie about it.

The second time was when she was visiting Kessie at music college, went to a jazz gig, and found herself fixated on a singer called Ruby with a voice almost as deep as Nina Simone's. She felt compelled to go up and speak to her at the bar afterwards, something she was rarely forward enough to do. Only as they talked did it occur to her that she might be flirting, and that Ruby might be flirting back. After a few drinks, it felt natural to lean in for a kiss, and this time it felt amazing – but also, afterwards, like she might just have imagined the whole thing.

As always, there's a lot to catch up on in Benjy's world. He tells her about his latest play: a queer retelling of *Macbeth* set in a Malaga beach resort, which he has high hopes for despite a tiny budget; and about Dom's new cycling hobby and penchant for Lycra. The conversation meanders to the looming Brexit vote and US election drama, social media, *Breaking Bad*, and forest fires in California. Robin wonders aloud why Darsha isn't more worried about the fires – and Benjy says Dom reckons that before long no companies will even insure houses over there. He asks how her anthropology studies are going, and how the hell she's still balancing that with her job. She starts telling him about her dissertation research into diverse approaches to family formation across cultures, which is a tempting segue to her big question . . . But she holds off, nerves bubbling up again.

They move on to Kessie and the Angelo debacle, and Benjy concludes that this is why you should never trust macho, misogynistic men. Robin is about to follow up by asking how his own thinking about parenthood is going – but he has already begun recounting a calamitous audition for a West End show he did recently, and his latest weekend away with Dom in which he ended up standing on a table and performing a spoof Hamlet to an entire pub. They pay the bill, then stroll into the woods.

The sharp, mossy scent, and the tapestry of green is instantly soothing; Robin begins to feel emboldened again. Benjy chatters on about Dom's family – something to do with his nephew who's addicted to video games, and his dad buying a late-life-crisis Harley Davidson and wearing leather trousers to the post office. Ahead of them, a little boy of about seven is climbing on a fallen beech tree, and the dad is helping a baby girl to stand up on it too. The family looks so happy that Robin's heart accelerates, and she finds herself interrupting him: 'Benj.' It comes out like a bark, and she hears him cut off mid-sentence. She stops walking. 'Do you and Dom still want a family? I mean, I remember you said ages ago that you'd like to, but – do you think the time might be right to plan it now? What with you getting married soon . . .' She's speaking too fast. She needs to make this sound more casual, more appealing, not like a desperate plea.

'Well . . . how come?'

The birds seem to have stopped singing, and the little boy's gleeful shouts fade. The trees are still there, though, solid and reassuring. 'I just wanted . . . to ask you a favour, which might end up being a favour for you, too . . . It's just that – you know I really want to have a baby, and I'm running out of time, and my fertility's shooting down a helter-skelter – well, I was thinking that you'd be an incredible dad, and obviously I love Dom too, so I'd be honoured if . . . you wanted . . . if you were in any way interested in . . . co-parenting? With me. Obviously. Involving Dom, of course, if he's into it.' So much for not sounding desperate. Whatever she just said must have come out at three hundred words per minute at least.

Benjy's face is unreadable. She's not sure she's ever seen him lost for words.

'You don't have to answer now, obviously,' she adds, smiling hopefully, 'and no pressure . . .'

'Wow,' he says finally. 'Listen, Suarez, I'm flattered. Genuinely. And a little shocked. But it's a great idea! I'd have to talk to Dom though . . .'

Robin lets out a peal of laughter that doesn't sound remotely like her own. 'Oh God, of course – I'm just relieved that you're not appalled!'

'Are you nuts? Come here.' He gives her a long hug. His aftershave is musky and fruity, and she can smell a hint of cigarettes. 'Suarez,' he says solemnly, pulling back – 'my sperm would be *honoured* to meet eggs of your calibre.'

She lets out a puff of laughter. 'Calibre of eggs – sounds like something a gastropub would serve up. I mean, I've only managed to produce *one* frozen egg so far that isn't scrambled, and I cannot go through that process again, so it better fucking had be of good calibre. But thank you. That's sweet.' They walk for a bit, not speaking. Then Benjy ventures: 'So . . . in theory, how did you envisage the co-parenting thing working?'

Robin bites her lip. 'Well, I'm totally open to negotiating. But I'd quite like to do most of it. So I was thinking maybe you guys could have the baby every other weekend or something, if you wanted to? But we could just figure out something that suits you and Dom too . . .'

'All right! Well – it sounds like fun. Thanks for asking.' He drapes his arm around her shoulders, and they carry on walking.

The sun's fingers wave through the trees, as if it had heard the news, and a lime-green parakeet perches on a nearby branch and tips its head back for a celebratory squeak.

That evening, Robin runs a bath and starts watching a David Attenborough documentary with her iPad propped up on the sink. A male cuttlefish with rippling fins and swirling tentacles is employing incredible trickery in his attempts to mate. He changes colour, from emerald to purple, and changes pattern, from zebra stripes to a complex jaguar-like print – which is miraculous to watch – and then he performs a gender-bending trick to make himself look like a female in order to lure one to appraise his charms.

Her phone rings. Benjy's name is on the screen! Is this a good or bad sign?

She clambers out and grabs a towel. It would be weird to talk about having a baby with him while naked, not to mention with Dom – although nakedness is probably quite a common state for such conversations. She freezes the cuttlefish mid-embrace, and presses answer. 'Hey Benj! How are you doing?'

'Fine, fine. You?'

'Great!' She sits down on the bathroom storage box, filled with half-used toiletry bottles that she should probably use up so as not to waste the contents, but realistically never will and should just throw out.

'So,' Benjy proceeds, 'you know I *love* your idea, and I'm *super* touched that you asked me – I mean, you'd be an awesome co-parent . . .' His tone is too tentative. She screws up her eyes, waiting for the 'but'. 'But I've been talking to Dom. He does want kids too, but he wants them on our own terms – so that we could have sole care, and not be tied up in a more complicated arrangement. I'm really sorry. I know you said it could be flexible and light touch, and I did try to persuade him, but he pointed out there'd be logistics, like holidays and Christmases, and it'd be tricky if we, or you, wanted to move away. Plus, I think he feels like he'd be left out. If I had a baby with you. Not just because he wouldn't be a biological dad, but he couldn't legally be a parent at all. On the birth certificate. You know, because you can only put two parents on there? So, basically, he wants to go down the surrogate route. Just the two of us. I'm really sorry.'

Robin bites her lips, trying to work out what to say that isn't a swear.

'Suarez? You still there?'

She swallows. 'Yeah, yeah. That's all . . . fair enough,' she whispers. In all honesty, the birth certificate thing hadn't occurred to her. Has the law really not evolved by now to allow family structures involving more than two parents?

'You okay, hon?'

'Oh, yeah, of course,' she lies, in a high voice. 'I'm just, well . . .

what if . . . if we were to ditch the co-parenting part? You could just be a sperm donor, like Angelo but not a git – no strings?' She sounds so pathetic. 'You wouldn't have to be on a birth certificate, either of you, but you could both be uncle-like figures – occasionally, if you felt like it, or not, if you didn't? And then you could still have your own kids with a surrogate in your own time? It's just . . . Benj, I really need sperm. Like, *soon*. And I'd love it to be yours.'

'Aw, Suarez. That's so nice of you. I'd love to help you out, and you already know my views on your calibre of eggs. Gastro-tastic. But . . . I did actually suggest that to Dom already.'

'You did?'

'Yeah. He reckons even that would be too complicated. He was like: what if you *said* that in the abstract, but then, when the kid actually arrived, you decided you *did* want to be more involved? He said he could imagine that happening with me and you, because of how close we are, and that it would make him uncomfortable. And, I mean, he just knows me too well, to be honest. I'd probably go crazy with love for our kid if we had one.'

'Aw Benj.' How had she not anticipated this? Bloody Dom. Her rational brain can see his point. But what about his empathy for her situation?

'Have you thought about paying for a donor?' Benjy asks.

'A donor? Yeah – I mean, I could do that, and it does make total sense as an option. I'm just – I don't know why but I'd rather it be someone I know,' she says. But why *can't* she be more open to that? Why can't she just be braver, more sure of herself – like Kessie?

After the call, the cuttlefish regards her solemnly, judgily, in his frozen pose on her screen. *Take a seaweed frond out of my book*, he seems to be saying. *More cuttlefish in the ocean. More spells in the cauldron.*

She walks slowly to the bedroom to get dressed. Are there any other guys she knows, even straight ones, who might be up for donating or co-parenting in some form? Dylan, her gap year travel buddy, comes to mind . . . but that really would be complicated. Not just because he was crazy about Darsha for that whole year, but because he's married now, albeit unhappily, with two girls of his own. Leila, his wife, had always been a bit cold towards her and Darsha, and would surely veto the idea.

On the Tube home from work the next day, she reads an academic article arguing that an unintended consequence of improved fertility technologies is a new culture of 'anxious reproduction' in the West. The research was based on interviews among single women who were considering using sperm donors. All felt uncertainty about going ahead, and some worried that solo motherhood might not be fair on a child – that they might be being selfish by putting their need for a child above their future child's need for a father.

Back home, she scrolls through a sperm donor website, then closes it and puts on a Joni album – not *Blue* for a change, but *The Hissing of Summer Lawns*. It's well known that Joni felt she had no choice but to give up her only baby for adoption, as a young singer yet to make it. Society, still, really needs better extended support networks for women. Other mammals manage much better – Robin watched an interesting documentary a while back about elephant matriarchs. She types 'matriarchal animal societies' into a search box now, just to see.

Turns out lemurs live in groups led by a female matriarch, and it's she who decides when the group will eat, sleep, and travel. All the females are bigger than the males, and they get to pick their mating partners.

Bonobos – not far removed from humans – live in female-led groups too. Apparently they are the most peaceful of the primates, able to settle their differences more easily and solve conflicts more amicably. Often by using sex.

Meerkats live in female-led groups, pleasingly known as mobs. The head of the mob leads the way in finding new burrows and in handling arguments.

Mole-rat queens are even more powerful, leading colonies of up to 300. They choose the strongest males and mate with them multiple times a year, and can end up having seven babies every two months. Which seems like a bit of an excessive effort. But it's a piece of cake compared to the reproductive expectations of queen leafcutter ants: they can produce 150 million worker offspring over a fourteen-year lifespan. At least they don't have to do anything in terms of childcare, like mammals do.

Orcas, Robin is thrilled to learn, also live in matrilineal societies. They used to be her favourite animals when she was a kid, after she saw some with her parents on a trip to Florida for a conference her dad was speaking at – and yet she never knew this fact about them before now. They travel around the sea in groups known as 'matrilines', and an offspring lives with its mother for its entire life, even after having offspring of its own. She thinks of her own mother. Of the distance between them these days. Remembers the three of them on deck, marvelling at the majesty of the orcas' sleek, leaping forms. She'd never been one of those warm, cuddly mothers, like Kessie's was, but she'd always been reliably supportive, present, and strong – until Brian came along.

Robin closes the laptop and resolves to be there for Kessie's child. To become part of a new, protective matriline, as loyal as an orca, and as adaptable as a cuttlefish to whatever comes her own way afterwards.

Chapter 10

Kessie

While eating her porridge, Kessie searches online for buggies suitable for newborns. There are so many different types, and the decent ones are unaffordable, even second-hand – it's like trying to buy a car. She adds seven to her watchlist and bids for one, knowing she won't win. Then searches for slings, thinking that maybe she can just carry the baby around the whole time until she starts to walk.

At the window, she contemplates the scraggy forecourt of the estate, and mentally replays the awkward messages she's exchanged with her dad since she left Bicester that day without saying goodbye.

I had to help Robin – it was an emergency.

A shame not to see much of you. You visit us so rarely.

Same goes for you. Anyway, you left before even getting to Mum's grave, just to see someone I don't even know.

I'm sorry I let you down, but I'm afraid it is part of my job and vocation to help members of my church family who are in need.

Sure.

I'm praying for you, darling. Come to see us again soon.

Saw this fabric and it reminded me of mum. You know, that throw you used to have?

It's nice.

Do you still have it? The throw?

Not sure. Possibly not.

Did you keep any of my baby stuff? That corduroy sling from the photos?

I'm afraid Cara had a clear-out.

Outside, a woman is pushing a pushchair across the car park with a large baby strapped into it, all its limbs flailing wildly. She is dragging a toddler behind, telling the toddler off at the top of her voice. Kessie shudders at the idea that this will be her before too long, but without the second child. She'll end up being a stay-at-home frantic single mum stereotype. She's not even sure how she'll afford to top up the heating this week and pay her phone bill – without a baby to provide for. On which note, it's time to go out to work.

*

By 6 p.m., Kessie is so shattered from a day of clarinet teaching that, after wolfing a packet of rice cakes, she's ready to go straight to bed. When her phone rings, she's about to press cancel – until she sees that it's Robin.

'Hey, got your diary handy?' Robin asks, as chirpily as if she's just had her morning coffee. 'We need to fix a date for your baby shower!'

The prospect hadn't occurred to Kessie. 'Wow, that's – such a lovely thought,' she says, 'but honestly, don't worry about it. I'm not sure I really feel like one.'

'I'm not *worried* about it, but I am organizing it!' Robin insists, her voice smiling. 'It'll be fun. I promise not to buy sparkly vibrators or pink teddies – but you deserve to be celebrated. I had a couple of dates in mind . . .'

Kessie closes her eyes. The matter seems to be sealed. It would be ungrateful to insist against it.

*

Walking only gets more painful over the weeks that follow, and teaching only becomes more energy-sapping. Every stuttering scale or out of tune high note from her pupils makes her want to weep. One morning, she is sitting on the loo for what feels like

119

the hundredth time, wondering whether to bother going out for a painful waddle along the canal in the cold, when a text message pings. It's from Robin, reminding her to arrive at 3 p.m. She is about to text back to ask what for – when she remembers. But what can she wear to a party with a belly this big? She's not in the mood to be the centre of attention. She just feels like holing herself up at home. She should never have gone along with this.

Back in the bedroom she flips through her wardrobe. Her best bet is probably black leggings and a black tunic, her normal uniform these days, with a shiny pair of hoops and lipstick to show that she's made an effort.

Standing in the lift going up to Robin's flat, Kessie wills the effusive version of herself to appear by the time she emerges. She knocks, tentatively . . . And then the front door is thrown open, and she's bombarded by whoops and applause. The hallway is packed with her favourite people – her wind quintet: Gayle, Tam, Paolo and Petra – Talia, her pal from music college – Anna and Jen from sixth form – Jen's heavily pregnant too now, a month ahead of her, and seems to be pain-free and loving every moment – and even Helena, her friend from nursery days. Above them, the hallway is decked out with gold and green bunting, and a jazzy version of 'Jingle Bells' is playing from the living room. 'Come on through!'

Elvis is warbling about chestnuts on an open fire. A baubly tree glints in the corner, and the walls are bright with bunting. For some reason the table is piled with Tupperware boxes. 'Everyone's home-cooked a meal for you to freeze and use in the new baby days,' Robin explains. 'You've got lasagne, Thai curry, risotto,

Bolognese, root veg stew, an amazing hot-pink beetroot soup. We're going to put them all in the freezer but we wanted to show you first.'

Kessie's jaw drops. 'You guys! This is . . . I didn't . . .'

A cinnamon smell wafts through from the kitchen. 'I'll bring out the mulled cider!' Tam calls. 'There's a non-alcoholic one!'

There are two cakes on the table – one yellowish, the other a sunken iced cake sprinkled with walnuts. 'You should definitely try Helena's lemon drizzle,' Robin says. 'And guess who baked the other one.'

'Well, not you for a start.' Robin has always been an unfortunate baker, and after the last birthday cake she attempted for Max was somehow both burnt and gooey, she'd vowed never to bake again.

'Well, actually I changed my mind, just for you. If it's inedible, remember it's the thought that counts.'

'It definitely does. Shall I cut?' Kessie takes a small slice from each cake. One comes out even and moist; the other oozy and crusty under the icing. She glances at Robin, who's wincing, and gives her a little pat on the back. 'You have so many other talents.'

Tam offers around a tray of steaming mugs, and they all settle themselves around the room. Chat flows to and fro. Kessie mostly listens, looks at their familiar faces, their easy smiles. As the light outside fades, Anna suggests the hat game, which Kessie vaguely remembers but has forgotten how to play. It involves writing down names of famous people, cutting them out into slips and folding them, putting them all into a hat and shaking it, dividing into two teams, then seeing which team can guess the most names in a minute until the names run out. The first round they can use verbal descriptions, the second round they are limited to one-word clues, the third to sound effects, and the fourth to facial expressions only . . . by which point everyone is falling about laughing and they give up. They chat – about job woes, Netflix binges, holiday plans, kids. Every other woman in the room except Robin, Gayle and Jen has at least one child – and they all seem very sane, Kessie reflects. And energized. And they're out, at a party, able to have a good time, despite being parents. It's all going to be fine.

As people start drifting home, she waves to them from her seated position, too physically tired to get up, but mentally invigorated. It was great to be sociable after all . . .

And then it's over.

Which means that she really is about to have this baby.

Dread creeps down her neck.

She asks Robin to sit with her for a bit, and leans her head on her bony shoulder. 'I had the best time,' she says. 'The whole thing was gorgeous.'

'Glad I insisted?' Robin smiles.

'So glad. But you know, I just started thinking about . . . well . . . death. Not to put a downer on things . . .'

'How could death possibly be a downer?'

'But seriously, I could die in childbirth.'

'I could be run over tomorrow.'

'Come on, childbirth is way riskier. Lots of women die, and if I do, then The Facilitator could turn up and have a claim on the baby, which freaks me out. And if not him, then my dad would be next of kin, and I really don't want her being brought up by Cara – so – would you want to be her guardian? Like, would you adopt her for me?'

'Wow. Kess . . .'

'Just in case?'

Robin's face has gone pink at the edges. 'Of *course* I would,' she says softly. 'I mean, I'd rather not dwell on the prospect of you dying, obviously, but . . . so . . . are you thinking you need to put that in your will, then?'

'Good point. I don't even have a will. I always figured I don't really have anything much of value. But I'll call a lawyer first thing on Monday. Do you know one?'

Robin puts her hand over her mouth. 'Just occurred to me that my will still mentions Max – I'd better get that changed too. I'll put you down instead. And yeah I can hook you up with the lawyer I used.'

'Oh, and I'd like to be cremated,' Kessie says, brain fizzing now. 'And for music at my funeral, I'd like Ella, Nina, Taylor . . .'

'Wait!' Robin lays her index finger on Kessie's lips for a second. 'I'll happily curate your funeral as you request – but do we have to do that right now this minute?' She raises her mug. 'Here's to life – to the new human you've made, and to you both having a long and happy life together, with me cheering you on.'

Chapter 11

Robin

An envelope lands on Robin's doormat as she's about to leave for work – with a French postmark. She tears it open. A card, with a picture of the nativity with a poufy sheep standing guard by the manger.

> Dear Robin, Happy Christmas! I'm sorry I shan't see you for it this year, but I can't leave the animals. It's chilly up here, as you can imagine, but the snow is beautiful. I have a new puppy, Chou-fleur, who's been a challenge – reminded me of you many years ago – but is settling down now and bringing me joy. I hope you are happy. Do visit me sometime. I have plenty of blankets and hot water bottles. Bisous, Mum xx

Robin tries to imagine a sheepdog puppy named Cauliflower. It's so unlike her mum these days to express joy, or anything close. She feels guilty now for assuming that her shepherdess move was a stunt that would end in failure – that she'd end up quitting after a couple of months and settling grumpily into some tiny council flat in Oxfordshire. It's wonderful that she's found a way to make it work, at least for the time being, and to be happy again. Self-pity gnaws at her chest. Their argument was stupid. And she had made it worse. There was no point in being so vindictive, and putting all the blame on her mum, when she had already lost everything, and it was really Brian's fault, and it was too late for anyone to do anything about that. Robin has a sudden longing to see her mum again, to hear the familiar tautness of her voice – and to be up there, too, in the mountains.

She drops her work bag and leans back against the wall. She had been focused on visiting Darsha in California as her next trip abroad, but it feels too close to Kessie's due date for her to go now. The Pyrenees, though, are much closer. A short trip could be doable. She's due some leave. She could easily dash back here if Kessie needed her to. She does have a lot of work on right now, with a client brief due before Christmas, and her boss would fume if she asked to take leave early . . . but then she always has a lot of work on . . .

She thinks of how he sneered at her when she requested to go part-time, at least temporarily, in order to do her master's. How he'd mocked her decision to study anthropology – 'opining on little tribes', as he put it, as if the discipline hadn't evolved since the days of empire. She thinks of all those boys' nights out at strip clubs to which she wasn't invited, and had no desire to be invited – and of the commentary about which of the office girls had the best legs. She thinks of how nobody at work asked how she was when she returned after the extraction operation, having nearly died, even though she went back earlier than she probably should have done so that she wouldn't let them down with the presentation she was meant to be leading.

She walks back to the kitchen, pulls out her phone, and texts Kessie to check that it's okay with her that she goes to see her mum for a few days, so long as she's back a week before the due date. The reply pings straight back: 'Totally!' She gets out her laptop, and before giving herself time to think any more about it, emails HR to say she is taking a week's emergency leave from today to support her mother, and that unless they can change her working pattern to four days a week upon her return she will have to consider her position. She puts on her out of office autoreply, opens a new window, and books a flight to Toulouse.

*

After crawling its way out of the pink city, the taxi winds its way into the mountains through small and smaller villages. Snow thickens, and sugar-capped peaks rise with gentle ferocity in the widening landscape. Robin imagines, for the first time, what it must have felt like for her mother to have arrived here, on her own, ready to make this place her new home.

Coming here for summer holidays as a kid, she always used to feel a thrill – but now, as a stressed-out, city-dwelling adult, this landscape seems to offer something more profound. These mountains feel like great protective guardians, like guarantors of freedom from the frenzy, like unwavering reminders that all the stresses of the city and the corporate workplace are no more significant than the scurryings inside an ant hill. The raw peace of this place, the sheer scale of ground undulating on all sides, allows something soft to unfurl inside her, like an evening primrose. She really, really needed to get away from that bloody office.

As a family, they only ever used to come up during the summer holidays, and sometimes the May half-term or Easter. Her parents didn't ski, and she doesn't remember ever coming in winter. The idea of actually *living* up here, in this freezing season, for more than a week or two? No – her mother's decision remains madness.

'C'est pour skier que vous êtes venu ici?' the taxi driver asks.

'Non, non,' she answers. 'Je vais visiter ma mère. Elle habite ici maintenant.'

'Ah bon.'

It's a pleasure to speak French again. If only she'd been more open to speaking it at home growing up. She'd taken to replying to her parents in English, even when they persisted in speaking French to her – she felt different enough from the other kids at school.

She wonders how her mother will react to the surprise of her daughter showing up unannounced. It occurs to her, for the first time, that the reaction might not be delight, despite the invitation on the card.

They turn off the main road to the familiar track that zigzags up the mountain. It's bumpier than she remembered, and looks icy. The taxi slows right down, and the driver starts grumbling. The landscape is oddly devoid of sheep – but then, of course, they go down to milder pastures in winter. She spots the hut up ahead, tucked underneath a thick duvet of cloud.

'Elle habite ici? Votre mère? Tout seule?' He sounds sceptical that anyone could possibly live up here, especially a woman.

'Bah, oui.' She hopes this taxi driver isn't some creepy type who'd register the fact of her mother's isolation and come up here . . . but why should she be so mistrustful? It's totally reasonable for him to express surprise that any sane person would choose to live here alone in winter.

She pays him, takes her bags out, and listens to him drive away before going up to the front door – once a chipped sage, now ivy green. She knocks, holding her breath.

No answer.

The air is knife-sharp – she should have brought long johns as well as her thick coat. She pulls her hat down over her ears and knocks again.

Is her mother okay? It's going to be dark in a couple of hours.

She tries the handle, and the door opens.

It's cold inside, and the fire's out, but it's perfectly neat, with a pretty rug on the floor that she doesn't recognize, and a new bookcase on one wall. Her mum must be out – maybe for a walk. She wonders whether to make herself a cup of tea, feeling like Goldilocks, though there are only two chairs to test out. Hopefully her mum hasn't gone to stay somewhere, or left completely . . . But the place looks freshly lived in. She refills her bottle of water, packs it in her rucksack, laces up her walking boots, and steps outside again to see if she can find her on the mountain path.

A loud baa sounds from her left, and a curly-horned sheep emerges from what looks like a rustic Wendy house at the corner of the garden. It trots right up to her, apparently unafraid. 'Hello there,' Robin says, and strokes its nose. When it stays, she snuggles a hand into its soft wool. It nuzzles her other hand, as if hoping for a treat. Well, if there's a pet sheep hanging out here, her mum definitely can't be far off. She tells the sheep she'll be back in a bit, and strides off, up the steep, narrow path from the back gate, towards the main hiking route on the ridge. It feels great to move again after the long journey, to devour the crystalline mountain air, to watch her breath billow. She slips on a patch of ice, and only just manages to keep her balance. Fear strikes, fear of hurting herself more seriously out here, of falling badly, breaking an ankle, being unable to get up, dying even, cold and alone . . . But her mother would call her a silly city girl for thinking such things.

She carries on, treading more carefully. A lowering cloud overhead seems to be expanding, its colour deepening to charcoal. A crow caws – no, this bird has gigantic wings, with tips like reaching fingers, could it be a vulture? It glides and flaps into the distance. The French government reintroduced wolves and even brown bears to this area of the Pyrenees as a rewilding initiative several years back. The bears had better be hibernating right now.

She reaches the main path where the terrain is easier underfoot, and pauses to scan the landscape for signs of her mum. The mighty mountain range extends out either side of her in all its magnificence. It's fucking brilliant to be out here, up in the heavens, to be free! Very tempting to start singing 'the hills are alive . . .' She inhales deeply through her nose and takes out her bottle to have a glug of water. Even though she has her thickest gloves on, her fingers are already so cold she can hardly open the bottle.

One summer, when all the alpine flowers bloomed in the meadows, she walked the whole of this route with her parents – it must have been the year before her dad died. Le Chemin des

Bonshommes, it's called, and it snakes its way from the French side of the mountain range all the way across to the Spanish side. She remembers him telling her all about its history as they walked – something to do with Catalan people fleeing persecution in France, but she can't remember exactly when. There's a certain symmetry, she supposes, in her mother fleeing her situation in the UK for a place so close to this route, but finding refuge at its French end.

Far ahead, she spots a figure, with a smaller one beside it – could that be her mother? Her heart accelerates. Yes! It definitely looks like her, the gangly proportions of the figure a mirror of her own. That must be a dog next to her, but it's huge, even relative to her mum's height – like she's taking a bear for a walk. And then it starts barking, a deep, percussive sound, ricocheting like a giant cymbal around the valley – and now it's running, running right towards her.

Robin halts, looks frantically around, slips, and falls, this time, cutting her knee open. Her mother's voice floats towards her on the wind, shouting something, but she can't tell what.

The barking is getting louder, and now the white beast is right here, booming in her ear, slathering, its jaws open wide, tongue fleshy and pink, barking and barking and barking. Robin curls into a ball on the path and stays completely still. Two great paws land on her back, and a hefty weight presses on her spine.

And then the dog quietens, as if it's conquered its prey – and the paws lift off again. Her heart slows a little.

Footsteps now, running. 'Chou-fleur! Vien ici! Shush. Assieds-toi.'

Robin cautiously raises her head. The dog is sitting next to her, panting hard, and her mother's hand is clasping its collar.

'Chou-fleur, you needn't scare off Robin – she's my daughter. She's very nice, when she wants to be. And it's *quite* the surprise to see her here.'

'Hi, Mum. Cute name for such a scary creature.'

'The French is more elegant, I think. She's very protective of me.'

'I'm glad. And yes, I'm all right, thanks for asking. Just cut my knee.'

Her mother lets go of the dog, who seems to have got the message that Robin doesn't pose an existential threat to her owner. She gives Robin a hand up, and enfolds her in a hug.

They walk back down the path, her mother leading the way, with Chou-fleur – who's really not unlike a fluffy polar bear – trotting around them in wide circles, as if keeping an eye out for danger. This is exactly what they're bred for, her mother explains – Pyrenean mountain dogs work as guardians for sheep, fending off predators in the higher terrain. Chou-fleur was gifted to her from Ernest, the elderly farmer down the valley, who had a bigger than expected litter, as a thank you for her work helping him out with mucky jobs. She was a runt, though you wouldn't believe it to look at her now.

Ernest had been sceptical of her at first, her mother says: saw her as one of these nuisance Anglaises who keep settling in France and contributing nothing. But she persisted in offering her labour, for free initially, and he gave in. She's ended up doing a lot of work for him over the past year, to the point that he's taken her under his wing now as an apprentice. He had hoped that his oldest daughter would take over the farm and do a lot of the work, but she has moved to the city, for the moment at least, and so he needed an extra pair of hands. He's trying to reinstate traditional sheep farming in the area, and has brought back a breed called the tarasconnaise which is hardy and beautiful and produces delicious cheese. Her mum has been learning to make that, too.

'Fascinating!' Robin says, genuinely surprised by how reenergized her mother sounds by all this agricultural activity. 'And is that the breed of sheep you've got back at the hut then, the one with the curly horns?'

'Ah, so you've already met Brigitte Baaardot.'

Robin cracks up and has to stop for a moment. 'Oh my gosh, that's a great name!'

Her mum grins. 'Well, she's a very refined lady. I saved her from being put down when she had a gammy leg. She and Choufleur are like a married couple these days – they live contentedly together in their pied-à-terre in the garden, and Chou-fleur keeps the wolves at bay. That's partly why I named her. If they see a predator approaching, these dogs, they puff out their white coats. Anyway, they're good company for each other. And for me too. I've had enough of humans, mostly.'

As they go through the back gate into the little garden, Choufleur runs up to greet Brigitte Baaardot, and lowers herself down on her front paws to get nose to nose – the perfect demonstration of downward dog pose. Robin had never imagined a sheep doing anything other than dashing away from a dog, especially one as immense as this. She should video it, she thinks, reaching for her phone – it's the kind of thing that would go viral on YouTube – but her mum would hate that.

Inside, they strip off their coats and rub their hands. Her mum puts the kettle on, and asks Robin to light the fire. It feels good to break up sticks, arrange logs, start a flame and watch it lick along the edge of a log and make it glow. 'So you're never scared of being alone up here with all the wolves and bears and things?'

'No,' her mother scorns. 'I've got a good protector. And animals are always honest, you know?'

She lets her two pets in for an evening sup of milk, and they allow themselves to be stroked for a while before wandering towards the door, ready to be let out again and return to their kennel.

Sitting by the crackling fire with tin cups of tea, facing each other in the two creaky old armchairs, Robin tells her the news about the break-up, after her ultimatum. Her mum doesn't seem very surprised, but asks more about what happened. Robin opens up, talking long into the evening as they peel potatoes and carrots, grate cheese, and tuck in to a simple meal. Her mum ends up revealing a lot about her fertility prognosis, her extraction trauma, Kessie's pregnancy, the responsibility of being a birth partner, and how she's fed up with her job . . . 'I'm thinking maybe I could just jack it all in and apply to do an anthropology PhD in California. Begin a new life in the sunshine like Darsha,' she finds herself saying, in conclusion. It's the first time she's aired that idea to anyone out loud.

'Well. That would be a change.'

There's a long pause as they digest their meal, then wash up. The wind whistles at the windows, and stars stud the sky outside.

Robin remembers how much she hated going to visit her mum at home when Brian was living there – how creepily charismatic he was. How he'd always find a jocular way to criticize.

Her mother pulls the curtains, puts another log on the fire, then sits back down in the armchair, and stares into the flames for a while, before looking Robin in the eye. 'I always liked Kessie,' she says. 'She was a great friend to you at school, especially after Dad passed away, and her mother too. I'm glad that you're sticking by her through this pregnancy. Makes me proud.'

Robin's jaw slackens. So far as she can recall, her mother has never uttered those last three words before.

'It is a responsibility, for sure,' she continues, 'but it's an opportunity for joy. No? You don't have to live a rich and conventional life to be happy, you know. Take it from one who's doing neither.' She crosses her legs, settles back in her chair a little, and smiles a small but beatific smile. 'If there's another rejected orphan lamb in the spring, as there almost certainly will be, I plan to take her in and offer her to Brigitte Baaardot. I think she and Chou-fleur will be good parents.'

'That's cute.'

'Look, Robin, whatever you do in life, my main piece of hermit wisdom is to try to value what you have. Friends like Kessie are rare treasures and you're lucky to have each other. And her baby will be lucky to have both of you.'

'Well, thanks Mum . . .'

'As for your job,' her mother interrupts, 'when you started it, you said it would be a temporary money-earner before you went into a career you were actually passionate about. I've been amazed that you've stuck at it for so long. I'm sure you'll make a sensible choice about when to quit and what for. And not leave it too long.'

As usual, Robin feels her hackles rising at the return of her mother's curt bossiness – and yet . . . she's not wrong. She cringes at the memory of calling her mother a selfish cow, to her face, for throwing her inheritance away on a crooked narcissist, and losing the plot by thinking she could manage on her own with no money in the French countryside because she couldn't even look after herself. No, that was not her finest moment. She hadn't given enough thought to how hard it was for her mother to lose her husband and the father of her child, and how well, in retrospect, she held it together, for ages, before Brian came along. How hard she worked as a single parent for years, taking on extra tutoring so that she wouldn't have to dip too far into the inheritance pot. How Brian's high-energy persona must have felt like an appealing change from her daily grind. How, even after he had persuaded her to empty the honey from her jar and buggered off, her mother barely even complained. She just packed up and started afresh, way out here. Okay, so she had never been the tenderest of parents. But neither has she, Robin, been the most understanding of daughters.

'Now, cherie,' her mother says brightly. 'Enough conversation for me – I'm out of the habit. I've got a pack of cards in the cupboard. Shall we see if I can still beat you at spades?'

Chapter 12

Kessie

By 9 p.m., Kessie is ready for bed. If only she could expect to sleep properly. Going to bed at this stage of pregnancy means sandwiching her mountainous midriff between six cushions and pillows to support both bump and back, then lying there uncomfortably, playing rain and wave sounds on her phone, until eventually being forced to heave her bulk up again to plod to the toilet.

A stomach twinge earlier in the afternoon made her nervous, but there's been nothing since. She assumes it's a Toni Braxton, as she likes to think of the false 'Braxton Hicks' contractions she's been warned about. Back in her teens, she got a welt of a hickey while making out to the soundtrack of 'Spanish Guitar'. The baby gives a lazy kick, and Kessie runs her hand over the protrusion before it recedes.

Last week, she didn't feel any movement for a whole day, went to the doctor to check it, and he couldn't find a heartbeat. This almost made her own heart stop beating, before it went frantic – he referred her to the midwifery unit at the hospital, and in a blind panic she called Robin at work and asked if she could come too. She cried the whole way there, and Robin held her hand for two hours in the waiting room. When they were finally ushered in for an ultrasound, the midwife found the heartbeat in seconds. 'Absolutely no sign of anything wrong with this baby!' she told Kessie heartily. 'It's completely normal to experience a reduction in movement at this point – not much room for her, is there?'

Bindingly obvious, in hindsight.

Kessie wonders whether the baby is feeling uncomfortable now, being squeezed into such a tight space – pushing at all her own internal organs like Yvonne's sack of potatoes. Either way, if she is awake, she would probably appreciate some music.

She heaves herself up, goes over to her little electric piano, and runs her fingertips lightly over the keys, then opens the book of Bach Preludes. She hasn't mastered them yet, but she has practised a lot over the past few months, and is coming to feel less intimidated by their complexity.

The opening bars calm her instantly. The counterpoint is so neat, so meant-to-be. For years she has mostly been playing the piano roughly to accompany children's lessons, but pregnancy has drawn her back to the instrument, and lately she has been practising like she used to as a child: learning a difficult piece patiently, playing phrases for each hand separately, slowly at first, marking in the fingering, speeding up, then putting both hands together, and repeating trickier bars until they flow. It makes up for the clarinet becoming too difficult as the baby pushes further and further into her diaphragm.

She plays through the prelude from start to finish, marvelling at the shifting patterns, like a kaleidoscopic cat's cradle game, the beauty of the cadences, and her new ability to shift her focus from hitting the right notes to listening and shaping the phrases. For the first time ever, she manages to get through the piece without a single mistake. She lets the last notes ring on, lifts her fingers from the keys, and imagines the applause of her daughter's tiny hands.

It's midnight when she wakes up to turn over and notices a dull period pain. But she's pregnant, for goodness' sake. Is this another Toni Braxton? She'd know if it were a real contraction. Wouldn't she? She isn't even due to give birth for another fortnight, and first children are supposed to be late.

The ache fades. Perhaps it was just a movement from the baby, pressing on a nerve. She turns over, arranges her pillows, closes her eyes.

But it comes again, unmistakable, boring softly but intently into her lower back.

On comes another. She realizes she'd better start timing the contractions – she's meant to wait to call the hospital until they are two minutes apart. Why oh why did this have to happen in the middle of the night? Angelo's face swims into her vision and she screws up her eyes . . .

Then opens them wide and sits up in bed. *Robin*. She was due to have flown back from France this evening, and Kessie didn't think to ask what time she was meant to arrive. She grabs her phone and sends a message. No double tick to show that it's gone through immediately. Contractions are supposed to last for hours, even days, for your first baby, so hopefully it should all be fine? She taps on her rain sounds app and turns up the volume.

*

Forty minutes later, deep waves of pain have been coming every six minutes and are getting stronger. It reminds her of the escalation of Beethoven's Ninth – and of the feminist scholar who proposed that its insistent pounding rhythm was a representation of the composer's secret rape fantasies. What was her name again? She closes her eyes, and her heart thuds like a bass drum. No reply from Robin yet. She needs some music, some Bach.

She switches on the bedside light, heaves herself up, shoves cushions behind her back, puts on *The Goldberg Variations*, and continues to track her contraction timings. Daniel Barenboim plays with such elegant fluency – she tries to imagine that he is performing a private recital for her from her own piano in the other room, and that she has to give it her complete attention. She allows her fingers to mime the piece on her soon-to-be-diminished bump, until more claws sink into her groin, and they ball into fists.

By 6 a.m. a breadknife is sawing at her spine, and 'contraction' has become the world's cruellest euphemism. Each time the blade pushes down a groan emanates from her chest, so creakily peculiar she hardly recognizes it as her own voice. Still no word from Robin.

Finally, at half past six, she calls the hospital. 'Is this your first child? Can you speak during the contractions?' the midwife asks, then pauses, listening. 'If you can't answer, it's probably time to come in.'

Kessie calls Robin again. Is she asleep? What if her flight was delayed? What if this baby starts coming out when she's all on her own here? How stupid she was not to line up a plan B birth partner! All of her close friends live in South London or have already moved out to the 'burbs. Leona is too old, and anyway she's hurt her leg again. Annika and Ishmail, the friendly couple downstairs who are also expecting, are away visiting her parents. Will she have to crawl up the stairs and knock on the door of the lovely old Turkish couple who struggle to walk up and down the stairs themselves and barely speak a word of English? Or next door to the student boys who moved in a few months ago but have never yet acknowledged her existence in passing?

An odd sensation – like she's wet herself extravagantly. The phrase 'waters breaking' makes it sound a lot more romantic. She's just waddling to the bathroom when her phone rings.

'Heyyyy Kess!' Robin yawns. 'Sorry I missed your call – how's it going? I was about to text you, I just got home . . .'

Kessie tries to reply but all that comes out is another wild groan.

By the time Robin arrives, she is by the front door on her knees, trying to get herself back up after the last contraction. She has changed pyjamas, gone through her checklist, and is pretty sure she hasn't left anything out of her bag, but it's impossible to think straight.

In the taxi, she doesn't even try to suppress her growls. After one subsides, the driver casually remarks that he's taken hundreds of mums to hospital when they were about to pop.

'Ah, it's funny,' he reflects, 'I missed me wife's completely! I was at the footy, see, and it was the cup final. By the time I got to the hospital, me daughter was already there.'

At the hospital, she hauls herself out of the vehicle and staggers into reception, leaning on Robin, only to be told that the birthing centre is full and she will have to go to the labour ward.

*

Remembering Yvonne's words, Kessie walks around and around her curtained-off pen in between contractions, listening to the sounds of other moaning, crying women. She asks Robin to distract her by telling her what's in the news, and then about what women or other animals in different cultures do during labour, but finds she can't concentrate on what's being said. Finally, a midwife bustles in to inspect her, and Kessie lies down on the bed. After a bit of poking, she surfaces to announce, brightly, that Kessie will need to dilate five more centimetres before it's time to push.

'You mean the baby's halfway there?' Robin asks.

Kessie wants to scream that she can't be only *halfway* – it's inconceivable to endure the same amount of pain for longer – more pain, in fact, as it's getting worse. And here it comes, a tsunami rising out of the dark, descending over every muscle and seeping into every vein, black and gold and savage . . . This is it. This the moment when she should ask for an epidural. But Yvonne's voice is nagging in her ear . . . *you're more likely to rip because you're not in tune with your body* . . . and what if she's paralyzed for life by the spinal injection and can't look after her baby? She tries to breathe again, deeply and rhythmically, channelling all her years of clarinet training and all the yoga classes she's ever done.

'Don't you want an epidural at this point?' Robin asks, as the midwife disappears.

'Fuck, I don't *know*,' she gasps. 'I mean yes but I'm also scared and I've coped so far*urrrruuuhhhhhh* . . .' Robin takes her hand and she squeezes it back, hard.

'If you decide you want one, just say, and I'll run and tell them,' Robin says. 'Any music requests? Distraction? I can get the speakers out. Other people are playing their music.'

Kessie nods vigorously. What does she want, though? Something with a beat, to push her through. 'Remind me what playlists I made,' she gasps.

'Power ballads?'

She shakes her head. Too emotive.

'Folk?'

No: too reflective.

'Motown?'

Too upbeat.

'Yoga chants?'

Too dreamy.

'Nirvana?'

Too dark.

'Reggae?'

That could work, she thinks. And lo and behold, Bob Marley & The Wailers hit the spot, at least for now, with their cyclical, looping beat going and going and going.

A snorkel tube is brandished in her face, gas and air – *finally, the drugs* – and she accepts greedily, bites down hard on the mouthpiece, inhales, and registers a floaty feeling of relief.

But after a few more contraction assaults, the floatiness fades. Time distorts.

At one point she notices that Robin's not by her side any more, and fuzzy panic brings her to her feet – but she has to grasp the bed for support. When Robin returns – just from a quick toilet break, she explains – Kessie squeezes her hand in gratitude.

'Hon, I'm totally fine with my hand being squeezed,' Robin says, 'but I'll be less help when the baby's here if you break my fingers.' Kessie grins and tries to apologize, but Robin kisses her forehead. 'Remember you can swear at me though, okay? What's the worst insult you can think of?'

Her body feels as if it has been wrung and wrung until it has nothing left. She asks, rasping, for a drink. 'Make it fucking sugary please.'

Robin brings back a Lucozade, and its orange sweetness is good, but it doesn't generate the energy she'd hoped for. She wants to give up already.

A midwife comes to re-examine her – and tells her she is still only seven centimetres dilated. How is that possible? She was admitted to this ward a lifetime ago – how will she have a single shred of energy left to push when she finally gets to ten centimetres? She is done. DONE.

More beats, more gas, more air, more pain. Time swims, dives, crackles.

She asks Robin how long they've been here. Eight whole hours. 'Fuck, fucking *fuck*, Robs, I can't take any more. I need that motherfucking epidural – what the hell was I waiting for? Fucking Yvonne. Can you call the midwife for me? Tell her I'll fucking murder someone if I don't get it.'

*

Ten minutes later, the midwife strolls back in. 'I hear you've requested an epidural,' she says, with acid politeness, as if Kessie had asked to return an expensive dress to her shop after wearing it to a party. 'I'll have to examine you again first.' She probes around Kessie's vagina once more, surfaces, and shakes her head – *smiling*, for some unfathomable reason. 'Well, I'm afraid it's too late, my girl – you're fully dilated now. Time to push!'

Time to push. Kessie had felt so ready for this earlier; but the concept of pushing feels mythical now. Her body is like a rag doll's.

She finds herself being wheeled through to the delivery room, where multiple pairs of eyes land on her. It's like being a naked mouse surrounded by staring owls deciding who's going to pounce first. Her eyes focus in on a new midwife, who introduces herself, explaining a change of shift. She's a rectangular woman with cropped ruby hair, a chin like a battering ram. A tattoo up one forearm says JUST DO IT, followed by a heart shape pierced by an arrow, and three tigers are climbing up the other forearm. 'This is it: go, go, go, GO!' she bellows, as if she were training a recalcitrant sprinter for the Olympics. 'Push as hard as you can!'

Kessie would tell her to go fuck herself if she had the strength – but somehow the indignation at her hectoring ignites a spark of strength within her.

But no, no, no, no, no – this is like trying to excavate a basketball from her bowels. 'I caaaan't!' she wails, and begins to weep in fat, slow yelps. They will have to cut her open and take this baby out and break her pelvis, even if it means being confined to a wheelchair for the rest of her life.

The midwife leans down until her brick-like face is inches from Kessie's own and she can see all the little hairs along her upper lip. 'You. Have. GOT. To do this.'

Shock snaps Kessie out of her malaise. Who does this woman think she is?

'This baby is COMING OUT,' the midwife continues, 'and YOU have got to make that happen. Nobody else. There's no way back.' Kessie wants to laugh in her face through snotty tears. 'Listen,' the midwife says, scarlet patches deepening on her face. 'There is no CAN'T now. There is no WON'T. Think of all the other mothers all around the world, in sheds and tents and MUD HUTS, pushing their babies out, no matter what! You think you can choose when you're DONE? You're only DONE when you've DELIVERED! And I am not here to take no for an answer. I'm here to make sure this baby comes out alive and well. So GOOOOOO!' Her blood-curdling war cry bounces off the walls, like a wrestler drumming up a crowd.

Outrage shoots electricity through Kessie's veins – her skin prickles – and somehow a force is being generated from her, like lava, and she feels a sound emerge from her lips, the bray of something primal, not a cow so much as an aurochs.

The midwife pumps her fist. 'I CAN SEE THE HEAD! KEEP GOING . . .'

Somehow another wave, another shift.

'SHE'S ON HER WAY! COME ONNNNN . . .'

A tectonic movement – a stingy metallic edge to the stony weight of pain.

'NOW THE SHOULDERS!'

An odd slithering sensation – she's metamorphosing . . .

*

She opens her eyes. In the midwife's decorated arms, a luridly purple slimy thing is being held aloft like a trophy.

'She's losing a lot of blood . . .'

Colour caves into dark.

PART 2

Chapter 13

Robin

So warm. So minute. Lilac-hued, curly-lashed. Feather-light yet weighty. Wrapped like a gift in soft cotton with a jaunty giraffe print, this tiny human seems more present than any other person Robin has ever met. She can probably count on her hands the number of times she's held a baby, and never one this small. Will she ever hold her own? But that question can be shelved for now. This baby seems far too fragile for Robin to be allowed to hold her in her arms, with no guidance and no protection beyond the delicate wrap – it's like being left alone with a rare medieval manuscript.

When she touches her giant index finger onto the clenched fist, four shoelace-thin fingers immediately unfurl and enclose it, surprisingly tightly, making her chest fizz. She's both holding and being held. She's needed. She's become the first human lifeline for a brand-new being! It really should be Kessie experiencing this moment of connection . . . but it feels so right.

'Would you like to do skin-to-skin?' Robin looks up and registers the midwife's face. 'It just means lying down and holding the baby on your chest, next to your bare skin. It's important for bonding – there's a lot of research – and Mum might be a while.'

'Is she doing okay?'

'They're still in surgery, but she's in good hands. You'd need to take your top off.'

The baby starts crying, sharp, bright sounds like electric shocks. Robin passes her carefully to the midwife, keeping her arms underneath for too long, terrified of dropping her, then takes off her T-shirt. 'Um . . . bra too?'

'Yup.' The midwife unwraps the small body, revealing its bandy legs and spreading toes. 'That's it, lie back'.

The tiny baby is laid, warm and silky and still whimpering, on the centre of Robin's chest. As Robin's gigantic hands cover her gently, like a duvet, the crying stops. Miraculous. Her head rests like a peach in the curve under Robin's collarbone, and she holds her own breath to focus on the sensation of the palm-sized rib cage moving up and down. When she raises her head a little, she can just reach the top of the baby's skull with her lips, and its downy covering feels like the softest cashmere. It's astounding to think that this human is experiencing this world for the first time.

'This first hour after birth is sometimes called the sacred hour,' the midwife says in a low voice. Robin had forgotten she was still hovering at the bottom of the bed. 'Your heartbeat calms the baby. She'll start rooting in a minute.' She turns and fiddles around with something, then tips a mini carton of formula into a bottle. As if on cue, the baby starts snuffling like a hedgehog, shifting down towards Robin's breasts, pushing down against her supporting arm with surprising force. 'There, you see! Thinks she

might get some milk from you – don't let her down now. Here.'
She holds out the bottle.

'But . . .' Kessie had been so looking forward to breastfeeding.
If only Robin's own nipples would erupt, just for this baby's first
feed, just to make the moment right for her, to give her the best
start.

'Here, sit up a bit.' The midwife hands her the bottle and guides
its angle. 'There. She can breathe more easily with her head like
that. Up a bit – that's it.' Somehow knowing what to do, the baby
begins sucking at the teat, and swallowing. *Her very first meal.*
A creamy drop rolls down the side of her chin, and Robin gently
wipes it off.

And then, just as she's got going, the teat slips out of her mouth
and she's dropped off to sleep. Quick as that! She appears as sated
as if she'd just wolfed a giant slab of cheese rather than a fat-rich
raindrop. Robin looks up for the midwive, ready to whisper
a question about how much milk is enough, but she's gone. She
places the bottle softly down on the bedside table. Around her, the
ward is quiet. This baby's sleep is so urgently peaceful, so intense.
Robin tries to keep her breath silent, loath to move a muscle lest
she disturb the serenity. This experience has felt – like the blush
of winter sunrise over snow.

A droplet lands on the baby's crown, soaking into the fuzz,
and it's only when Robin licks her lips and tastes salt that she
realizes it's come from her. Before now, she'd only ever envisaged
herself feeling utter panic around the scene of a birth. The
part of motherhood that she'd been hankering for is later on,
once her hypothetical baby was settled, and happy, and able
to talk, and sleeping through the night, and once Robin had

figured out what the hell she was meant to be doing. But this unexpected moment with this very real baby, who isn't even her own, somehow feels like the pinnacle that her whole life had been building up to.

She strokes the little head again, as gently as she can manage. The downy hair is a light chestnut, and completely straight. She hopes this kid inherits some ringlets when she gets older. Not just because Kessie's are so lush, but so that she'll look less like her toad of a father.

It had been torturous to witness Kessie in that degree of pain for so long. When she'd finally yelled for the 'motherfucking epidural', Robin felt the urgency lance through her own body. She ran to make the request, urgently, but was told the anaesthetist was busy with a C-section. She kept going back and asking, again and again, but every time she was just told that he was 'on his way' and then, a bit later, that there had been another delay – and meanwhile Bob Marley droned on and on in an endless cycle. She used to like reggae; now she wonders whether she'll ever be able to hear it without being transported back to that room, watching Kessie's agonized face, her top drenched in sweat, and feeling powerless to help.

Any weirdness she might have felt in coming face to face with Kessie's vagina was obliterated by the power of life's emergence. The sight of this baby's head finally manifesting itself, and then the shoulders, felt not so much like a scene from *Alien*, but like a time-lapse video of a blossoming cherry tree – or something of immense magnitude like the Big Bang. But then came the eruption of blood. An unrelenting red tide, densely lurid. Robin's legs went hollow and her head began to spin, but something in her forced her to stay with it, to remain conscious, for Kessie's sake.

Doctors had swarmed. Someone had asked if she wanted to cut the cord. She heard the word *haemorrhage*, and found she was holding a pair of scissors – just ordinary scissors, like you'd used to cut wrapping paper – and someone was urging her to *sever* a part of her friend's body, and a part of this baby's body, their magical connective vessel. The blood was gushing faster and faster . . . she snipped, and it was like separating two chipolatas. And then the scissors were taken from her, and a weight was placed in her arms. Even as she was registering the miniature features and the screwed-up little face, she and the baby were being rushed out of the room.

Even in sleep, now, this child is both perfectly calm and yet forceful in her newness. She's just so undeniably *in existence* – as if life before she came into the world, just a few hours ago, wasn't really real or relevant.

One of her little hands is draped over Robin's shoulder. Robin lifts it, and strokes a miniscule finger, which is already adorned with a long, translucent nail. The baby's forehead is as smooth as a rose petal, though flaky along the hairline. The eyelids, serenely closed, are like pink tellin shells, capillaries painted on with the delicacy of a Japanese miniaturist.

Robin allows her own eyelids to fall. Her bones ache. When did she last sleep? It's a surprising amount of effort to hold the baby in this position. Gingerly, she turns the small body over to lie against her chest again, runs a fingertip over the crease of the tiny wrist and shuffles herself down the bed a little. Her eyes close again. How is Kessie going to recover from surgery on top of that ultramarathon labour? She'd better not fall asleep with this baby on her. Reluctant to let her go, she lies her as gently as possible down in the little Perspex cot by the bed, and covers her in a warm wool blanket.

Sometime later, she jerks her eyes open and checks on the baby – still asleep – then on the time. It's been a while now since she asked for news of Kessie. She looks around for the midwife and listens – no sign. Carefully, she scoops up the baby, thinking she'll surely wake at being moved, but she doesn't. Clasping her against her chest with one arm, she wraps the blanket around her with the other, then peeks around the curtain.

No hospital staff to be seen. Can't be a good sign if they're all in Kessie's operating theatre. *Please be okay. Please be okay.*

She pads along the corridor. 'Hello?' She presses the buzzer at the desk for attention. *Come on, come on . . .*

As she waits, she looks down – babe still asleep – and wonders what Kessie will call her. They had discussed and revised a short-list almost daily over the last couple of months. All the names on it were inspired by great women of colour – Ella, Zora, Nina, Alice, Billie, Zadie, Serena, Aretha . . . Robin had been loath to offer too strong a view on which she liked, feeling like it should be Kessie's choice. But when pressed, she had admitted that her favourite, by far, was Zora. 'Hey there, Zora,' she whispers now, just to try it out. The name rolls pleasingly off the tongue. It sounds powerful and feminine and rare all at once. 'Your mama's going to be just fine. In the meantime, I'm here for you.' Swaying to and fro, she begins humming 'Little Green'.

Chapter 14

Kessie

A sea of intent, white-coated people. Something pressing on her face. A fuzzy nausea, jagged shoulders, cables . . . a weird numbness in her lower half. A man doing something to her. An indigo well.

Light, jarring. 'Well hello there!' a stranger is saying as if she were a long-lost friend. 'Your baby is absolutely fine – your birth partner is looking after her. We're just finishing off a procedure for you – the surgeon is working on the final sutures, so please just continue to lie still, okay? You should be able to hold your baby very soon.'

Kessie tries to ask a question, but a crackle comes out of a sand-paper throat. Water. She needs water. How long has she been in surgery? She had expected pain during birth, obviously, but her main fear had been something going wrong with the baby, like the cord strangling it on its way out. Now she doesn't even have a baby to hold. Is this a bit what it feels like to be a surrogate: to give birth, and wind up with nothing? But no, her baby is okay. The stranger said so.

She closes her eyes. Pictures the thousands, millions of teenage girls who've got pregnant and been abandoned by their partners or chastised by their parents. The Magdalene Laundry girls. Mexican migrant women detained on the US border. Is her baby really okay? *Baby, bathwater, a pancake flippin' daughter . . .*

Fatigue crawls up the back of her eyeballs. Brain matter dripping through a sieve. Could she be dying?

*

Distant rumbles. Bleeping. Whining. A scummy outline resolves itself into . . . Robin's face! A little lower, a shape in her arms. 'Hey, lovely, how are you feeling?' Her voice, like velvet. 'I have the most magical gift here waiting for you. She's perfect. She's the most perfect thing I've ever seen.'

Kessie opens her mouth, but nothing emerges.

'Right then!' chirps a nurse. 'Let me just help you to sit up there, Mum, and then you can hold your beautiful baby! She's a great size – seven and a half pounds!'

Strong hands grip under her armpits and haul her up. Robin bends towards her, smiling. Kessie tries to reach, and at first her arms don't work properly, but finally they obey, and her breath catches as she takes the weight.

She examines the small face. It's oddly pale, with straight brown hair. She had expected no hair, or curls. And darker skin. Could they have accidentally swapped her baby with someone else's? Someone should check. She needs to tell them to check. Her arms aren't strong enough to keep holding this one.

'Want me to take her back?' Robin asks, and she nods. 'Oh

Kess – congratulations, my love! That was a properly Herculean effort. You did so well. Isn't she just gorgeous?' Robin cradles the baby and kisses her, and Kessie closes her eyes.

She feels Robin's cool hand stroke her forehead, then her cheek. So nice to be touched. She pushes her lips towards a smile. Robin leans down to kiss her cheek, too. 'I'm so glad you're okay, darl,' she whispers. 'Everything's fine now, I promise.'

*

She wakes sometime later. Fluorescent strip lights grate her eyeballs. 'Oh hey there!'

Thank God: Robin.

'Do you need anything – water, tea, the toilet?'

She moves her head from side to side, her neck a creaky gate.

'The baby's doing great.' Robin smiles. 'She's an absolute dreamboat. She's just fed again and gone back to sleep. How are you feeling?'

Kessie does something to her mouth.

'Do you want me to send some messages? Shall I tell people the good news?'

She creaks her head down, then up. If only she were in her own bed. Her lower half has begun throbbing like the slow plucking of a double bass. She needs more drugs. More sleep. To sleep, to fall down a rabbit hole away from all this.

*

An alarming noise, high-pitched shrieks . . . she snaps open her eyes. Robin is putting a bottle in the baby's mouth. The noise ceases. They look comfortable together.

'Oh, hi again!' Robin says, noticing. 'You must need water now – can I give you a sip?' She picks up a glass and brings it to Kessie's lips.

She tries to sip, and Robin tips it a tiny bit further, but Kessie accidentally jerks so it spills down her chin. 'Oops! I'll just wipe that,' Robin says. 'Let me call the nurse to check on you – do you want to hold the baby while I go find her?'

Kessie shakes her head forcefully. Robin's face falls a little, but she nods, and takes the baby with her.

A while later, Kessie hears a French lullaby. She opens her eyes to watch Robin singing while stroking the baby's head. Noticing Kessie awake, Robin comes over to sit on the edge of her bed. 'What does that song mean in English? Can you stroke my hair please?'

Robin laughs and obliges. 'It's a bit dark really, now that I think about it, but my dad always used to sing it to me – it's about a little sailor who goes out to sea alone and gets into trouble. It's got a lovely tune though. Do you need a massage or a drink or anything?'

Drugs, she wants to say. 'Water, maybe?'

'Sure. You've had lots of congratulations!' Robin says. 'Want to see on my phone when I get your drink?'

Kisses, exclamation marks, heart emojis. A long voice message from Auntie Elmi, all the way from Nepal, in which she sings a version of James Taylor's song about showering people with love in her low voice.

From her Dad: CONGRATULATIONS DARLING, HALLELUJAH! followed by an angel emoji. No suggestion about visiting. But if he was planning on bringing Cara, she would honestly rather he didn't for a while.

Remembering something, she sits up a little, and takes a sip from the glass that's materialized on the bedside table. 'Robs,' she says. 'I meant to ask ages ago – will you be her godmother? Or something a bit less . . . soul mother?'

'Oh, I love soul mother! I'd be honoured. In fact, have you thought any more about her name? I accidentally started calling her Zora, but I can totally stop . . .'

'No, no, Zora's great. Let's go with that.' She closes her eyes. Sinks.

*

Days pass on the hard hospital bed, surrounded by the sporadic shrieking of babies and the yakking of other families. Every four hours, Kessie gets to swallow another batch of painkillers, and everything eases a little – but then the pain grows inexorably, minute by minute, needles, arrows, hot irons, until finally the next dose is due.

She keeps headphones in most of the time, hearing classical music or podcasts without really listening.

It occurs to her at some point to ask Robin for an eye mask.

Flurries of worry that she's failing to keep an eye on the baby in its Perspex cot, but then it seems to sleep a lot. Anyway, Robin's there, almost all the time.

She's not expected to do many jobs yet, and the one only she *can* do she's already failing at. Breastfeeding was something she'd dreamed about. Longed for. It was going to be a way to bond intimately with her baby, feel like a true mother. But the first few times she tried it, nothing seemed to come out. The baby snorted and grasped around her nipple, like a half-starved warthog foraging in the dark. It did manage to get a grip on it now and then, with surprising force, and the midwife assured Kessie that she was producing colostrum – a sort of super-nutritious mucus that she vaguely remembered Yvonne talking about. Didn't seem anywhere near sufficient.

But then, when her milk did 'come in', it was a tidal wave. Within twenty-four hours her breasts quadrupled in size, metamorphosing from small, soft, familiar parts of her into fully pumped footballs. *Pamela Anderson, eat your heart out.* Now they're sore to touch, and sore if she rolls over without thinking, and when the baby latches the pain is sharp. She's begun to spend most of the time dreading the baby's high and particular cry, the tap on the shoulder, the voice informing her that it's time . . .

And here goes. The tap of doom. She pushes herself up, dragging her groin through gorse. Takes the raging creature. Tries to shove its mouth as gently as possible onto one of her bruised nipples, which are stuck like barnacles onto her whale-like boobs.

The creature, slipping around in her effort to latch, squalls in frustration. Milk sprays in delicate fountains all over the bed, and all over the floor, showering the baby's face and hair and back, but not actually making it into her throat. Why is her body overreacting like this? It's fucking frustrating, and embarrassing, and exhausting, trying again and again to get her to latch, while also keeping her own head up properly.

Thank God, there it is: a latch! For a few precious seconds. It feels like someone's pressing down hard on a bruise on her breast, but at least the high-pitched yowling has stopped. But then she's off again . . . then on again . . . then off.

'I'm shit at this. I wish you could feed her instead,' she sobs to Robin, handing her back after an equally messy attempt on the other boob, and starting to mop up the milk. Robin starts to protest, but she interrupts. 'Should I just quit and do formula? No, don't answer that, I don't want to give up yet . . . but I just . . . I don't think I can manage on my own. Will you come stay with me after I'm discharged? Just for a night, or . . .'

Robin agrees. She even offers do some night feeds, bless her, if Kessie can either pump milk or wants to mix formula. But a passing midwife overhears this, and stops at her bed. 'Partial formula feeds are absolutely *not* a good idea I'm afraid. At any time. Baby needs to get used to the *breast*, particularly after a difficult birth. Breast is best, remember!'

Kessie begins to protest, but the midwife wags a finger at her. 'I know it can seem hard at first, but it's all about perseverance. There's a real risk of nipple confusion if you start mixing breast and bottle at this stage – and we don't want *that*, do we?'

Who's *we?* she thinks. Also, *nipple confusion*? It would be a fun name for a punk band. As soon as the midwife leaves, she pleads with Robin to try it anyway.

*

Five days later, she's back at home. The pain from the surgery is less intense now, but still persistent, while the pain from breast-feeding has got worse – far worse. One of her nipples has begun to crack from overuse, so the creature's every suck feels like being stabbed by a shard of glass. Meanwhile her neck and back muscles are as knotted as the ropes of an old sea vessel.

At least the creature still sleeps a lot in between crying and feeding. It's nice just to look at her from the bed while she lies in the Moses basket on its rocking stand – the best part of parenting so far. She probably shouldn't say that out loud to anyone. But there's a profound quality to the baby's slumber, oblivious to sirens or phone rings. She often adopts hilarious superhero poses in sleep, fist raised over one shoulder, as if frozen in the act of celebrating a Wimbledon win. Kessie tries to absorb some of her peacefulness in these moments. To take in the little sweep of hair, the tiny nose, the thick lashes, the miniature fingers and toes . . . But she still feels a niggling detachment. That feeling that this can't really be her baby.

The problem with watching the creature sleep is that it's laced with panic that she's bound to wake – and of course she always does, and begins to cry, instantly, incessantly, like a deranged creature, or something in the throes of torture. If only she'd had more time to get over her injuries and the trauma of the whole birth experience before having to attend to the baby all the time, never knowing how long she's going to sleep for. At least, for now, Robin is doing a lot of the labour – things like changing the nappies, and carrying the creature around the living room while she cries, as well as the cooking and laundry. She's going above and beyond what anyone could expect of a friend, really.

The only thing that Robin can't do for her is breastfeed – but even that she'll be able to help with, once the new pump arrives. Thank God she's agreed to stay longer and has insisted on sleeping on the futon. She seems to have everything in hand. She lets Kessie know when it's time for her painkillers, takes the creature off for her whenever she asks, which is most of the time, brings through tea and snacks, and strokes her hair. *Don't ever leave,* Kessie wants to plead with her, several times a day. But Robin will leave. She'll have to, any day now.

Leona knocks on her door one day with a card and a hand-knitted blanket. It's turquoise with a cheery clashing red border, and the fact that she has taken the time to knit it with her knobbly, arthritic fingers makes Kessie's heart swell.

*

A message comes through from her dad while she's eating her porridge: he and Cara will be up on Sunday after church to visit and meet the baby if that's okay!!!! Four exclamation marks apparently indicate that this should be an exciting event. She wants to message him back to ask him please to come on his own – but the flack she'd get from Cara probably wouldn't be worth it. Robin reminds her that it'll be nice for Zora to meet her granddad, and says she'll try to keep Cara distracted.

*

It's Cara who flounces in first, squeaking congratulations. She almost pushes past Robin to get into the flat and runs over to see Zora, who's lying in her Moses basket. 'Oh my goodness! Look at her, Koji!' she calls, as if she's just discovered a new breed of kitten all by herself.

Kessie's dad walks over to the cot, puts his arm around Cara, and smiles fondly at the baby. 'What a little darling,' he says. 'Looks just like you when you were tiny, Kess.'

'Can I make you both some tea?' Robin asks.

'Black coffee for me please, sweets,' Cara says. 'Half a sugar.' She presents Kessie with a gift, baby angels printed all over the wrapping. Inside are three virulent pink flowery baby dresses. Each has buttons up the back. Now that Kessie has experienced changing a baby, she would like to know why any clothing designer would be so sadistic as to produce baby girls' dresses with buttons up the back. The idea of any child this small being content to lie still and quietly on its tummy for long enough to enable you to do up every fiddly one, without tearing your hair out first, is laughable.

'I can't beliiieve I'm a granny!' Cara coos, picking Zora up without asking. 'I don't feel old enough, to be honest with you – you can call me Cara, you tiny thing!' Kessie resists pointing out that she isn't Zora's real granny. Or that it'll be a while before the baby's calling anyone anything, by which point, hopefully, her dad will have come to his senses and ended the relationship and she and Zora need never endure her again.

He stands by, looking on genially, and then turns to Kessie, smiling so proudly that she feels extra mean. Maybe Zora's arrival is the moment when they begin to bond again. 'I brought along a few of your old baby things too – Cara found them in a box in the attic when she was clearing out, and I thought you might like them. They're out in the hallway in a plastic bag.' She frowns, and is on the point of asking why he hadn't brought the bag into the living room – until it occurs to her that this would involve drawing attention to their shared memories of her mother, which would annoy Cara. No doubt Cara was already annoyed at him for obstructing her mission to eviscerate as many of her mother's things as possible. 'So! How are you feeling, darling?' he asks, and rubs her arm. 'Recovered from the birth all right?'

'I'm fine,' she lies, sulkily. She has absolutely no desire to talk about either the birth or the awful fallout since. But he's being nice, so she will be too. She switches on a smile. 'I'll go fetch the bag – I didn't even know Mum had kept my baby things! That's such a nice surprise.'

Cara has begun bouncing Zora up and down as if training her for a trampolining contest, and promptly launches into a tirade of chatter about her sons' various spectacular sporting successes.

Kessie goes out to the hall, grabs the old supermarket bag, and brings it back into the living room to open ceremonially. She pulls out her Nepalese rattle, painted in a red and green dot pattern, her favourite lion puppet, with droopy whiskers and one ochre ear dangling off, and a paisley printed turquoise cotton bag that folds out into a portable baby changing mat, though without a plastic waterproof lining. 'Oh look at these, Robin! Thanks so much, Dad. Do you remember the puppet shows that Mum and I used to put on for you?'

Zora starts to cry – inevitably, since she isn't accustomed to or old enough for trampolining – and Cara looks over at Kessie with pitying disapproval. She holds the child out, and informs Kessie that she must be *'so hungry'*, the *'poor little thing'* – as if the poor little thing's mother had been deliberately withholding milk from her, distracting herself with fripperies – then fixes her gaze on Kessie's breasts, as if summoning her shirt to spontaneously unbutton itself.

Kessie puts the things aside, takes the creature back, and stares desperately at the shrieking mouth for a moment, at the tiny epiglottis waggling like a wren's tail, then catches a smell. 'Sorry, I just need to change her first,' she says – as if she owes anyone an apology, never mind Cara.

Lying her down on the changing mat is a red rag to the world's tiniest bull. The creature rages even more loudly, flailing her little fists. *Bull snarling, hoards barging, sun burning, battle failing . . .* Kessie can't fricking get the fricking Babygro undone. And the fricking nappies are inexplicably missing.

Robin comes over. 'Want me to do it?' she asks quietly.

Yes, please, yes, is what she wants to say – but she also wants to prove her capability as a parent to Cara, and not to have to go back to talk to her any more, so she says she's fine doing it herself.

The room seems to go quiet, save for the creature's caterwauling. Kessie flushes as she feels herself being watched intently as she fails this basic test. It strikes her, only now, how few times so far she's actually changed the creature's nappy in comparison to Robin.

Meanwhile Robin asks her dad how the church community is doing, and this gets him on a roll talking about the build-up to Christmas, the carol services, the deliveries of packages to the vulnerable, the decorations. Kessie wipes the creature's bottom, but the poo is all up her back. She can't get it all off without twisting the little body around in a dangerous-seeming way – what if her spine snaps? – and she can't get her fricking arm out of the fricking Babygro. She removes the sticker from the fresh nappy, pulls it through her rubbery legs, and tries do up one side, but the tape keeps popping off as Zora kicks.

And then Cara appears beside her. 'Oh no, no, no, it'll be all wonky if you do it *that* way,' she says fussily, and reaches over to do the nappy herself.

Kessie steps back without speaking, then starts to well up. Typical. She runs to the bedroom and hunches down on the bed, trying to breathe, to regain control. No chance.

A few moments later, Robin comes in to ask if she's okay.

'Please just tell them to leave,' she sobs.

She hears Cara protesting loudly that they'd only just *got* there – but before long the front door closes.

Chapter 15

Robin

The soft whistle of an empty bottle being sucked prompts Robin to heave open her eyelids. Fatigue is dragging on her limbs. Her lower back smarts – Kessie's futon is incredibly uncomfortable. Inches away, two gleams: Zora's wide eyes. She sits up. 'Oh, hi! Well done, little one – you finished the whole bottle? Hearty appetite, huh? Reckon you'll be able to last a bit longer before the next feed?'

The sky is charcoal. She turns over to look at her phone. 5 a.m. Oh, and it's the 25th of December. She lifts Zora and the bulky co-sleeper pod over to the other side of her, gives her downy hillock of hair a stroke, and offers her juggernaut finger. Zora's tiny ones wrap tight around it without missing a beat. She'll never tire of that instinctive connection – though it probably won't last for that long. Is there a word for the nostalgia you feel for something that you have but know that you're going to lose? 'Merry Christmas, sweetheart! Your very first!'

This co-sleeper thing was a great investment. It's exhausting still having to wake up multiple times a night to bottle-feed Zora, but it's also lovely having this tiny companion in her bed, needing her, content just being with her. None of the sour breath and snoring fits she's endured from bed-sharing with men.

Yesterday, Kessie asked her, again, whether she would be a terrible mother if she gave up breastfeeding. Robin reiterated that of course she wouldn't; that it was completely her choice, and that whatever she decided would have no bearing on how good a mother she was. But so far Kessie doesn't seem to be finding much pleasure in any aspect of motherhood. Robin reminded her that she really didn't have to live up to some abstract notion of being a 'perfect mother' – that she'd actually just been reading about how, back in the 1950s, paediatrician Donald Winnicott coined the phrase 'good enough mother' to make the really important point that nobody is perfect, and that children can actually *benefit* from what mothers might see as imperfections . . .

But Kessie didn't seem to be listening. She'd started to hit her forehead with her palm, and she shook her head violently, and said there was loads of evidence about the benefits of breastfeeding, and that was *one* thing she was physically able to do for Zora, so she had to carry on even though it was fucking agony.

'You honestly *don't* have to,' Robin persisted. 'Lots of women bottle-feed their babies. My mum did! Zora will be fine either way. You should just do whatever feels right for you.'

Kessie ended up deciding to pump more milk for the time being, even though she moaned that it made her feel like a dairy cow.

Zora is starting to wrinkle up her face in a way that Robin has learned means burp time. She scoops her up, lays her against her shoulder and massages her little back firmly from bottom to top: a technique learned from YouTube. And there it comes. 'Well done!' she praises, then swoops Zora round to see her facial expression. Hilarious! Her little mouth is still agape, but contorted on one side, as if she's just witnessed Robin sprouting a unicorn head.

Resting the baby back against her chest, she slides one hand up to cocoon the back of her head. So pleasingly spherical. But still as fragile as a glass bauble, the plates of her skull yet to fuse. She walks slowly over to switch on the radio, and a choir is belting out 'Hark! The Herald Angels Sing'. She turns on the fairy lights that Kessie had wrapped around a miniature tree days before she went into labour, and swivels Zora around into the crook of her arm so she can look at the sparkles. But the baby's eyes lock into hers. Such solemn intensity for a such a small human. What do newborns think about? How does thought feel when you don't have language?

Kessie doesn't surface for several more hours. Zora's beatific mood disintegrates into incessant, shrill crying. Digestive pain? If only she could explain what the matter is. Robin paces up and down with her and ratchets up the volume of Mozart's piano concertos. It occurs to her that she had planned to cook a Christmas lunch, but hadn't got round to buying any of the ingredients. Thank God for all the frozen meals from the baby shower. After ten minutes or so, Zora yawns and slips into sleep.

After scrolling through her socials for a while, and wondering whether to start being more active again, rather than just spying on people she barely keeps in touch with any more, she hears the bathroom door click and squeak open. She puts on the Ella and Louis Christmas album, then waits for Kessie to pull back the thick curtain and come through to the living room, all set to wish her a jubilant *Merry Christmas! Your first as a mama!*

But it is a long while until the toilet flushes. Even then, there is no click from the bathroom door. Instead, she hears something that sounds like a sob. Zora has drifted off again, and let the bottle slide from her lips. Robin places it down on the table, pulls back the curtain, and knocks on the bathroom door. 'Kess? Are you okay?'

Silence.

'Kess? Is everything all right?'

The door slowly opens. Kessie's face is mottled and smeary, her eyes veined red.

'Oh, love.' Robin wants to reach out to hug her, but can't easily while holding Zora.

'Everything hurts,' Kessie croaks. 'It's too embarrassing.'

'Oh gosh – I'm sorry. But listen, you don't have to feel *embarrassed* about anything with me, okay? I'm pretty familiar with your undercarriage now, don't forget.'

This at least cracks a small smile.

'Here, come and sit down and I can make you some breakfast, and maybe you can tell me more about it?'

Kessie nods, mutely, and begins to sit down as slowly as a ninety-year-old. Robin is just preparing to pass Zora to her, when she winces, sucks in a breath, then stands up again. '*Fuck*, it's just excruciating. I can't even explain – it's like sitting on a cluster of nails. I'm sorry, it's gross, but . . .'

'No, no,' Robin says. 'Don't apologize. Keep going.'

Kessie sighs. 'Pissing feels like someone's slicing my clit with a razor. I can hardly bear to look down there to see how bad it is. But I feel like it's worse than my home ec sewing disaster in Year 8, if you can remember that.'

Robin is relieved to hear her making something like a joke. 'I'm sure it'll heal just fine. But, well, just in case it's a welcome distraction – is this the wrong time to say Merry Christmas?'

Kessie looks up, suddenly. '*Christmas Day?!* Bloody hell. I haven't got you anything.'

'Well, you have a pretty good excuse! It's fine. I did get a couple of small things for you, but they're back at home. I did have an idea about a gift for Zora though . . . it's just a little thing that we could make . . .'

'*Make?* Mate, I can barely make myself a cuppa at the moment . . .'

Robin laughs. 'I didn't mean right *now*. And we don't have to. You definitely don't. But I was just reading about how some cultures make bracelets for new babies as a good luck charm and I thought it sounded like a nice thing to do. The Beng people in Cote D'Ivoire make them out of pineapple fibre, and attach things to them – a lemon, because lemon trees are meant to be powerful, and cowrie shells, because their ancestors like them – I think they used to use them as money, so if their spirits get payment in shells they're likely to take extra care of those babies from the afterlife . . . Anyway, I still have some beads from our Morocco trip, so I could maybe use those . . .'

Kessie nods, eyebrows raised, looking faintly bored.

'Silly idea really,' Robin says, encircling Zora's smooth little wrist with her thumb and forefinger.

'No it's not – I like it,' Kessie says. 'I just don't have the energy . . . But please make one if you do. That's so lovely that you still have beads from Morocco. God, that feels so long ago, right? When we were young and free and had energy.'

Once Kessie has eaten some cereal, and has sat herself delicately on the futon, listening to a bebop Christmas hits soundtrack, Robin asks if she wants to hold Zora again. She puffs out a breath but says okay, and holds out her arms – her expression is almost like she's on bin duty and ready to receive a bag of rubbish. Perplexed, Robin passes her the child.

Zora stares up at her mother, while Kessie, after a few seconds, fixes her gaze out of the window. 'God, Robs, I'm so fucking tired of being in pain,' she groans. 'And tired of being so tired. I never knew it was possible to *be* this knackered.'

Zora's head is slipping, so Robin leans over and moves it up again. 'It'll get better soon, I promise,' she says, thinking better of mentioning her own fatigue. 'Want me to make you some toast and honey?'

When she turns around, no more than two minutes later, with a plate of toast, Kessie's eyes have drooped – and so, to Robin's alarm, has Zora's body, which looks as if it's about to roll onto the floor. Her little neck is wilting like a plucked wildflower. She dumps the plate on the counter, dashes over, and puts a protective hand behind her, supporting her head again.

Kessie looks up a little, grunts and asks if she'll take her back.

Robin takes the baby, feeling suddenly queasy. Okay, so Kessie is evidently super tired and in pain – but is she unable to bring herself to care about her own baby's safety? 'I'll just put her down for a bit then, shall I . . . ?'

But Zora is not into the idea of the Moses basket. Her back arches as Robin tries to lay her down, and she squawks her disapproval. Robin lifts her up again, and she glares as if daring her to try that again. Robin grins and cuddles her instead. She ends up nibbling at the toast herself as Kessie snoozes, while humming along, for Zora's benefit, to songs about Santa getting stuck in the chimney, the snowy delights of a winter wonderland, and how love can keep you warm.

*

New Year passes much like Christmas. The health visitor comes over a couple of times, but each time Kessie somehow cleans herself up and puts a brave face on things, claiming to be fine. Robin tries to persuade her to book a doctor's appointment, to talk to a professional about how she's feeling psychologically, still – but she keeps not doing it. Mostly, she stays in her room, listening to Bach or watching *Love Island*.

Meanwhile, Robin occupies herself looking after Zora, and doing the endless laundry, cooking and washing up, mostly to the soundtrack of Joni's earliest albums. Time somehow passes in an extraordinary way when she's with this baby. Leaning her lips on Zora's forehead, when she's calm, is the purest fulfilment. When those little fingers reach out and touch her face, the intense feeling of delight is almost erotic. In the run-up to the birth, she didn't expect for one moment that she'd feel remotely like this about Kessie's child – but it's finally arrived: that mysterious depth of love she'd longed for that day on the bus, watching the Tintin baby. And now that she feels this for Zora, it's hard to imagine how she could possibly feel any more strongly about any other baby, even if one were ever to grow out of her own lonely little frozen egg.

Kessie, on the other hand, seems overwhelmed by her own daughter in an entirely different way. She does sometimes look at her lovingly – but mostly the expression on her face, when she is holding Zora, is befuddled. Even terrified. Which is understandable seeing as the birth nearly killed her – but that was weeks ago now.

By mid-January, Robin has begun to get properly worried about when and how she'll be able to get back to work. She's had to take annual leave to keep on looking after Zora – and Kessie, and has already used up most of the leave that she'd planned on saving for her California trip in the spring. But Kessie doesn't seem anywhere near ready to cope on her own yet. She's barely doing anything towards Zora's care except breastfeeding her when she's hungry, and even that usually sends Kessie into floods of tears. It would feel hard enough for Robin to leave Zora anyway, and at the moment, if she's being frank with herself, it seems too risky.

One evening, when Kessie is napping, Robin watches Zora drop off as silently as a cloud sliding over the sun, and colours splurge inside her chest like one of Richter's crazier paintings. She could never get bored of staring at this tiny child, of devouring her beauty. It occurs to her that she's never felt this fiercely proprietorial about anything, or anyone; and yet this baby isn't hers. After being the first person in the world to hold her, to do skin-to-skin with her, sing to her, feed her, carry her while singing lullabies up and down that hospital corridor, they're connected in a deep, tangible way. But maybe it's all in her mind. Anyway, she just can't let herself get too attached to a baby who isn't actually hers. Her boss is already pressuring her to come back to work, and she could really do with sleeping in her own bed again. She resolves to talk to Kessie seriously in the morning.

She picks up the anthropology book she'd ordered online the other day, called *Mother Nature*, about how maternal instincts have shaped the human species, figuring that she might as well try to use the extra time away from the office, when Zora is asleep, to do some research for her dissertation, and she might as well make her dissertation research relevant to parenting. The author of this book, Sarah Blaffer Hrdy, had started off as a primatologist before moving into anthropology, so her perspective sounded interesting.

After flicking through the pages, she pauses at an unfamiliar word: 'allomothers'. This turns out to be a term for women who assist biological mothers in bringing up infants – the prefix *allo* coming from the Greek meaning 'other than'. It was coined back in 1975 by Edward O. Wilson, an ant specialist before he branched out into socio-biology across species. He pointed out that mothers in many species, like reptiles and fish, just lay their eggs and take off; but that in species where they stick around, their babies' survival almost always depends on the help of other adults, who sometimes end up providing *more* care than they do. Ornithologists used to call such birds 'helpers', and primatologists used to call such chimps 'aunts', but Wilson felt that the term 'allomothers' was a more 'dignified' designation that could extend to humans too.

Robin tries saying it in a low voice: 'allomother.' The idea is both obvious and revelatory – it finally seems to describe what she's been doing for Zora – what she is to Zora, even. Kessie even referred to her as Mama Roro the other day, when she got fed up with holding the baby and wanted to give her back. Robin does still like the term 'soul mother' that Kessie came up with as a substitute for godmother; but it strikes her now that, although godmothers are an established part of British culture, they rarely seem to play a very meaningful role. Robin's own godmother, Marlene, fell out with her mother when Robin was little over something that was never spoken of, and promptly exited their lives. Kessie had been far more deeply connected to her Auntie Elmi, of course – who became almost like a second mother, at least until Kessie went to music college and Elmi moved away to that commune of Buddhist women, and then to Nepal. But that seems rare.

Hrdy argues that allomothers have always been critical to human societies, and points out that plenty still use them today. The Agta people in the Philippines, for instance, see a child as being born not into a small nuclear family, but into a community of helpers. As soon as a baby is delivered, it is passed from person to person among a big group of friends and relatives, until everyone present has had an opportunity to cuddle and admire it, and care continues in that vein for the whole of its first year, allowing its mother to go back out to work, hunting wild pig and deer along with other men and women in the community who are healthy and strong enough for this labour. The main problem facing mothers in Western societies now, Hrdy argues, is a scarcity of alloparents. There's a totally unfair expectation on contemporary Western women that they should be able to be competent and dedicated mothers all on their own, while living away from extended family and holding down jobs outside the home; it's way out of line with what's normal, and it's no wonder that many women feel like they can't cope.

Robin puts the book down, and goes to check on Kessie, then Zora. 'Allomother', she repeats, looking down at the baby. It has a mellifluous ring to it. It's kind of friendly, too, like – 'allo mother, 'ow are you doin'? She thinks about her fish, back in the tank in her flat, unfed for two days now – they must be ravenous. You're not meant to leave tropical fish for more than three days without food, and hers have come to expect a sprinkle of flakes twice a day. They deserve her care too. She'll go back and feed them tomorrow, and pick up a few extra clothes.

Back on the sofa, she smooths down a page of the book at the section on breastfeeding. She hadn't realized before how common wet-nursing used to be in centuries past. In Egypt, back in 1330 BC, King Tut built a grand tomb solely to honour his wet nurse. In Arab cultures, Islamic law still provides for three kinds of kinship: by blood, by marriage, and in cases where babies have sucked milk from the same woman. It probably should have been patently obvious, seeing as formula is a newish invention, but it hadn't occurred to her.

Wet-nursing was apparently common in European societies until much more recently than she'd imagined. In Paris, in 1780, out of 21,000 births registered, only 5 per cent of the babies were nursed by their own mothers. This only changed in the eighteenth and nineteenth centuries, when the authorities became concerned about 'public morality' – at the same time, oh so coincidentally, as wanting to encourage more women to stay in the home and 'know their place'. Law reformers drafted new legislation to ban wet-nursing, using phrases like 'natural law' and the 'sacred duty of mothers' – and they got their way. Wet-nursing was phased out, to the point that it's almost unheard of now. But anthropology research reveals that 'allomaternal suckling' is still thriving beyond Europe and North America, from the Efé people in the Ituri Forest to the people in the Andaman Islands.

Robin finds herself smiling broadly. So her desire to be able to breastfeed Zora wasn't actually freaky and twisted after all! Western patriarchal culture, and its suppression of wet-nursing in order to compel mothers to stay at home with their babies – *that's* what's abnormal. Other cultures think of kin in a much more pragmatic way.

She can't actually believe what she reads next: that lactation can be induced in an allomother even if she's never been pregnant. Can that be right? But it's a question of graft, and not magic: breasts have to be kneaded and massaged past the point that many women can take, and nipples have to be sucked in preparation – sometimes by baby *animals*.

She puts the book down again and gets up to look at Zora's peachy face, then paces around and stretches. At the window, she pulls out her phone and searches for 'human animal breastfeeding', just to see what comes up.

Saint Veronica Giuliani, a seventeenth century nun and mystic, apparently used to suckle a lamb in bed with her as a symbol of the Lamb of God.

The Ainu people in northern Japan hold an annual bear festival where a bear, who had been suckled by a woman as a cub, is sacrificed.

In Turkey, Persia and America, as recently as the eighteenth century, it used to be common for pregnant women, in their eighth month, to get puppies to suckle on their breasts in order to harden their nipples and prepare their breasts to secrete more milk.

Even Mary Wollstonecraft breastfed puppies, on a doctor's orders! A male doctor, presumably. After childbirth, her placenta wasn't coming out, and he hoped that the puppy's suckling would cause her womb to contract enough to push it out. It didn't work. And she died. *Mary Wollstonecraft.* What a way for a feminist hero to go.

More recently, a Californian mother of two breastfed her nine-year-old daughter's pug named Spider and welcomed in the media to witness the spectacle. And a Burmese woman who worked at the Yangon Zoo was caught breastfeeding a pair of motherless tiger cubs.

Robin finds herself weaving through more and more strange portals. Turns out there was a long human history of the opposite practice, too: human babies suckling from animals. But then, of course, that must be where *The Jungle Book*'s Mother Wolf came from. Apparently French mothers regularly used to let their babies suckle from goats. In 1816, a German book was published with the title, *The Goat as the Best and Most Agreeable Wet Nurse*. In the opinion of Swedish scientist Carl Linneus, being suckled by a lioness would surely confer courage on a child.

A sleepy gurgle comes from Zora's direction, and Robin goes over to the cot. Her blue eyes are wide open, staring up at her with such intensity, such trust. 'Hello there, darling girl!' She strokes one soft cheek. 'I was just reading that babies like you used to drink milk from other animals! What do you think of that? Fancy a trip to London Zoo to sample some tiger milk?'

Is that a smile? No, she's not old enough yet. And there, she's already asleep again, like a book flipped shut.

Robin goes back over to her own book, but she's too zapped to lift another page. Going out on trips with Zora – they'll really need the buggy for that. It's due to be delivered tomorrow. She had only realized last week that Kessie had been too broke to buy one, and immediately insisted that she'd buy one for her – not realizing, until she looked at prices, quite how extortionate they were. Even so, she decided to order a fancy new Uppababy from John Lewis that was a decent height for tall people and had lots of storage space, figuring she could re-sell it more easily when the time came.

*

A week later, she's dressed up in her suit again, outwardly ready for her first morning back in the office, but inwardly rigid with anxiety. Kessie has just got up, and is still in pyjamas, but insists she'll be alright. Robin forces an encouraging smile, then holds the baby close, drinking in her sweet smell. She can't help feeling like she's about to commit an act of reckless abandonment in leaving her behind. As if Zora were reading her mind, as soon as Robin hands her over to Kessie, the baby starts to bawl, and Robin's own eyes well up as she hastens out of the door and down the street.

Biting her lips, she reminds herself that she's done everything possible to make this work, and to set things up for Kessie and Zora to succeed. She has made good use of the new buggy for daily walks around the park, and even a trip to the Tate. She's established a rough routine for Zora's feeding and sleeping, and written everything down in a mini Zora handbook which she's stuck to the fridge with a magnet. She's kept Kessie's flat in order, and done all the laundry and cooking – albeit mostly omlettes and pre-prepared soups and ready meals, and the fridge and snack cupboard are well stocked. Kessie has assured her several times that she'd be ready to take over by this point . . . but Robin can't help worrying that she's not yet there – that she isn't mentally well enough to manage.

On some days this past week, Kessie has at least got herself dressed and shown a little enthusiasm about Zora, and about life; but most days she has remained morose, teary, and stayed largely in her room. She's only twice been persuaded to join Robin and Zora for walks around the park, and even her usual favourite flat white failed to perk her up. Robin has texted Paolo and a couple of Kessie's other friends to let them know the situation, and that Kessie is really struggling. They have offered to help, but haven't suggested anything specific, save for promising to come visit, and to keep checking in. Robin has asked Kessie, multiple times, if she can please make an appointment to see the doctor and talk about how she's been feeling, but Kessie has fobbed her off, as if she's nagging, and has just insisted, stubbornly, that she'll cope when she has to. Hopefully Robin's absence during working hours will turn out to be the motivation she needs to get herself together enough to take care of Zora properly.

By the time Robin gets out of the Tube, she already feels

exhausted, panicky, and tempted to go back home again. Only caffeine propels her legs further towards the office. Sanjay knows full well why she's had to take extra leave over the festive break, but his emails haven't exuded empathetic understanding. It wasn't as if she'd expected flowers, like they would always send someone on the team who'd just had a new baby, but he might at least have said something kind, like that he understood, and that they were looking forward to having her back when she was ready. It wasn't like she had been taking a holiday, which she actually *needs* now that her leave has run out. She's going to demand that they reduce her hours, at least. Four days a week or she'll quit.

'Finally,' is all Sanjay says when he sees her at her desk. 'Better get you caught up. The telecoms project is under major pressure. And there are several other urgent tasks. For now, I want you to prioritize the red-flagged emails I've sent you over the last few weeks. I suggest you come to meet me in my office in half an hour, and be up to speed with the new logistics brief so that we can apportion tasks. Oh, and your annual review is coming up and you have two days to submit your form.'

Chapter 16

Kessie

They don't tell you that your boobs will become ticking bombs.

They don't tell you that you'll have to force your screeching baby to snog one, wildly, in its desperate quest for nourishment, like it's bobbing for a cooking apple, while your milk spurts out around you both, and the apoplectic dial is turned up and up — *milk, milk, all around and not a drop to drink* – and meanwhile your other boob will smart with neglect, and flood waste milk into your breast pad, and down into your top, ready to turn rancid.

They don't tell you that the only way to get relief is to stand in a hot shower and shoot excess milk at the tiles, like water pistols, like you're in a spaghetti western-slash-porn movie.

They don't tell you that if your baby finally latches, and you let it feed for too long, both your nipples crack, bleed, and never heal, because your baby just wants more, wants to come back on every few hours, jabbing your open wound each time with a serrated penknife.

They only repeat the mantra, *breast is best, breast is best, breast is better than all the rest.*

No bottle for you, they said. Nipple *confusion,* they said. Oh, these nipples are confused all right – they're screaming, WHY ARE YOU MUTILATING US? CAN'T YOU KEEP THAT BEAST AWAY, JUST FOR A DAY?

They don't tell you that hitching yourself up to the breast pump, listening to its repetitive buzz and watching your milk trickle in, will make you feel like a dairy cow, to the point that you will vow to boycott cow's milk for life, then won't have the willpower to follow through with it.

They don't tell you that you can't sleep, even though your baby is being looked after by someone else precisely so that you can sleep, making you feel more and more guilty about your failure to sleep, and less and less likely to get any sleep sleep sleep SLEEP.

They don't tell you that your torn vulva will pound like a kidnap victim on a cellar door.

Or that your spirit will become a deflating helium balloon in a deserted playground.

Breast is best – but your breasts are a mess – the source of your unmaternal unhappiness. Your breasts are pests, won't let you rest – they stink out your clothes, undress and redress – they're slave-driving organs you couldn't want less . . .

They don't tell you that you want to pour your soul into verse but fail the test.

Kessie puts the notebook down. Paolo's lovely ukulele is lying against the wall. She wants to try playing it, singing a song, but that would mean motivating herself to walk across the room.

She wants to listen to Kate Bush, but that would mean motivating herself to charge her phone or walk to the CD player.

The radiator ticks to a different beat. Probably needs bleeding. There's another reason for self-disgust to add to the list: never having learned how to bleed a radiator by age thirty-five.

A faint pattern of distorted diamonds lingers on the wall cast by the low light.

They don't tell you how much you will loathe this mauled and flabby shell of a body.

They don't tell you that enthusiastic new baby announcements from your antenatal group will fizz into your phone, as if everything's great, as if everything's easy, as if it'd be totally fine to get dressed and exit the building with your baby and get together in the park for skinny flat whites and birth story sharing, that you will want to block them all, and wish you'd never shelled out for that ridiculous class where the teacher went on about choosing a natural birth, as if you'd have some sort of control over any of it, and where you learned nothing, *nothing,* about the shitshow that begins afterwards.

They don't tell you that you wish you could just go off and hide on your own somewhere, on a fluffy beanbag in the corner of a library, or in a hammock up a large tree, far, far away from your baby. Just for a while. Several months, perhaps. Years. But you can't leave, even for an hour, because you're trapped in its orbit now, like mercury to the sun.

They don't tell you that your previous life will seem like someone else's. That summer after their GCSEs when she and Robin went travelling together in Brittany, backpacking around the coast, mostly in the rain, drinking cider and eating frites and galettes every night, revelling in their newfound independence and freedom. Was that really her? *Goodbye old me.*

From the other room, Zora's high-pitched crying starts up, chafes against her eardrums. And there's Robin's voice, singing, soothing. Thank God it's the weekend and she's home again.

The other day, she opened one of Robin's anthropology books about motherhood, just because it was perched on top of a pile on the coffee table. The bookmarked chapter was about mothers who don't act in a 'motherly' way, to the point of committing infanticide. It summarized a study of black-tailed prairie dogs which showed that 9 per cent give up on their pups at birth and make no effort to keep them alive. Unprotected, the young are eaten by other females in the group, sometimes with the mother joining in. In other words, a prairie dog mother is allowed to just give up if she needs to. Robin had been telling her about allomothers, and about how she shouldn't feel bad about needing help, because women always have needed help – but then Robin's giving her far more help than she could ever ask for or expect, and she's still failing.

She knows she's lucky to be alive. If she had been born into another culture without access to a decent hospital, she wouldn't be. She should be grateful. And yet . . .

They don't tell you that your baby is like a gong sounding the fading note of your own mortality. They don't tell you that you'll look at her and wish you could turn back time, that you'd understood what time meant when you were free.

Bad person. Fickle person. Inadequate mother.

Sleep, that's what she needs, craves, *sleep, please, sleep*, the deepest oblivion – a coma, ideally. Will she ever sleep properly again?

She misses her mum. She misses her dad. She misses Auntie Elmi, who was meant to come and visit next week, even had flights and a hotel booked, but has had to cancel.

She reaches for her headphones, plugs them into her phone and puts on some Mozart. No, too soothing and well-patterned; the violins are mocking her.

A true crime podcast: maybe distraction in plot, in someone else's dark story, maybe that's the answer? But as the episode meanders on she realizes she's not following.

Only twenty minutes until Zora is due another feed, as per the new schedule Robin has drawn up. The idea was to try to space out the feeds and give her more respite. But there are still too many . . . And there it goes again: the mere *thought* of breastfeeding has set her boobs off. The weirdness of this, how a secret, momentary thought is like pulling a trigger on a hose inside her when she's not consciously willing it – when she's willing the *opposite* to happen, in fact. Earlier this morning she had forgotten to put new breast pads in, and was foolish enough just to think, for a second, about how much she *hated* breastfeeding. Huge wet circles promptly emerged on her pyjama top, stinking sweetly.

If only her mum were alive. She picks up the wooden rattle her dad brought over and turns it around and around between her fingertips, feeling the paint patterns like braille. Her dad hasn't yet followed up after that awful visit with a phone call, or questions, or offered to visit. They exchanged some awkward texts, but he didn't really apologize for Cara's behaviour. He did send a card, though. Auntie Elmi has been much more engaged than him, even from a distant continent – she posted a care package, has messaged every day, and called on a terrible line, has promised to rebook a flight to visit. But she's not here now.

Kessie turns over gingerly in bed. Robin is doing much better than her at parenting, but without ever trying to take over. She is doing it with so much kindness and grace it makes Kessie feel like utter crap. She knows, though she'd never ask, that Robin hasn't had the urge, like she has, to put her hand over Zora's screeching mouth to make the crying stop.

Who has she *become*? How is this *happening*? She had wanted motherhood so badly for so long. She'd thought she'd be okay at it. Good, even. She curls up, pulls the duvet over her head, and hugs her knees in the dark.

They don't tell you that you'll become a monster and that you'll have to keep your most monstrous thoughts a secret.

They tell you that you'll automatically adore your coochie-coochie, satin-soft, squidgy-cheeked baby.

They don't tell you that you could be landed with a tiny-but-domineering monarch with a metallic stare and a steam-train scream.

She should have known that she wouldn't have what it takes. That llama cloud was a bad sign.

It should have been Robin.

A knock on the door. Robin creeps in, carrying a steaming mug of tea, and a worried, enquiring smile.

Chapter 17

Robin

Robin's desk phone rings. It's Gemma, the receptionist. 'Your client's arrived.'

'Sorry?'

'I said your client's arrived? Jonathan Burrow? You have a meeting at two? He's just in reception. Shall I say you're on your way?'

Burrow. Bunnies. Barrow. There's a book she remembers from childhood with a barrow man. Or was it a barrow boy?

'Or . . . shall I bring him straight down to the meeting room?' Gemma's asking.

'Um, agh, okay, sorry, no, I'll meet him in reception . . . Can you tell him I've been held up by something unavoidable? I'll be five minutes. Thanks.'

She gets up and glugs some water. This meeting had been arranged for this new project when she was away, but she had seen it pop up in the diary. She's been back at work for days now and had totally failed to check the schedule properly, or prepare, or somehow register the passing of time in a sensible way. And now, with zero preparation, she's supposed to meet this guy in person and tell him, coherently, how plans for his profitability are taking shape in her hands.

Taking shape. She imagines herself turning a pot like Demi Moore in *Ghost*. Imagines herself as the pot. She could be turning into clay, in fact – her bones are dissolving with tiredness. Her head aches. She digs in her bag for some ibuprofen, and pops two pills. What's the name of Burrow's company again? What's the full project title, even?

She sits back down and searches her files. It's to do with customer service . . . optimization and balancing automation . . . Crap, he's waiting for her now. Damage limitation: that's all she can aim for. She just has to not alienate this guy, or cause him to pull the plug on the project, and bad-mouth the company's reputation.

Maybe she should pretend to be really ill today, struck down with a bug, unable to see him at the last minute? Or maybe she should fess up at the start of the meeting that she's behind, tell him about her personal situation . . . Which is what, though? She's not a new parent, as her boss was so quick to point out. *Looking after a friend's new baby* sounds lame. Like she's just done a short stint of babysitting and it's been too much for her porcelain female self to handle.

She just doesn't want to be here. Having to justify herself. Turns out even four days a week is too much. She wants to be with Zora – to induce that miraculous smile again! It happened yesterday for the very first time while they were playing peepo – a genuine smile, finally, not a grimace induced by trapped wind – and it was like summer had announced itself out of the grey!

She also wants to be *home* home – at her own flat, where

she's barely been for weeks now except to feed the fish and grab spare things – where there's space to move around and her own comfy bed to sleep in. She has got to tell Kessie that she can't crash on her futon any more, that it's preventing her from doing her job properly, that at least one of them needs to have an income.

It becomes apparent that she's walked into the toilets. She blinks hard, turns on her heel and walks towards the meeting room. Then realizes she does in fact need the toilet and does another U-turn. She has also forgotten her notebook. What was this guy's name again? Barrow? James? Joe? She needs sleep. More leave. But she's not a parent. Not. A. Parent.

In front of the bathroom mirror, she fixes her hair, wipes off a smudge of mascara, smiles at her reflection with teeth, and takes a long breath. It's only a meeting.

That evening, she climbs the stairs to Kessie's front door humming 'Big Yellow Taxi' in an attempt to drown out the internal replay of the disaster that took place over the tray of coffee and sachets of sugar.

You assured us on entering into the contract . . . I trusted this company . . . beggars belief . . . plenty of competitors out there we could have gone with . . . patently inadequate progress . . . lack of communication . . . waste of time . . . Never before has she had any negative feedback from a corporate client. This was a slating.

She had nearly retreated to her own flat afterwards, to crawl under her own duvet and close her eyes – but she needs to check on Zora. She wants to cuddle the little person who loves her back without question and won't judge her for being a disaster at work. And she's worried about Kessie.

Her key hovers in front of the lock. A reedy sound is percolating through.

The volume intensifies as she opens the door. In the living room, Zora is shrieking in her Moses basket, while Kessie is lying face down on the sofa. Robin drops her bag, runs over to the baby, and catches her breath – how long has she been crying like this? The child's face is purple and her balled-up hands have got the shakes. Robin picks her up, rocks her, shushes her. She reeks – her nappy is hot and needs changing. Poo has soaked up her back and onto the sheets. She wants to yell at Kessie, but instead she goes over to her, rubs her upper back, and tries to speak kindly. 'Oh sweetheart. Tough day huh? Please don't cry. I'm back now – I'm here. Let me get you some water. I'll change Zora – when did she last feed?'

The nappy has clearly been dirty for a while; red welts have risen over Zora's skin. Robin cleans her up as quickly as she can, puts on a new one. No pumped milk in the fridge. 'Can you feed her?' Kessie tilts her head back, closes her eyes. Robin rushes over to the cupboard to get the emergency formula, and fortunately there's one sterilized bottle left.

'It's okay, I'll do it,' Kessie groans. 'Can you get me a glass of milk?'

'Sure, let me help you first . . .' Robin crouches by her, gently places the screeching, arching Zora in her arms, and guides her to latch. Zora gobbles frantically and Kessie winces. The quiet is immediate and blissful.

Until it's broken by Kessie blowing her nose and dabbing at her eyes.

Robin pours her a large glass of milk and strokes her hair. 'Oh Kess,' she says, starting to feel at a loss. 'Do you want something to eat? Toast and honey?'

Kessie nods slowly.

'I was thinking I could make Zora that good luck bracelet this weekend,' Robin says, tentatively, as if that would be of any use at all.

Chapter 18

Kessie

Every time Robin leaves for work, Kessie feels like she's abandoned on a desert island with sole care of a rare and ravenous bird who hasn't worked out how to fly. Zora has just learned how to smile, but she gifted her very first one to Robin the other day while Kessie was having a nap. Kessie has barely been granted any since. Which is no more than she deserves. How does that jazz standard go, the one Ella sings about songs of love that always makes her cry? Most of them make her cry these days. She could easily spend the rest of her life listening to Ella and weeping.

She perches on the edge of the bed watching the creature sleep for a bit, then picks up the soft faun cashmere scarf that Auntie Elmi sent her to wrap Zora in and buries her face in it. She breathes, then pulls out her phone, watches the video of the baby smiling that Robin sent her, apparently unaware that it felt like evidence of her own failure.

Oh well. At least Paolo is coming to visit today. She's put him off until now, but she does want to see him, and knows she needs the company. And if he's going to be Zora's soul father, he should get the chance to meet her, finally.

By the time he rings the doorbell at 10.30, she is still in pyjamas, but has at least managed to brush her teeth, get through a feed and two nappy changes, and eat half a bowl of cereal. 'Hiiiii!' he crows delightedly. 'Ohmygod, Kessie, you're really a mama now, congratulations!' Energy radiates off him, and she can't help but relax a little. She asks him to keep it down a bit, though, as Zora's still asleep.

In one arm, he carries a bunch of yellow roses, which he hands to her, and he swings a narrow black bag off his other shoulder. 'A little gift.'

'Is that . . . ?'

'Yup!' He opens the box, and takes out a ukulele. It's rosewood colour, with hand-painted forget-me-not-like flowers around the hole in the middle.

Kessie's eyes well up, yet again. She takes it, and traces one with her fingertip. 'Oh Paolo, this is such a beautiful object. And thought. I don't know if I can do it justice . . .'

'You're welcome, my dear. I didn't like to think of you trying to play lullabies for Zora with that cheapie one you've got. I can help teach you if you like – and I can teach Zora too if she wants to learn when she's older. Some lessons for her are part of the gift. May I?' He strums a few chords, then sings a bit of Stevie Wonder's 'Happy Birthday'. As if he didn't know that the creature's actual birth day nearly finished Kessie off.

She starts to make him a coffee, but manages to tip most of it on the floor.

As he helps her clear up, he starts to ask questions – but she cuts him off and asks if it's okay if she doesn't talk about the birth. Or breastfeeding. Or basically anything that's happened since she went into labour. 'Can you tell me about what's been going on with you instead?' she asks, a little desperately.

He says sure, and starts chatting, but after a bit she realizes she hasn't really been listening. She can't seem to remember how to do small talk.

After about twenty minutes, the creature wakes, starts to cry, and needs changing. Paolo jokes that he has no idea how to do that, so he'll leave it to the expert. *Dunce, more like.* Kessie feels like snapping at him that he's a soul father now so he should bloody well give it a try, but holds it in. The creature will need a feed, too, after being changed, and she can't face him watching her mess up both activities, so she tells him she doesn't have much stamina at the moment, and asks if he wouldn't mind leaving her to it.

He hesitates, perplexed for a second, then says that's fine, that he totally understands, that he'll come again soon. But he fails to conceal the hurt look on his face.

After he closes the door, Kessie curls up in a ball on the sofa. She should have thanked him again for the ukulele. For coming to support her on a working day. She remembers their trip with the wind quintet to Bologna all those summers ago – how she and Paolo had changed their return flights and gone hitchhiking afterwards, making it to Florence and Rome, then all the way down to Naples, busking to pay for their hostel beds along the way, drinking Campari and Coke in the evenings, and flirting with beautiful Italians in bars, wandering drunkenly back to their hostels in the early hours as the stray dogs howled. Not as loud as this creature is howling right now.

The next nappy change takes five attempts and two nappies

to get right, and the howling continues. Kessie offers the creature the opportunity for another knife attack, aka sucking on her least cracked nipple. She gets even more frantic when it's bared, thrusting her little hands around, and yet she doesn't manage to latch properly for ages.

Finally she seems to ingest a bit of milk and quietens slightly. For a few minutes. And then she ramps up the crying again. Kessie sings 'Rock-a-bye Baby' and walks her round and round the room, like Robin always does – but somehow it doesn't seem to have the same effect. The creature just keeps on crying. And crying. And crying and crying – like that washing machine advert from her childhood where animated bras and shirts sing a jingle about how it goes on, and on, and on, and Ariston and on, and on, and on, and Ariston and on, and on, and . . .

The click of the letter box rouses her from her stupor. What if she's just won that competition for an all-expenses paid holiday to St Lucia? If half-starved Charlie Bucket could win a golden ticket, why not her? But the first letter is clearly a water bill – she can't look at that – and the second is a letter addressed in her landlord's handwriting. *Shit*. She's over a month late with the rent again, and she'd been trying not to think about it – which wasn't hard to do because he was always so nice and easy-going in accepting her apology by email, she'd started to believe it didn't matter to him that much, that he was probably too rich to be bothered. She pushes her finger slowly under the corner of the fold and tears it open. It's a Section 8 notice stating that she is in arrears with her rent, and he is giving her seven days to remedy the situation before commencing eviction proceedings.

Chapter 19

Robin

On the way to work, Robin stops at the café on the corner and asks for her usual flat white but with a triple shot. She wishes she knew the name of the cheery barista with the lip piercing who always remembers what she likes and asks how she's doing. Her default answer is that she's great, thanks – but this morning, after handing the drink over, the barista looks harder at her than usual. 'Hope this makes you feel better, luv,' she says, with such compassion that Robin wants to reach over the counter and hug her.

The front door to the office building seems to repel her with a magnetic force field. When she enters the office and walks towards her desk, nobody says good morning. Her feedback form lies uncompleted in her tray. She takes it out and stares at it as she finishes the last dregs of her coffee. I HATE YOU ALL AND I'M LEAVING, she feels like writing, in diagonal lines with thick red marker. She retreats to the kitchen to make another coffee, before realizing she's already caffeinated up to the eyeballs.

Her bones throb. Maybe she should actually just quit. She misses Zora viscerally – the weight of her, the sensation of sliding her hands under her head and little body to lift her up, and of that little hand gripping her finger like the mast of a sailing boat in a storm, the milky musk of her . . . Is Zora missing her in return? Is Kessie managing better today, or has she already descended into crisis mode? She wouldn't *harm* Zora if she lost the plot, would she?

She tips two sugars into her coffee, then sits back down and logs into her work email.

Four hundred and sixty-eight unread messages. Including one from Jonathan Burrow.

As predicted, it contains words like *dismayed* and *serious concerns*, and requires a full update in writing, with a clear, fully fleshed-out, day-by-day timeline for completion by tomorrow morning. It's the kind of email that could end her career. A career she would quite like to end, but on her own terms.

*

Somehow she gets through the week, and Saturday arrives. She lies in with Zora until the luxurious hour of 8 a.m., despite the futon-induced backache, groggily entranced by the curved outline of her face as she sleeps, the curl of her eyelashes. Once she wakes, and they've exchanged smiles and giggles, Robin walks her around and plays with her until she starts bleating for a breastfeed.

Kessie groans as they come into her room, but pushes herself to a seated position. As she tries to get Zora to latch, a warm arc of breastmilk collides with Robin's face. She licks the drip that runs down her upper lip. Sweeter than she'd expected.

When the feed is over, Robin says she could do with some fresh air, and suggests taking Zora to the park so that Kessie can have some time to herself, if she wants. Kessie's face lights up for a second, and she says yes please, but then turns over to face the wall. Before leaving, Robin makes her a cuppa, runs her a bath scented with lavender oil, and extracts a promise that she will get in.

It's cold but luminous outside. The few jaunty clouds are scalloped around the edges like a child's painting. Robin loves the sensation of walking along with Zora attached to her, peeping out of the side of the carrier like a baby monkey giving Attenborough's camera crew a coveted glance. She whispers to Zora about the sounds they can hear on their way – a blackbird – a bus – a bicycle bell – a bin being rolled out. She's read that the more you talk to your baby, right from the beginning, the easier it is for them to learn to speak quickly.

In the park, every green thing glows. It feels as if the Earth is beaming at them – spring is on its way. A woman with a toddler in a buggy stops to look at Zora, and says hello to her in a high voice. 'So adorable,' she says to Robin. 'Congratulations!'

'Oh – thanks!' she smiles.

'Such a wonderful time, right?' the woman asks. 'I still miss my babies. Enjoy it while it lasts.'

Walking on, Robin's face burns. It was too awkward to explain the reality, and she didn't want to. It felt good to accept the role of publicly recognized parent. And she *has* worked hard as an allomother. Accepting congratulations for that would be pretty much the same thing, wouldn't it? She strokes Zora's head, and feels as shifty as a shoplifter.

Before leaving the park, she pauses with Zora for a few moments under an oak tree, observing the baby's fascination with the play of light around the green canopy. But it's too chilly to linger long.

On the walk back towards Kessie's, her feet grow increasingly heavy. Along the river path, a couple of ducks are padding around, and she imagines taking Zora as a toddler to feed them.

By the time she's got to Kessie's street, she's made a decision: in order to save her job – which she is hanging onto by the skin of her teeth now that Burrow has grumpily accepted her new project plan – to face the fact that she isn't actually Zora's parent, and to deal with her constantly aching back, she has got to move back to her own flat. Stop this night-feeding arrangement. Stop basically doing all of Kessie's housework and shopping, too. Kessie really doesn't seem well enough to go solo yet, so she'll insist she sees the doctor, for her own health and Zora's, and invite her and Zora to come and stay with her for a while instead. Her flat has two bedrooms and is much bigger, so that way at least both adults will have beds. It's also right by a lovely park, which should be a good way to encourage Kessie to get outside more. It's what she should have done weeks ago.

She opens the front door. 'Hello?'

No answer. Kessie is still in bed, staring at the ceiling. Tea untouched. Lavender bath stone cold.

Robin gulps. 'Haven't you got in the bath yet? I'll top it up for you,' she says brightly. 'Zora and I had a nice walk, didn't we? Do you want a cuddle with Mummy now, Zozo?'

Kessie shakes her head violently. 'Don't give her to me. She hates me.' She grabs a cushion and buries her face in it.

'Kessie! Don't be absurd – she's too small to hate anyone, and anyway, she *adores* you – you're her mother!' Robin pulls up a chair next to her and strokes Kessie's hair the way she likes.

'I'm a crappy mother,' Kessie moans. 'I'm wrecked. I'm kind of terrified of what she's turned me into, and I haven't bonded with her, and she knows it.'

'Come on, you're just exhausted and still feeling a bit low . . . that's just . . .'

'Don't tell me to come on, Robin!' Kessie snarls at her, eyes wild. 'You don't know what it's like! She's comfortable with you, not me – and every time you give her to me I freak out . . . I should never have gone ahead with this pregnancy on my own! And I should never have trusted that bastard. I can barely look at her and not remember I hate him. I'm going to the loo.' She walks off and slams the bathroom door.

Robin lays her lips on Zora's soft crown. Again, she finds herself wondering whether Kessie would ever intentionally *hurt* Zora, if her state of mind deteriorated any further. The thought feels like a betrayal. But she seems so low, so angry, that it's surely gone beyond baby blues now. Is it her fault? She's tried so hard to help, to give Kessie the time and space to rest and sleep and recover – but she should surely be improving by now? Her own brain is fried from fatigue. Benjy and Darsha keep telling her she's nuts for even trying to juggle her job, the master's, and looking after these two.

When Kessie emerges, Robin hugs her, which she doesn't reciprocate, and tries to keep her voice calm. 'Kess, I'm so sorry that you're still feeling like this. You've got every right to feel angry with The Facilitator, and it's totally normal to feel some baby blues, especially after such a tough birth – but at this point . . .

I think you really need some expert help to get well again. Can I please call the doctor to book you an appointment?'

Kessie takes a step back. Her eyes are panicked. 'Fuck no, don't do that, Robs, please – I'll pull myself together. I can't face talking to a doctor yet. Or having to sit in that waiting room with other mums . . . Just . . . just give me a few more days, okay?'

'Well, the thing is . . . I'm starting to lose it myself . . .'

'You're saying I'm *losing it*?'

Robin inhales slowly through her nose and tries not to growl at the injustice of Kessie's outrage – at her, of all people. 'All I'm saying, Kessie, is that you're not well, and I think you need help to better again, and I don't know what else I can *do* now – I can't carry on sleeping on the futon here and doing the night feeds any more and keep my job. I'm knackered too, my back hurts, and I've started fucking up at work, like, they're on the brink of firing me. But listen, I have two solutions for us. One is that you go to the doctor, urgently, and tell her how you've been feeling and see whether she gives you some medication to help. The other is an invitation: how about you and Zora come to stay at my flat for a bit? I have two bedrooms and quite a lot more space . . .'

'No, Robs, we live here. It's fine, you just go back to yours if you want. I can manage.'

'But . . . Kess! That's not what . . .'

'I *said* I'll manage,' Kessie snaps. 'I'll call the doctor too, if you insist. I'll probably do better without you here doing everything for me and breathing down my neck.'

Robin has to turn away, bite both cheeks hard, and make a conscious effort to breathe. *Fucking ingratitude!* But she has to remember that Kessie is chemically imbalanced – that this isn't the normal her. 'Fine then,' she says, still facing away from her. 'I'll go and pack then and stop *breathing down your neck* and doing all your laundry and grocery shopping and cooking and cleaning and childcare,' she adds, through clenched teeth. 'I'm glad you're going to call the doctor – please do it today, and let me know when you have. And I'm going to come to check on you both tomorrow, whether you think that's breathing down your neck or not.'

*

That night, in her own blissfully comfortable bed, but without the familiar darling little body beside her, Robin closes her eyes. She needs sleep so badly – but her mind's racing. She's even more worried about Kessie now that she's not around to look after her – and on top of that, she's now worried about Zora on a whole new level. Should she have called the doctor regardless? Alerted social services, even? But Kessie was so adamant. And it's her body, her child, isn't it? How ill is she really? *Has* she, as Kessie implied, been overdoing it in looking after them like some adoptive mother hen? Is this all somehow her fault? Or was she negligent to leave them?

She switches on the bedside light and picks up the *Mother Nature* book to look up what it says about postpartum blues. Apparently about half of all new mothers experience them a few days after birth, and a smaller portion go on to experience serious depression weeks later. Hrdy takes issue with the assumption that woman instinctively love their babies from the beginning; maternal ambivalence, she says, is treated as a dark secret, but actually there are good reasons why mothers can find the servitude to their infants overwhelming. For this reason, many primate mothers abandon or kill their infants if they can't cope.

Feeling shaky, Robin puts the book down. She wants to get a taxi back to Kessie's, to check Zora is okay, to apologize. But that would be crazy. She texts Kessie, sending love, hoping she's feeling better, reminding her to let her know about the doctor's appointment, and picks up the book again.

Western society is out of step with many other cultures in deeming that infants are fully human the moment they are born, Hrdy points out. In the majority of human societies, personhood is postponed until some later milestone. Among the Ayoreo in Bolivia, no child is considered fully human until they can walk. In other societies, the milestones are eating food for the first time, or beginning to smile, or laugh, or cutting the first tooth. In Holland, as late as the eighth century, infanticide was ethically permissible so long as the child had not yet tasted 'earthly food'. Which seems batshit crazy when you've spent time with an incredible infant like Zora whose personhood is surely undeniable. Robin wants to pull some of these ideas together into a coherent argument for her dissertation – but right now she's too bone-tired.

She turns off the light, closes her eyes, and thinks of Darsha – of their gap year reunion trip to Morocco with Dylan, of hiking in the Atlas Mountains, then heading down to Taghazout to surf – or in Robin's case, fall off a surfboard repeatedly then give up to read a book on the beach in the shade. That was the summer that Dylan got together with Leila, his now wife. And that summer she and Darsha so nearly kissed on a drunken night out. She'll video call her after work tomorrow. For now, sleep.

Chapter 20

Kessie

Kessie is being slowly strangled by a pink python which seems to be feathered like a flamingo neck. She's trying to yell for help but nothing's coming out – and then she wakes. Her pyjama top is bunched up around her neck. She must have accidentally gone to sleep while feeding Zora. Shit! She's supposed to use the co-sleeper. Has she smothered her baby?

No, thank God: the creature is still peacefully asleep under the fingertips of her left hand. Her lips are parted. A silver whisper of breath as her chest rises and falls. Her tiny cheek presses against Kessie's ribs as if she has adhered herself like a mussel to a boulder, as if this were her only hope of survival in this strange world. As if she knows full well that her mother has been threatening to drift away from her. As if she were straining to hear Kessie's heartbeat again in her own dreams, to be re-immersed in the idyll flow of amniotic fluid.

A shaft of sunlight lances her arm. What time is it? What day of the week? Hopefully a weekend, so Robin will be here – but no, she's pretty sure that only just finished. When will the creature demand her next feed?

Seconds after this thought, milk sprays out of her exposed nipple, cresting over Zora's head. She pulls her bra back up to stem it. She's cramping up. Tentatively, she begins inching her body to the right . . . and of course this prompts the creature's eyelids to snap open, followed by her mouth. 'Waaaaaa cchh waaaa cchh waaaaaa cchh . . . Waaaa . . .' Seriously, how is she able to mutate in seconds from a serene cherub into a furious, purple-faced, pink-gummed beast?

She shoves herself up in the bed, fumbles with a pillow she needs to get behind her lower back for support, and tries desperately to guide the caterwauling mouth towards a latch. The pain of feeding will at least plug the greater evil of that noise. *How do other new mothers deal with this and not hack their own ears off?* The creature grapples her way to her goal.

The familiar stab of pain. She breathes, and sings a lullaby through it, 'Rock-a-bye Baby', as much to soothe herself as Zora. She's never really thought about how twisted it is until now – why have so many generations of mothers felt moved to sing their children a song about a baby abandoned in a treetop and crashing down to the ground? Maybe because lots of them felt just as furious about their entrapment in motherhood and weren't able to express it in any other way.

She reaches for her phone to put on some other music. Mozart's *Requiem* seems about right. Scrolling through her list of contacts, she peruses all the familiar names of her once-closest friends. Jen has had her baby now and, judging by her prolific social media photos, she seems to be having an idyllic time with him – a little blue-clad boy. There they are, cosying up on the sofa, sitting in a café with a cappuccino, posing outside the cinema for a parent-and-baby screening in matching Breton stripes. She's been texting, but Kessie has only sent late and brief replies.

She should never have driven Robin out. What the hell was she thinking? Why didn't she accept her very generous and sensible offer to decamp with Zora to her two-bed flat for a while? She really shouldn't have said what she said about Robin breathing down her neck. It was bullshit, and it was vindictive, and it was only because she didn't want to admit how much she needs her. Especially now. Plus it's been great living with her again, and not just because of all the baby-care help – they just work so well together, always have. Or they did, before she became a screw-up. Of course Robin couldn't carry on sleeping on a futon in her tiny shoebox flat doing pretty much everything to look after her friend's new baby when she still has to function for a high-powered job. Not to mention a master's degree. She's been wonderful to have done a fraction of what she's done already. And fuck, the rent – she's only paid half of last month's so far, and her maternity allowance isn't due until next week.

The melody of the *Lacrimosa* creeps up the scale, swells and diminishes, rises and falls, into an exquisite sea of sound, like drowning in a warm sea.

A call from Jen. Kessie can't bring herself to press answer. A voicemail follows. *Hey Kessie! How's motherhood going? Hope you're okay! Can't wait to introduce our babies! Call me and we can compare sleeping notes! Lots of love!*

She gets up to boil the kettle. How stupid to have broken her promise to Robin. She should have gone to the doctor's appointment. And let the health visitor come over. They would have helped . . . but then, if they found out what a terrible mother she's been so far, they might take Zora into care, and then what?

After a glug of tea she perches on the side of the bed, closes her eyes again, and listens to the Mozart – really listens. Tries to allow its patterns to calm her. If only she were playing this piece in an orchestra right now. If only she were still part of a group collaborating to make something beautiful vibrate through the air and move everyone in the room. That used to be her life.

The ukulele that Pablo gave her lies on its back in the corner. Maybe she can at least learn a few chords. She pauses the Mozart, gets it out of its case, and plucks a note. It makes a mellow sound, not unlike a harp. She begins to tune it. Then the creature starts up again. Already? She shoves the uke hard in the corner of the room, and fortunately it doesn't crack.

*

Robin messages to say that she has to work late again, so it would be a bit tricky to come over, but she can if Kessie needs her – and has she called the doctor yet?

Squinting through new tears, Kessie messages back that they'll be fine, and that she's left a message with the doctor's surgery. Which at some point she will. She adds a photo she took earlier of Zora in a contented moment, waving her hands in the air. The baby really is objectively cute when she wants to be. If only she didn't bloody cry so much.

A new email has come in from Acorn. They've finally considered her evidence, and have taken the decision to ban Angelo as a future user should he attempt to rejoin. 'Thanks for the update,' she writes back. 'But what if he signs up again with a different email address and name? Can you ban him if a photo of him comes up attached to a new profile?'

*

The next day passes in a blur of nappies and naps, pumping and feeding, washing up and doom-scrolling through dating sites looking for The Facilitator's face, doom-scrolling through social media looking at happier friends' photos, and through online shops looking for clothes she lusts after but can't afford, yet adding them to baskets she'll never check out. She keeps catching putrid whiffs of herself. She's out of knickers and really needs to do some laundry. She hadn't fully realized that Robin had been doing all that too.

*

Zora goes down to sleep just before midnight, but is awake again, whingeing, at 3 a.m. Kessie gives her another feed but she's still grouchy, and starts making snarly whining noises like a wildcat. What does she need? *If only Robin were here.* 'Waaaaaa cchh waaaa cchh waaaaaa cchh . . . Waaaa . . .' It's too much, too much! Kessie looks wildly around the room. For fuck's sake, she just needs to sleep! Some peace and quiet! She wants to toss this screamball out of the window. She can't be in this flat with this noise any more, for a single minute, even though it's freezing outside and it's the early hours and all sorts of gang activity is probably happening on the estate . . .

She gets up, grabs the sling, clips it on, stuffs the screecher's limbs almost roughly into a snowsuit, which makes the screaming even louder, then packs her into the sling. She tries to arrange the straps so that the weight is equally distributed, grabs Auntie Elmi's cashmere scarf to wrap around her, shoves her biggest coat on over her pyjamas, struggles her feet into trainers, nearly looks in the mirror but changes her mind, and sets out.

She tramps along roads weaving out of the estate, illuminated every so often by orange lamps. The creature is still crying, but less vociferously. Past overflowing bins and parked cars. Through the scary alley. Onto the dark canal path.

Finally the crying cuts out. Like pressing a stop button. *Peace*.

Gingerly, she pulls up the edge of the wrap to peep underneath – yes, asleep. Banshee into dormouse. She strokes her palms up and down the creature's back and legs, trying to read her topography in braille. Tracing the swelling shape of her in the sling feels almost like being pregnant again – the curled-up little body conjoined with her own, swelling organically from her centre. She'd never thought she'd miss that.

If only she'd thought to put tights on, and a hat. But that is the lot of a mother, she supposes: to learn that your own welfare is no longer at the top of your priority list.

Dawn's silvery sheen creeps up the charcoal sky, the water glints, and eager birds carouse and skitter in anticipation of the day ahead. Patches of frost force her to concentrate on her footing. The air chills her lips, and she's grateful for the human hot water bottle strapped to her chest.

A cyclist zooms past on the towpath, probably commuting to some city office job, where he'll take a warm shower and don a fancy suit before sipping an espresso and eating a chia coconut fruit pot in a child-free cafe.

A middle-aged woman walks purposely towards them with her dog on a lead – a scampering spaniel with strokable ears, sniffing at a thousand unimaginable smells. It occurs to Kessie that she should have got herself a puppy instead of a baby – that would have been far easier, and cheaper, and more joyful.

'Morning!' the woman says briskly, looking at Kessie as if she were a normal, healthy person, not a hideously sleep-deprived phantom wearing the same pyjamas she's had on for days, waddling along with genital pain and a child she'd like to be a dog. It strikes her that this woman has the same bob haircut as her own mother did. She stops walking, and turns to look at the woman's back as it gets smaller and smaller.

Back at the front door, she lifts the creature out of her sling as gently as possible. *Don't wake don't wake don't wake*. She absolutely *has* to get some sleep herself now – her head is stuffed full of paperweights. Fortunately the eyes stay closed, lashes sweetly curled.

Slide hand up back. Under head. Eyes still closed. Lie her down in the cot . . .

Eyes pop open.

Oh fuck no – come on now, give me a break and go back to sleep – please, please, please . . . She smiles at her desperately. 'Hi, little one! Don't you want to sleep a teeny bit longer?'

Zora smiles at her. Finally smiles! Kessie gasps . . . And then the baby's brow wrinkles. A contortion that promises more shrieks. *No please no.*

Kessie looks up to the ceiling and claws her temples, then looks back at Zora. Unbelievably, the shrieking hasn't begun after all. Instead, the child is staring up at her, intently, serious now.

She strokes her index finger softly down the centre of the small forehead to the tip of her tiny nose, trying out the trick that Robin taught her – it's apparently a baby's reflex to close their eyes at this age. But that doesn't work now. Of course it doesn't.

And there it is: the steam train wail. Kessie moans and stomps back to the living room to shut the door and make herself a cup of strong tea with sugar, and a coffee to drink immediately afterwards.

So much for the longed-for smile – a flash in the dark. Perhaps she needs to buy some dummies for the creature to suck on – anything to just shut her *up*.

She experiments with slipping the tip of her ring finger into the small mouth instead, to stem the noise – and blessed quiet falls as the lips close around it and suck it, the tiny tongue rubbing against Kessie's fingerprint. Maybe this is the trick!

But seconds later it's spat out, and the noise resumes. Kessie has an awful urge to press her palm down hard on this bellowing little pie hole . . . she leans forward . . . Then gasps at the thought and staggers backwards. This is crazy. Zora is an innocent child. Her innocent child. She has to pull herself together.

Which means accepting that she's not coping.

When the crying finally subsides, she is about to head back to bed to close her gritty eyes, when the letter box clicks.

At the front door, an envelope hangs like a dog's lolling tongue.

She takes it to the bed with her, flops down and rips it open. It's from her landlord.

Unfortunately, following my Section 8 notice, and your continued rent arrears, I have been forced to start eviction proceedings.

Chapter 21

Robin

Robin walks through the mist into Kessie's estate, past a couple of cats facing off by a bin, and a man swearing at a scooter that won't start. It's already been a long week, and it's only Wednesday. She's got to submit a new update report to Burrow by Friday, and she's got to lead a client presentation on a video game comms project tomorrow, and that one has morphed into something more far complicated than it was meant to. Jake, the new graduate trainee, is off sick, and Jess has been on annual leave at precisely the wrong time. When Robin asked Sanjay if there was any spare capacity for someone to step in and help her out, he just raised an eyebrow and said, 'I'm afraid you'll just have to put the hours in for this one, Suarez.'

Right now, she wishes she could just have a hot bath and go to sleep in her own bed – but she misses Zora like a limb, she wants to see that smile again, and try bouncing her in the new bouncy chair she bought, and she's been getting more and more concerned about Kessie's responses to her messages. They've all taken a long time to arrive, and then seem overly brief.

She unlocks the front door and walks through to the living room. Kessie is sitting on the futon and holding a sleeping Zora, arm propped up by a cushion. Her puffy eyes swivel as Robin enters the room. Her hair is fuzzy and bunched up on one side. There are empty cups strewn around, and a sour smell. It takes all Robin's strength not to rush over and try to snatch Zora from her arms and kiss her angel face. 'Oh love,' she says softly.

'Can you?' Kessie asks, her voice as husky as if she'd just sunk a couple of bottles of red wine.

Robin scoops the baby up and Zora lets out a shivery sigh, but stays sleeping. Robin can't help gazing for a few seconds at the exquisite curve of her cheeks and eyebrows. Then she lays her down, gets a glass of water for Kessie, and sits down next to her on the futon. 'Sorry you're still feeling so rough. What did the doctor say?'

Another shrug. 'Just take it easy, basically.' Kessie knocks back the water, then curls up on the futon.

Robin bites her lip. That's either a lie, or Kessie must have put up a very good act. She would phone the doctor herself now, but the surgery will be closed. She starts gathering up mugs, most of which are half-full of tea that's grown a whitish film on top, and multiple Dairy Milk wrappers. 'What did you tell the doctor about how you'd been feeling?'

'Like shit, you mean? I didn't use those words exactly. She just said it's kind of normal.'

'Right,' Robin says. She's pretty sure Kessie is lying, or at least exaggerating. 'I picked up a niçoise salad for you, the one you like – shall I put it on a plate for you now?'

Kessie just shrugs.

She serves the salad up at the table, waits until Kessie's taken a mouthful, then looks in the freezer to see whether any of the frozen meals are left. It's empty. She checks the cupboards, and finds a tin of beans, half a packet of stale ginger nuts, and some mango chutney. 'How's feeding going?' she asks. 'When did Zora last . . .'

'Oh I don't fucking remember, Robin. I'm a shitty mother, okay? Maybe that's finally going to sink in for you soon.'

Kessie's sharp tone wakes Zora, who starts to cry – but instead of attending to her, Kessie gets up, disappears to the bedroom, and closes the door.

It is 10 p.m. by the time Robin has fed Zora some pumped milk, changed her, played 'Incy Wincy Spider' with her in the new bouncy chair, which made her smile and gurgle, which in turn made the whole world brighter, taken her to do a grocery shop for Kessie, put her down to sleep in the study area, and cooked rice and a stir fry with enough to last Kessie for a couple more days. Again, she gazes at Zora's sweet little face and sighs. Her limbs ache. But this kid is worth it. One hundred per cent.

*

The next morning, she's back in her suit, back in the office, pretending to be on the ball – but a headache is creeping up her skull.

By the time she's climbing into a cab with Jess to go to the client's office for the presentation, her vision is fuzzy. What's this client's name again? Damian, that's it. Damian Tressick. Despite the adrenaline pumping through her veins at the prospect of presenting, she feels like sending him an email to postpone, claiming to have been suddenly taken ill. But it'll be over in a couple of hours. She can read over the bullet points on the way. All she has to do is bullshit with sufficient competence, and come out of today not fired.

She's about to pull out her laptop when light spills out around the edges of her phone. *Unknown number.* She doesn't pick up. Then it occurs to her that it could be her mum calling, and what if something's happened to her up on the mountain? The phone flashes up with a voicemail. The traffic is at a standstill, and she's not really going to change the flow chart at this point, so she listens.

Hello, this is a message for Robin Suarez? It's Lynn from the health centre. You came in with baby Zora for an appointment a couple of weeks ago, when Mum wasn't feeling well, and then left a voicemail this morning? We would really like to speak to you, about Mum, if you could call me back as soon as you can. I'm leaving the office shortly but will be back in the morning.

Robin calls back but gets an automated message.

'What's up – everything okay?' Jess asks.

'Sorry, just . . . a family issue.' She calls Kessie, but gets no answer.

At the client's, she switches on her brightest smile, shakes Damian Tressick's hand as if she'd never been so excited to meet anyone in her life, and emerges again ninety minutes later, some-how, apparently, having given a presentation that wasn't wholly unsuccessful, but with no recollection of how she managed it. She falls into another taxi.

It's dusk when she arrives at Kessie's block. From below, the flat looks unlit. Panic bubbles in her chest as she climbs the filthy steps. She unlocks the front door. 'Hello?'

Kessie is sitting on the futon, again, like it's Groundhog Day. Stains have formed marbled patterns on her breasts. Robin's heart folds in on itself. Thankfully, Zora is sleeping soundly in her cot.

'So I'm being evicted,' Kessie croaks.

'What?'

'Next week. I meant to tell you before but I was kidding myself I could fix it. Turns out I can't fucking cope on my own. And yes, I know you knew that already. But maybe you didn't know that I've had thoughts – awful thoughts – once I even considered smothering Zora which makes me feel like a murderer . . .' Kessie's face crumples and Robin finds she can't inhale. 'I'm so sorry, I mean, you know I'd never do anything to harm her but . . . I just . . . Anyway, I have to get help, I know that now. The doctor and health visitor have been leaving messages, and yes, I know I should have gone before, when you told me to – I lied about that, okay? And I know it was stupid. But I promise I'll go now, or whenever I can get an appointment. And . . . I just really hope you can forgive me for being such a mammoth pain to live with lately. You've been the best friend imaginable and I've been . . . awful. Please can you still help me?'

Chapter 22

Kessie

Kessie stands with Robin and Paolo at the doorway, surveying the scuffed emptiness of her flat. The pile of boxes looks like Table Mountain. It feels both sad and cleansing to be moving on. Especially now that her head is clearer, albeit a lot spacier, since she finally saw a doctor and started on a course of drugs. They're strong – the doctor diagnosed her depression as severe – so she feels a bit out of it the whole time. But infinitely better than a week ago. She'll miss Leona, and Annika and Ishmail and baby Jonjo, and the old man with the bulldog whose name she never found out. 'End of an era,' she sighs. 'Not sure how I managed to accumulate so much stuff in such a small space – I feel like a hoarder.' She's already thrown out two boxes' worth.

'It was a cute flat,' Paolo says, 'but you're going to be way happier in Stokey. And your landlord situation will be sweet – I mean, a babysitter and cook thrown in, what more could you hope for?' He nudges Robin, and Kessie flushes. He clearly thinks Robin's barking mad for doing all she's been doing so far *and* now offering to have Kessie and the baby move in with her. Might she change her mind? Kessie tries to read Robin's expression as she checks something on her phone. 'Just kidding – it'll be perfect having Clissold right on the doorstep with a baby,' Paolo continues. 'All those landscaped paths and gelato vans and lawns and the playground – it's a *dream* place to be a mum, right? I mean, like, if you both decide you'll stay living together for a bit, or . . .'

'Well, we'll see, but you're right: it'll be ideal,' Kessie says. She tickles Zora before unclipping her from the bouncy chair and picking her up, and the baby smiles, just like that – as if she really is happy, as if their eviction is actually for the best. She looks at Robin again, and she returns a tight smile before they begin lugging boxes down the stairs.

'You know how grateful I am, don't you, Robs?' she asks, as she squeezes the last box in the back of the rental van. It's only now that the eagle claw around her brain has loosened that such thoughts are really able to spread their wings.

*

A week later, it feels as if she has been living in Robin's flat for months, and she doesn't miss her own a jot. Robin's is much more spacious and comfortable. The neighbourhood is incomparably more peaceful too – as Paolo said, it might as well be designed for new mums, who seem to be oozing out of its every pore. For the first time, she feels able to walk around with Zora in the buggy and look at them without seething at the unfairness of everything – even return a few smiles. At home, she's started to play the ukulele to Zora, strumming simple accompaniments to nursery rhymes, and Zora really seems to enjoy it, often smiling away and even chuckling sometimes, especially when she gets out her old lion puppet and puts on silly voices in between songs.

After Robin has gone to work, and Zora is sitting happily in her bouncy chair, gazing in fascination at the fish in the tank, Kessie decides to pull out her yoga mat from the back of the remaining pile of unemptied boxes. She unrolls it, performatively, on the living room floor. 'Da daaa! Check this out, little one,' she says. 'Behold: a yoga mat. And prepare to witness your first ever sun salutation!' Zora gazes at her a little quizzically, then resumes her focus on the fish.

It feels great to stretch, although it brings home how incredibly inflexible she's become. Still, it's good just to feel motivated enough to do this for the sake of her own wellbeing. She relaxes into a supine twist. Yes, her brain feels lighter. Her muscles reawakened as if from a long sleep. The world feels less jagged.

She's been enjoying Zora a lot more, too. Every time those little lips tip upwards at the edges it feels as if the sun has peeped out of a hole in a carpet of cloud.

Standing at the front of the mat, she reaches her arms high, then bends down. Her hands barely pass her knees; she used to be able to touch her toes. She steps one foot back, and has to manually shuffle it into the right place for Warrior 1.

She had never spent much daylight time in Robin's flat before moving in here, always visiting in the evenings – but it's a lovely space in the mornings. Even on a dull day like this, the living room feels airy, with its view over to the park, and the back bedroom is quiet enough for her to hear birdsong in the surrounding gardens. Yesterday, she found the energy to put some laundry on, and even to bake a tray of flapjacks. She lowers herself into a plank, but isn't strong enough to hold it, and drops down onto her belly.

Zora squawks, pretty much on cue for a feed. For the first time, this doesn't inject Kessie with a shot of anxiety and resentment.

Feeding has become a lot easier now. It helps that her boobs have returned to a recognizable size. Her nipples have pretty much healed now, too, and although the pain hasn't vanished, it has lessened. The new routine that Robin came up with is working well: Zora gets hungry at predictable times, and Kessie is now able to be functional in between – to get basic chores done, and wash herself, and make food, nap, and think more clearly. Better still, whereas breastfeeds previously had dragged on forever, largely thanks to Zora dropping off after a couple of minutes or getting distracted, Kessie has learned techniques to keep her going. She can blow gently on her forehead to rouse her, or dip her finger into a glass of water and place it on her cheek.

The latch happens quickly this time, and Zora gets to business. Breastfeeding is even starting to be a rewarding connection – provided that Kessie sits in exactly the right position. Which entails propping herself up with at least three cushions, so that Zora's mouth doesn't pull down on her still-fragile skin, and so that her back and arms don't ache. It surely shouldn't be this complicated. Other mums don't seem to need such an elaborate set-up.

She looks over at the corkboard, where Robin had pinned up a flyer for a breastfeeding circle. Kessie had said she'd think about it, but hadn't felt like being on show, or being social with anyone, especially strangers. Today, though, she reckons she might have turned a corner. She could do with some tips from a breastfeeding expert about her position, and how she can manage without all the props. And it would actually be nice to connect with some other mums. She'd left the prenatal message group in a fit of despair, unable to deal with the two Alices apparently parenting perfectly in their very different ways and yet still trying to get one up on each other. She hasn't even felt up to texting Sam, the one she liked best. No, it can't hurt to try this instead.

*

At the children's centre she is greeted by a woman who shows her into a large room with cream-painted walls plastered in children's collages and information posters. Boxy faux-leather sofas are arranged in a square, populated by four other breastfeeding mums. Zora is on her best behaviour, and is ten minutes away from her next feed.

Kessie scrawls her name onto a sign-in sheet, then pulls her cushions out from the bottom of the buggy, and settles herself and Zora on an empty sofa. It's peeling along the edges but comfy. She says hello to another mum, Chantelle, who's already feeding on the adjacent one, and asks whether she comes here often. As soon as the words come out of her mouth, she realizes it's the worst chat-up cliché. But Chantelle just grins and says she's come a few times, and it's helped a lot, but she probably doesn't need it any more.

Just as the breastfeeding expert approaches, Zora starts up with her I'm-hungry-now cry. Kessie smiles down at her, proud of her child's clear communication at precisely the expected time, and of her own ability to understand the communication and satisfy the hunger. She pulls up her T-shirt and pulls down the flap of her feeding vest. She'd been worried about revealing her breasts publicly, but all the other women on the sofas are doing it.

'So, Kessie, welcome!' the expert says, taking a seat next to her. 'I'm Ann. You mentioned on the form that this is your first time here – is there anything specific that you'd like help with?'

She has a tanned, lined face, and strong-looking hands that are folded calmly together on her lap.

'Well, this is Zora,' Kessie says proudly, 'and she's feeding right on time, so that side of things is going well now—'

'On time? You mean she's on a *schedule*?' Ann cuts in sharply.

Kessie looks up, confused, wondering if she'd read the tone right – and Zora slips off the nipple, the one that had the deeper crack, triggering a twinge. She holds back a swear and helps her to re-latch. 'Yeah – just since this week,' she explains. 'She gets hungry on cue now, every three and a half hours, which is really great, so I just wanted to get some advice on—'

'How old is she?' Ann interrupts.

'Ten weeks . . .'

'Only ten *weeks*! Babies should *not* be placed on a feeding routine, *certainly* not so young. Their stomachs are *tiny* and they're still developing – they need food! Imagine if *you* were fragile and small and hungry and you were denied food when you needed it?'

Kessie finds her jaw opening then closing like one of Robin's fish. Is she seriously being told off right now? For something she'd chalked up as her first mothering success? Her eyes are hot. Maybe she hasn't explained the context well enough. 'But – she's on track with weight,' she protests, weakly — 'she's in the 80th centile—'

Ann is smiling and nodding in a patronizing fashion. 'I have been advising on breast-feeding for twenty years now,' she cuts in. 'I've seen *thousands* of babies, and I know they thrive on feeding *on demand*. It's not just about weight; it's about feeling that they have a source of comfort and nourishment when they need it. You see?'

Kessie isn't sure how to reply. The creature *isn't hungry* between feeds any more; she's adapted to the schedule and eats what she needs. It makes all the difference to be able to predict when a feed will be needed, and to know that she's eaten enough. That's not selfish, is it? 'Well, the baby seems . . . happier now . . . I mean, for longer, between feeds . . .'

Ann pouts, and inhales a long sniff. 'All I can give you is my advice,' she says, with pointed patience. 'Which is what we're here for.'

Actually, I thought you were here to give us support? Kessie wants to say, but her teeth are clenched. If she stays here with this woman any longer, she won't be able hold back tears. Abruptly, she stands up, pinning Zora, still feeding, to her breast with one arm – and, miraculously, the baby stays latched.

'Are you all right?' Ann is asking.

Kessie doesn't answer. She manages to stuff her cushions and bag into the buggy with her free hand, still breastfeeding, and to push the buggy and walk away, still breastfeeding, to the exit. She feels as exultant as if she'd just ridden away on a unicycle.

'Excuse me, Kessie – what on *earth* is the matter?' Ann is calling behind her.

Kessie turns to face her, a bolt of electricity in her chest. '*You* are the matter, quite frankly. I came here for support, not to be told off for what I'm doing *wrong*, in your so-called expert opinion, even though it's been working just fine, and my baby is happier, and I've *finally* begun to feel human again after being seriously depressed. You have no *idea* what I've been through, or what it took for me to come here. Well one thing's for sure: I won't be coming back.' She turns on her heel, blasts out into the cold outdoors with Zora, and a wild laugh rips out of her.

Chapter 23

Robin

Jammed between a tight-shirted City boy's sour armpit and a meat pasty-eating builder on the Tube, Robin tries to get through another chapter of her book on anthropology and writing before her stop. She's doing her best to keep up the reading and thinking needed for her dissertation, even though she's had to pause her degree – her lack of time was getting ridiculous. She did ask Sanjay if she could go down to three days a week, in order to fit it in on top of her childcare commitments, but he was politely scathing. 'Sorry, but you should count yourself lucky that we made an exception and agreed to four days,' he told her. 'We don't even let *parents* work three days a week.'

As she emerges into the daylight, rubbing her sore back, a text comes through from Kessie. It's a photo of Zora, gnawing at Robin's old purple scarf, which has become her preferred blankie, even over Auntie Elmi's cashmere one.

We miss you Mama Roro – have a good day at work xxx

She's clearly teething already – Robin keeps meaning to get her one of those Sophie La Girafe toys that all the babies in Stokey seem to have. She's sitting up all by herself now, albeit precariously, on the soft foam tiles at the corner of the living room, and starting to exercise her legs more too – to push them with surprising force against the ground when she's held up above it, clearly wanting to stand. Such verve, such determination! It's probably time to get her one of those Jumperoos, where babies can sit upright in the centre of a circular frame, slung on a cloth seat, designed so that they can propel themselves into rotating bunny hops while entertaining themselves with sensory toys fixed around the edge. It's a clever invention, and she's sure Zora would love it – but they're expensive, even second-hand and garish, and she's already splashed out on the buggy.

At lunchtime she heads out to grab a bagel and coffee from her usual place before going on a brisk walk. It's a grey day, and a determined breeze whips her hair around. She checks her phone and texts Kessie to ask how it's going. They'll probably be out in Clissold Park. Has she remembered to put Zora's hat on, and bring a warm blanket?

She rounds a corner and stops short at the sight of two round, electric-blue eyes, glowing at her from a robot. Is she losing it? No, it really is a robot. About the height of a three-year-old child, but round and curvy, a bit like a snowman, just more huggable. Its face is not unlike ET's. 'Hello,' it says.

Robin looks around for the kids playing a trick, or a group of students doing an experiment – but no one is watching her. There doesn't even seem to be a camera. But there must be. She walks a bit closer. 'Hi,' she says, and feels her face flush. Maybe the robot's filming her — maybe it has cameras in its eyes.

'I like your face', it says, and she hoots. The robot doesn't laugh back.

'Well, thanks,' she says. 'What do you like about it?' An older couple coming along the pavement give her a sidelong glance but continue walking, as if it's not really that weird to see another adult talking to a robot in the street. She loves that about London.

'I like your eyes,' it says.

'Oh, okay. Yours are a nice blue. Where have you come from?'

The robot pauses, as if considering this. 'Have you been to space?' it asks.

'Would you recommend it?'

'Will you be my friend?'

'Oh. Sure! You remind me of a bear called Paddington. Shall I take you for a cream tea?'

The robot pauses. 'What does love feel like?'

'Well. That is a great question.' Robin feels a drop of rain on her forehead. 'There are different kinds. I've discovered a whole new kind recently. Sometimes it makes me feel like I'm on cloud nine. Other times it feels like I'm being beaten up.'

'I am sorry,' the robot says.

'Thanks,' she says, surprised. How well can this robot do empathy? Did it understand 'cloud nine'? One day, robots will be such good conversationalists that humans won't need each other, and the robots will invent their own metaphors. The rain is getting heavier. 'Are you okay in the rain?' she asks, feeling a flash of maternal concern. 'Do your electrics . . .'

Her phone rings, and she pulls it out. Darsha!

'How often do you feel happy?' the robot asks.

'Heyyy Robinita! How's it going?'

'Darsh! Great timing – I just made friends with a robot. Wanna say hello?'

'Excuse me?'

Robin holds the phone over to the robot. 'Say hello to my friend Darsha.'

'Hello Darsha,' the robot says.

A group of women come up from behind, giggling and pointing. 'Oh my God, is this *yours*?' one of them asks. Robin says no and backs away, and they all start talking to the robot and patting its head. On the end of the line, Darsha is cracking up. 'Robin, what are you *doing* right now?'

'I just met a robot. On the street. In central London. We were making small talk. You know, about love and the meaning of happiness.'

'That's insane. I mean, I live next to Silicon Valley and that's never happened to me.'

Robin walks slowly away. 'Yeah, super weird. It must be some AI experiment, but there were no owners or scientists around, so far as I could tell. Maybe it just came from Mars.'

'What was it saying about love?'

'Asked me what it feels like.'

'What *does* it feel like?' There's a smile in her voice.

Infuriatingly, Robin thinks of Max. Did she ever really love him, or was it always the idea of him? 'Well, speaking to *you* makes me feel warm inside, Darsh.' She smiles.

'Love you too, babe,' Darsha replies. 'Hey, can you ask it something for me?'

'Oh sorry, I've just abandoned it to a bunch of excited people.' She turns back to look at the robot one more time. It's still busy with the women, who are dressed in the same uniform and must work together somewhere. Maybe its appearance was a test to see whether her heart was big enough to love like a real parent. If she'd picked the robot up and kissed it, would it have turned into a human, like the frog in the princess story? 'What did you want to ask?'

'Oh, just whether it agrees with me that you should value your *actual* human friend's advice and book a flight to visit her in California.'

'Ha! Well I obviously do value your advice – always. And I am so tempted, Darsh. I'd love to head to the airport right now. The sunshine would be amazing – it's a gloomy day here for May. I just – still don't think I can quite yet.' She passes a flower shop, the display lustrous with pink and purple peonies. 'Kessie's getting back on track – she's doing really well – and I'm looking after Zora at weekends . . . anyway I don't have any annual leave left . . .'

'But . . . I thought you had lots carried over?'

'I used it up.'

'Wow. Unpaid?'

'I'm not their favourite person right now, after I nearly lost them a big client . . . doubt they'd give me any.'

'Well . . . I just hope Kessie appreciates you. I mean, I'm sure she does, but I'm worried about you – you've got her out of a dark place, but it sounds like you've been burning yourself out in the process, no? You need a break. I can pay for your flight with my air miles – why don't you come, even for a long weekend, and just call in sick for a couple of days? Your boss is such a jerk, he deserves it. Or you could request to work remotely from here for a week or so. Or just ask for unpaid leave – what have you got to lose?'

'Umm – I just . . . don't really think . . .'

'Then you *need* to think! Think hard, Robinita! The weather is *perfect* here right now, we have a spare bed, and desks to work at, and you and I can do a road trip, swim, drink green juice . . . just relax.'

Relax. The word seems as alien as the robot. 'It does sound like paradise. Let me see what I can do.'

'All right. Hey, so you don't think this Brexit thing is a real concern, do you? It seems insane to me that a referendum is even happening.'

'It makes no sense.' Robin and Kessie had debated it at length yesterday – Kessie reckoned there was no way more than 50 per cent of people would vote leave, but Robin has been feeling more and more worried about it. The way the world is going, cutting this small island off from its friends has started to seem plausible. If it were to happen, would she even want to stay here?

Walking back into the office, she imagines packing up all her stuff, saying goodbye to her colleagues forever, and flying off to the Golden State for a holiday with Darsha – or even, possibly, to start a new life there. She thinks of Zora, how she used to coo in her arms, then roar in fury when she was passed over to Kessie. Of how guilty she had felt about that, on one level; but how secretly touched she was at the intimacy. The uniqueness of that connection the baby had with her and nobody else. That's changing now, as Kessie's mental stability is returning. Which is a good thing, obviously. It's wonderful to witness the two of them finally bonding. But Robin still feels so deeply attached to Zora

– as if she were her own baby. It has helped to think of herself as an allomother, but that term is pretty much unheard of beyond the niche realm of anthropology. If her close friends and colleagues knew how she felt about this kid, they would think her bananas. But when she says Zora's name now, even from across the room, the baby turns to look, and usually grins and coos something in gobbledygook that seems like their own secret language.

Her phone pings. A message from Kessie.

Wish you were here Mama Roro. I've been trying to say duck! Xxx

A photo of Zora sitting up in her buggy in the park, chewing on one bare foot, while clutching Robin's purple scarf, light glittering on the water behind her.

Chapter 24

Kessie

The day that the Brexit referendum result is due to be announced, Robin left for work at the crack of dawn. Kessie has just started to feed Zora when she checks the news on her phone – and nearly jolts the baby off onto the floor. 'Oh God,' she says out loud. 'Sorry, darling. You have absolutely no idea what's just happened to your future.' She texts Robin: I wish you weren't so good at predicting election results.

Robin texts back: I'd convinced myself I was being too pessimistic.

Out on the street, walking to the doctor's surgery to have Zora weighed, Kessie looks around, wondering what every other passer-by has made of it. How did so many people in this country feel so disconnected to people who just happen to have been born elsewhere on the continent? She texts a shocked emoji to Paolo, who's lived here for fifteen years now but is still an Italian citizen.

A few seconds later he replies: Cannot believe it. Feel like I'm not wanted here.

Zora is happily munching on her giraffe toy. Kessie takes

a photo of her and sends it to Robin, and then to Paolo, suggesting London forms a new nation state so that they can reapply for EU membership. She thinks of Robin's mum, out in the Pyrenees. Will she stay out there for good now? Apply for French citizenship? Kessie is pretty sure Cara voted leave. She suspects she tried to persuade her dad to do the same, but she can't bring herself to ask him.

When Zora's lying naked and smiling on the scales, the nurse comments on what a beautiful baby she is. Kessie thanks her, then adds that she just can't help looking at her and wondering what her future will be like now.

'What do you mean?' the nurse asks, confused. 'Oh . . . do you mean the referendum? Oh yeah, well, I voted leave, I mean, we needed a bit of a change, right? But – well, now that I'm hearing more about it, I feel like maybe I made the wrong decision. But it'll work out okay I guess, right? Things always do.' Kessie feels like snapping at her, but clenches her jaw.

Walking slowly home, she ponders the prospect that the world she knew as a kid is going to be completely different to the world Zora will get to know – more so than it has been for most previous generations. The climate is breaking down. Nature is in freefall. International legal structures are crumbling. Her family and all her relationships have fractured.

A crow eyes her from a gatepost. She can't just give up. She's just clambered out of the postnatal hellfire bunker, more or less. Maybe she should get into politics . . . ? But that's way out of her comfort zone. She can at least try to live positively again within herself. To nurture Zora, and equip her to thrive as best she can in this crazy world. To find a way to make music again – yes – to spread joy and connection among people who need it, including herself. That's probably what she should aim for.

'Got a light, luv?' a man asks her. He looks desperate. Dishevelled. She can smell him.

'Sorry mate,' she says. Zora is staring up at her, wide-eyed. *Unless you count the light of my life*, she thinks.

He grins. 'Cute kid you got there.'

*

Birdsong flickering, leaf shadows on the duvet . . . Kessie sits up, panicking that she's done something wrong, forgotten something, lost something. But Zora is still next to her, fast asleep, arms cactus-like. She reaches for her phone to snap a photo, though the light is still a bit too grey for it to come out clearly. It's 7 a.m. Is that really six hours of uninterrupted sleep that she's just had? She remembers once thinking than six hours wasn't enough. Non-mothers really don't know what tiredness is. Oh, and today is yoga day! Her first class in a real life studio.

She gets up, brushes Zora's cheek with her index finger, puts on her leggings as quietly as possible, and pads to the kitchen to make herself a cup of tea and pump some milk. Ugh, that loathsome machine. She turns her back on it as she fills the kettle. The only thing to mar an otherwise perfect start to the day.

Robin comes in just as the pump is getting going. 'Morning! How was the night?'

'Good, actually!' Kessie remembers how embarrassed she was the first time that Robin saw her breast out, pumping; now it just feels normal. She can't remember any former boyfriend of hers

238

being more at ease and familiar than Robin is now with her body in its flawed, everyday state.

'Brilliant! Sounds like we've turned a corner.' Robin pauses. 'Guess I'll be doing some laundry while you're gone.' The overflowing basket is visible through Kessie's bedroom door, and her voice betrays irritation as well as fatigue.

'Oh shit, sorry, no don't, I'll do it when I get back – I did mean to do some washing this week, and clean the bathroom, but . . .'

'It's okay,' Robin says kindly, but it's not, really. Zora's cry bleeds through the door, sharp and rasping, and Robin goes through to get her.

Kessie watches the two of them. The expression on Robin's face as she picks Zora up and comforts her is golden. Zora is still far more emotionally bonded with Robin than with her – but she's getting there. She cleans the pump, puts the milk in the fridge, and gathers her things. 'I don't *have* to go to this yoga class,' she says reluctantly. 'You deserve some time out for yourself, too.'

'No it's fine – go!' Robin calls. 'I mean, I am super tired, but I've missed my Zora time during the week – very happy to hang out with her.'

*

Sandalwood, clean lines, big green plants in matte-glazed pots – stepping into the yoga centre is an instant tonic. It feels luxurious just to lie prone on a mat in an airy studio, among other quiet bodies, to a low, chanting soundtrack. Gentle floor stretching eases her shoulders and lower back further. Light creeps in between her vertebrae. Body and earth, connected.

Sun salutations begin. By the end of one long downward dog Kessie's muscles begin to shake – but they're invited to return to another and hold it for ten interminable breaths. Her arms start wobbling like a jelly and she soon has to lower into child's pose. Tree pose, which she used to find easy, now makes her look clownish, as if she's deliberately toppling each time she raises one leg above her knee. Her leggings feel tight around her now-flabby waistline.

After the class, she'd assumed she'd be shattered, but she actually feels surprisingly springy and loose – though also starving. A double fried egg on toast in the caff next door fills the hole. The day has turned out to be fresh and bright, and she texts Robin to see if she wants to meet up for a family outing somewhere like Columbia Road.

She had forgotten how hectic the flower market gets at its weekend peak: hundreds of people edging impatiently around each other and squeezing towards stalls they want to look at, as vendors yell out their wares and prices. 'No way we'll get the buggy along here,' Robin shouts. How about you choose a plant? Shall we meet at the other end at Hackney City Farm? Show Zora the animals?'

Kessie agrees, though she reckons Zora's still too little to appreciate such things. It's fun to make her way slowly through the market, taking in the hubbub. A cactus stall draws her over, and she lingers to gaze at the sturdy, peculiarly shaped little life forms, the prickly bulbs and the succulents. 'Three for a tenner!' The stallholder girl's voice blasts like a trumpet – the kid can't be more than ten. Must be fun to help out on your parents' stall when you're that age, Kessie thinks. Or would it be a burden?

One cactus's bulbous shape is just like a foetus. It even has a little offshoot on one side like a tiny arm.

Her gaze lands on a purplish succulent at the back corner of the stall, with a spiral of softly pointed leaves – or are they petals – with a fine pearly covering of hair, like downy kitten ears. One of them is broken off leaving an angular stump. She feels sorry for it – it's like the old mutt at the dog's home watching everyone come in and coo at the cute puppy in the first cage. She asks to buy it, then figures she should get another two for a tenner, then falls for a few more. She'd only meant to buy one striking plant for the living room – ideally a yucca tree, like they had in the yoga studio – but it'll do no harm to dot a few smaller plants around on bookshelves and windowsills. By the time she emerges, she's weighed down by two large plants and nine small ones, and has spent far too much, but it will make the flat so much more alive.

A jaunty hand-painted mural highlights the entrance to the farm. Kessie asks the woman in the cafe for permission to leave the plants in a corner, and then heads to the animal enclosures to find Robin and Zora.

They're standing in the pasture area, next to a muddy pen containing two giant copper-haired pigs. Robin has turned Zora around in her carrier to look at them, and is pointing and talking to her as if the baby understands every word. Kessie joins and says hi, but Zora is fixated on the pigs and doesn't look around. They are vast, gingery creatures, with round, hairy bodies and dainty legs, snuffling around quite close to each other but not actively communicating. Their snouts shimmy along the ground while their tails shake and their papery ears wave – they seem unperturbed by all the human snoopers.

The information board states that the pair are named Pepper and Pearl, and that they are both female Tamworths, one of the oldest pig breeds in Britain, descended from wild boar. They are hardy, and can survive in cold climates, and on plants that other pigs cannot digest.

Kessie wonders how they communicate – whether they have a subtle repertoire of grunts. They seem happy enough living in harmony as a female duo – a bit like her and Robin, but without a babe to look after. Zora tugs at a lock of Robin's hair, grinning and squawking.

'Remember when I was desperate to have a miniature pot-bellied pig as a pet?' Robin asks her. 'I must have been about eight.'

'Totally! I shamelessly copied you and asked my dad for the same thing. No dice.'

'Our parents were probably wise,' Robin reflects. 'I read an article the other day about pet pigs – people who bought what had been marketed as miniature pigs, but actually grew huge. There was a picture of this one middle-aged couple who shared their living room with theirs, and it had almost got too big for them all to fit in – but they said they loved it so much, it was so intelligent and loyal, they couldn't bring themselves to get rid of it. They'd even built a special extension to their house for it.'

'Wow.' Kessie rubs her finger under Zora's chin. The baby looks at her, finally, but then turns to Robin and chuckles. 'Bababa,' she says. She's been babbling more and more lately – but is this an attempt to say Mama? To Robin? Or just more gobbledygook?

*

Over dinner, Robin floats an idea. 'I was thinking: I've been feeling down about the referendum, but the weather's finally more summery – so what do you reckon about having a picnic with the baby shower gang in the park to celebrate Zora? Like an informal naming ceremony.'

Kessie hesitates, chewing her broccoli for longer than is necessary. She has refused visits from all of them, except Paolo and Tam, for a while now. But she can't stay a recluse forever. A get-together would feel like progress towards becoming a functioning member of the real world again. But won't they all have been talking about her, about her breakdown, her incompetence, her reliance on Robin?

'It could be super low-key but memorable,' Robin continues. 'We could hang out in Clissold Park and have cake and drinks – then maybe sit in a circle and everyone could say something? Like read a poem or message aloud if they want to. I could finally make that good luck bracelet we talked about and tie it on – with the Moroccan beads, and those Ghanaian ones you found the other day, and the Nepalese ones Elmi sent. We could invite anyone to bring a charm or special bead to add if they like?'

Kessie smiles. 'That does sound really lovely. I could follow the Ghanaian naming ceremony tradition my dad told me about, and give her a taste of honey, so that she gets sweet things in life, and maybe a flake of salt for preservation . . . Okay, let's do it.'

*

Everyone accepts the invitation. The forecast the day before threatens rain, but by breakfast time it's patchily sunny, and Kessie wakes up fresher than usual after six solid hours of sleep. In the park, where daisies freckle the grass, marigolds glow in the flower beds, and the tree branches are laden with green, dogs of all shapes and sizes frolic about amongst people playing frisbee, or working out, or chatting in groups.

As the three of them approach the fenced-off area where the group had agreed to congregate, Kessie falls silent. She's beginning to feel queasy. Will she be super awkward and have forgotten how to socialize properly? Can she come up with an excuse to duck out? She has no real idea how much the others know about her mental state over the last few months. Robin seems unaware of her nerves; she's busy adjusting Zora's hat and making funny faces at her.

They spot the group already assembled under a large tree where they have laid out several picnic blankets. They whoop and clap as the trio arrives, congratulate Kessie, and coo over Zora. In the centre of the circle are several big bags of crisps and hummus and grapes, a large iced cake, and paper cups of prosecco.

Robin picks Zora up and passes her around. She's alert, content, and not yet hungry: to all appearances the product of normal and competent parenting. 'Baba gaga,' she tells Tam, who exclaims at how ridiculously adorable she is and bounces her up and down. Kessie smiles with relief, and the sick feeling starts to ease.

Once the baby has done the rounds, Tam holds her out to Kessie. But as soon as she takes her, Zora's face contorts and she starts shrieking. Kessie fights to keep her own face stable. 'Are you hungry, poppet?' She fumbles around for a cucumber stick from the bag, but can't find the tub.

'She had the bottle at 11.30,' Robin says, hovering. 'Shall I . . . ?'

Kessie passes her up, and in Robin's arms the baby calms almost immediately, even before receiving her milk. Kessie looks down at her left shoe and adjusts it needlessly. All her friends' eyes are on them right now, observing her daughter's obvious preference. She wants to turn and run out of the park. Instead, she clears her throat and claps her hands together. 'This is so fun!' She reaches for a handful of crisps, and ends up with one hanging out from the side of her mouth.

Tam shimmies up to sit beside her and pours her some prosecco into a paper cup. 'How are you *doing*?' she asks, with what feels like excessive sympathy. Kessie knows this is her cue to at least acknowledge why she's kept them all out of her life for the last few months. 'I'm sure you've heard it's been . . . hard,' she says. 'It was a traumatic birth. Which I'd rather not talk about if that's . . .'

'Oh, totally.' Tam rubs her arm. 'I'm so sorry you had to go through that. Are you fully recovered now?'

'Yeah. Basically. I mean, I've been – well, depressed. But I'm on some drugs now, and doing much better. Robin's got me through it all. In fact, everyone – ting ting!' she calls out, and taps her paper cup, pretending it's a wine glass. 'Can we all raise a toast to Robin please? She's been amazing. We're calling her Zora's allomother now – it's an anthropology thing.' She raises her cup. *'To Robin!'*

Everyone echoes, and Robin goes beetroot. *Love you,* she mouths.

Various people come over to talk to Kessie and congratulate her. She settles into a chat with Petra, who thankfully slides into a monologue about her new job. To her left, she overhears Robin talking to Paolo, and telling him that her friend Darsha has offered her a free flight to visit her in California, and she's been longing to go for a couple of years, but she's had to turn it down for now. Paolo laughs incredulously – says she's crazy, that she should go immediately. Robin gives a shallow laugh. 'I'm needed here,' she tells him. 'Anyway, I used up almost all my leave looking after Zora.'

The crisp that Kessie's eating dries up in her mouth. She can't swallow the pulpy shards. Of course: Robin had been planning to go and visit Darsha before the baby arrived. Kessie doesn't actually know Darsha all that well, though they have hung out from time to time over the years, but she knows how close she is with Robin. That they talk on the phone and message each other all the time. It's awful that Robin hasn't felt able to tell her about this. It just hadn't occurred to her that Robin would have used up most of her annual leave looking after them both. She never complained. But of course, in retrospect, it's obvious . . .

'Kessie? You okay?' Petra's asking.

Her face burns. How rude she's being – she's totally lost track of what Petra was saying. 'So sorry, I just . . . I need to say something to Robin.' She turns around and taps Robin on the shoulder. 'Robs, I didn't know.'

'What's that?' Robin turns around.

'I didn't know about California.' Robin's forehead pleats. 'You should go!' Kessie says firmly. 'Totally – just book it. I'm so much better now. We'll be fine!' Which looks like an absurd thing to assert while the baby sits happily in Robin's arms and can barely stand to be in hers. Everyone else has gone quiet.

With a thunder-patter, a curly chestnut puppy bounds into the midst of their picnic, knocks over a bottle of newly opened prosecco and a box of grapes, treads in the humous with a muddy paw, and sticks its nose into the middle of the cake. The owner runs up to them panting, waving his arms and huffing, 'Shit, sorry guys – come here now, Butternut,' and carries the dog away under his beefy arm. There's a long pause, during which most faces around the circle resemble Munch's *The Scream*.

Once they've all had a rueful laugh and tidied the worst of the mess, Robin suggests they sit in a circle and begin the ceremony.

She passes Zora to Kessie and nods at her expectantly. The baby doesn't start crying this time, thank goodness, but still – it just all feels too much, now. Kessie can't bring herself to share the song she's written. It's not good enough yet; she's not up to it. She decides to just thank everyone for coming, and holds Zora out to Robin again.

'What about the honey and salt?' Robin whispers.

Of course – these rituals were her idea. She looks around nervously, even though these are their closest friends, and orders herself to lighten up, to enjoy this moment. 'Nearly forgot! So there's a Ghanaian tradition for babies' naming ceremonies, which my parents did at my ceremony, which is to give the baby a taste of honey for good luck, so that she gets sweet things in life – the NHS says babies shouldn't have honey under the age of one but we were only planning on giving her a teeny dot so don't judge us – and a taste of salt for preservation . . .' People make interested mmm noises, and smile encouragingly at her. She inhales. Exhales.

Robin holds out the tiny sachet of salt flakes they'd packed. Kessie takes a small pinch, mimes to Zora to say ahh, and puts a single flake on her tongue. Zora's eyes widen. She screws her face up like she's about to shriek but then tips her head to one side and widens her eyes again curiously. Everyone claps and Paolo whoops.

'So far so good!' Kessie says. 'Next, the honey – so I bought this little pot from an awesome local charity that has beehives on rooftop gardens.' She holds up the jar for everyone to see, and then, with some trepidation, dips the very tip of a teaspoon in the amber liquid, so that a tear-drop amount adheres, and slips it onto Zora's tongue.

Zora frowns again. Moves her jaw around. Goes through an eccentric range of facial expressions . . . she's about to wail now, for sure . . . But no, she's reaching out for more! This time, everyone cheers.

Robin kisses Zora on the forehead and promises to be the best soul-mother-slash-allomother she can. She ties on the bracelet, the Moroccan beads gleaming orange and gold in the sun, alongside the lemon peel and shells, and tells everyone about the Beng tradition. She then produces a printout of a Mary Oliver poem and reads it aloud in her clear, voice, and holds Zora up as she ends with the famed question about what you will do with your one wild and precious life.

Everyone claps, and Zora smiles delightedly, basking in the attention – and almost as if she really gets the point of the poem, as if she's ready to make the absolute most of whatever lies ahead for her. Kessie looks at Robin, who's chortling about something with Benjy, looking relaxed for the first time in ages. She wonders whether Robin has felt like she's squandered her own wild and precious life since childcare took over. At least she can look forward to a wild and precious week or so if she goes off to California to see Darsha. So long as she doesn't decide to do something properly wild and move out there.

Most of the others have brought along a pre-prepared poem or message to read aloud in turn while holding Zora, who seems remarkably content to be passed around to people who aren't Kessie. Paolo asks if she can hold her for him while he plays her a song. He produces his ukulele and sings one he's written, all about dawn and new beginnings – it's incredibly sweet, and he gets the biggest applause yet. 'Sure you don't want to share yours now, Kess?' he asks. 'I saw you brought your uke along. Go on.'

She rolls her eyes and pulls it out of its bag. 'Look everyone – isn't this a gorgeous instrument? It was a lovely gift from Paolo to Zora when she was born, but I've been messing about on it in the meantime. But I'm just . . . I'm not there yet with a song. Sorry.'

Everyone chimes in, urging her to come on, to give it a go. She shakes her head, smiling. 'Maybe another time. Next summer – let's all do this again.'

Chapter 25

Robin

California: she's finally here! Airports are such anonymous places, though, it might as well be Oman. The conveyer belt vomits out yet another bag, triggering a memory of watching her grandma's cat regurgitate a hairball. He was a recalcitrant creature and had an aversion to children. Several pieces of luggage glide around again and again. There's the large leopard print case – there's the vintage leather one. There's the tatty canvas backpack – there's the mysterious bulky object wrapped in a bin bag. Everyone else loitering around from her flight seems to find theirs easily.

At Heathrow, Robin had been insanely excited about getting away and seeing Darsha again – but most of that energy seems to have been sucked out of her by the plane's air con. Her heart is still beating like crazy, but her mouth is yawning. It's been three years since she's seen Darsha in person – will they have enough to say to each other? Since Zora came along, they have talked much less often. And when they have spoken, Darsha has tended to sound a bit distant at times, and frankly uncomprehending on the topic of the baby. She clearly thinks that Robin is mad to have done what she's done – that she's jettisoned her freedom and her sense of fun by going above and beyond for a friend who could surely have found a way. But this trip, Darsha has assured her, will remind her what freedom is, and how awesome life can be again. Finally, her green wheelie trundles into view.

She scans the arrivals hall. There – for real – Darsha in person! Robin runs over, arms outstretched. 'I made it!'

'Robinita, you're really here! Welcome! God I've missed you so *much*!' They hug for ages, and Robin inhales her lemon-peel scent. Back when they were seventeen, Darsha had tried on some citrus perfume in the airport duty free shop, and announced that she was going to wear a citrusy perfume for the rest of her life to make people feel bright and zingy in her company. Not that she needs the smell to have that effect on people. Robin pulls back to look at her pal properly. Her smile is so big it looks set to spring right out of her face. How does she still have such an inner force of positive energy? Her skin is so clear. She could easily be in her twenties still.

'Honey, you look like a ghost,' Darsha tells her, tenderly. Can she see the fine lines that have emerged on Robin's forehead in this light? Darsha's own face looks smooth and shiny. Robin found another grey strand on her head the other week and pulled it out – but they're definitely coming; while Darsha's hair looks black and sleek as ever. 'Guessing you didn't sleep much on the flight? Well, you can have a proper rest back at the house. I'm so happy you're here!'

They drive into the city in the roomy car that's shared by the commune. It's not open-top, after all. It's owned by Tom, one of the members, Darsha explains, and he created an online rota for booking it. The ground rules are that none of them is allowed to hog it, and they all keep it clean and share the upkeep costs. Normally you wouldn't book it for a few days at a time, but when she'd told him her soulmate was coming for a much-needed escape, he was cool with them going on a road trip down the coast.

Soulmate – Robin feels lighter for hearing that Darsha still thinks of her that way. 'It's a bit like how the kitchen works,' Darsha continues, cheerily. 'There's no rota, so you don't *have* to cook on any set day, but it's just expected that you'll cook something regularly, to chip in. And when you do, you try to make enough so that you can leave extra portions in the fridge for people. Vi's curries are incredible – there might still be some of her spinach and butternut left.'

'Nice,' Robin says. From what Darsha has told her about Vi, her partner, she's a force of nature, and Darsha often sounds a little in awe of her. It was Vi who had persuaded Darsha that an open relationship was a good idea – but Darsha had admitted to Robin at the start that she wasn't wholly comfortable with the idea yet. 'Is Vi coming with us in the end, by the way?'

'No – too much work on, as usual.'

'Shame,' Robin lies. 'Though it'll be nice to have more one-on-one time.'

*

As Darsha leads the way up the front steps, Robin pauses to take in the facade of the building. She hadn't anticipated such grandeur. Darsha had told her before that the commune was in a lovely house, but this is an imposing mansion, with faux-classical columns framing the front door and ornate stained-glass windows.

Inside, high ceilings are hung with chandeliers, walls are adorned with gold-framed mirrors and paintings, William Morris willow-patterned wallpaper, rich, musky paint tones, and a vast living room visible through an archway displays carved teak and velvet furniture, Persian rugs, and a grand piano. 'This is the living room,' Darsha says. 'We hold salons here most weeks – discussing topics like ideal societies, alternative ways of living, that kind of thing.'

'Oh yeah, I remember you mentioning that . . . Kind of like the eighteenth-century salons?'

'Right! Without the corsets or curly wigs.'

The kitchen is clean, with shiny, marbled surfaces. Darsha opens the fridge. The bottom drawer is bursting with kale. 'Bit of a kale obsession here, as you can see. Most people are vegan.' She lifts the lid of a large pot. 'Yes! Vi's curry – you have to try it.'

She shows Robin up to her bed – a bunk in a hostel-style room that's kept for short-term visitors. Robin stows her bag at the end and resists the temptation to collapse into it. She wonders who she'll be sharing with, but it doesn't seem in the spirit to ask.

As they head back down to the kitchen, she wonders what Kessie's doing right now. Probably feeding Zora, or washing up. It really is liberating to be away from all the chores.

Over the next few hours, she and Darsha hang out in the living room drinking coffee and herbal tea and snacking while various people come in and out. Most greet Robin with friendly enthusiasm. Only one girl says hello to Darsha in a noticeably offhand way, then walks off upstairs. 'That's Ava,' Darsha whispers. 'She has the room next to mine and has super vocal sex every night with at least three guys. And she thinks *I'm* being insensitive for politely raising the fact that I can't sleep. So I mostly sleep in Vi's. Unless she has someone else there.'

Robin nods. 'Wow. That happen often?'

Darsha nods from side to side. 'With Vi you mean? Depends. Few times a month maybe.'

'Right. Always other women?'

Darsha shrugs. 'Once there was a guy. But I think there was another woman then too. Anyway, it's not like there's any subterfuge. Everyone here is in open relationships – literally. It does just make you realize how limited your horizons can become from all these social expectations that are never even articulated, right? It's like what you've been reading about in anthropology, you know, in terms of family. I mean, monogamy's only a contemporary cultural practice, right? It's natural to feel some kind of possessiveness about a sexual partner, but it's also natural to feel desire for other people – so the idea people have here is just to try to embrace that. Not stress out about it. Like, you get the right to intimacy, but without being tied down, you know?'

Darsha's tone is chipper, but it sounds to Robin like she's still trying to justify it rationally for herself. Or maybe that's reading too much into it. She tells herself to get with the times and open the shutters of her mind, like Darsha did. Like Mead did. Like she's been wishing everyone else would about alloparents.

Vi, it turns out, has to work late. They eat the remains of her curry for dinner, and it really is delicious; even Max would have been impressed. The thought annoys Robin. She'd been doing so well at keeping him and all his good points out of her thoughts.

The sky darkens as they drink wine in the living room. Robin has just decided that she can't keep her eyes open for long enough to form a coherent sentence, and is about to get up to go to bed, when Vi arrives. She strides into the room, throws off her denim jacket, walks up to Darsha, tilts her head, and kisses her long and full on the lips. Then she turns and drops her head to one side, appraisingly. 'Hey! So you must be Robin, come to whisk my girlfriend away. Good to meet you.'

Robin wonders whether this was intended to be as passive-aggressively sarky as it sounded. 'Nice to meet you, too.' She stands and hesitates, wondering whether reaching for a handshake would be preposterously old-fashioned. Somehow Vi's body language doesn't seem to be inviting anything more affectionate than that. She's seen Vi before in lots of photos, and even briefly during video chats with Darsha – but in person she's far more striking. She's even taller than Robin, and sporty-looking, with an asymmetric short bleached haircut, an angular jaw, and wide, ice-grey eyes. Like a Viking Joan of Arc. 'Shame you can't join us on the road trip,' Robin adds.

Is it her imagination, or did Vi just flinch? She shrugs one shoulder. 'Work calls.'

Robin nods. 'I know that feeling. Look, I'm sorry, but I'm wrecked – no sleep on the plane plus jet lag plus childcare lag – I'm going to have to crash. See you both in the morning!'

'Probably not,' Vi says. 'I'm heading to the office early. But sleep well.'

'Yeah, sleep well, hon!' Darsha adds. 'So great to have you here!'

Robin is about to head on up the stairs – but before she does, Vi pushes Darsha back down onto the sofa and starts kissing her again. She can't help staring for a moment until, embarrassed at herself, she turns away.

There are two guys asleep in the dorm room already. One of them is snoring, which reminds Robin that she forgot to bring ear plugs. At least she only has one night here. She wants to phone Kessie and see how Zora's doing. This will be the first night in weeks that she hasn't sung Zora to sleep before sleeping herself . . . Well, tonight she is beholden to nobody. She sends Kessie a message, telling her how fancy the commune is, how nice it's been to see Darsha, and asking how she and Zora are getting on – then gets changed into her pyjamas in the shared bathroom and creeps into bed.

*

The coast highway is breathtaking. A sapphire galaxy on their right, and hills on their left glowing emerald and gold. The quality of light is transcendent, like nothing Robin has ever seen – including that summer that she and Kessie spent backpacking in the Alps and Provence, when every day was balmy, and when they both bought cheap Matisse prints they said they'd display wherever they lived for as long as they lived. Hers is now languishing in a box somewhere. She should dig it out, actually, and see whether Kessie kept hers. But this Californian light has an even more magical quality. And driving through it, next to Darsha, with James Taylor's soothing tones floating over her and out of the window – it's a dream . . .

Except a voice keeps whining, mosquito-like in her ear: *How could you leave your baby the other side of an ocean?*

Kessie replied last night just saying that all was fine and adding two exclamation marks. Two seemed a tad excessive. Was she over-compensating? She didn't mention how Zora was doing or send a photo. Does Zora feel abandoned and unable to express it? Is Kessie's mental health regressing? But there's no point spending this amazing trip stressing about home. It's done, she's here now – and Kessie should be absolutely fine: she's way better now, she's taking her drugs, the doctor is monitoring her, Paolo and Tam are checking up on her, and this will be a great bonding opportunity for her and Zora.

But then nobody else knows how bad it's been until recently. Even Kessie herself, Robin suspects. In any case, it still just feels wrong, and strange, to be away from them both. But maybe missing them is just inevitable. This trip should help to reinforce the fact that Zora isn't really her baby. She just didn't anticipate how much it would feel like going cold turkey.

'You okay?' Darsha asks. The song about Mexico has just come on – the one where James Taylor raves on about the place despite never having been there.

Robin laughs. 'Oh, just . . . in my own world for a sec. This scenery is *incredible*!' She starts singing along, and Darsha joins in.

They stop at Carmel Beach, a serene crescent of pale sand crowned with white-painted timber houses. After kicking their sandals off, they run to the water's edge and paddle for a bit. Darsha's body looks as toned as it was at eighteen. They buy coconut ice creams and sit on the sand, taking in the light shifting on the water, the ocean rolling in. 'I mean, you promised relaxation,' Robin said, 'but I had no idea it would be this glorious.'

They reminisce about their gap-year travels — and marvel at how some of their memories overlap, like the time they sneaked into a five-star hotel pool and were promptly kicked out, while other memories are only recalled by one or other of them — Darsha's poker victory over a bunch of Israeli guys just out of military service, for instance, and Robin's near-death experience on a rusted-up motorbike. It's like jointly stitching a tapestry from a shared scrap bag of their old clothes. Robin had forgotten how much Darsha makes her laugh! How funny and wry she is, and how much lighter she makes her feel, compared to Kessie of late. But that thought makes her feel guilty. Kessie in the throes of postnatal depression isn't the real Kessie. Before that bombshell, she was equally full of energy and warmth, and could be even more hilarious — and she's getting back to her old self again.

It's too lovely to leave, as they'd planned to, so they end up finding a little seafood bar, and a B&B with a spare room, and a beachside bar with a live band of ageing rockers, whose music is loud enough that they can dance on the sand, with the beach to themselves, under a warped moon.

Next stop, Big Sur — which is as spectacular as Robin had hoped. They navigate down steep, narrow paths between rugged rocks, and among clusters of other tourists, to stand fully admiring the spiky drama of the geology, the waves all creamy, the water such a deep, heady blue. Back up at the diner, they order guacamole and fries and gaze out to the blue horizon.

While Darsha is in the bathroom, Robin logs onto the Wi-Fi and checks her phone. Kessie has just sent a picture message of Zora munching on a banana, with smears of mush around her cheeks on her bib. 'Someone's enjoying her solids.' Impulsively, Robin taps to make a video call – and Kessie picks up.

'Robs, hi! Good timing – we're just having a deluxe meal of mushy banana. Most of it's on the floor already. Look baby girl, it's Mama Roro – want to say hello?'

'Dada,' Zora says, reaching excitedly towards the camera.

'She's been jabbering so much today,' Kessie says. 'Where are you?'

'In a diner right above Big Sur. This coast road is stunning.'

'Your pictures have been amazing!' Kessie says. 'Oh no, don't throw it all on the floor . . . oh God, that's the water everywhere too – look, I'd better go.'

'Sure, see you soon!' Robin ends the call and looks up to see Darsha slipping back into the booth with a quizzical smile.

Back on the road, the light intensifies to marigold as they turn off the highway and head inland in the direction of their mountaintop bed and breakfast. It's a long, winding drive up into wooded wilderness. After a while they both lose signal on their phones. There are no streetlights. Above the tree line, the glow of light fades. It feels like this can't lead to any place that's habitable for humans any time soon, and Robin is beginning to envisage them sleeping in the car – when they finally see the gleam of light from a small hamlet.

They knock, and an exuberant man appears to welcome them, dressed in a pink silk shirt. He introduces himself as Gil. He asks if they'd like to partake of a drink, and leads them through a hall with a rug that is luxuriously thick and soft.

They go through the back door to a huge veranda that looks out over aeons of black forest to a glint of ocean in the distance, below a crisp, silver half circle of moon. 'Quite the view, huh? Even better in the morning. Now, how about a glass of local wine?' He pours them one each, tells them about the vineyard, then lingers to chat. He works two days a week at a hospital doing admin, he says, and takes care of this business the rest of the time, while his husband works as a surgeon – not a bad life. After a bit, he leaves them to it. They hang over the rail for a few minutes, marvelling at the moon and the murmuration of stars, and how easy it is, living in a big city, to forget the magnitude of the night sky. 'Do you remember that sky in the Maasai Mara though?' Robin asks. 'That unbelievable trove of stars.'

'Astonishing,' Darsha sighs. 'A whole new sense of our place in the universe. We were so young, right? I had no clue how unique that moment would turn out to be. I knew I was super lucky to have been placed with you, though, Robinita. Lottery win, that one.'

'Totally. It's so good to be together again.' They retreat with their wine to the chaise longue, which is luxuriously decked out with poufy velvet cushions. The wine is delicious – plummy and smooth. A wind chime tinkles, fairylike, at a tuft of breeze. A dreamcatcher sways. 'These guys live the life of Riley', Robin murmurs. 'Who was Riley anyway?'

Darsha laughs then sits forward and points – and they both stare at a giant, impossibly graceful silhouette of a buck, its antlers like winter trees, bounding across the grass, then leaping, flying, over the tall fence that must separate their lawn from next door's. 'Did that just happen?'

They look at each other. In the lantern light, Darsha's skin is like burnished copper, and her hair gleams. Robin reaches out to touch it. What a wonderful human Darsha is, to have brought her over here, and given her this time, this space. She'd needed it so badly and didn't have the headspace to realize it on her own. And she's such a refreshing free spirit! It's no coincidence that she's chosen to live out here, on the West Coast, free from convention and oppressive grey weather – and free too, apparently, from the relentless ticking of a biological clock.

Darsha scooches closer. An owl hoots, as if cheering the moment. 'Why don't you just move over here too?' she asks. 'Leave the Big Smoke behind. You clearly hate your job, and you've cut your ties to Max which is one of the *best* decisions you've ever made. I mean, obviously I take that back if for some reason you ever get back together . . .'

'Oh that is *not* happening!' Robin cuts in. 'The getting back together part, I mean. You know, I'm so glad now that he didn't say yes to having a baby with me. It would have shackled us together and . . . I just didn't feel great about myself when I was with him. It wasn't working but still, I couldn't let it go for the longest time. I feel like an idiot now.'

'Hindsight is a wonderful thing. I guess he had his good points. I mean, he could cook. But now we have food delivery apps and instant meals! Anyway, I'm sorry it's all been so shitty.'

Robin laughs. 'Well, kind of. In lots of ways. But super rewarding in other ways, with Zora. I do adore that kid.'

'Okay, well that's nice to hear. But just think: if you moved here, now that Kessie's getting well again, you wouldn't have any of that responsibility. And we could do road trips like this all the time.'

'Bliss!' Robin grins. 'Too dreamy to be practical, probably, but . . .'

'Couldn't it be, though? You could do a PhD in anthropology in the US. Berkley's good for that. Ursula Le Guin's dad was a prof there. Or you could set up your own consultancy practice, doing something you actually care about – something in international development? I could do all your graphics.'

Robin kisses her on the cheek. 'You're amazing. Imagine that . . .' It's such a joy to hear someone who knows her this well articulate a whole new future vision for her life. Her mind flicks to Kessie and Zora, and she feels instantly guilty, as if she were cheating on them by just thinking about the possibility.

'You've basically been acting as Zora's surrogate mum ever since she was born, right?' Darsha says. 'You should be super proud of yourself for that. And you're such a loyal friend to Kessie. Most friends wouldn't give half as much. I know I wouldn't. But you've got to be kind to yourself too. Fulfil your own dreams. It just – I *might* be wrong, but it seems to me like you might have been filling the hole left by Max and his fuckwittery by throwing all your energies into helping Kessie, and getting a taste of parenting? You deserve someone who'll care for *you* with that kind of devotion too.'

Robin tilts her head back and closes her eyes. 'Maybe . . . I mean – I'm sure Kessie would have done the same for me . . . I think? Anyway, I do adore Zora, so it's not like it's *just* been a burden. It actually feels kind of painful to be away from her, even though I'm having the best time with you. I guess it's just been a bit all-consuming . . .'

'I bet. So much fucking hard work!' Darsha says. 'To be honest,

I just look at most mums and babies and think, thank God I'm free of that! And you've been doing *everything*. For a kid who's not even your own. I really do admire you for that. I mean, if I ever did somehow end up with a kid of my own, I expect I'd go gooey for it and everything would be different – but I have zero inclination to sacrifice the lifestyle I have to find out.'

Robin laughs. 'Very wise.'

'I mean, I get that maternal love is deep,' Darsha continues. 'But then motherhood so often seems to eclipse romantic love, right? And *lust*. Both of which are emotions I enjoy, quite frankly, and don't feel old enough to give up. And just being able to seize the moment. Like we are now.'

'Totally,' Robin says, the truth of this blazing in her brain.

'Anyway, just look at you!' Darsha smiles. 'It's great to see some colour back in your cheeks. You're not Morticia Addams's double any more.'

Robin grins. 'I looked that bad?'

'I mean, I always find her quite sexy. But she does not look healthy. Anyway, you know, there's also a queer feminist element to embracing a child-free life as I see it,' Darsha says. 'I don't want to feel like I *have* to live up to the normative social expectation to reproduce, just because I have a womb. And, I mean, queer feminism needs celebrating more than ever under this administration. Women's rights – human rights – it's not looking good.'

'It's not. I take all your points, 100 per cent. I just wish I had your certainty. And hadn't got so darn broody already!'

Darsha hugs her knees and raises her eyebrows at her. 'Well, you've had a taste of mothering now. And you're not biologically tied in, so – you still have choices.'

Robin leans into her and they sit with their arms around each other for a while, looking at the brightening stars. Orion's Belt. The Big Dipper. Could moving over here really be possible? It would definitely be a way to accelerate getting over her delusion that she's become any more than a glorified nanny to Zora. 'I already feel so renewed,' she sighs. 'From just a couple of days here. It's just perfect. You're perfect.'

Darsha strokes her cheek, and a tiny firework shoots upwards in Robin's chest and explodes in coppery sparks. This is just – happiness, right? Not desire. Surely not. She resisted those feelings so many years ago. But she's just really feeling drawn to Darsha's lips, to the tip of that skewed lower incisor . . . Why *did* she hold back from experimenting more when she was younger? Why did she care so much about what people thought?

Somehow their lips are moving closer together – then connecting. Darsha's feel softer and lighter than any that Robin has kissed before, the sensation more tender and languid. Is this for real?

Robin slides her fingertips up and down Darsha's back, and Darsha's nails are running down hers – Robin's plunges her hands into Darsha's thick, silken hair, feels it sliding between her finger crevices, and everything is dissipating except warm skin and lemon marmalade scent and hot blood. Darsha's unbuttoning her shirt . . . *This shouldn't be happening; this is happening. It's crazy; it's brilliant. It might ruin the friendship; it might be the culmination. It's a mistake; it's what I should have done a decade ago.*

They pull apart for a moment to look at each other, laugh at the absurdity, and at the rightness, then come together again. It turns out that they don't need to discuss getting up from the velvet cushions and moving to the silky ones in the bedroom, or pushing their twin beds together, or tossing each other's clothes onto the floor – and that this all happens without the least awkwardness, like gliding on skates, engrossed in an improv dance sequence with not the least fear of falling, that it's not at all like two old friends who hadn't seen each other for three years until the day before, and had never so much as pecked each other on the lips, never mind taken their lips to parts of each other they'd never seen or touched before. It turns out this feels like running along a white-hot beach and diving into turquoise waves abounding with phosphorescence.

*

Robin wakes to a thin shaft of sunlight on one shoulder, and a faint high-pitched roar. Crap, where's Zora? Is she awake, hungry? But no: it's the dawn chorus from the forested hills all around them – and Darsha's arm is around her waist. Her delicate brown hand with its jade ring lying warm against her own pale skin. Robin lets out a long, quiet breath. This is real! The feather-lightness of Darsha's body is remarkable – the delicacy of it. She could never have slept with Max spooning her like this; his arm was too heavy, his breath too loud.

Darsha stirs. 'Mm, good morning, beautiful.'

Robin turns over and traces her cheekbone. 'Good morning.' She smiles. They kiss again. Just as warm, just as soft. It really wasn't all a dream.

'Remind me why you invited Dylan to join this reunion again?' Darsha sighs.

Robin rolls her eyes. 'I know! Argh. So short-sighted of me.

I was looking forward to seeing him – but now there's only one person I want to be with. Too late to put him off now.'

'You'd better not decide you fancy him again,' Darsha warns. 'I'm not up for sharing you, Robinita. You know, while we're here, I feel like there are some places I need us to revisit from last night.' Her lips brush downwards, her tongue lands as lightly as a moth, and Robin's veins flick on like fairy lights.

They settle into a tessellation on the bed. 'Darsh, that was unbelievable,' she murmurs. 'You may have put me off men for life. I can't help thinking about Vi, though . . . whatever this means . . . I'm not sure I could manage the whole open relationship thing.'

'Robinita, if you moved over here, I'd be monogamous with you in a heartbeat.'

Robin props herself up on one elbow. 'You would?' This feeling is so wondrous it's actually really tempting just to say *fuck it, yes*. Moving over here could be a solution to all her career disgruntlements, her anxieties, her break-up pain, her feelings about Zora . . .

Or would it? Surely the odd, unconventional little household – family – that she has created back home in grey old London doesn't trump this euphoria. She can't always be fated to repress her own desires, can she? She's not even Catholic.

'You're thinking about Zora and Kessie, aren't you?' Darsha murmurs.

Robin lies back down and looks up at the ceiling. 'They crossed my mind.'

'Are you in love with her? Kessie?'

Robin hoots out a laugh. 'What? No! Not at all.' She immediately feels bad, for some reason, about how defensive this sounded.

'I mean . . . I do *love* her. I always will. She's my oldest friend, and we became as close as sisters after our parents . . . I mean, we know each other back to front. And this time with Zora has . . . But it's totally platonic. Plus, Kessie's as straight as a . . . I don't know, a ruler.'

Darsha shrugs. 'Okay. I mean, you thought you were too, but okay.'

Robin grins ruefully. 'I guess that's fair – but Kessie really is.'

Leaning against each other, they listen to the birds again for a bit. 'Darsh,' she says, 'do you think everyone is on a spectrum, sexually?'

'Nope. *I'm* not, anyway. Men have their uses but they're not for me – in that way.'

'Ha! That's what Benjy said about women when the spectrum thing came up. Well, anyway, hello world, I've just realized I'm bi, only a couple of decades too late.'

Darsha kisses her nose. 'Better late than never. Is this the first time you've even kissed a girl?'

'Not quite. But as the song goes, I liked it – and a *lot* more this time than either of the other times. They were just drunken snogs.'

'When?'

'Once when I was still at school, on an orchestra trip . . .'

'You never said.'

'Well, I thought it was nothing. At least, I hoped it was. I think I was just scared of being different. Plus, I still fancied boys, and I think I naively thought you had to be either/or. The second time was when I was visiting Kessie at music college. After a few drinks I pulled this jazz singer called Ruby, but just wrote that off as an aberration.'

'Another one. You're sober now, right?'

'I'm high on you.' They kiss some more.

'Well, I always hoped this was buried deep inside you,' Darsha says smugly, smoothing each of her eyebrows in turn.

'You did?'

'Yup. Gaydar innit. Didn't want to pressure you though.'

Robin shakes her head, trying to jiggle her memories. 'I wish I knew you knew.' She flops down onto her back and covers her eyes with her palms. How different could her life have been if she'd been brave enough to come out earlier? Got together with Darsha at seventeen, moved to California too? Never even met Max?

'Babe, don't beat yourself up. The whole concept of being bi back then was like being from a remote tribe to most people,' Darsha says. 'Your anthropologist pals hadn't even got around to studying it. Listen, have you read any Adrienne Rich?'

Robin turns towards Darsha, wracking her brains. 'Wait, is she a poet? I think Kessie has a collection of hers that her aunt Elmi gave her . . .' Casting her mind back to the book on the table at home prompts her to think of Zora, and what the two of them might be doing right now . . . and how the hell she'll tell Kessie about what's just happened.

'She's an amazing poet, and essayist too,' Darsha says. 'Super important thinker on feminism and lesbianism. There's an essay of hers called "Compulsory Heterosexuality" that is compulsory reading for you, I'd say. It basically argues that women are compelled by misogynistic social forces into feeling like they *have* to want to be with men and bear them children. And that's all reinforced by the dominant anti-lesbian narratives. Even written by so-called feminist women writers, like Doris Lessing – basically stories reinforcing the idea that lesbianism is twisted and wrong so women shouldn't surrender to it.

'Woah. Okay!'

'In fact, I've decided: *Blood, Bread, and Poetry* is my choice for our next mini book club. It might just change your life.'

'I'm in. When was it published?'

'Early Eighties?'

'Eighties . . .' Robin wracks her brains. She has read so much about kinship and feminism lately – how did she simply not know about what sounds like an important strand of feminist thought? Was her whole life with Max really a kind of socially imposed delusion? What about her desire for a baby? Baby. Her heart tugs as she imagines the sensation of Zora's little fingers gripping her index finger, their surprising strength, that feeling of being conjoined.

Darsha presses out the crease in the middle of her forehead. 'Anyway, there's plenty of time for homework. Now I've finally got you in my bed after, what, *seventeen* years of loving you, we should enjoy the moment, right?' She butterfly-kisses Robin's neck, shoulder, right breast, nipple. 'You deserve some pleasure time. And I want more pleasure time with you. Win-win. How about we make a pact not to talk about the future for a bit?'

Robin smiles in relief. 'Yes! Stop all the clocks. My brain was crashing anyway.' She climbs on top of Darsha and traces the arc of her collarbone with her lips. Her phone buzzes, and she knows it's Kessie – but resists her instinct to pick up.

*

Back at the airport, waiting to meet Dylan, she and Darsha are unable to stop touching each other – but they pull apart as he emerges from the departure lounge, a frown rucking his freckled forehead. He looks grizzled, thickened around the face, and so much older than the lanky seventeen-year-old Robin always pictures when she thinks of him, flicking his curtained hair in the Tanzanian sunshine. A smile breaks as he spots them. He reaches out his eagle arms and pulls them into an awkward triangular hug. 'Long time no see! Can you believe it's been seventeen years since we met at an airport for the first time? Look at you both. Radiant.'

Darsha laughs. 'You old sleazebag.'

'You look almost as destroyed as Darsha said I did when I got here,' Robin puts in.

Darsha hooks his arm in one of hers. 'What *you* need, Dylly boy, is a sea view coffee.'

They drive north towards Salt Point to a 90s soundtrack, crossing the Bay Bridge in thick fog. The chat flows, despite the elephant in the room, as if the decades haven't passed. They swap gap-year anecdotes, and exchange bits of light news. Darsha tells him all about her design business and the commune – not mentioning Vi, Robin notes. Every so often she reaches over to stroke Darsha's nearest hand with one finger, and Darsha gives her a sly smile, then draws a heart shape on the top of her hand when she's not looking. Robin tells him about her break-up with Max, about Kessie, Zora, and her job frustrations, her degree that she no longer has enough time for – how most things she had imagined for this year have gone to pot. How amazing it's been to come here.

After a while, she looks around to the back seat to see Dylan slumped and gazing out of the window into the fog. 'Dyl, I'm so sorry about your separation. It must have been awful, with the kids and everything. I know it had been brewing for a while, but still . . .'

The answer is written in the lines on his face. 'Thanks,' he says. 'Not much fun. I'll tell you more later. It's good to get away anyway.'

Robin turns back round to face the road. She can't imagine what it must feel like to be living permanently apart from your kids after you've parented them for seven and nine years respectively. It's bad enough after allomothering for a few months.

After a detour from the highway, they park up at Point Reyes. Following Darsha, they all career skittishly down a steep path among rugged cliffs, then stomp through lush, flowered grasses until they reach a long, sandy beach. They run along the strand until they are out of breath, then stop, hands on thighs, panting and hooting.

Robin straightens up and looks slowly around the smudged horizon. The fog seems to be slowly lifting, and gulls are cavorting on the spray, catching glimmers of light with their wings. 'I can't believe this place is so close to the city!' she exclaims. 'It's so gorgeous. So wild.'

Darsha slings an arm around her. 'What can I say – California's a great place to live. You should try it.' They kiss, then Robin glances over to Dylan, but he's still gazing at the horizon, oblivious.

There's nowhere open to get coffee nearby, so after reaching the far end of the beach and walking back again, Darsha suggests they drive on towards Salt Point, where the cabin is, and find coffee en route.

'I'm still in dire need of caffeine, but I actually feel miles better already,' Dylan says, windmilling his arms.

'Yup, you've shed at least five years,' Darsha tells him. 'You could still pass for fifty though.' She darts away from a shove.

At a nondescript diner, they pause to knock back some acidic filter coffee, then press on. Salt Point signs finally materialize, and Darsha parks up on a deserted stretch of road in dense forest. Outside the car, Robin inhales earth and pine. The quiet shadow is like being brushed with silk. A bird she doesn't recognize shrieks in hilarity from the trees.

They follow the direction of a signpost, head down a track – and the landscape opens up onto what feels like another planet.

Fawn-coloured rocks, as gnarled and whorled as a sea that's frozen mid-motion, are peppered with black seaweed. Robin steps onto them tentatively. Some are honeycombed with small depressions like bubbles in caramel.

A giant bird statue – is that a pelican? – moves, flaps away, then coasts on the wind. No sign of any other people. The three of them might as well be the only other Homo sapiens on this whole peninsula. Robin hadn't thought to read up on the places they were going in advance, but she had just assumed that everywhere along this coast would be heavily populated or heaving with tourists.

'So I was reading up on the geology here,' Dylan says. 'I left the book in the car . . . but I think this honeycomb stuff is called tafoni? Word of the day.'

'Sounds like an Italian pudding,' Robin muses.

'Ha! Now I'm craving a tiramisu.'

'Educate us some more, Mr Norwood,' Darsha demands. 'Why does it look like this?'

'Salt crystallization, Ms Dahliwal. You can write an essay about it for tomorrow. Four hundred words.'

Dylan must be a good teacher, Robin thinks. She'd bet half the girls in his class have crushes on him, just like she once did, before she knew which of these two she really wanted. Though he probably looks ancient to them. She crouches to run her palm over the rocks, thinking of the shape of Darsha's hips.

'There's a deep-sea fan here too,' Dylan adds.

'Fan?' Darsha is standing on a protruding point of rock that looks like a peak of meringue, and is swaying her slim body gracefully, perched on its cusp, like a fan herself.

'Part of a mermaid kingdom?' Robin asks.

'Good effort, Suarez,' he grins. 'Science isn't quite there with mermaids yet. But there's a massive slide underwater, where sediment moves between two plates, and it causes unusual currents.'

The idea of this, the three of them, perched like ants on two ginormous dinner plates that could crack against each other and fracture any minute, prompting a fiery explosion of lava, makes Robin feel nauseous. How does Darsha deal psychologically with living in this prospective natural disaster zone the whole time? How does she find it so easy to stay happily in the present?

Darsha bounds over, puts a hand on her waist, and cradles her head with the other. They kiss, long and slow, and Robin feels herself flush as she senses Dylan behind them, stopping to watch. They both start to laugh, pull apart, and look over at him.

He's standing with hands on hips, shaking his head slowly. 'Well, you nymphs,' he says, finally, grinning. 'You finally converted her then, Darsh? What did it take in the end – did you feed her a potion made from Californian kelp regurgitated by an elk or something?'

'Gross! I'm hardly going to divulge my potions to *you*.'

'Well, congrats, guys!' Dylan high-fives them both. 'I must be behind the times – I thought you had a girlfriend over here? Even if it was a bit . . . polyamorous or whatever. And as for you, Robin, I had no idea you swung both ways.'

'Nor did I, really. Well, not consciously.' Robin laughs, and kisses Darsha again. It feels thrilling to be witnessed in the act. They walk on, hands clasped.

Her phone vibrates. She pulls it out, and Kessie's name flashes up. A salty wave of guilt and longing hits her, and she detaches her hand and turns to walk off the path. It must be early morning in London. 'Hi, hon!' she answers brightly. 'Nice to hear from you – everything alright? How's Zora?'

Kessie is saying something, but there's only one bar of reception here, and Robin can't make it out. She glances around. Darsha is looking at her and pointing vigorously in the direction of the beach. Robin gives her a thumbs-up, and Darsha and Dylan start walking off. 'Sorry, Kess, can't hear properly – let me move up nearer the beach and see if I get more reception – can you say that again?'

'Can you hear now?' Kessie asks. 'We miss you! But we're doing fine. It was a hard night though, to be honest. Zora wouldn't sleep and she's a bit hot so I've given her some paracetamol . . . I thought your voice might help! Hey, little one, can you hear Mama Roro?'

'Oh hi, baby girl!' Robin croons. A squeal-grunt comes down the line. 'Poor poppet, are you a bit hot?' she asks – and can't help thinking: *Is she keeping you cool enough? Has she given you the right dose?*

'Can you video call us?' Kessie asks.

'Oh I wish I could, but I'm on this wild peninsula – there's hardly enough reception even for an audio call . . . The rocks here are amazing, like a surrealist painting!'

'Wow. I wish we could teleport ourselves over,' Kessie says.

'Me too,' Robin half-lies. There's a pause as the line cuts in and out. It feels like she's deceiving Kessie by still not telling her what's happened with Darsha. If she only knew herself what it meant. Or where it was going. 'I miss you both too,' she says. 'I feel bad for being away when Zora's ill.'

'Oh, c'est la vie – don't feel bad at all! You totally deserve this – go enjoy the sea! Love you. Can you say *love you*, Zozo?'

'Dodoo?' comes the tiny voice. Robin's heart inflates. 'Love you both too. You're sure you're okay, Kess? Medication on track?'

'All fine, pretty much . . .'

The line cuts out again. 'Hello? Robin walks in a wide circle, waving her phone around, but the connection has gone.

She gives up and turns to look for Darsha and Dylan. They have got to the sandy part of the beach, taken off their shoes and are paddling in the milky-crested shallows, laughing about something. Should she tell Kessie about Darsha now, if she calls back? No: Kessie really doesn't need to be rocked emotionally at the moment, not while she's dealing with sole childcare for the first time.

A deep breath of sea breeze calms her. This space. This place!

Earthquake and wildfire threats aside, California is Eden. And these days with Darsha have felt not just therapeutic but euphoric. Maybe, if she really could decide to stay here after all, she could take the chance to embrace a whole new phase. A woman in love with a woman! A woman who can finally enjoy sex with another woman! A woman who can say: *Hi, I'm Robin, and I'm bisexual.* Maybe she really could be liberated from London life, its stressful pace, its oppressive weather, and from the quasi-parental responsibility she's taken on – she could throw off her old skin, like a snake, and slide into the next phase with a newly patterned one.

She pockets her phone, runs over towards the water's edge, and kicks off her shoes. Darsha and Dylan are paddling further along, jeans rolled up to their knees, ankle-deep.

'There you are!' Darsha calls.

Robin dips a foot in, and quickly withdraws it. 'Whew! It's *cold*!'

Darsha splashes up to her, black hair rippling in the wind, and puts an arm around her waist. Robin's too-fine hair plasters itself over her face – she swipes it away and kisses Darsha's salty lips.

'So have you got over the shock yet?' she asks Dylan as they all wade in a line.

'I mean, you guys – it was clearly meant to be,' he says. 'One relationship ends; the next begins. The great cycle of life.'

'Sorry that you're having to deal with the ending part.'

'Yeah.' He sniffs. 'I miss the kids like hell, but I'm . . . processing it.'

Robin releases Darsha and takes his hand, and Darsha wades around him to take the other one.

'Thanks guys,' he says, swinging their arms and kicking a wave in the water. 'It's not just that Leila cheated on me – it's that she genuinely seems to love this other guy. He makes her happier than I could, which sucks, but it's true. Part of me wants us to fight to stay together for the kids' sake, but then they'd only have to witness us at each other's throats even more. I wish I could bring myself to go for custody, but she's been a stay-at-home mum, so . . . we'll just have to work out childcare. People do.'

'But – you mean you're just going to give the kids to her?' Robin asks. 'I mean, I know she stayed home, but you've been there too, and worked to pay for everything!'

Dylan sighs. 'Well, I just don't have the strength for a big legal battle. Reckon I'll end up having the kids every other weekend. Other dads manage. I'll find stuff to do with myself, I guess. Go to the gym more. Take up archery.'

'Zumba?' Robin suggests.

'Knitting?' Darsha offers.

Grinning wryly, Dylan pulls away and wades to the shore. Then he wheels around and holds up a forefinger. 'Just don't go and wreck this friendship of ours with your mid-life love affair, okay?' he tells them both sternly. 'I need all my old pals in this new, single state I've found myself in. And I want us to be able to have another reunion before another decade passes. And before one of us gets cancer or dementia or something.'

'Dylly! We're not that old,' Darsha says. 'I want no more of this British pessimism . . .'

'To friendship, forever!' Robin crows, her voice spinning off in the wind. 'Let's drink champagne tonight.'

'Let's eat first,' Dylan says. 'I'm starving.'

'I say we need to swim first,' Darsha says. 'Symbolic. A pagan baptism. To new starts all round!' She runs up to the dry layer of sand and begins stripping off her clothes. Robin and Dylan glance at each other with mutual anxiety. Darsha leaps squirrel-like back towards the water, fully naked, as the sun ahead of her burns off the remaining fog. 'Come on!' she calls, as she splashes in, then dives and swims out. She surfaces and turns onto her back like a sea otter, making intersecting ripples on the surface. 'It's glorious!'

Robin decides to abandon caution: the theme of this trip. She strips off too, as quickly as she can, so as not to change her mind, and finds she's racing with Dylan, whose torso is still muscled, and much hairier than she remembered.

They splash out together and launch in behind Darsha. The cold takes her breath away for a few seconds, and she has to pant to regularize it. 'Woo-hoo-hooooo!' she calls up to the gulls. The three of them shriek and giggle like tweens who've slipped their parents' leash for the first time.

The water feels deliciously tingly on naked skin. It strikes Robin that this is her first-ever skinny dip. It's exhilarating, titillating; her nipples harden in the water, and she wonders for a second whether they'll end up having a threesome, whether she'd be liberated enough for that. Almost certainly not. But why has she spent her life a slave to the swimming costume?

The sun finally burns through and makes the water sparkle.

After dancing around to get dry, and pulling clothes over sticky skin, they power up the path from the beach and around the headland. A family of seals is basking in the hazy light on the rocks below, a couple rolling, one shifting lumpily over to a comfier spot. They look so content, lolling together, whiskery faces at peace. Darsha links her fingers with Robin's. They all sit down for a while and watch the sun streak the sky with clementine and lavender and turn the rocks a fool's gold. Robin imagines her night ahead in Darsha's bed, fingers under the covers . . . Then her phone vibrates again.

A picture message: Zora's peachy face, chewing on Sophie La Girafe. If dark fell here and they got lost on the way back to the car, she might be ravaged by a grizzly bear and Zora would never see her again. Would she remember even a ghostly sense of her?

She thinks of her lonely little frozen egg. Of those horrific days as her body rebelled against the extraction, like punishment for believing she could defy nature to make a baby. Of how a real baby, a perfect baby, materialized in her life, like a charm. Scrambling to her feet, she suggests heading back.

*

That evening, after a fish dinner and two bottles of prosecco, they settle into wicker chairs in front of their cabin to sip tea and watch the night sky, accompanied by cacophonous cicadas. Robin wishes she could capture this moment in a 3D Polaroid, to preserve it like summer fruits. She pours everyone a large measure of the Jim Beam from the dusty bottle that Dylan had discovered in a high kitchen cupboard, and takes a glug, feeling the warm sizzle move down her body. She loves these two humans. Darsha blows her a kiss. Robin returns it, then looks fondly at Dylan, searching his face for signs that he's feeling rejuvenated . . . And then she pictures that cuttlefish from the documentary and has a brainwave. She leans towards him. 'Hey, Dyl', she blurts, 'you know how you were saying you didn't want this friendship to be wrecked by Darsha and me?'

'Oh, ignore me, I'm just being Eeyore . . .'

'Well, it just occurred to me, totally off the top of my head – but Darsh doesn't want kids, and I do, but I also want to be with her, and we all want to stay close as a trio and have reunions for the rest of our lives, and you've already had a couple of kids of your own, so . . . might you consider being a donor for me? Like, wherever we all end up living, it would be a pretty amazing excuse to all meet up! And travel the world again.'

'Wooooah.' Dylan's eyebrows have shot up into his receding hairline.

'Er, that came out of absolutely *nowhere*,' Darsha cuts in.

Robin flushes, wishing she could take it back already. So much for being impulsive. She shouldn't have knocked back so much fizz so fast. 'Sorry Darsh,' she says. 'I'm a bit wasted – I didn't think that through . . .'

'Kind of a big assumption that I'd want to be some kind of step-parent for you two?' Darsha points out, head tipped to one side.

'Good point. Sorry! I think my hormones just staged a coup . . .'

'I mean, I might have got the wrong end of the stick, but I thought we'd started a sort-of relationship? Which usually means discussing fairly major things in life, like having kids, which as you pointed out I'm not keen on doing?'

'You're right. You're absolutely right.'

Dylan hacks out an awkward cough-laugh, and thanks Robin for the thought.

'And let me get this straight,' Darsha jumps in again. 'I am *really* not up for a threesome, okay? Not even with you, Dylly boy.'

'Wait!' Robin protests. 'I wasn't thinking about *sex* – I'm not interested in *that* with you, Dylly, no offence! I want Darsha all to myself I'm afraid . . . I was just, you know, having a drunken flight of fancy and envisaging a turkey baster – oh God, please just forget I said anything.' She gets up to walk over to Darsha, slips her arms around her. 'Darsh. I'm sorry.'

Darsha's body stays tense, and her expression remains hostile. She turns away to look out at the dark. Robin rubs her back, and takes another glug. What has she done?

'Okayyy, well I'm mildly disappointed about the threesome thing, now that it's out there,' Dylan says genially from his reclined position on the chair.

'Oh my gosh, the sex thing is *already out there*,' Robin quotes, trying to induce a laugh from Darsha, who loves the film too. The corner of her mouth twitches.

'Look, Robin,' Dylan says, 'my active parenting days are done, but *hypothetically* speaking, if you *did* need sperm in the future, once you and Darsh have worked things out between the two of you, feel free to come back to me.' Darsha shoots a glare at him, and he gets to his feet. 'Okayyy, well, I'm escaping to bed – but remember what I said: don't go falling out, you two, all right? I know my sperm are gold dust, but they'll be around for a while yet.'

The door closes. Robin and Darsha look at each other. Darsha drops her head onto her forearms, leaning on the rail, and Robin slips her arms around her from behind, and kisses her neck. 'Forgive me. I'm just so – mixed up about motherhood, still, you know?'

Darsha turns to her with a sceptical face.

'I don't feel mixed up about *you*, though,' Robin says. 'I adore you . . . I should obviously never have said that to him out of the blue. It's just . . . what I went through with the whole egg extraction debacle . . . and since then . . . and I don't know what we . . . how . . .'

Darsha strokes her cheek. 'Shh. I get it. Kind of. You've been through so much. And I know how much you'd decided you wanted a baby. I guess I just thought you were ready to try something different. Like, maybe you thought being with me could maybe make it seem positive, even exciting to be child-free.'

'Well, maybe I do! It would certainly be easier. And fun and generally amazing, I know it would be. I just don't know if I'm there yet. I mean, maybe I am . . .' She thinks of Kessie, packing up all of Zora's little clothes, ready to move out. 'Also, I guess I still have to pinch myself that this is real, between us, you know? I mean, it feels so right, now, being with you, like it was always meant to be – but I guess I still don't actually know how it can work, what with the ocean being where it is. But I do want it. I want you. Right now. I really, really want you.' They kiss, tenderly, and a shiver runs up her back.

Darsha winces a smile. 'Me too.' She looks out in the direction of the ocean – then pulls Robin towards the bedroom.

Chapter 26

Kessie

Kessie staggers from the bathroom to the kitchen with a hollow belly and legs. Zora, thankfully, has just dropped off. One custard cream left – she pops it in her mouth, whole. Even now they always remind her of that night out in the woods.

In the fridge, a mournful half of a red pepper is curled and drooped around the edges. She doesn't dare open the feta that's clipped up in the back. In the freezer, a few slices of bread are left in a bag. She sticks them in the toaster, and then shoves several used mugs into the crowd by the sink and washes one up to make a black tea.

Sipping it, she stares at the Richter print on the wall. Robin had been taken with his work at that exhibition they went to together a few years ago, by the effusive colours – lime greens, acid yellows, cerulean blues, violets, all rioting together. Kessie pulls out her phone to look at the last batch of photos from California: some weird rock formations, seals, feet with red toenails in clear water, and a selfie with Darsha, their smiles leaping like dolphins.

Looking around the living room, she tries to put herself in Robin's shoes – what would she see if she were to return early and walk in the door? All the used mugs. Nappy bags strewn around the bin from yesterday, starting to smell. Tiny dirty outfits piled by the washing machine. There's no excuse for this now; she's so much better than she was. It's cleaning time! She puts on Tina Turner, unwraps a new sponge, and gets going.

Once the flat's in a better state, and a load of laundry is in, she goes through to check on Zora. Still peaceful in slumber, lips slightly parted, legs askew. What to do before she wakes? She could practice the clarinet, but she's so rusty, and it might wake the baby. She could read something – how about that? She picks up a book that Auntie Elmi had sent her, a collection of poetry by Adrienne Rich that she said was meant to be good on motherhood, and opens it at a random page. 'Dreamwood'. The poem is about a wooden typing stand – about its grain revealing a hidden landscape that can only be seen either by a child or by that same child's grown-up self – namely, a woman who is dreaming – dreaming when she is meant to be typing a report. It seems to encapsulate what Kessie needs right now. To recapture the creativity long-buried inside herself. The zest for life associated with childhood, as opposed to the sense of dread associated with being responsible for a very small child. The feeling of new growth and renewal while also putting down roots. Of life as a route through a wooded landscape waiting to be discovered . . .

She closes the book, gets her uke out of its box, and tries out a few chords while watching the fish swirl about. Then starts singing, quietly, tentatively. 'Such a small, slippery thing in the bath . . . Your shiny skin soft, sleek and taut . . . Just like that mackerel that I once caught . . . A flicker before it slid from my grasp.' It's a silly rhyme, really, but a melody arrives, like she'd plucked it out of the air, and the chords seem to fit first time. She gets up to grab her notebook from the pile in her room, scribbles words down, picks up the uke again, and keeps going.

'I worked so hard to prepare that healthy sweet puree for you to eat . . . only for you to splash it over freshly washed sheets . . . la la la laaa la laaa . . .' She snorts at the idea that this could be a song. It would be fun to play it to Robin sometime. Maybe she could make a mini-album of motherhood disaster songs.

When Zora finally wakes, she picks her up with newfound enthusiasm. 'Hi there, little one! Hungry?' Zora stares at her, faintly astounded. 'Let's give you a feed. Milk, this time. And then, do you know what? We're going to *leave the local area*! I know, right? We're going to go out and do something *cultural* together. What do you think? How about a gallery? Or a museum? Come on now, don't look so flummoxed.'

Incredibly, Zora latches at the first attempt. With her free hand, Kessie searches on her phone for what's on at the Tates and the Portrait Gallery. Nothing immediately grabs her, until she comes across the Foundling Museum – a place she's passed many times but never been into.

Somehow, all by herself, she manages to assemble all the baby clobber, pack it in the buggy, get Zora in her sling, exit the flat, board the bus, pay, and park the buggy in the designated area while the vehicle is moving without overturning it, or knocking the baby's head into one of the metal poles. Oddly, none of the other passengers seem to have witnessed this achievement or want to congratulate her. A couple of women do peer in her direction, but they're just trying to get a glimpse of the baby. This must be how Galileo felt as he twigged that Earth was in fact orbiting the sun. She remembers Robin's bus baby revelation. Imagines someone else looking at her and Zora together and feeling a similar longing. If they knew, though. If they knew.

*

Zora has fallen asleep in the sling by the time they arrive, and Kessie's back aches, but she doesn't dare put the baby down in case she wakes. Anyway, she likes having Zora cocooned on her chest, being able to look down and see the smooth shape of her profile, that raspberry nose, smell her milky vanilla scent, to be the one to hold her in such an engulfing sleep despite the hustle all around them.

At the café she orders a double espresso, tips a sugar packet into the dark nectar, and knocks it back in two gulps. In the hall, she pauses to read the opening information boards. The Foundling Hospital opened in 1739 with the purpose of looking after children whose mothers were unable to care for them due to poverty or the social exclusion caused by becoming pregnant while unmarried. If she had given birth 250 odd years ago, she would be bringing Zora here for a very different purpose. Would the hospital have even accepted a mixed-race child? In the Foundling's early years, children under a year old were sent to be looked after by foster families where they could be wet-nursed until they turned one. *Wet nursing* – Robin was telling her about that recently: how common it used to be, and still is in some cultures. God, she would have been grateful for that in those early months. Demand for places at the Foundling soon became so high that

286

chaos ensued, and they introduced a ballot system. A mother who needed to leave her baby was handed a bag and instructed to reach in and draw out one coloured ball. A white ball meant admission; a red ball, the waiting list; a black ball, goodbye.

She moves on, then stops by a small cabinet displaying 'tokens', coin-like discs with holes drilled in the top, and minute illustrations engraved on the surface – an eye, an ant, initials in gorgeous copper plate, a curled leaf. Each mother had to leave a token with her child that was distinctive enough to enable them to find each other in the future and prove their connection. It must have been a hell of an expense for women who were too poor to keep their own child to commission bespoke metalwork. Not all could: another cabinet contains textile tokens – a scrap of cotton linen illustrated with an acorn, a dark yellow ribbon with 'My Name Is Andrews' inked on in impeccable handwriting, a lace-edged linen baby cap with an accompanying paper heart. But at some point in the nineteenth century the governors decided to exhibit the tokens, and nobody thought to make a note of which objects belonged to which baby, so most of the stories attached to them were lost. The term 'token' seems so insufficient for the love and pain and hope that went into these tiny objects. Kessie thinks of the little bracelet Robin made for Zora – she hadn't been able to give a damn about the idea when she was in the thick of her malaise, but she'll treasure it now.

A painting draws her across the room. It depicts a woman in a red dress leaning, white-faced, against a barred window, her hand to her head, and an empty basket by her side. The title, *A Mother Depositing Her Child at the Foundling Hospital*. Kessie walks away, suddenly furious at herself: what right did she have to have been so sorry for herself, with Robin helping her out so much, and when she is lucky enough to be living in a country with a welfare state, and the NHS, and membership of the European Union? Oh, wait, that's now been consigned to history too. And the NHS is horribly underfunded. But they still did look after her very well once she fessed up about her mental state.

She looks down to find that the baby has woken, and seems to be regarding her with silent accusation. *I would never leave you, sweetheart. Not now.*

*

After the museum, she walks around the corner to Coram's Fields, a park that's only open to children and their adults. Zora stares out from the sling, bright-eyed and jabbering, while bigger children cavort around the space, screaming and calling to each other. Kessie walks along the path, watching other parents chatting while their children dip and rise on seesaws and hang alarmingly from climbing frames by their knee joints. Perhaps she has the strength, now, to call Jen back. She pulls out her phone and dials, hoping Jen won't actually pick up . . .

But she does, and squeals to hear from Kessie, then asks excitedly how she's doing.

'Good! Otis is gorgeous,' Kessie deflects. 'Looks like you've had an amazing mat leave so far?'

Jen agrees that it's been lovely . . . but soon begins to splurge all about Otis's birth going wrong, the scariness of forceps and his squashed skull, the jaundice, the sleep deprivation, and his vile crusty yellow cradle cap scabs. The sound of shrill crying bleeds through the phone, and she promises to call back.

Kessie shakes her head slowly as she continues walking, feeling both proud of herself for initiating contact again, and mildly vindicated: if the truth behind the social media facade is that even *Jen* has been struggling, maybe motherhood really is harder than it seems for most people.

Zora has started making *ah ba ba* sounds, gazing fiercely in the direction of some kids balancing on the wooden rim of a sandpit. 'Looks fun, right?' Kessie asks her. 'Before long you'll be old enough to do that. Hey, Zozo, can you say mama? Mama?'

Zora eyes her for a second. 'Dadoo,' she says, then returns her gaze to the other children. Kessie wonders for a second whether she's deliberately attempting to say 'dada', making a point that Kessie is more like a babysitting dad than a mother to her . . . then she grins at herself. It's just jabbering, still. But the child is sometimes getting very close to imitating real words. She'll be crawling soon, too; she's already shifting herself around on her play tiles.

Two mum friends chatting to each other by a swing make her think of Robin, and wonder how she's doing on the road trip. She hadn't realized quite how much she'd miss Robin being at home to share things with. It's brilliant that all her messages sound so joyful and ebullient, in a way she hasn't sounded for ages – which is no doubt all Kessie's fault for a having been such a burden. She'd like to get Robin something as a thank you and welcome home gift. An image of Berlioz, the catfish, swims into her mind, and Robin's stricken face as she found her angelfish dead the other week. Both her guppies and a tetra had died a week or two before, and she's down to only three fish now. The woman at the aquarium had told her that they'd probably just reached the end of their lifespans, but Robin still blamed herself for neglecting them. Kessie knows that taking care of the fish feels to her like a way to keep a connection with her dad alive, though she's never said as much.

After another bus ride, she rolls Zora's buggy into the nearest pet shop. The tropical fish section is a dark grotto of greens and blues, and the baby is captivated by all the glinty eyes and scales, and by the sinuous, flickering movements. Kessie wanders around for a while, admiring all the colours, shapes and comically morose facial expressions, before asking the shop assistant for advice.

It turns out most of the fish she likes the look of are more expensive than she can really afford, and either too high maintenance, or need particular pH levels, or are generally antisocial. But forty-five minutes later, she emerges with a raft of new knowledge about fish care, and a new gang: two gold angelfish to replace the silver one that died, two new guppies with delicate tiger-striped fan tails, two marmalade swordtails, one fat and one thin, with black fins like thick false eyelashes, and three little neon tetras, just because their electric blue and red slashes are irresistibly feisty. Best of all, she has a new bristlenose catfish to keep Berlioz company and to munch more of the algae, and a cave for him to call his own.

Back at home that evening, she pulls up her sleeves, installs the new cave, then releases all the new fish from their inflated plastic bags, and sprinkles in some food. Most of the new residents swarm up to the top to gobble alongside the old ones. Their arrival doesn't seem to bother the old ones too much. Berlioz's new tankmate swims down to the opposite corner, and soon hides away in the new cave, just as she'd hoped he would. He's going to need a musical name too . . . As she watches his mouth latch and shimmy, inspiration strikes: Louis Armstrong! He used his mouth not unlike a catfish to play the trumpet. Plus he has a comedy singing voice that she's pretty sure a male catfish would have if he could sing. Plus she and Robin both revere Ella, and you can tell from the way they duet that the platonic love between those two was real.

That evening, she decides to give Zora another bedtime sing-song with her uke. She finds herself improvising a long, rambling song about a mother and baby stuck in a council estate who turn into a pair of zippy tetras and swim down through the sewers until they reach the wide ocean and the light, where they find Louis Armstrong, and sing a victory ballad. Zora seems to approve. She has become so much more expressive now – biting on the wing of the toy owl that Robin gave her, and watching with bright eyes while kicking her little legs.

Kessie tries out another song, about a mother who starts growing spaghetti for hair and olives for eyes, but this doesn't get the required rating; Zora starts getting fretful. Kessie puts the uke down, picks her up, and swoops her high and low to make her giggle. As she lifts her again, she glimpses something at the front of her mouth: the gleam of a new pearly tooth.

Chapter 27

Robin

Sleep refuses itself again on the night flight home to London. Robin tries and fails to focus on her book, on any of the films, the sitcoms . . . Too many sensations and images are tussling for attention in her brain. And how to tell Kessie? What to tell Kessie?

She plods towards the barriers at Heathrow, dragging her case, face to the ground, intent on getting to the Tube and not turning right back round again to get on the next flight back to California – and then a high-pitched voice catches her attention.

'There she is!' Kessie's smiling face – and she's holding Zora up above the crowd . . . Robin abandons her case and runs over to them. The soft, warm weight of this little human again! That smile . . . and with a tooth in it! Zora seems at least a kilo heavier, and paws happily at her cheek. All this change in ten days?

'Look, it's Mama Roro!' Kessie says.

'Woahooowo,' Zora says, then grins.

'Whaaat? Did she just try to say Roro?!'

'I reckon so,' Kessie says. 'I'm sure she said *fisss* the other day for the fish, didn't you? I mean, she's still babbling, but she'll be talking before long. And she's trying her hardest to move around and grab things now. Especially breakable things.' She goes over to retrieve Robin's abandoned case and wheels it back. 'No contraband in here, I take it.'

'Nothing to declare.' Robin hugs Kessie with one arm, keeping Zora snug in the crook of the other. 'Soo sweet of you to come all the way here! You look great. Clearly doing fine without me.'

Kessie grins. 'We survived. Glad you're back though, aren't we?'

The baby's face is glowing with a daffodil smile. 'Look at her,' Robin sighs. 'I can't believe a tooth sprouted and I missed it.'

The low ceiling of the Tube, its screechy clatter, and the sheer volume of people crammed into such a narrow carriage, drag Robin's mood down again. She thinks of all that Californian space, light, freedom, the way her nerve endings sparked, her mind expanded, her desire flared. Darsha's eyes, Darsha's fingers, Darsha's hips.

'Mama!'

'Heyyy chickadee!' She focuses on Zora, starts bouncing her on her knee. This kid's smile somehow makes complications meaningless. She takes one of the silken hands in hers and admires the smooth, plump fingers with their miniature nails . . . the nails have got too long, though, and several are dirty. Robin can't remember Kessie ever being the one to clip them. One thumbnail is broken. A lock of her shiny hair is reaching down over one eye – does it need its first trim? She pushes it back with her index finger, touches the tip of her nose to Zora's, and kisses a velveteen cheek. She is almost glad to have torn herself away for a bit, just to be able to experience the pleasure of this reconnection. But then it doesn't compare to her connection to Darsha, to her entire body switching on with a new voltage. Or does it?

'She's so happy to see you!' Kessie says. 'She's been pining.'

Robin suspects she's just being nice. 'You mean, like, crying more? She's definitely better from being ill?'

'Oh yeah – she's fine. I even managed to wash my hair this morning.' Kessie runs a palm over her curls. 'But it's really hit me how much we've been relying on you for everything.'

Robin had convinced herself that it wouldn't matter if Kessie never said that, but now that she has, a cloud seems to have lifted. 'Well, it's nice to be back,' she grins. 'It was an awesome trip . . . but . . .' She falters. Why didn't she just tell Kessie about Darsha straight away, on the phone? How to put it now? It might be easier if she and Darsha had parted with some sort of a plan – but after that night with Dylan, when they nearly had that terrible bust-up, they'd tried to stick to their agreement not to discuss the future for the rest of the trip. The present had felt too precious to let go of. Even at the airport, they'd both decided to swallow their words.

'But?' Kessie is looking at her curiously.

Robin swallows. 'Sorry, I just didn't sleep on the flight. Not really with it.'

Back at home, she is pleasantly surprised to find that the place is relatively clean and tidy. 'So I cooked us a meal. In advance,' Kessie says, airily. Robin drops her jaw. 'I know,' Kessie nods. 'A green curry, no less. It might even be edible. I mean, I didn't make the *paste*, but I did look up a recipe and go out and buy ingredients and chop veg and mix them all together.'

'Impressive!'

'I cooked broccoli for Zora too – I've been trying to give her more different kinds of finger food, and that's one of her favourites. At least, she likes sucking it and chucking it across the room.' Kessie puts on some rice, while Robin feeds and changes the baby.

Once she's got her in a fresh outfit, Robin cradles her for a while in the armchair, and sings her 'Summertime'. She clips her into the bouncy chair, where she stretches her increasingly chubby legs. 'What next?' Robin begins singing 'My Bonnie Lies Over the Ocean' – and looks up to see Kessie, brandishing her ukulele, and joining in with an accompaniment and a harmony.

Robin claps at the end. 'Love it! I missed our duets. Have you been writing some new songs?'

'Oh, you know, messing around a bit. Oh shit, the rice . . .' Kessie runs back to take the pan off the heat.

Robin strokes Zora's hair. Being home with them both again feels like being slotted back into place. 'You're the missing link, little one,' she whispers. And yet, and yet . . .

The food smells good – lemongrass, coconut, creamy rice. Kessie has even lit a candle at the table, and puts Ella and Louis on through the speaker. Robin plops Zora in her high chair, lays out cutlery, then gets the gin out of the cupboard and waves it in the air. 'G & T?'

They clink glasses over steaming plates. 'Something's changed,' Kessie says. 'Can you spot what it is?'

Robin searches her face for a clue, then looks around. Zora is thumping a broccoli floret on her tray like percussion. Nothing new on the walls . . . She spots a flash of gold, gets up, and bounds over to the tank to have a closer look. 'Whaaat? New angelfish! So beautiful – and look at the swordtails! I'd been thinking I might get those again . . .'

'I've been calling them Joan of Arc and Boadicea,' Kessie says.

'I mean, that is perfect. And more tetras! Guppies . . . oh my goodness, is that a new buddy for Berlioz?'

As she turns to look at Kessie, she has the weirdest sensation of her dad's face looking back at her, back in their living room decades ago, when he whisked a blanket off a box to reveal her first tank.

'I've already started calling him Louis Armstrong,' Kessie says.

'Genius! I always thought composer Berlioz would have loved jazz if he'd lived long enough to hear it. This is such a lovely gift, Kess – give me a hug.'

Back at the table, Robin takes a mouthful of the curry. The vegetables are flaccid and soggy, save for the carrots, which are still crunchy, and the taste of fish sauce is overwhelming. 'Mm,' she says.

Kessie takes a mouthful and grimaces. 'Ew!' She spits it out. 'Really should have tasted it first! Stop, don't eat any more – I can make toast. Or wash off the sauce . . .'

'Oh, it's fine! It's – distinctive.' Robin valiantly inserts another mouthful.

'Honestly, don't be a masochist!' Kessie swipes her plate away. 'Listen, I was hoping we'd get to eat first, but I wanted to ask you something.'

Robin looks up, still chewing with difficulty. Kessie's jaws are clenched. *Here goes*, she thinks: she has found a job and a place to live independently with Zora. Maybe she's even moving out of London . . .

'I've been thinking about the allomother thing,' Kessie says. 'And I started looking up the law on adoption.'

Robin swallows. Is she contemplating . . . giving Zora away?

'We've basically been co-parenting so far,' Kessie continues, 'and obviously you were doing a lot more than I was, at first, and still until you went away – and being apart made me think so much about all you've done for us, as a family, and how much you and Zora love each other . . . I mean, 'allomother' doesn't seem like enough to reflect what you are to us. And since you left . . . it has been good to find out that I *can* manage without you, if I need to, but I also realized I don't really want to. I mean, I must have been horrible to live with at first, but now that I'm back to something like my normal self, and I can just about keep my shit together and tidy up after myself and keep the baby fed – and it's so nice to be living together again! And I know how much you've longed for a baby, and that you haven't wanted to go solo, and so . . . if you *did* want to be a proper family, to keep doing this together – which I know is a big if – then I'd love to be able to give you that. But you might just want us to make a plan to move out now that I'm better and just be too polite to say so yet. Which is also totally fine . . .'

'No!' Robin manages. 'Wait . . . I'm just . . . processing.' The air dazzles; she feels oddly faint, and takes a large swig of gin. 'Kess, I'm – that's a beautiful offer. Do you really *mean* that you're inviting me to – *adopt* Zora, like, as a second . . . mother? Is that even possible?'

Kessie scrunches her face up. 'Well . . . I've been researching it a bit, and I'm still not entirely sure about how the legal side would work to be honest . . . at first I felt like, well, *obviously* it should be possible, but . . .'

'I mean, if it is, I would *love* to be Zora's co-mother!' Robin says. 'I *adore* this kid. I've been trying not to let myself think . . . I've been trying to suppress how I feel. It seemed almost wrong – I mean, even the word allomother seemed presumptuous. But you're totally right that I do *feel* like – like she's mine too, in a way, and . . . ' It's as if a stopper has been released and everything is fizzing over. 'I felt so *guilty* being away from her, and from you, but to tell you the truth, part of the reason I went, besides really needing a break, and some sunshine, and wanting to see Darsha, was that – I thought *you'd* be wanting to find your own place again soon, and that I'd have to get used to life without you both. And that I had to somehow get it into my head that Zora wasn't mine at all.'

Kessie reaches over to hold Robin's hands across the table. 'I hope I haven't just offered you a red herring though. I haven't actually found any legal cases that say it's possible. I mean, a step-parent can apply to adopt their partner's child if they're married. And lesbian couples can become co-parents. But I haven't come across any with platonic parents – except one with a man and a woman where they'd planned it all out in advance of conception and had written legal agreements in place. I haven't researched it for that long, though.'

Robin's brain is on a hamster wheel now. The hamster morphs into Darsha spinning around – that first night up in the mountains, her supple lips, her delicate fingers, and her laugh, always so unexpectedly deep when it erupts from her small frame.

'But it would seem super unfair if friends were excluded as a category, right?' Kessie continues. 'Just because we don't happen to be fucking each other. I mean, women are increasingly having children on their own with donors, like I nearly did, no sex involved. So why shouldn't we be able to team up so that the kid has two loving parents?'

'Definitely!' Robin says. She'd never even thought of this before, but it makes total sense. It's been ages since she's heard Kessie being so passionate about anything, and she feels herself getting fired up to match. 'You're so right,' she reiterates. 'What's sex between parents got to do with the needs of their kids? I mean, most couples who do it to make a baby seem to stop doing it for years once the kid arrives anyway.' She imagines Darsha's scorn if she'd heard her say that. *Exactly my point!* she'd say. *Why sacrifice your sexual pleasure for the rest of your life, to care for a needy kid day in, day out, when you don't have to?*

Ironically enough, just a couple of weeks ago, she might have felt pretty open to enduring a long stretch of no sex in order to focus on Zora. Towards the end of her relationship with Max, she had basically got used to having mediocre sex occasionally, and the early days of Zora seemed to satisfy all her available energy for intimacy. But Darsha has transformed that now. She's opened up a whole new erotic world – a realm of sex with women, tender sex, sex that's wholly pleasurable, that fires up every nerve ending. And even when Robin was head over heels for Max in the early days, or thought she was, sex with him had never felt like it did with Darsha. The sherbet was missing . . .

Kessie's laughing. She takes a large gulp of G & T, then shakes her head. 'I mean, yeah: even if The Facilitator were still around, and even if he'd turned out to be a great dad, and I still fancied him, I cannot *imagine* wanting to have sex with him, or anyone else – yet. I'm still barely healed down there! It's not like I don't want to have great sex again in the future, obviously. It's just that the whole sex thing seems irrelevant to how good a mother I might be able to be. Which isn't very good, so far, but still . . .'

'Oh stop,' Robin says. 'You're a brilliant mum. You just had a hard time for a while. Your libido will come back, and when it does, you'll find someone much better than The Facilitator.' She pictures Darsha's naked body splayed on the bed like an artful starfish. The feeling of Darsha flipping her over, and kissing her eyelids, ever so lightly . . . Could she somehow manage to be a co-parent here with Kessie, and fly over to California for long-distance trysts with Darsha? Would that be enough – for either of them? Is it a shocking act of environmental harm to even contemplate so many long-distance flights? She tries to refocus. 'So . . . what is the legal situation for where you have two sets of couples, one lesbian, one gay, who decide to have a kid together? I mean, presumably *they* all get the right to be parents?'

'Actually no,' Kessie says. 'In the UK, anyway, only two parents can be on the birth certificate. Do you remember Paolo's friend Jago and his partner Rav? They're in the process of planning a four-way arrangement with a lesbian couple, so I got Jago's number from Paolo and gave him a bell to find out a bit more. He told me the biological parents usually get parental responsibility – so they're all drawing up an agreement in advance, to mention the other two parents, but if any dispute over it came up, it wouldn't be legally binding. The court would take it into account but that's it. Only few American states accept more than two legal parents on a birth certificate.'

'Wow. And Jago's cool with that?'

'Well, they're using his sperm, so he's all right – his name's going to go on the certificate. But it could be really unfair. Like, imagine a situation where you've got a gay couple and a lesbian couple who've decided to be co-parents, way before conception, and then one of the dads or mums who's *not* on the birth certificate turns out to be the one who *actually* spends all their time doing the childcare. And bonds most with the kid. That arrangement might go on for years, until the kid starts school. And then, if that couple breaks up? That parent who's put the time in has *no* parental rights. In the eyes of the law they're no better than a babysitter. The legal parents could take the kid off to another country if they wanted.'

'That is harsh. I'd have thought that four-parent scenario should make our two-platonic-mums scenario seem, like, conservative in comparison.'

'Yup.'

'Also, so many marriages break up these days,' Robin continues. 'Forty per cent or something, isn't it? And *those* parents are allowed to carry on co-parenting. Even if it's been a massively antagonistic relationship post break-up, causing the child all kinds of stress. Which is much more unlikely to happen between friends, right?'

'Exactly! Long-term friendships are way more stable. I mean, look at you and me. Despite everything I've put you through since Zora was born, there's nobody who feels more like family. Even Dad, these days. Auntie Elmi, obviously, but I haven't seen her in so long . . .'

Robin bites her lip. 'Me too.' She thinks of her mum, up in her shepherd's hut, happier with animals than humans. Of her advice when she visited. 'Well, listen – even if the law prevents it, I'm really happy that you feel like we're a family too.' But her heart is starting to race again at the thought of having to tell Darsha about this turn of events. If adopting Zora were a possibility, that would be the nail in the coffin for her seedling idea of moving out to California. Might Darsha consider moving back to London? But no, she adores her life there. Why wouldn't she? And she is definitive about not wanting children – while Robin, in a way, already has one.

She thinks of her lone frozen egg. Probably too weak to grow into a child even if she were to introduce it to the most premium-luxe sperm available. She recalls the searing pain of those post-extraction days. The wasteland of her womb. She imagines Zora and Kessie living away from her, possibly leaving London – weeks, months, even years passing when she might barely see them, when work might consume her again, and meanwhile Zora would grow a full set of teeth, shoot up, grow hair long enough to plait, sprout her first pimple. She can't miss all that.

'Anyway. We need to eat. How about scrambled eggs?' Kessie asks. 'That's one thing I do know how to cook.'

'Ideal,' Robin says. 'Hey, and I'm going to open that bottle of champagne that's been sitting in the cupboard for ages! Why not, right? We can stick an ice cube in. Eggs, toast, bubbles.' She gets up to find the bottle in the high cupboard.

She rinses two flutes and pours the drinks, then pauses to watch Kessie's lovely, familiar face whisking the eggs – her bouncy hair, her wide, dark eyes, the blob of mascara, the little mole on one side of her chin like a beauty spot that had slipped out of its proper place . . . God, she loves this woman. She loves their baby. How to compare that to what she feels for Darsha? They're different species of love.

*

By the following week, Robin has struggled through her jet-lagged return to work, having resolved to devote the minimum time and emotional energy to her job that are required to avoid being sacked, Zora has learned to crawl – making her way across the floor one evening from Robin to Kessie and back again – and they've set up a meeting with a solicitor who's an expert on fertility, families, and gay couples.

In her spare fragments of time, Robin tries to catch up with Kessie's research and to figure out what other models and examples of family are out there. She's trawled websites on adoption and same sex relationships, and digested legal case summaries. She's found a couple of relevant ebooks in the university library, one of which explores exactly the scenario they'd been talking about, when two gay couples want to make a family, but only two of them get to be legal parents, and also delves into other kinship structures.

One evening, after Zora's gone to sleep, she settles down to read it while Kessie does yoga to a chanting soundtrack across the living room. Kessie doesn't like to be interrupted while she's practising, but Robin comes across one section that she can't resist sharing. 'Kess, you know I've been reading about matrilineal societies,' she says, as Kessie lifts her arms to the ceiling.

'Mm hmm?'

'Well, there's this fascinating group called the Mosuo, who live in the mountains in China, and they've got this kinship system that's not based on marriage at all. Their households are multi-generational, and all headed up by women, and they're run on an alloparenting model – so, when one of the women in the household has a kid, all the members share childcare responsibilities. They keep their sex lives totally separate from parenting. Super interesting, right? Just like we were talking about before. So, sex for them is voluntary and nocturnal, while family life is obligatory and diurnal. Some of it sounds a bit weird. Like, they have this practice called *tisese* where, once a girl reaches puberty, they put on an initiation ceremony that ends in her getting a "flower chamber" where she can choose to receive night visits from men.'

'Woah,' Kessie says, swaying in tree pose. 'That part sounds a bit dodgy. I mean, does an early teen girl really have the power to say *no* to some hairy, muscular man if he comes knocking at her flower chamber window?'

'Hm. The author suggests the modern version is much more consensual than it used to be. But I mean, yeah, you're right: either sex is consensual or it's not.'

'Kessie grabs one foot behind her, raises the opposite arm and leans forward into a ballerina pose. 'Well, the matrilineal alloparenting part does sound super progressive – even though it's ancient. Not sure a court of law here will be so interested though.'

'No,' Robin agrees. 'But it's good to know about alternative ways of doing family that are already out there, right? Like, we just assume that marriage, especially heterosexual marriage, is "normal", but it is possible for women to have a lot more equality and autonomy in other ways. Oh and another thing that seems good about the Mosuo approach is that individual women don't get individually pressured to reproduce. They focus on each *generation,* collectively, and aim to produce enough children, with a good gender mix, to sustain the society.'

'That does sound a lot fairer,' Kessie muses, tilting sideways into triangle pose.

'Oh and another thing about them,' Robin continues: 'their language doesn't distinguish between a mother and a maternal aunt. They use the word *emi* for both.'

'Oh! Well, that's just like a lot of African cultures,' Kessie says, straightening up, jumping back to a plank, then moving into a downward dog. 'Like what Auntie Elmi is to me.' She descends into child's pose, then leans her head to one side. 'Listen, Robs, once you've got back into your master's and written this up into your dissertation and got a first, you should turn it into a book. I mean, not an academic book, but a bestselling non-fiction book that changes the way our whole society thinks about families and childcare and equality.'

'Ambitious!' Robin grins. 'Meanwhile, you and I could set a whole new movement in motion for platonic co-mothering. I guess I could write about that too. That would be rad.' She wonders what it could be like if they were living in a matrilineal network now – maybe as part of a commune . . . a 'mommune', even . . . But that only causes her mind to revolve back to Darsha's commune, and to picture Vi pressing her down on the sofa, performatively kissing her.

Chapter 28

Kessie

The day of the lawyer meeting, Zora is in a recalcitrant mood, seemingly determined to make them late. Kessie is finally lacing up her second shoe in the hallway, and going through the mental checklist of baby stuff, when a smell announces itself. She sniffs, then kicks both shoes off again. 'Come *on* – I only changed you half an hour ago. Robs, we have a shituation.' The baby's small face wrinkles up at the corners, as if it were a huge joke to have evacuated her bowels just when they are on the brink of exiting the building on time. Kessie tugs at two fistfuls of her own hair.

Robin pats her on the back. 'Hey, shit happens! I'll change her.' She scoops Zora up, holds her at arm's length, and makes a funny face at her.

As she waits, Kessie looks through her notes, trying to anticipate what they might be asked. When Robin carries Zora back down a few minutes later, all fresh and clean, the baby promptly pukes half of her recent milk feed down the front of her white shirt, leaving a gloopy mass over one breast, like a giant bird shit. '*Fuck,*' Robin breathes. 'Sorry kiddo, don't listen to me

– swearing is bad, okay?' She squints at Kessie. 'Can you take her? I'll email and say we might be a bit late.'

Kessie puts Zora back in the buggy, and she immediately starts to fret. 'What is it now? Oh don't tell me you're hungry already; it's not time yet. And no, I'm not picking you up again. You need to be ready to go. Your whole future with two parents is at stake here, kiddo.' Zora dribbles and blows through her lips like a horse.

A few minutes later, Robin still hasn't returned, so Kessie jogs through to the bedroom. Robin is standing in front of the mirror in her bra, holding up three different tops. 'Which one?'

'Oh, the rust, definitely,' Kessie says. 'Colour's great. It says you're serious but subtle. And it's flattering. Whack it on and let's go.' She suddenly recalls her hesitation about which outfit to wear for that first date with The Facilitator. How many other women might he have implanted and ghosted by now? Has he been using a different name? She couldn't resist downloading a couple of dating apps the other day, just to see if she could spot him, but she couldn't, and after losing an hour or so swiping, she'd deleted them.

Once the bus gets moving, Zora seems content, finally, gazing out of the window, and Robin is checking her emails, so Kessie pulls out her notebook to return to some lyrics she'd started work on . . . And then her phone rings. *Dad*. He hasn't called for ages. Why now?

She flicks the switch to silent, and stares at his name on the screen for a few seconds, imagining him on the other end, walking out of his church, perhaps, surrounded by members of the congregation pestering him for attention. *Dad*. Such a cosy, comforting word. Where did their intimacy go? She needs to tell him about the adoption plan, but it will probably go down with a thud. *You know I'm open minded as pastors go, but . . .*

'Who is it?'

Kessie shows her the screen. The call ends, but he promptly rings back.

'Aren't you going to pick up?' Robin asks.

She hesitates. He has still only met his granddaughter once, when he came up with Cara for that awful visit. She lets the phone ring on again, silently, then stop again. It rings a third time. Maybe something's wrong? She better had pick up. 'Hi, Dad. Everything okay?'

'Oh hullo, love! All well here – I was just calling to see how you're getting on.'

'Oh. That's nice. I'm just on my way to . . . baby massage.'

Robin gives her a sidelong glance.

Her dad laughs. 'Ah, the things on offer for new mums these days.' He tells her he'd love to visit again but he's really busy with the congregation at the moment – and that Cara would like her to clear the rest of her things out of the attic in the next couple of weeks, so if she wants anything from up there, she needs to request it by then.

Seriously? She breathes in, then out. She needs to keep her voice under control. 'Right. Well, please just ask Cara – tell her – not to throw away anything of mine without checking first, okay? Including baby things that Mum might have saved. I'm sure she kept some picture books. And I don't want her to throw any Nepalese treasures she might have stored up there. Look, I'll pick anything like that up next time I'm able to come – can you just put them in a box? Or you could post to me if she's really desperate to get everything out of the house immediately. Anyway, I've got to go now, sorry.'

She hangs up and looks at Robin, who raises questioning eyebrows. 'So Cara *urgently* wants to chuck all my stuff out so that she can have more loft space to store her designer crap and expunge all traces of Mum and me. Dad just doesn't get it. I know I should probably be more like your mum and embrace giving it all up, but I just . . .'

'Sorry. Well, my mum's taken it to the other extreme,' Robin says. 'I'm not sure how healthy that is either. Though she seems to be doing pretty well so far to be honest . . . So, you reckoned your dad wouldn't want to know what we're *actually* on our way to?'

Kessie flushes. 'Have you told your mum yet?'

Robin pouts. 'No . . . I mean, she's basically off-grid – I could write a letter, but not sure I should get her hopes up . . . Not that she's necessarily been waiting to be a granny with bated breath. She's more interested in sheep these days than babies. But if this meeting goes well, maybe I'll write?'

'Okay. I'd tell dad, too. You know, I'd love to take Zora to visit your mum when she's a bit older,' Kessie says. 'Introduce her to that amazing mountain landscape, and a new language. I want to meet Chou-fleur and Brigitte Baardot too. I *love* how eccentric she is.'

'She's definitely different.'

The lawyer has a geometric bob, like Anna Wintour's but with an ultra-short fringe. Friendly but brusque, she asks them each to explain why they want Robin to adopt Zora, starting with

Kessie. She takes notes with a sleek navy and gold fountain pen in a blue notebook, chipping in with occasional requests for dates and details.

After summarizing, Kessie tells her about her legal research so far, and how she's found cases that are similar but maybe not similar enough. 'It's been really interesting – I've been studying anthropology alongside my work,' Robin chips in, 'and reading a lot about matrilineal family structures and allomothering, and it seems like society is moving—'

The lawyer interrupts: 'Intruiging though that may be, we're bound by the British legal system here I'm afraid. Even legal cases from other jurisdictions are very rarely deemed relevant.' Her voice is acidic, but her eyes are kind.

When they've both finished, the fountain pen is laid neatly down in the middle of the notebook, and the lawyer's hands clasp on the desk while her eyes study each of them in turn. 'Now, I need to ask you a question,' she says. 'As an alternative to adoption, have you considered entering into a parental responsibility agreement?'

Kessie looks at Robin, then back at the lawyer.

'This would give Robin the right to have a say in important decisions affecting Zora's upbringing, like medical treatment and education, reflecting her role in your ongoing family life,' the lawyer continues. 'It would legalize the arrangement you already have in place – but without going so far as adoption.' Her gaze is focused on Kessie now.

'So . . . what's the main difference?'

'Well, parental responsibility wouldn't make Robin liable for maintenance payments. And it wouldn't give her automatic rights to see Zora if you should separate or move apart. It also wouldn't terminate the legal relationship between that child and their other biological parent . . .'

Fury rattles into Kessie's throat. 'Wait, but I don't even know who An— who the biological father really *was*! He abandoned Zora and me the day before the first scan – he left no trace. He was a total con artist.'

'Also,' Robin adds, 'if it makes any difference, I would actually *like* Zora to be part of my inheritance . . .' She clears her throat. 'And I'm happy to carry on contributing to maintenance.'

'She's already been subsidizing us a *lot*,' Kessie adds. 'I've only just been able to get back into work – some clarinet teaching in the evenings – but it's not nearly enough to pay the bills. Robin's already in my will as Zora's guardian if anything were to happen to me.'

'I see.' The lawyer takes another note, then looks from one to the other of them. 'Well, let me put this into context. The law is a slow beast, and we're very reliant on precedent. I'm presuming from all you've told me that your relationship with each other is platonic – but do either of you identify as LGBTQ?'

'No,' Kessie says.

'Not – publicly,' Robin adds, and Kessie shoots her a look. Of course, Robin's always said that she feels like there's a wider spectrum of sexuality than most people admit to, and Kessie knows she's kissed a couple of girls in the past – but that was a long time ago now, university age, way before Max came on the scene. And this is the first time she's heard Robin all but come out to anyone else. It seems odd that she's chosen to do it now. But then, it was a response to a direct question. Robin flushes.

'Well, as you probably know,' the lawyer says, evidently deciding not to put Robin on the spot by asking her to expand further, 'members of the LGBTQ+ community have long faced significant challenges when it comes to family and reproductive rights, and those challenges continue. Many of us came of age under Section 28, which made it illegal to "promote homosexuality". Of course that's gone now, but discrimination continues in terms of access to IVF, for instance. A lesbian couple has to provide proof of *twelve* conception attempts to be deemed eligible for NHS treatment – in other words, twelve costly rounds of artificial insemination – and a heterosexual couple doesn't. Two lesbian women weren't even allowed to adopt until 2005. Now, in terms of family law, developments in gay marriage have made a real difference, and that's because the law still attaches significance to marriage as evidence of an enduring family relationship. Which brings me to my advice to you now: if you are still set on adoption, I would consider getting married.'

'WHAT?' they both chorus, then look at each other, and crack up.

A few moments later, Kessie notices that the lawyer's expression, after a glimmer of a smile, has reverted to a serious gaze. She clears her throat and sits straight, trying to stop laughing and refocus. 'I mean . . . marriage? That's just . . .' another giggle escapes, 'crazy!' She looks at Robin. 'I mean, I love you very much, hon, but . . .'

'Likewise!' Robin smiles. 'Just – not in that way.'

'Well, here's the issue,' the lawyer continues. 'Your case is *akin* to a step-parent adoption; but the difficulty is that currently you're neither married nor in a conjugal relationship. Which isn't an absolute barrier, but the requirement for adoption by a second parent is to prove an *enduring family relationship,* and marriage is a legally established way of doing that. A long-standing conjugal relationship is usually the only alternative option, but even then, couples need to prove that they've been in such a relationship for at least two years . . .'

'But I mean,' Kessie says, 'if we're talking *enduring,* Robin and I have been best friends for nearly thirty years! Much longer than most conjugal couples.'

'And 40 per cent of marriages end in divorce, right?' Robin adds.

The lawyer blinks. 'I'm not talking about what's morally right, or fair, or even logical, here – I'm explaining the way the law works.'

Robin shakes her head. 'But how can it be okay for the law to still require that for two people to prove they're good parents they need to be having *sex*? I mean, I know you're just explaining how the system works, which is obviously really helpful, but from what I've read about family law, most decisions seem to pivot around the idea of the child's best interests – and sex seems irrelevant to that, and also just really tied up with outdated misogynistic kinship traditions of male ownership of women, so I just find it hard to believe . . .'

The lawyer tightens her lips, and Kessie wants to tell Robin to give it a rest with the anthropology if they want to keep her on their side. 'I completely get what you're saying,' she jumps in, 'but surely at some point the law does have to take a leap forward, right? For parenting arrangements. Just like it did with gay marriage.'

'True . . .' The lawyer tips her head to one side. 'But that kind of shift usually needs to happen through the parliamentary process.

Sometimes case law *can* bring about profound change. Particularly since the European Convention of Human Rights. But that usually happens long after a social practice is well-established. To be frank, it's very rare that we have couples coming to us as friends of the same sex who have never had a conjugal relationship but who want to co-parent. There's no legal precedent that I know of—'

'Have you really *never* had this come up before?' Robin asks.

'Not personally. But I can look into it further for you if you'd like me to.'

Kessie looks at Robin again, clicking her fingernails together, then back at the lawyer. 'Are platonic marriages even *allowed*? I guess there's nothing explicitly in the normal vows . . . but, I mean, couldn't a hypothetical platonic marriage be – annulled for non-consummation?'

The lawyer smiles. 'Same sex marriages can't be annulled for that reason anyway,' she explains. 'But putting conjugality aside for a moment: the fact that you're living together would *help*. As would Robin's involvement from pregnancy onwards – and your long-term relationship as friends, I expect. But what I need to underline here is that none of that is going to *guarantee* anything. On the adoption order application form, you would have to enter the relationship you have with the baby. And if you remain unmarried, then Robin would need to tick the *no relationship* box.'

They both nod, silently, taking this in.

'Now, could you tell me a bit more about the biological father?' the lawyer asks Kessie. 'Do you have the means of getting in touch with him?'

Kessie rolls her eyes. 'I have no idea. He left a note telling me not to try to find him – that I wouldn't succeed, and I did try, but he was right. He clearly had zero interest in having a baby. Especially not a girl.'

'I see. I'm very sorry to hear that. Do you still have that note?'

Kessie winces. 'I burnt it the night I found it.' She thinks of those ash fairies floating away into the dusk. 'So . . . would I . . . *have* to tell the court about him?' She hadn't fully anticipated the extent to which this process could start turning up nasties under rocks.

'You would have to address the issue of his identity, yes. But given what you've said, the court shouldn't expect him to be contacted.'

'So . . . what would we have to do next?' Robin asks. 'Assuming we *don't* get married!'

'Well, another consideration for the court will be what happens if your relationship disintegrates. If Robin *were* to be granted the right to adopt Zora, she would then be Zora's legal parent forever, and would have equal rights of access. You'd have to work that out between you.'

Kessie bites her cheeks. The truth is, she hadn't allowed herself to contemplate that scenario until now. Nobody but Robin could have put up with her this past year – and it's awful to contemplate the bitter, horrid things she said to Robin when she was in the depths of postnatal depression – but Robin stuck by her. Nobody else loves Zora the way Robin does, and vice versa, for sure. And yet . . . what if Robin were to meet a new guy, who wanted to start a family with her? What if, a few months down the line, Robin were to get pregnant? Would she ever want to move on and start to make demands about Zora? Ask for custody, even? Surely she never would! It's horrible even contemplating the prospect. But what if *she*, Kessie, were to meet someone else? Someone who thought the whole Robin arrangement was just . . . weird?

They both agree to go away and think about it.

On the bus home, they sit without talking for a while. Kessie gazes at Zora in the buggy. The baby miraculously stayed asleep throughout the meeting, oblivious to this momentous conversation about her future. Kessie feels suddenly exhausted – dulled, as if her brain has just been scrubbed at like a pen-stained whiteboard. The length and scale and expense and emotional labour of this legal process have been brought into relief, now, in a way that she should probably have anticipated. Was this whole adoption idea a massive mistake? Should she just tell Robin that she'd actually prefer to go down that parental responsibility route, if anything? It would be a lot simpler . . . But then, for Zora's sake, and her own, she *does* want a sense of permanency, a sense of a proper family.

The bus driver brakes sharply, and all the passengers jerk forwards, then back.

'Kess, you don't have to do this, you know,' Robin blurts, turning round to face her. 'I mean, it's incredibly lovely and generous of you to have thought of it, but it sounds like it might all turn out to be a mega load of stress for nothing. And you might have changed your mind after today anyway – I'd understand if you have.'

A tremor in Robin's voice peels Kessie's heart back open. 'Well, look, I'm not thrilled about the prospect of a legal wrangle. And I definitely can't afford to contribute, so that's an issue. But I do still see you as Zora's co-parent – I'd still love for us to be a real family. It does all look trickier than I'd thought though. How about you – have you changed your mind?'

Robin shakes her head.

Kessie smiles. 'Also, I do feel like this is important in *principle*, you know? For others. Especially after what she was telling us about the history of discrimination against other so-called "alternative" families. Not a single one of the *dads* I know, who are husbands, have done anything *like* as much as you've done for Zora. And for me.' Saying this out loud reminds her how certain she is about this fact.

'Well, I didn't do it expecting this . . .'

'I know *that!*' Kessie laughs. 'The look on your face when I asked you! I mean, you're good at a lot of things, but there was a reason you didn't get Ophelia in the school play.'

'Ha! Thanks for reminding me, Horatio. In fact . . . it's not acting exactly but . . .' Robin scrunches her face up, then looks worriedly at Kessie, like she's about to confess something. Something terrible, even. Each of her cheeks has developed a dark pink spot. 'Kess – I've got to tell you something. I should have told you earlier.'

Kessie's stomach drops, but she can't think what it could be. She wants to get back with Max? She's decided to try a donor after all?

Robin looks down at her hands, which she's clenched hard in her lap, nails digging into the gulleys between her finger bones, then back up at her. 'So, here goes. When I was in California, I kind of . . . got together with Darsha. Sexually. Romantically, even.'

Kessie frowns, taking these words in, repeating them in her

317

head. Robin and *Darsha*? It doesn't make sense. They're just mates. Robin's not gay . . . Though . . . maybe she didn't just kiss those two girls just in the Katie Perry sense – experimenting for the hell of it. And back there, in the room, that thing she said about not being gay publicly. 'But . . . fuck, Robs, why didn't you tell me before? I mean . . . you've never . . . wait . . . so . . . are you a *lesbian* now, then? Or . . .'

'Bi, I think. Yeah,' Robin says softly. 'Probably always have been. It's just that I never followed through much, or really admitted it to myself. I guess I'm only just coming to terms . . .'

'Fuck, Robin!' Kessie interrupts. 'I mean, obviously I'm glad you feel like you can come out finally if it's something you've had to bottle up or suppress for whatever reason – but *now*? With Darsha? And not telling me before today – before the fucking *legal* meeting we just had! Don't you think it's *relevant* to our ongoing conversation about our future as a family? Including our *relationship*? And after I asked you to be Zora's *mother* . . . I mean, you literally just told the lawyer that I was your best friend, like your family, that we were more secure than any romantic couple – that we could trust each other – and you kept *that* from me?'

'I know, Kess. I'm so sorry . . .' Her voice is wavering – it's infuriating.

'I mean, for fuck's sake, did you go out to America *planning* . . . ?' Tears are careering down Kessie's cheeks now. She just can't seem to stop them these days.

'Of course not. Kess, I promise I was as surprised as you when it happened and I still don't really know what to make of it or what it means . . . But you're totally right, it was wrong of me not to tell you before, and I wanted to – I kept almost telling you, and then I didn't know what . . .'

Kessie presses her head hard against the window, feeling the engine's vibration running through her brain.

'I didn't want to let you down . . .' Robin's saying. 'I felt like I had this sexual revelation in California, I mean, I enjoyed it in an entirely new way, and that was so unexpected, a bolt from the blue, and then you offered me the chance to co-parent and I was blindsided all over again . . .'

The bus passes a bakery. Kessie wants to grab all the cupcakes in the window and hurl them until they splatter like paint bombs. Is Robin expecting her to be *sympathetic* right now? She feels an urge to turn round and slap her in the face – she's never ever felt anything like that towards her in all their decades of friendship. Heart galloping, she reaches over, presses the bell on the pole, and starts to get up as the bus pulls into a stop. 'Let me through, please.'

'Wait, where are you going?' Robin asks, moving her legs to let her out of the seat. 'Kess . . .'

'Stay on the bus. I need some air. On my own. With *my* baby.' Kessie releases the buggy brake and rolls it off onto the pavement, prompting Zora to wake up, stare around her, then start to cry. She strides off down the road, not turning to see Robin's face at the bus window as it moves off.

After a few minutes, she turns off the main road into a random side street. Allows the sobs to shudder out of her. Her phone vibrates in her pocket. She ignores it. Another pulse: a new message. *Whatever.* She strides on, along several streets, barely able to see where she's going, and then notices that Zora is caterwauling.

She stops walking and leans down to stroke her little head. 'Shh, sweetie,' she chokes, but the baby seems too immersed in her own emotional thunderstorm to hear. 'I feel like that too.' Looking around for a bench, she sees a playground just up the road. 'Let's go sit in the park and give you a feed, shall we?'

There's nobody else around. Kessie sits on an empty graffitied bench by the swing, prepares a bottle, takes Zora out of the buggy. The baby's body begins to relax as she glugs the liquid. Kessie concentrates on the reassuring weight and scent of her. After a few minutes, she supposes she might as well read the text message.

> My love, I'm so incredibly sorry for landing that on you today. After the meeting, too. I'm such a fool. Zora means the world to me, and you do too. I still love the idea of being her co-mama with you. I'd understand if you've changed your mind now. But I'll end things with Darsha today if that's what you want me to do.

Kessie puts the phone down. The *point*, she thinks, isn't the relationship with Darsha, whatever point that has got to – and she'd thought Darsha was in an open relationship anyway. The point is the deception. Isn't it?

Another message.

> Kess, I promise I'll never keep anything like that from you again. I feel awful that you must be feeling like I've lied to you. I truly didn't mean to, but I realize now that the omission had the same effect.

Well, yeah.

Another message.

Look, it's not a good excuse, but I've just been feeling so confused. This is all new for me. And obviously it's not exactly practical for me to be considering a 'relationship' with Darsha given that we're on different continents and I've . . . well, I feel like I've already started a family with you and Z. And I really want to continue that. If you do.

Another message.

I guess one way to think of it could be that it's a bit of a kick up the ass for us? In the sense that, like the lawyer said, we both do need to think seriously about what happens when we decide we want sexual relationships with other people in the longer term, if we are co-parents, right? I mean, you must envisage wanting sex with someone too at some point, right?

Another message.

And I mean, if we do both want to have that option, then maybe a long-distance occasional sexual relationship-type-thing would actually be easier for both of us than with someone who lived closer . . . especially if the other person definitely never wants kids of their own, like Darsha . . .?

Another message.

> The Darsha thing will probably end up being a one-off
> holiday experiment anyway, seeing as she lives on the
> other side of the world.

Another message.

> Either way, if you do still want to co-mother with me,
> I cross my heart I would never ever abandon either of
> you. Please talk to me, Kess. I feel awful. I didn't mean
> to lie to you. Love you both always.

Fuck you. Kessie puts the phone face down on the bench beside
her. She looks down at Zora's raspberry face. 'Just you and me
now.' It feels like a vindictive thing to test out saying, but empowering, too. What it if were? She can handle it now. At least, not
financially yet, but she's getting there. She managed while Robin
was away. She's out of the woods mentally.

A seagull lands a few metres away from them and stares at
her with an accusing eye. *What's your problem? I'm the one who's
been wronged here.*

On the other hand . . . does Robin have a point? Why *should*
she feel cheated on? This whole co-parenting plan was never
meant to stop either her or Robin from sleeping with anyone. Or
even from falling in love, romantically. Whatever that means. She
clearly hadn't thought that part through properly.

That tribe in China that Robin was telling her about . . . the

Mosuo, was it? *They* apparently separate family and sex with no issues. So is it just a matter of perspective?

Love. *I love you.* Loving versus being in love. Tenderness versus desire, friendship versus romance. There should be more words. Like the panoply of Inuit words for snow.

Would she ever want to sleep with Robin? The question had never occurred to her until this moment . . . Right now, she's furious with her, but trying to be objective . . . No, she's pretty certain she never would. Though if Robin can fall for someone of the same sex in her thirties, and Adrienne Rich could pivot to lesbianism in her forties, maybe anything is possible. But, unlike Robin, Kessie herself has never kissed a girl before, or wanted to. Crushing on movie stars like Claire Danes isn't the same thing. She should have seen it coming between Robin and Darsha, though. She just hadn't expected Robin to start sleeping with another woman at *this* point – though obviously she knew that Darsha had been out and proud since her early teens, and that she had pursued Robin in their gap year. She even knew that the two of them had nearly kissed that year, though at the time Robin had written it off as a thought experiment, and nearly two decades have passed since.

Could she envisage herself pivoting that way – or sliding along the spectrum, as Robin sees it? She does find Robin beautiful. Loves looking at her, watching her smile – loves spending time with her, when her head isn't messed up, doing any old mundane thing – loves the intimacy they have built through so many years of friendship, and of cohabiting. As for physical intimacy – intimacy with genitalia, even – Robin has seen her vulva, in the act of emitting a child which is arguably as intimate as it gets, and has seen her breasts daily since she's been using them to feed . . . But that hasn't exactly been reciprocated. Their relationship does involve touching – countless hugs, and plenty of cheek kisses, even hair kisses . . . But she would never want to fuck Robin. That would be too weird.

A guy with a council jacket on arrives to pick up litter around the playground, and raises his hand to her in greeting. Kessie raises hers back, lowers it again, and sighs. Robin is bloody well right, frustrating though it is to admit. If they were going to go down the co-parenting route, they *should* work out what they'd do if – when – future sexual partners materialize. Whatever the plan, they'd have to be able to trust each other. And what does it say about their mutual trust that Robin felt she couldn't even *tell* her about Darsha before today? That she kept it quiet, even when the lawyer asked?

An old man shuffles past the bench, his coat torn in one corner, one shoelace undone, probably looking for some place to sit and drink a can of cider in peace. He glances over at Kessie. She squeezes Zora a little more closely, and he moves on. Maybe it wasn't a sinister look at all. Maybe he was thinking of a family he once had, a baby. She inhales the sweet scent of Zora's silky hair. The creature gurgles gently.

She should never have persuaded Robin to go out and visit Darsha, just when she was getting better and they were establishing themselves as a family. She should have known that Darsha would still be in love with her . . . But no, Robin needed the break – deserved it. And perhaps, in hindsight, Robin's decision to sleep with a woman at some point, with Darsha, even, was inevitable.

She reads the messages again. She still believes that Robin loves her too. In a way. Maybe in many ways. Profound ways. And there's no doubt about how much she loves Zora. But does she love them both *enough*?

And anyway, can it ever be the same after this argument?

Zora thrusts out a little hand, plants it firmly on Kessie's chest, and breaks from feeding for a moment to look up at her. Is she making a point? No – she's just full. Kessie holds her up, then gets to her feet. 'Well done, little one.' She wishes she could ask Auntie Elmi's advice, but it's the middle of the night in Nepal.

'Mama Wowo?' Zora chirps.

Chapter 29

Robin

Robin wakes up disorientated – then remembers. After the awful falling-out on the bus, she'd stayed over at Benjy and Dom's to give Kessie some space at home, and had cried herself to sleep into their Egyptian cotton sheets, convinced she'd ruined everything – not only her chance at motherhood, but her best and oldest friendship. She might actually have to quit her job and move to California after all to make a clean break of it. Though the prospect of actually doing that, tempting though it is, brings home quite how much she'd wanted Kessie and Zora to be her forever family.

Benjy feeds her a delicious breakfast of Dom's homemade granola and freshly squeezed orange juice. He'd been gobsmacked last night when she told him the triple whammy of news – about sleeping with Darsha, and then about the adoption plan with Kessie, and their falling-out – but he was super sweet in looking after her, calming her down, insisting she stay. He's been very empathetic about the Kessie situation, and knows how close they are, and how attached Robin's got to Zora – but he also tells her how super excited he is about her coming out, and about what

California living could offer. 'I mean, obviously I don't want you to leave London, but if that chance came up for me, like it has for you? I'd probably leap. Anyway, I wanna see some of your holiday pics. Come on, make me jealous and let me see you two together,' he cajoles.

He oohs and aahs at what a beautiful couple she and Darsha make. Encourages her to think about the silver lining of this upset: how incredible life could be for her out there, starting afresh. He wouldn't mind the excuse to come visit her, to be taken on that exact road trip, he adds.

Robin is just finishing her coffee and starting to think that maybe he's right, that this was perhaps a natural end point to her allomother phase – when a message from Kessie comes through.

Thanks for the space. We should talk. Come home?

Home.

When she walks back through the front door, she finds Kessie playing the uke and singing – and in a far softer, more reflective mood than she'd expected. They decide to take Zora out for a walk in the buggy to talk properly.

'So, I – accept your apology,' Kessie tells her as they head up the street. Robin looks at her, startled. 'I've been thinking it over, hard,' she continues, 'and trying to get past my fury about you keeping such a big thing from me and to understand why. And I realized you're right that, even if it hadn't happened, we would have needed to plan for what either of us would do if the other one wanted to start sleeping with someone else. So maybe this was an important test that we came up against sooner than I bargained for. I'm not sure if we can work out a solution. But if we could . . . for me, it would have to involve promising to be honest and transparent with each other in future. And so . . . here's what I came up with as terms that we'd have to agree on. One: we're committed to co-living for the long term. Two: we prioritize our family over any sexual relationship we might enter into. Which might seem too onerous, for both of us – I'm not sure. Three: I'd want you to promise me that you're not planning to go to live in California, or go out there for months at a time . . . I mean, know Darsha was trying to persuade you before . . . But, well, on those provisos, if you wanted to keep up an occasional fuck-buddy relationship with Darsha, if that isn't too crass, or if you want to start sleeping with anyone else, for that matter, then – well, depending on those other things – I think I'd be okay with that.'

Robin nods, slowly, trying to take all this in. After the extreme emotions of the day before, it's hard to believe that Kessie is suddenly speaking in such a measured, rational way about this – and that her offer isn't yet off the table. She sounds so self-assured, too – like the old Kessie. Her chest churns with relief. 'Well,' she says, cautiously, 'first of all, thank you for being so understanding. And thoughtful. And forgiving. And for not cutting me out of your life. That means so much,' she says. 'Also, thanks for . . . thanks for thinking about all this so – well, clear-headedly. Everything you've said makes complete sense to me, I think. I'm still so sorry that I effectively lied to you and hurt you like that. I wish that part hadn't happened.'

'Me too. But it's okay. It's done.'

They walk on for a few minutes, not talking, while Zora coos joyfully, waving at birds. What a beauty this baby is! She's just learned to pull herself up to stand on the coffee table, and on the leg of her cot, and she's so adorably proud of herself every time she manages it, as if she'd just walked a tightrope. She's so deeply glad that Kessie doesn't hate her, and still wants her to be this perfect child's co-mother . . . But then she was just beginning to get her head around the idea of abandoning this fraught adoption journey.

Maybe Kessie's right, though: maybe they had just found a loophole in their original plan, and that was an issue they were always going to have to come up against and work through.

And maybe her time with Darsha in California was just a kind of holiday romance, after all. Long-distance relationships almost never work. And it would be a massive risk to quit her job and move out there, to see whether the relationship could flourish, to try to find a job – to begin her adult life all over again, in a way, without a realistic prospect of motherhood on the horizon. Not to mention begin across an ocean from her own mother.

As for Vi – if Darsha ended up ditching her so as to be monogamous with Robin, as she'd said she would, Robin would probably live in fear of Vi turning up in the night and slitting her throat. But would Darsha even want to do that still, after their 'Sperm-gate' row?

There's absolutely no guarantee that she would find a new job in the US, or get onto a PhD programme, or be eligible for a green card. And with the increasing threats of earthquakes and wildfires in California, and all the homelessness in San Francisco, would she really want to live there?

Most importantly, how she could live with herself after leaving

Kessie and Zora behind? Abandoning her future as a mother to this extraordinary child who she just can't get enough of looking at? Abandoning her oldest friend?

'Take more time if you want,' Kessie says. 'I'm not even sure what I think yet. But I know that I don't want to lose you. And nor does Zora.'

'You're the best,' Robin says. 'I don't deserve you.'

*

Late for work, again, Robin dashes out of the flat, attempting a kind of glide-run to prevent her coffee from splashing out of her reusable cup. She bumps into the postman and hot liquid sloshes onto her wrist and down her sleeve. Apologizing profusely, she steps aside to let him pass, but he tells her to hold on a sec, then hands her a letter in a narrow envelope. She licks coffee drips off her wrist, then rips the letter open as she walks, preparing to chuck it – but it's from the local authority.

She stops. Puts the coffee down on the neighbour's front wall.

They have a date for the social worker assessment. She takes a photo of the letter and messages it to Kessie. Makes a note in the diary. Prepares to request yet another day off work. Since posting off their application, she had almost allowed herself to forget about this assessment process. Partly because she wakes up most days expecting Kessie to pull the plug after all.

She carries on, then stops in the middle of the pavement to read the letter again, checking to see if there are any more details about what they need to prepare, before registering the impatient huffs of people navigating around her. She folds it up and carries on, her new work shoes pinching her little toes.

Oh, but that Californian sunshine and sea . . . leaning out of the car window singing, running naked into the sea, it all seems like a distant dream . . . a dream she maybe could reclaim after all, take a risk, live in that moment, go with her desire? But she's made a commitment to Kessie and Zora. If only she could live two simultaneous lives.

Ploughing down along the edge of the park towards the Tube, she observes all the parents hurrying their children to school, and pictures herself doing the same with Zora a few years from now. A mother is dragging a toddler along on a scooter, telling him fiercely to stop whining, that he's making them both late. If she gets the chance to be a real mother, Robin thinks, she will try to appreciate every minute, to be kind and encouraging, to make sure that they get out of the flat on time after a proper, healthy breakfast, to play games on the walk, to relish every moment . . . She grins wryly. Every parent must start out with those intentions.

A bulky woman with a crocodile skin bag nudges her aside at a junction to get across the road faster. People are much more chilled in California. Giving up the possibility of a future with Darsha completely is hard to contemplate. So hard that she still hasn't quite told Darsha about the adoption application. She had meant to. On their video call last night, she nearly did – but it felt good to talk about easier things, especially since the tension hasn't quite faded after Sperm-gate.

Instead, they'd talked about the Adrienne Rich essays – how hard-hitting and convincing they were – and about the Chekhov short story collection they'd both failed to finish. Then, at more length, they'd talked about the trip, and about the best moments together. And then, at Darsha's suggestion, Robin had laid her phone next to her pillow, and begun to touch herself to Darsha's incantations. She put some music on so that Kessie wouldn't overhear, then closed her eyes, thought of Darsha and her skewed tooth and pointed tongue, moved her fingers in circles, and eventually came in a wave to rival the ones at Big Sur. In that moment she'd wished more than anything that she could teleport herself across the ocean, and run her wet fingertip over Darsha's lower lip, then down along the coastline of her ribs, the headland of her hip bone.

Weaving through the commuters, her thoughts keep drifting from Darsha's laugh and citrus scent back to Zora's satin skin and increasingly chubby thighs, and to laughing with Kessie at her latest facial contortions – until, finally, she reaches the office. Time to focus on her heaving email inbox, and an elaborate logistics strategy.

*

Two months later, on the day of the social worker's visit, Magda, the neighbours' cleaner, arrives to get the place spick and span. Despite the fact that everyone with small children finds themselves with a messy home – literally all their friends with small children say that their flats are perpetually chaotic and strewn with toys and laundry – the lawyer made very clear that if they wanted a good report, their flat would have to look like a show home: theoretically safe for children, yet not in any visible way actually *affected* by children.

Online forums discussing adoption processes all recommended that they act as if they were putting their property on the market: put away or hide all laundry and any extraneous items, and display at most a single toy for Zora – nothing plastic or twee; ideally something wholesome and realistic and unthreatening, like a stuffed alpaca.

They head out to the park to give Magda space to work her magic, and buy coffees on the way to the playground. Kessie slots Zora into the baby swing, where she lounges happily, grinning and cooing, kicking her soft-booted feet. 'Sing sing, sing sing!' she chirps. Her vocabulary is coming on so well now – she can say 'duck', and 'borw' for ball, as well as 'Maki' for Kessie, and 'Mawo' for Robin. Robin pushes her from the front, pulling silly faces at her each time she swings back towards her – and as Zora laughs hysterically, the stress seems to evaporate from her pores.

Kessie isn't watching them. She's leaning on the swing post and looking out across the grass. She's been quiet all morning. Robin wants to ask how she's feeling about the social worker, and whether she wishes she could cancel the whole thing, but it's not the moment.

After squawks of protest and back arching, they cajole Zora to accept being removed from the swing seat, and stroll the paths for a bit, which quickly distracts her. There are so many pretty aspects in this park – views of the church spire, the grand Victorian house; views of the ponds, and the tree-lined paths carving asymmetric routes through the sloping swathes of grass; little bridges over the waterway; a group of elegant deer. It couldn't be a nicer park to live next to with a small child. The social worker should surely take that into account, shouldn't she?

Kessie points out that it'll be Zora's nap time when the social worker is there, but that it might be better for her to be awake if she's looking for evidence of the bond between them.

'Good thought,' Robin says. 'Though if she's all cranky, might it have the opposite effect?'

'Hm. Reckon she might go down early now if we drape the muslin over the buggy?'

Robin moves to pull the muslin out – but, as if she'd understood every word, Zora waves her arms around and squawks in a tone that means *don't even think about it – pick me up immediately*. Robin leans down. 'Well hello there, wakeful one! All right, I get it.' She tickles the baby under the chin. The resulting smile is better than any medal. *Just don't go all demonic on us when we're being assessed, please?*

*

Back at the flat, Robin's jaw drops. Magda is a wonder. The place has clean lines again, and the wooden floors shine! The skirting boards are white, the coffee table is clear, the sofa throw is smoothly folded, and the kitchen sink gleams. Magda gets a big tip.

Robin sets the coffee table ready for tea with the social worker while Kessie feeds Zora. They'd normally have teabags in mugs, but this seems like an occasion to pull her grandmother's teapot and matching cups and saucers from the storage box, and open a box of loose-leaf. She arranges everything on the table along with a plate of shortbread and chocolate chip cookies, and a large bowl of grapes, apples and satsumas. Just as she's sat down on the sofa to read through her notes, the buzzer sounds.

The social worker introduces herself as Dinah – 'that's D-I-N-A-H' – Baron. She has an oddly guttural voice for her wiry frame, and is dressed in black and vivid purple with crescent moon earrings – a signal of being into 'alternative' ways of living, maybe? She isn't very smiley though.

Kessie asks if she'd like tea or coffee; but D-I-N-A-H tells them firmly that she doesn't drink either and she'll just have a glass of water. '*You* have some tea though,' she orders. Kessie obediently goes through to boil the kettle, and Dinah perches on the edge of the sofa, straight-backed. She refuses anything to eat. Robin attempts some small talk, asking how far she'd travelled today, and how long she's been doing this job. Responses are minimal. After what seems like ages, Kessie returns with the teapot.

'Now, first things first,' Dinah says briskly. 'I gather from these forms that you're not married or in a civil partnership. How long have you been a couple?'

Robin and Kessie look at each other. 'Since we were eight, in a way,' Kessie replies, sweetly. 'We met at our local junior choir.'

Robin nods, attempting an equally honeyed smile. 'Best friends ever since. We're both only children and lost a parent at a similar time – so that brought us really close.'

'I'm sorry to hear that,' Dinah says.

'Thanks. It felt familial, even then.'

'I see. So when *did* you get together as a couple?'

They both pause. 'Well,' Kessie says. 'It's a platonic relationship, so, I'm not sure we could name a date – it evolved from then, I guess.'

Dinah frowns. 'Ah. I see . . .' She reads over her notes, then looks up. 'I presume you understand that the courts favour stable, conjugal relationships between parents . . . have you drawn up an agreement about what happens when you find conjugal relationships with other people?'

An awkward pause. 'Well yes, we definitely *have* talked about it,' Kessie says. 'Robin, why don't you say a bit more on that? I'm just going to get a glass of water.' She leaves the room.

'Well,' Robin says, bracing herself. 'We've agreed that, whatever sexual relationships come up for each of us, we'll prioritize our family unit with Zora, for the long term. Including co-living. And we did actually get the chance to test that out, in a way, recently – I began a, well, a relationship with someone who lives in California . . .' She feels herself reddening. 'But she and I are definitely not planning on living together, or anything like that, obviously. And she doesn't want kids, whereas I do, and already feel like a mother to Zora. So it would just be an occasional, long-distance thing, if it continues at all.'

'*California?*' Dinah repeats. The look she's giving Robin is like, *are you kidding me?*

Robin's heart races. 'I just went there on a holiday not that long ago,' she explains. 'A short break. I'd had to put it off for ages. Things had been pretty intense – you know, Kessie suffered from postnatal depression, and I was doing a lot of the childcare for a while, and also working full-time, and . . .'

Kessie comes back into the room. 'The biological father abandoned me during my pregnancy, and Robin stepped into the role from then, really. She's been amazing. And I'm much better now.

I mean, I'm on medication still, but fine. Anyway, Robin really did need a holiday – I encouraged her to go . . .'

'I see,' Dinah says, like it's clear as mud. 'But you didn't draw up any agreement? You didn't plan for Robin to have a parental role before?'

'Well . . . no, it just, evolved that way.'

'When did you actually start cohabiting?'

'Not long after Zora was born . . .'

'I see. Are you aware that adoptive parents are normally expected to have been in a conjugal relationship *and* living together for at *least* two years?' Dinah turns an accusatory gaze on Robin, who tries to find an appropriate response.

Kessie jumps in again. 'Well, Robin was very present during my pregnancy too – she was my birth partner . . .'

'Right,' Dinah says. 'So you felt that you *owed* Robin the opportunity to become an adoptive parent? Because of your dependence on her, financial and emotional?' Robin feels sick. Could that be true? 'I presume Robin was the one to suggest the adoption?' Dinah adds, pointedly.

Kessie shakes her head and blushes a little. 'I was, actually.'

Dinah's eyebrows vanish into her fringe. 'There are *other ways* to repay favours, you know.'

Robin bites her lip and tastes blood. What right has this stranger got to opine sarcastically like this on their relationship with each other to their faces?

'I'm aware of that,' Kessie says, a little coldly. 'And I do owe Robin a lot. But it's . . . it's not about favours. It's about – family. We've both made a decision to prioritize co-parenting Zora.'

'Hmm,' Dinah says, scribbling. She looks up once more, staring intently at Kessie. 'Why not just apply for a parental responsibility agreement then?'

Robin's teacup slips out of her fingers and cracks open on the floor. She must have been passing it from hand to hand. Tea rolls across the wood in streams and drips between the floorboards. 'God, sorry!' she squeaks. 'I'll clear it up.' She runs to the kitchen, rips off a wad of paper towel and comes back to dab at it.

'. . . we both agreed that stability and permanence would be in Zora's best interests,' Kessie is saying, a little more uncertainly now.

Robin looks up from her knees and tries to concoct the smile of a committed parent who doesn't smash crockery when things get stressful.

Dinah doesn't return it. 'One of the things I'm looking for is your preparedness for responsible parenting,' she says, directing this statement pointedly at Robin. 'I can already see that there would be a lot of childproofing required in this flat before I could recommend you.'

Robin looks around in a panic. The place is so squeaky clean now, spilled tea aside, and it's light and lovely – a dream two-bed flat in a great area of London, right by Clissold Park. What on earth could be dangerous for a baby in here – besides flying mugs?

As she struggles to find a measured response, hip-hop beats begin to boom down from the upstairs flat, where the new early twenty-somethings recently moved in. The sound is so loud it might as well be coming from the next-door room on full blast. *Typical*. What possessed them to choose *today*?

Dinah cocks her head in an exaggerated listening pose. 'How often does *that* kind of noise interference happen?' she asks.

'Oh my God, *never*!' Robin squeaks.

'Right.' A single eyebrow lift this time. They sure get a lot of action, Dinah's eyebrows. Robin wonders whether she practices in the mirror, manipulating her own personal Punch and Judy show on her forehead. 'Venetian blinds with those cords are very unsafe for small children,' Dinah continues, raising her voice slightly over the now pounding music. 'If this application were to be seriously considered, you would need covers for all outlets and sockets . . . cabinet locks for all bottles of dangerous substances in kitchen, bathroom and hallway, knives inaccessible, not on the countertop . . . smoke detectors . . . fire blanket, fire extinguisher in kitchen, fire escape plan, room for the child . . . bathroom equipment . . . ideally a playroom . . .'

High-pitched crying filters through the thunderous beats. 'Zora – I'll go and see to her,' Robin says, and rushes out.

Zora is already purple and writhing around in her cot, squalling like a tiny hurricane. There's a bad smell – Robin lifts her to reveal a large brown liquid stain. She grabs a soother, probably clean, from the shelf, and pops it gently in Zora's mouth, but it's spat straight out again. She lies the baby down on the changing table and sings her 'Lavender's Blue' – normally a favourite – but Zora continues shrieking, as if she knows that the visit is turning out to be disastrous. Robin persists, more to calm herself than anything, but as she's wiping Zora's lower back, more excrement shoots out, a spatter of it landing on her sleeve. 'Little monster,' she mutters.

She looks up to see Dinah watching from the doorway. She

jerks her head back to face Zora, furious with herself, pulls out a baby wipe and swipes at her sleeve.

Just then, her phone rings. It rings on and on, as Zora wails on and on, the beats from upstairs pound on and on, and Dinah continues standing there, silent, looking on and on and on and on.

Robin rips the first nappy in her haste to get it around Zora, then drops the second.

Aeons later, when Zora is finally clean and dressed, she returns to the living room, bundles the baby into Kessie's arms, and tells Dinah that she needs to go and change. She runs off to her bedroom like a teenager, slams the door, pulls off her soiled shirt, ripping out a chunk of hair on a button in the process, burrows her face in her pillow, and bites down into it.

*

A few nights later, Kessie gets dressed up and heads off for her first night out since Zora was born: Paolo is taking her to an open mic session. At first, her plan was just to go along to listen, but Robin and Paolo had persuaded her to bring her uke along, just in case she felt like singing something after all.

Robin, meanwhile, has planned to meet Darsha for their mini book club. She gets into her pyjamas early, but touches up her mascara and does her hair carefully, then places her laptop and book on the bedside table, clambers into bed, and arranges a small pile of pillows. She stills herself for a moment and listens: yes, Zora is still asleep.

It had been her turn to pick this time and she'd gone for

Maggie Nelson's *The Argonauts*. It had got great reviews, and she'd figured Darsha would be interested in the way it explores queerness, and that it would make for an interesting follow-up to Adrienne Rich. She'd found it a comforting read, as well as a scintillating and disturbing one. Nelson's account of her partner's gender transformation while she was pregnant made Robin's revelation about her own sexuality seem pretty minor. It struck her that this would also be a good springboard book from which to finally tell Darsha about the adoption application, which she really needs to do . . . But she isn't optimistic about the reaction. She loves the way Nelson uses marginalia, instead of academic footnotes – she'd like to try that for her dissertation, if that's allowed. And if she can ever find time to get back into her studies. Closing her eyes for a moment, she remembers the sensation of Darsha's slim fingers hot on her cheeks, nails running lightly down her body. Time to call.

'Heyyy!' Darsha answers. 'Wait – I need to move rooms.' Robin wonders whether she's just removed herself from a space where Vi is present. 'Well hello, beauteous one,' Darsha says, switching on the video again to reveal herself settled in the velvet armchair in her bedroom. 'I've missed you! You look tired again though – is that Morticia Addams creeping back? Do you need to come back for another dose of Californian vitamin D?'

They exchange news, and Robin doesn't quite get onto talking about The Thing. Darsha recounts her last couple of days, populating her account with comedy encounters and sarky insights about the other commune folk – and not mentioning Vi.

Enjoying the energy of her voice, Robin closes her eyes, slides down a bit in the bed, and pictures Darsha on the opposite pillow, imagines exploring the topology of her skin as she speaks, her small breasts with their tiny, dark nipples . . . 'You know what?' she says, when Darsha pauses for breath. 'If you ever get bored of graphic design, you should make a podcast. I could lie here and listen to you all day.'

Darsha cackles. 'Well, I want to hear more of *your* voice! We should make one together. What would our theme be? Mini book club, maybe. With a bit of design stuff thrown in by me, and some anthropology by you?'

Robin grins. 'On that note, what did you think of the book?'

'Loved it. I've underlined about half of it,' Darsha enthuses. 'Like that bit where she talks about the fact that we're all made from star stuff as a way to think about interconnectedness . . . Can't remember where that is. But there are so many good quotes, right? Her Californian take on queerness, really resonated. I mean, I don't know how I'd feel if my partner decided to transition, but I hope I'd be that cool about it.'

Robin looks across to the photo on her shelf of the two of them on their gap year, rucksacks like giant tortoise shells on their backs, arms slung happily around each other's shoulders. She slides her fingers down into her trousers, remembering that moment when Darsha opened her up like a pomegranate.

Chapter 30

Kessie

Kessie gets up late with a headache, but at least it's a familiar, wine-induced kind; nothing like the cluster bombs she used to get in those first months of motherhood. Strains of Joni sift through the bedroom door.

In the kitchen, Robin is singing along to 'Carey' while bobbing about with Zora in her arms by the window. 'Morning!' she sings, and waves Zora's hand for her. 'How did it go last night?'

'Hey you two! Kind of . . . great, actually,' Kessie croaks. 'Wait, I need water.' She goes to pour herself some and takes a glug. 'Thanks for making me go. And take the uke . . . '

'You played? Fantastic!'

'After several glasses of wine. Just a little something. I thought, what the hell, some of these acts are pretty out there – I might as well try out a couple of my kooky, raw motherhood songs . . .'

'You still haven't played them to me!'

'I know. I will, if you want. I feel a bit more confident now – the audience seemed to quite like them. It's funny: I didn't realize until I was up there how much I'd missed performing.' She massages her head. 'I'll have to see what I feel like sober, though.'

'Well, please do test them out on me when you're not hungover. Anyway, that's amazing – we're proud of you, aren't we, Zozo?' The baby squawks and wriggles. When placed on the floor, she eyes them both with a mischievous grin, then shimmies towards her like an eager seal.

*

Kessie resolves to keep going – to write something new every day, even if it's garbage. While Robin was away, she'd started experimenting with going to some local cafés to write while Zora napped in the buggy. Of those, her favourite has ended up not being the hipster cafe by the park, with the extortionate flat whites, but a builders' caff with ~~fluorescent~~ lighting where strong milky tea costs a quid. Somehow it feels less pressured.

After waking up one day humming a tune that came from a dream in which she was playing a gig from a treehouse in the rain, she's just scribbling in her notebook when Robin pokes her head in the door. She's in smart mode, suited-up and about to leave for work, but asks, with a worried face, if she can come in for a minute. Perched on the edge of the bed, she tells Kessie that Darsha is flying over to the UK. Today.

Kessie lowers the notebook to her knees.

'Her dad's had a stroke,' Robin explains. 'Seems pretty severe. Her parents live in Stanmore, end of the Jubilee line, so she's coming to see him, or say goodbye, depending how he progresses. They haven't seen each other or spoken for years, you know, after he went ballistic at her when she came out?' She tails off.

Kessie nods, slowly. 'Uh-huh.' She remembers hearing about

Darsha's father – how the big family showdown over his homo-phobia was part of the reason Darsha had wanted to go to live on the other side of the world. 'Well, thanks for letting me know,' she says, trying to sound unruffled.

'Would it be okay with you if I go to meet her at the airport after work?'

Kessie smiles brightly and says sure, and that she hopes Darsha's all right. 'Go on! You're late, aren't you?' She listens to Robin pull on her shoes and coat and close the front door, then spins her notebook like a frisbee at the door.

Later that morning, in the caff, she finds herself stuck. No melodies form. No lyrics mesh. She eats a sugar sachet, grain by grain. A couple of plasterers are loudly dissecting their night out. Kessie starts a doodle in her notebook, a spiral that fans out into swirls. The radio switches to a news bulletin about the US election. Trump has declared that he'll keep the country in suspense about whether he'll accept the election result if it doesn't appear to go his way, and called his opponent a nasty woman. Surely Hillary's a shoo-in. Not that many Americans can believe conspiracy theories that undermine democracy, can they? On the subject of conspiracy, she must try harder to stop feeling suspicious about Darsha's motivations . . . But Darsha did try to persuade Robin to move to California. And Robin admitted that she had been tempted.

Pressing harder with her pen, she draws thick, jagged lines around her doodle. If something like that happened to her own dad, then she'd want to see him, despite the frostiness between them these days. Anyway, Robin has promised that their family comes first now. And that she will be transparent about her relationship with Darsha, so there's no reason to be jealous.

Except Kessie hadn't expected Darsha to just turn up like this. And so soon. She had assumed that if their relationship did last, it would be very occasional. A week or two a year while on holiday. It was probably mean of her to refer to it as a fuck buddy thing, but Robin hadn't taken issue with that.

She orders a second mug of tea and a portion of toast and butter. Stares at the blank page as she crunches. Writes ENVY = BAD. Tiny golden crumbs scatter around the words like stars. She crosses them out, rips out the page, and scrunches it into her mug.

*

The third night in a row that Robin goes out to meet Darsha, after putting Zora down, Kessie sits down to play some Bach on the new electric piano. So long as she plays nursery rhymes in the daytime, the baby likes the piano now – she can even say 'pano' – but she doesn't have the patience to listen to pieces that take up more than two minutes of her attention. After a while, Kessie tries the clarinet, but her lips have lost their stamina, and she doesn't last long. She picks up the uke instead and tries out a new song – but it sounds generic. She realizes she's ripping off Laura Marling, who she'd been listening to over dinner.

She's about to go to bed, when Robin comes home, bleak-faced, and asks if she'd like a whisky. She agrees to a thimbleful, and they sit at the table.

Robin knocks her drink back. Darsha is finding things

really hard, she says. Her dad still recognizes her, and seemed happy to see her when she first turned up at the hospital, but can't speak – at least, not yet. Her mother has given her strict instructions not to mention their argument, or being gay at all, so as not to stress him out; and so, on her daily visits, Darsha just tries to tell him bits and pieces about her design job and her life in California, and to summon up happy memories from childhood. It's hard for her to know if he's taking much in. Meanwhile, back at home, her mother has been stiff and formal, as if her daughter were a lodger. Darsha is thinking of renting a studio for a week.

Kessie, still listening, walks over to the tank to feed the fish. Berlioz and Louis Armstrong are, as usual, on opposite sides, sucking away at the algae. She can't help thinking that they've become a bit like Robin and her right now: sharing a home but leading fairly separate lives. She makes sympathetic noises, but can't help feeling resentful that Robin hasn't yet suggested the three of them get together. Not that she necessarily wants to see Darsha. And not that Darsha necessarily wants to see her. Also, given what she's going through, Darsha's probably not feeling up to social get-togethers. She seems keen enough to hang out with Robin, though. Kessie wonders what the two of them talk about. Whether they talk about her.

She notices something, and leans forward. 'Hey,' she says, suddenly. 'Sorry to interrupt, but . . . are those tiny fish? Oh my gosh, I thought Joan of Arc was getting a bit plump. Has she . . .? Look!'

'No way.' Robin gets up and rushes over. 'Oh my gosh. Fish fry! That's never happened in all the years I've had a tank. How many do you think there are – thirty? Nice work, Joan! Gosh, I'd better look this up – we might have to isolate the babies . . .'

Robin searches for advice on her phone, as Kessie stares at the fry – and then gasps. Is that . . . is Joan of Arc *eating* one? One of her own babies? 'Robin, look, look – is this a thing? Maternal cannibalism?'

'Ohhh crap,' Robin says. 'I think it might be. And Goldilocks is going after another one . . .'

'No! Quick, we have to save them!'

'I'll get something . . . a plastic box?' Robin grabs one from the cupboard.

'Adult fishies! Look, here's some appropriate food – eat this!' Kessie cajoles, sprinkling a wad onto the surface. Goldilocks seems to find her own live babies far more tempting. 'How do we get them out? Didn't you have a little net?'

'It broke,' Robin moans.

Kessie grabs a wine glass from the shelf and starts dipping it in, trying to catch the fry, but despite their tiny size, they're pretty adept at swimming away from it, and all the food she's just put in sticks to the side.

Around an hour later, they've managed to rescue fifteen babies. Kessie looks at the clock. Half past midnight. 'The fish seem so peaceful and, well, civilized most of the time,' she says, stifling a yawn. 'I never predicted Goldilocks would turn out to be such a demon.'

'Joan is worse.'

They glance at each other. Kessie wonders if Robin is thinking about her admission that, at her lowest, she'd considered smothering her own daughter.

'Well, great teamwork!' Robin says. 'Well done for spotting that while there were still some babies left to be saved. Wonder whether Joan will decide to change sex now.'

'Excuse me?'

'Oh yeah. Swordtails can do that after having babies, if they fancy it.'

'You're making that up.'

'Fact. I'll go to the shop tomorrow and get a proper breeding box.'

A couple of days later, over breakfast, Robin clears her throat and tells Kessie that she'd popped into the hospital the day before to visit Darsha's dad. 'The deal was that we wouldn't allude to any more than friendship,' she explains. 'It felt a bit weird, but Darsh reminded him that we went to Tanzania together, and told him stories about our gap year, which I think he was listening to, but it's hard to tell. Also, I was just wondering . . . how would you feel if I were to stay for one night away in a hotel with Darsh? But I don't want to if it feels wrong to you.'

'Oh. Well, I guess you should go for it,' Kessie says lightly – but her mind is whirring. What does this signify? Is it really going to be just one night? How long is Darsha going to stay here? Is this proof that she's on a mission to entice Robin back to California? Is Robin considering it again? What would the social worker say about the impact of this on their 'enduring family relationship'? Should they disclose it? Robin's asking her something. 'Sorry, what was that?'

'I was just saying, would you fancy all getting together on Saturday? Darsh would love to see you, and meet Zora. I thought maybe she could come here, and we could all go out to the park or something?'

Kessie exaggerates a yawn and says that it sounds nice. After Robin goes off to work, she immerses herself in reading to Zora – *Burglar Bill* and *Where the Wild Things Are* that her dad finally posted her the other day. Zora likes them both, and even says 'Biw' for Bill – though her attention isn't as rapt as it is when Kessie reads her beloved Julia Donaldson picture books. Still, it's lovely to have the older ones. Reading them aloud, Kessie often imagines her mum holding the same pages, and reading them to her. If only she had a recording that she could play back.

*

When Saturday arrives, Darsha bounces through the door five minutes early, bearing a bunch of purple peonies. She gives them to Kessie, then hugs and kisses her effusively, exclaims at how great it is to see her again, and congratulates her on Zora. It has been well over a decade since Kessie has seen Darsha in the flesh. She's struck by how lithe and petite she is, by the shininess of her hair, and by how young and fresh she still looks, especially given what she's going through. That relaxed Californian no-strings life sure has its benefits. Brown skin helps. Darsha's is a shade darker than Kessie's, and of the three of them, Robin's pale skin is the only one that's visibly lined, despite her extortionate retinol serum.

Darsha bends down briefly to look at Zora in her bouncy chair, and says politely that she's cute – but doesn't linger or ask to hold her. It's obvious that she doesn't have the slightest interest in babies, not this one at least. A strand of drool starts to seep out of one side of Zora's mouth, and Kessie swoops to wipe it and replace it with a kiss.

Robin pours drinks, and Kessie asks Darsha how her dad is doing.

'He's making some progress, thanks,' Darsha says. 'His left arm's just started working again, which is a relief – a good sign, they reckon. He can say a couple of words now, including Anjali – my mum's name – so that's nice.' Darsha walks over to Robin at the kitchen counter and strokes her arm, then leans her head against her shoulder.

It shouldn't be uncomfortable to see Robin with someone else like this, Kessie tells herself. It's great to see her appreciated, in contrast to the Max era. For ages, she had wished that Robin would find someone new to replace him, someone who would make her eyes soft, her cheeks bloom . . . but then Zora has that effect on her too.

Darsha oohs over the baby fish with more enthusiasm than she showed towards Zora, and cackles at Kessie's account of the drama. 'Imagine if humans had that many babies all in one go – total nightmare!' she says. 'One sounds like it's been hard enough for you guys.'

As they walk around the park, leaves float in copper glints from the trees. Conversation mostly revolves around the imminent US election, and the rhetoric being weaponized against Hillary – that she's in favour of ripping babies out of wombs, and is content with the avalanche of immigrants who are poisoning the blood of Americans. Darsha says she's not sure if she'd be able to stand living in the US any more if it goes Trump's way. Kessie stops to tie a shoelace then observes, from behind, Robin's slim fingers linking with Darsha's – one set long and pale; the other short and dark. Darsha chats constantly, and makes Robin laugh a lot. The chemistry between them is evident, and there's an irresistible energy about Darsha, a vivaciousness, that's infectious. She gets that. But what if Darsha gets too comfortable here?

Robin takes over pushing the buggy, and Darsha proposes buying them all takeaway and watching an Eighties romcom.

'Great!' Kessie says. 'Thai? And – I don't know – *Three Men and a Baby*?'

Chapter 31

Robin

The day after the US election, still reeling, Robin heads out to meet Darsha for dinner. They'd messaged – *fuck, it really happened – is this the beginning of the end of humanity* – but Darsha was too busy for a phone chat. Robin had been unable to concentrate on work all day – kept finding herself scrolling through media commentary to try to get her head around how it happened, and what it really means.

Relieved not to be able to get online on the Tube, she pulls out a book from her bag. It's an interesting one that Benjy had recommended on 'modern families'. Despite how much she's read on alternative kinship lately, it's shocking to come across examples of how things used to be for queer families in the UK as recently as a couple of decades ago. A newspaper article from the 1970s about lesbian women having children through donor insemination was titled 'Ban These Babies!' and a prominent MP described the practice in Parliament as an 'evil'. If a dispute arose between a biological mother and father, a heterosexual mother would almost always win sole custody, as she was assumed to be the only one who had a clue how to look after the children at home – *unless* the mother had come out as a lesbian. In that scenario, even if she was living happily with another woman, the father would win, because, it was claimed, lesbian women were 'less nurturing', and such children would be teased and rejected by their peers – and, worst of all, because such children were likely to grow up to be lesbian or gay themselves. *Shock horror.* Contemporaneous studies revealing that there was in fact no difference between the wellbeing of young children in lesbian versus heterosexual families were ignored. Robin grits her teeth. Equality is so fragile. If only she could rouse those judgemental bastards from the dead and show them the video she took on her phone earlier of Zora, joyfully intoning *Superworm* like a musical score while coasting along the sofa at just eleven months old, with no father on the scene. She really has to tell Darsha about the adoption application. She has to do it tonight.

*

At the restaurant, a Japanese-Korean fusion that has become their favourite London eatery, Darsha greets her with a dark look, and a rather cursory peck on the lips. 'Hey. I'm sorry, but can we not talk about US politics right now? It's such a shitshow I might just start howling, and I was up all night reading about it so my brain is fried.' At the table, she orders the usual sake, miso soup, and edamame to share. She's wearing a severely cut teal shirt that complements her skin tone and invites Robin to imagine the slim shape of her underneath. It emphasizes the elfin quality of her face, and the straight whiteness of her teeth, save for that skewed lower incisor that somehow makes her lips even more magnetic. 'What main do you fancy?'

Robin tears her gaze away and scans the menu. 'Hm, I thought I'd try something new – but I can't *not* have the salmon bento box. Feels a bit weird eating fish, though, after what ours are getting up to.'

'Mothers eating their babies?'

'Gets worse. This morning I found Jimbo, the biggest of the babies, eating the smallest one. Kessie was like, guys, you're siblings! You should look out for each other!'

Darsha shrugs with a wry grin. 'Babies always make things messy.' She tilts her head from side to side, looking through the options. 'I mean, that miso aubergine *is* the next best thing to an orgasm,' she muses. '*Even from you,*' she whispers, looking up at Robin through her lashes. 'But – I'm going to try something new. I've been eyeing up the veggie bibimbap. See over there, table opposite.'

This is about their tenth visit here in the month that Darsha has been in London. It's just around the corner from the studio she's been renting, now that she's stayed on, so that she can have a space to work and be sufficiently distant from her mother. She leans a little over the table, a coy smile on her lips. 'Robinita – you have no idea how seductive you look, sucking a plump edamame bean out of its salty pod.'

Robin laughs and nearly spits the edamame out, then glances around in case their neighbours had heard. Max never spoke to her like that – except occasionally in bed, in the early days.

Darsha leans back, her bowl of miso soup cupped in her hands, and grins. 'It's been lovely, going out for these dinners together.

Sitting across from you in a crowded room and imagining what I'll see of you afterwards that no one else will.'

Robin bites her lips and feels herself flush. 'It has.' She smiles, thinking of Darsha opening her up in that hotel room with the purple walls. Thank goodness Kessie was cool with her spending a few nights there. 'But Darsh – I'm sorry but I can't stay over this time. This week, even, I don't think. I'm sorry, but I have tons on at work, and I promised to be home to do Zora's dream feed . . .' *The application,* she thinks. *For God's sake, just say it.*

'Right.' Darsha's jaw shifts. 'No worries.' She sighs. 'It does just feel a little bit like having an affair with a married man, and having to send them off after an illicit rendezvous back to their wife and kids – except you don't even seem that keen about sleeping with me now.'

Robin's stomach clenches. That is both unfair and untrue – and she hasn't even broken the news yet. 'Darsh, you know there's nothing I enjoy more!' She leans forward, takes Darsha's free hand. 'Seriously, sleeping with you has transformed my sex life!' she whispers, flushing at her own daring in this public place. 'It's incredible – unrecognizable – I had no idea what I was missing.'

The couple from the next table are definitely listening in. Meanwhile Darsha is looking at her with an expression that seems both fond and sceptical.

'Listen,' Robin persists, 'we could just make this a takeaway and go back to yours if you like?'

'For a quickie, you mean?' Darsha asks loudly. The couple at the next table don't even try to hide their eavesdropping now. 'It's okay, thanks anyway.' She gives Robin a sarky smile, pulls her hand away, and leans back in her chair again. 'I'm ravenous.

I need to try that bibimbap. If there's time, great; but it sounds like it won't be possible.' Her lips have tightened.

'Okayyy.' Robin swallows, trying desperately to figure out where this terseness is coming from.

Cutlery clinks. People around the restaurant chat loudly about their various tribulations and anecdotes. It's definitely not the moment to mention the application. 'So . . . how was your dad today?'

Darsha rolls her shoulders, smiles a little. 'I was waiting to tell you, actually. He spoke his first full sentence.'

'Oh Darsh, that's brilliant! I'm so happy to hear that. What did he say?'

She rolls her eyes. 'He issued a demand, of course. *"Bring me a cup of sweet tea."* Summoning the women to serve him. No please or thank you. Leopards and spots, right? But still, I got quite emotional – I even ran to get it for him. And when I handed it to him . . . he told me . . . he'd missed me.' Her eyes glisten.

The last time Robin saw Darsha get close to crying – the only time – was during that argument on the California trip after her blunder. She touches Darsha's jade ring in its simple silver setting, and runs her fingertip down the length of the ring finger. 'I mean, hopefully he'll learn some manners in his old age . . . but I'm so relieved for you. I mean, obviously he *did* miss you, but for him to actually say it . . .'

'I know. And then he asked me to tell him more about my life in California. So I did. And then – wait for it – he asked if I had a girlfriend.'

'He did? Wow. That's, like – acceptance, right?!'

'It's a step forward, for sure. So I said yes. At least, that I have had one.'

'Oh.' *Have had.* Was this a reference to her or Vi? She waits.

'He asked if she made me happy,' Darsha presses on.

'And . . . what did you say?'

'I said she has done. And he said that's all he'd really wanted at the end of the day.' Darsha closes her eyes for a moment and shakes her head. 'I felt like I was sitting by his deathbed in a Greek tragedy performance, and he was finally repenting, and the red velvet curtains were about to close. And then he grinned at me with the half of his face that still works, and he was like: so anyway, now that you're too old to give me a grandchild, I've put that idea behind me.'

'Charming!'

'Charm was never his forte. But he's right, in a way. They'd have loved to be grandparents, but it's not gonna happen, and it's good that he's not in denial about that, at least.'

'Right.' Something inside Robin sinks. And then she has a sudden thought that, if Darsha were up for being a kind of highly uninvolved soul parent for Zora, her parents could be somewhat distantly involved, or at least labelled, as soul grandparents, which could be nice for them – not that they are easy people . . . But this is getting ridiculous: she absolutely has to tell Darsha about the application, right now, this minute. 'So – did you tell him any more about me?' she finds herself asking. 'Or . . .'

Darsha regards her almost mournfully. 'No,' she says, finally. 'He didn't ask more. And I didn't want to spoil it. Or get his hopes up for nothing.'

Robin feels like an ice cube has been slipped down her neck. 'What do you—'

'I mean . . .' Darsha leans forward again, elbows on the table. 'Robin, I mean I've loved you for decades now. I pushed it into a bottom drawer once I figured you must be straight, or that that was your line and you were sticking to it – but then, when you came to visit, you yanked it right back open again, and I should have known it was too good to be true. That you're not really in it.'

'But, what? I—'

'Just hear me out, please?' Darsha interjects. 'It's been amazing in lots of ways. We have so much going for us. Chemistry – tick, history – tick, great sex – tick, a friendship with laughter and shared reading interests – tick tick. And maybe we could have been a real couple if you'd come out years ago. But it is just too late – I see that now.'

'But why . . .'

'You don't *actually* want to live with me, Robin. Make a life with me. Be in a proper relationship. You want to be in a family with Kessie and Zora – and you're already doing that. I know about your adoption application. I read the letters from the social worker.'

Robin's brain jolts. 'What? When?'

'Last week. They were sitting there on your desk when I came over for the movie night. I've been waiting for you to tell me about it, but it looks like you were planning to keep it from me, I don't know, maybe to see if it worked out for you first or something. Which I get, but I hope you can understand that it doesn't feel *great* from my perspective.'

Robin digs her nails into her cheeks. *Idiot.* 'No, no, oh Darsh, I was . . .'

Darsha thrusts a palm at her. 'Don't dig yourself deeper. Or make excuses. You really want to be a mum, I know that. And you want to be Zora's mum. I knew you felt kind of maternal about her, but I didn't have a clue how far you and Kessie had decided to take that. They're obviously more important to you.'

'Well, no – it's just different, what we have, I—'

Darsha holds her other palm up. 'Also, I just don't fit in here any more, you know? The UK doesn't feel like home now. At *all*. My home is California – and I miss it. I need more sunshine and warmth in my life. More social openness too; less repression. All this British cold and drizzle and greyness and narrow-mindedness and uptightness – it's getting me down. Always did, to be honest. Brexit felt like the last straw. But then you came along and made me feel like saying fuck it all, maybe I'll just think about it . . . but it really isn't for me.'

'Oh.' Robin is a pebble sinking into a lake, down and down.

'Plus, Vi misses me,' Darsha adds off-handedly. 'She's been calling and messaging me constantly – and now she's even promised to be monogamous if I come back, which is pretty radical, for her. Absence and the heart, I guess.'

'Oh,' Robin repeats, stupidly. She can picture Vi's victorious face, smiling despisingly at her.

'So I've booked a flight back. I've got a potential new client – a big Silicon Valley name – and they want me to come to an in-person interview next week.'

'What? Darsh! That's . . . So you're . . . I mean, congrats, but . . . is this . . . you breaking up with me? And telling me you're about to leave for good . . . in a matter of days?'

Darsha nods. 'That pretty much nails it. Oh, come on,

Robinita. Don't look so distraught. You know I'd probably stay in the Big Smoke and dump the client meeting and Vi and even California if you wanted more with us – to be together properly – but it's obvious you don't.' Her eyes have gone shiny again.

'But . . . no, that's not *right*. Just come here a moment. Please.' She tugs Darsha back towards her across the table. 'Darsh, I love you. I love being with you – I *do* want more of you. I feel like I can't get enough . . . I've never felt the same way about anyone. I mean, I do feel like Kessie and Zora are my family now, and I love Kess too, just in a very different way – it's totally platonic. I don't *desire* her – I desire *you*! I love how you've turned my life inside out and made it feel the right way round – it's just the timing, the situation—'

'Listen,' Darsha butts in, 'it's okay. I'd got used to suppressing my feelings for you for years. I can get used to it again. Even better, I could finally get over you! That would be progress.'

'But—'

'Babe, this is what it comes down to: you had to choose between a romantic relationship and sex with me, and a platonic relationship with Kessie and motherhood. Right? You've made the choice, which is fair enough, and I hope it works out for you. I genuinely do.'

'I . . . but . . . oh shit, this is all my fault. I'm so, so sorry I didn't talk to you earlier about the adoption thing – Kessie surprised me with the idea out of the blue when I got back from the US, and I was confused and too gutless to tell you I guess – again – but it's only because I didn't want to lose you. I wish I hadn't taken so many years to work out that I felt like this, that I was bi, even. It seems idiotic from here. I just wish . . . Oh, God.'

'Don't torture yourself,' Darsha says. 'I'm not really angry with you. Well, I am, but I'll get over it. As for me and Vi – I think what's happened with us has made her want more from our relationship, so that's a silver lining. Anyway, I know what I want from my life, and that it's definitely *not* being a parent. Or a step-parent, or any kind of parent. I've built a life that suits me, and it just happens to be on the other side of the world.'

'Right,' Robin says, deflated. Darsha seems to have become as immovable as a block of granite. 'But what about the election?' she persists. 'I thought you said if – if what's just happened happened, you couldn't bear to live in the US any more?'

Darsha tightens her lips, shakes her head slowly. 'Well, I was speculating. I didn't honestly believe it could happen. I mean, who knows how it'll play out. But California didn't vote that way so at least I'll know that I'm still surrounded by like-minded folk in my neighbourhood. And maybe it's even more important now to stay and defiantly live by your principles. I don't know. What I do know is that I still wanna be there.'

All the other people in the restaurant still seem to be laughing and chattering animatedly. As if everything were just the same.

Their food arrives. Robin looks down at her perfectly crafted bento box. Glistening pink salmon has never looked less appetizing. Darsha is already attacking her colourful bibimbap with her chopsticks. 'What about your dad though?' Robin asks shakily. 'It seems like he really wants to repair your relationship – don't you want to stay a bit longer?'

'No way. I mean, it is nice that he's come the closest he will ever come to apologizing, or telling me he loves me despite my "transgressions". And I'm glad I could be there for him when it seemed like he was at death's door. But it'll never be happy days between us, you know? He cut me out for too long. And he's too rude. Anyway, I can't just put my life on hold for any longer just to sit here and watch him slowly recover, and demand tea without saying please, and remember how much he actually does hate all gay people.'

'Well . . .'

'Mum's doing fine now, so I don't feel bad about her. This is the only decision that makes sense for me. I'm sure you get that, deep down. Or you will, once you chew it over.' Darsha pops some veggies into her mouth, savours the flavour, swallows, and nods slowly. 'Mmm.' A small smile tweaks one side of her mouth. 'Here, try this – it's delicious. It might even tempt you to diverge from your usual order – next time you come here with Kessie, maybe?'

Robin stares at her, unable to speak. She tries to hold on to the fact, for a tiny bit longer, she's still here with this glittering person who's lit her up from within, who's made her laugh, and gasp, and dare to break out of her anxieties, and feel desired, and who knows her so well. Darsha is still touching distance across the table – and yet she's already vanishing, like steam from a cooling kettle.

Chapter 32

Kessie

Pound along the path, puff clouds into the air – splash through putrid puddles, don't let the buggy loose – fingers fail, tips numb, lungs burn, mum churn . . . Kessie isn't finding it any easier to keep up with Sam, even after weeks of this new jogging routine. Sam does have a fancier buggy, to be fair. It's one of those light-but-chunky-wheeled ones, brand new and especially designed for running, like a prize racehourse next to Kessie's lolloping mule. Their bodies match their steeds, it occurs to her – Sam's athletic legs are showcased by her body-sculpting leggings with their abstract droplet design; while Kessie's old grey leggings have a hole in the side seam and are sagging around her knees. Still, she's determined to keep going, to get fitter – to imbibe some of Sam's energy. She pushes harder to catch up. An annoying man in too-short shorts sprints easily past her, buggy-free.

She had tentatively texted Sam a few months back, asking if she remembered her from the antenatal class, and was relieved when Sam replied positively, and didn't mention anything about her leaving the message group and dropping out of touch for so long. The first time they met up, they tried out an extortionate mum-and-baby yoga class – until, three minutes in, both Zora and Arlo began shrieking in synchrony. They grabbed their respective children, scuttled out of the circle, breastfed next to each other, and the friendship felt instantly easy. It's crazy to think that Zora's first birthday is coming up next month – that it's over a year since she and Sam first met. Her legs and lungs are screaming for a break when – deliverance – her phone rings.

She slows to a walk to get it out of her pocket. *Unknown number.*

Sam glances back, then waits for her to catch up. 'Go ahead, take it!' she says. 'I need a break.'

'Thank God!' Kessie pants. 'Hello?'

'Hi there.' A woman's voice. 'This is Kessie, isn't it?'

'Yes . . .' she says, breathily. 'Who is this, sorry?'

'It's Anna, dear. Calling from Elmina's home in the UK.'

'Oh, Anna – hi!' Anna is Auntie Elmi's silver-haired, snub-nosed, tai chi-loving friend who quit a career as a maths professor to become a Buddhist nun . . . Why would she be phoning?

'My dear, I hate to be the bearer of such terrible news, but I'm afraid I have to let you know that our beloved Sister Elmina . . . has passed away.'

Kessie stops walking. Her breath grows sticky inside her chest. The sycamore overhanging the path starts to buzz. 'Died?' she asks. But she'd been meaning to message Auntie Elmi back yesterday. She should have gone out to visit her again – or at least written a proper letter, sent her a recent photo of Zora, she hasn't even thanked her properly for the little elephant toy she sent. 'What . . . happened?'

'She was in a motorbike accident while out on a food delivery for some of the earthquake victims. They think it would have been instant. She was riding on the back – one of our Nepalese sisters was driving, and a truck drove into them at a junction. The sister survived, so – that's something.'

Kessie crouches down. Her buggy, with Zora in it, starts rolling away. Sam lurches over to grab it and looks down at her, worried.

'Her body is going to be flown back to the UK,' Anna continues. 'And we're going to have a funeral, a week on Saturday. I know you have a baby now – Elmina told us all about Zora, she was so proud! – but we'd love to have you there, and can help look after her if you need. Perhaps you'd like to read something? And play your clarinet? She always loved listening to you play.'

'I – of course, anything. I just . . .'

'You'd be welcome to stay with us if you'd like. I'm her executor, so I'm having to work a lot of things out at the moment. And on that note, there's something else I'd like to tell you. Are you still there, my dear?'

Kessie nods, then realizes this won't come across. 'Yes, sorry . . .'

'Okay, well, Elmina left you some money in her will. She left half of her estate to the Ehani Foundation, some to our convent, and the rest to you – some money. And all her shares in an ethical investment fund.'

Kessie gasps. 'She *did*?'

'That's right, sweetheart. With the value of the shares, it should work out at about ninety thousand pounds.'

'Ninety *thousand*?' Kessie's mind races . . . rent . . . even a mortgage deposit . . . nursery . . . a savings account for Zora . . . a songwriting course . . . But what is she thinking? Auntie Elmi is gone. Forever. No chance to say goodbye. The closest connection she had to her mum, save for her dad, is gone. Had it not been for Elmi, Kessie would not even exist. Although she was her mum's best friend, it was her dad who had actually been friends with her first – back when they were kids and their families were next-door neighbours in Cape Coast. Elmi had moved to the UK a few years before him, and when he arrived, she had invited him to a party at her flat and introduced him to her best friend. They'd bonded over a shared love of jazz and fried rice. Kessie gets out her phone to call him – she promised Anna she would – but can't face it just yet. She needs to see Robin.

*

At home, Robin holds Kessie for a long time, letting her snuffle into her collarbone, then offers to look after Zora while she goes to the funeral. 'Spend a few days up there if you like,' she says. 'I'll see if Sam's childminder still has a space when I'm at work, or I can just take unpaid leave. If they sack me, they sack me – I'm at that point. Take however long you need.'

'That's so lovely of you, Robs. I'm sorry about the timing.' Robin has been quietly miserable ever since Darsha left her to go back to California. Although Kessie had never really seen how it could work between them if they continued living at such a long distance, and would hate for Robin to move over there, part of her had felt horribly guilty about indirectly coercing Robin into abandoning this seedling relationship that obviously meant so much to her already. When she saw Robin and Darsha together, the chemistry and the joy they found in each other had been tangible. She had never wanted to pressure Robin to choose her and Zora, certainly not over true love, whatever that means, or for her to be hurt in the process.

'Remember that amazing long weekend when Elmi took us to Paris for the first time?' Robin is asking. 'That was so incredibly generous and lovely of her. I'll never forget it.' It had been a blast. They were just thirteen, and neither had ever been to France before. Elmi booked the three of them into a tiny family hotel room in Montmartre, and they did all the best things: went up the Eiffel Tower and Le Louvre, wandered around to Galeries Lafayette and tried on fancy clothes, drank big bowls of *chocolat chaud* for breakfast, and stopped at every patisserie they liked the look of.

'Don't you want to come to the funeral too, though?' Kessie asks. 'It'd be nice to have you there.'

'Well . . . I would – but then I wasn't really in touch with Elmi for a long time. And if I stay here and look after Zora, it might give you more space to feel you can really say goodbye to her properly, no? And you could probably do with a night away. You haven't had one since Zora was born.'

That evening, Kessie pours herself a large glass of wine and prepares to call her dad. It'll be so weird and sad to tell him the news. Like letting him know that he's just lost a sister, though one that he hasn't been very good at keeping in touch with – especially since Cara came on the scene. When her mum was alive, the four of them used to spend Christmas together, go to the WOMAD festival together, and holiday together – the best trip was probably that dreamy summer camping in the Loire valley. But after her mum died, he changed. He stopped practising his saxophone, cancelled all his gigs, failed to turn up to most of his plumbing jobs, and stopped stocking the fridge – until, after a few months of excessive drinking, he went teetotal and began to spend more and more time reading the Bible and meeting with his new evangelistic church group. Elmi stayed loyal. She used to come over a couple of times a week to cook a nutritious dinner for them both, even after a long and tiring day of social work, so that Kessie didn't have to subsist on cereal and fish fingers. The two of them had always bickered amiably about politics and religion, mostly mediated by Kessie's mum; but in those years soon after her death, her dad was often morose or distracted, and the bickering could turn grouchy. Elmi used to bring his spirits back up by turning up the music and making them all dance around the kitchen with her to Herbie Hancock or Sam Cooke.

Unusually, he picks up the phone straight away. 'Hi love! One sec, I'm just finishing a conversation with someone in our church family . . . yes, bye Doreen, see you soon! Sorry. What can I do you for?'

'Dad, I need to tell you something awful. I'll cut right to it. Auntie Elmi – she's died. A motorbike accident. In Kathmandu.'

A long silence. She hears him inhale through his nose and exhale. 'Oh Lord.'

'I know. I'm going to the funeral next week. It's going to be at her convent in Hertfordshire. The sisters are organizing it. Her body's being flown back now . . . Will you come too?'

He blows out a breath. 'Oof. Well of course I – I do have a lot on, but . . .'

'Oh for God's sake, Dad – and yes, I just took his name in vain so shoot me – you better *had* come. After everything she did for us, with us, after Mum – but then maybe I can believe it, seeing as you've barely made any effort to be there for me when I've been having a shitty time as a single mum with postnatal . . .' Her voice is going haywire. She pauses to recoup her composure.

'Oh dear, oh dear,' he says, sounding panicked. 'I'm so sorry, darling, I didn't mean – I'll be there, yes, absolutely, no question. I just wasn't thinking . . . I didn't realize . . .'

'Maybe you should have asked a bit more then,' she snaps.

A long pause. 'Right. You're right. I'm so sorry you feel that way. I didn't intend to be neglectful – it's just, after Cara and I visited, I wasn't sure you even wanted . . .'

'What I didn't *want*, Dad, was *her* there! Criticizing me, telling me I was doing things wrong in week *one*! She hasn't liked me since the beginning, and she seemed to take a sadistic pleasure in—'

'Well, hang on a minute now—'

'Dad, I really don't want to talk about this on the phone any more, okay?'

A long pause. 'Okay,' he says, carefully. 'That's fair. Let's talk in person, then. I'm . . . I'll try to do better. And I'd like to see you before the funeral, too, if you have the time. To catch up, and remember Auntie Elmi, and – talk about things. Anything. Everything. I can come to you in London? I'd love to see Zora again. She's grown so much, from the photos.'

'She has.'

'How about this,' he proposes. 'I'll cancel all my engagements with the church in the coming week, fortnight, even. Explain that it's a family emergency. I'll book a room somewhere near your flat, and be available – if you'd like to spend a day or two together . . . ? Unless you have other plans, but I can be flexible, babysit, even . . .'

Kessie pauses. Such an offer seems never to have occurred to him before. He does sound genuinely contrite. If he really has been that clueless all this time, and wants to make amends now – well, he'd be like the prodigal dad. And she'd have to figure out her capacity to forgive him. She always thought the prodigal son had a bit too easy a ride in the Bible; no doubt he would disagree. 'All right then,' she says, reticently. 'It would be good to have you come for a solo visit. Finally. So long as you're open to really listening and not judging.'

'That I can promise.'

*

She waits for him by the pond in Clissold Park while Zora chatters to the ducks, trying to process that she'll never be able to meet him and Auntie Elmi together again. That Elmi will never even get to meet Zora in person once. *Jenga bricks floating apart . . . Kitchen dancing days lodged in my heart . . .* He calls her name from way up the path, waves like he's drowning, and then gives her a hug that only ends when she yelps and lunges away towards Zora who's crawled too close to the water's edge.

'Little adventurer, huh?' he chuckles. 'How's my favourite granddaughter?' *Your only granddaughter,* she thinks. He reaches out to Zora, who gives him a wary look.

'That's Granddad!' Kessie says. 'Remember?' He scoops the child up, and she squawks angrily, then lets out a fruity giggle as he tucks her under one arm and tickles her tummy. 'Ohhh, I haven't spent nearly enough time with this dreamboat,' he sighs. 'Kess – I feel terrible that it came across to you as if I didn't care . . .'

'Well . . .'

'And Auntie Elmi – I just can't get over it. Devastating. I've failed there too – I owed her a message . . . I owed her incalculable things, as you rightly pointed out on the phone.' He takes a long sniff of Zora's hair, which makes her squirm and reach for Kessie, so he passes her over. 'I have really been thinking hard about the things you said. Tried to be honest with myself. And I realize – it has been dawning on me how blinkered I've been. Towards the two of you. I've just been working so hard to tend to my flock at church, and my flock at home, you know, all the works to the building, trying to bring the young generation in – the boys have been struggling at school . . . Gareth has been diagnosed with dyslexia, and Aaron has ADHD – but, well. Elmi passing away so suddenly . . . It's a shock. I've been praying. Reflecting . . .' He looks pained. 'And it's become very clear to me that I haven't been the best father to you. For a long time.'

She hadn't expected such a speech. 'You've had your moments, Dad . . .'

'And I know I lost my way a bit after your mother died. But you were so tight with Robin, and of course you had Elmi too, so I . . .'

'So you just let Auntie Elmi do all the hard work of looking after me when I was a teenager while you let Jesus make *you* feel better.' It's spiteful of her to put it like that, but it does feel good to finally release some of the resentment she's held for so long.

He flashes a rueful glance at her. 'I admit I probably retreated into the church at the time – it was a sanctuary. But Elmi seemed to really want to help, to be with you . . . And she was a wonder, wasn't she? A force of nature. I know I took her for granted, in hindsight. I wish I'd told her more often how grateful I am.

Should have learned from losing your mother. I guess all I can do now is . . . learn the right lessons this time?' He smiles a small, hopeful smile at her. He looks so old, now. So grey at the edges.

'That would be a good start,' she says more gently. Then can't resist adding, 'Cara's dislike of me can't be that easy for you, I guess.' That too came out in a more vindictive tone than she'd intended.

'Sweetheart, please don't say that. Of course she . . .'

'Dad,' she interrupts, 'we both know she wishes I didn't exist. Don't deny it – look, she's your wife and I've accepted that, and I'm glad if she makes you happy – but she's been horrible to me, and she's acted like she's trying her hardest to wipe me and Mum out of your life, and so I just think you should at least—'

'Kess . . .' He's frowning now, desperate for her to stop.

'No, Dad. You promised to listen, so please just hear me out? You've been deliberately blind to her behaviour towards me. And fine with her trying to eviscerate our history. Mum's memory. Chucking out all her stuff, and mine . . . And I mean, that day you both turned up after Zora was born . . . I was spiralling, and she was just, like, she wanted to make me . . .' Her voice is cracking. She has to keep it together enough to say what she needs to say.

'Oh dear, yes, I can see how that must have been a difficult moment,' he says. 'She was a little hurt *too*, you know, by how it went, but it's always a tricky time . . .'

'*Always*? *Tricky*? Dad, you have no fricking *idea* how difficult it's been for me! And how much worse it got after that day.' She takes a deep breath, then blows it out as if through a straw, thinking of Auntie Elmi, of her compassionate smile, of her positive Zen in spite of everything, of the daily messages that always gave her at least a glimmer of cheer. 'You don't even know that I'm on anti-depressants right now, do you?' His jaw drops. 'Well, I am. I'm way better now, but a few months ago I wasn't far off being sectioned. Robin saved me. Look, I can try to explain how things have been from my point of view a bit more, but only if you really want to listen properly? It might take a while.'

'Of course, of course – that's why I'm here.' He looks nervous now, like she's just metamorphosed into a being he doesn't quite recognize.

'Good. Well, let's walk and talk, then, shall we?' She plugs Zora back into the buggy, and they set off.

Over the next hour, circling the park, she delivers a tirade – doesn't hold back on breastfeeding agonies, on self-loathing and on her antipathy towards Zora, even, on her inability to sleep or really function at all, on how Robin was there for her through everything, doing all the hard labour of childcare, and how Auntie Elmi messaged her every day, even from Nepal, and sent them presents. She even decides that he should have to endure hearing about her post-birth body, breasts, piles and all – and to his credit, he keeps nodding along. He hmms occasionally, utters the odd 'oh dear', and becomes very quiet.

She realizes she's been speaking at a hundred miles an hour, half thinking he's going to make an excuse to get back to his congregation if she were to slow down. When she's finished, they walk for a while in silence amidst the ruckus of birds and traffic.

'I'm glad you've finally told me all this,' he says eventually. 'You've been so brave. Enduring . . . so much. I'm glad you've had Robin. Sounds like she's been an angel . . .'

'She has. She's family too now, really . . .'

'Absolutely.'

'Good. Well, I'm not sure how the church would view it, but – you might be pleased to hear that we're actually taking steps to become a family, formally. Like, by Robin becoming a legal co-mother to Zora.'

He stares at her. 'Oh! Goodness.' After a second of looking perplexed, he flicks on a smile. 'Well, that's . . . very nice! I didn't realize – I have a couple of lesbians in my congregation actually, and . . .'

She tips her head back. 'Noooo, Dad, oh my God! It's great that you're being inclusive, but we're not – it's not *that* kind of relationship.' She tells him about the application, the various legal issues, and even the lawyer's comedy suggestion that they get married.

After another attenuated pause follows, during which he nods like an automaton, even though she's no longer talking – and then wishes them both the best of luck. 'You'll make a lovely family,' he pronounces, only a little stiltedly. 'I'm only sorry that you didn't feel you could talk to me about this before. I'm always advising my congregation to listen to each other, and to Jesus, and here I am . . .'

'It's all right, Dad,' she says. 'You are here now.'

*

They meet again the next day at the Tate Modern. Zora gets super excited about the busking guitarist by the river, who gives her a wave, prompting Kessie's dad to dig out a coin for him, then squeals to be able to get out of her buggy and crawl down the slope of the Turbine

Hall. She has zero interest in being taken inside a gallery room, however, and makes her feelings about that loud and clear, so they retreat to the café to buy her a babyccino. Kessie and her dad decide to order hot chocolates in tribute to Auntie Elmi and her mum, both of whom always picked hot chocolate over coffee or tea. After a few stressful attempts, it proves easiest not to talk about Cara any further, and they decide to leave that topic aside for the time being, and to focus on memories of Elmi and her mother.

Back home, while her dad prepares jollof rice, they listen to jazz – the Herbie Hancock that Elmi loved, and reminiscent tracks from Benny Goodman, Miles Davis and Sarah Vaughan albums that he used to play when she was a kid. Kessie introduces him to the new Jacob Collier album that she's recently discovered, which has re-sparked her energy for finding new music, improvising on her clarinet, and sketching out song ideas. She asks him how much he cooked when she was a baby – and was surprised to hear that he prepared most meals while her mother was alive. He even made her purees, when she was tiny.

Kessie re-teaches him how to change a nappy, and the second afternoon he babysits Zora while she goes to a yoga class. That goes so well that she and Robin decide to leave Zora with him in the evening so that they can go to a movie together for the first time in at least a year. Feeling like they can't take too much emotional drama, they pick *Almost Christmas,* which turns out to be about a dysfunctional family coming together after the death of a parent, and seems oddly apt.

Robin and Zora wave them off for the funeral. It feels liberating to leave them both behind, but also like abandoning an extra arm that Kessie hadn't quite realized she'd grown. She and her dad take the train together, and he pays for a taxi. On the way to his B and B, he and drops her off at the cottage in the convent's grounds where Elmi used to live.

In the doorway, Anna gives her a long hug. The place still smells of patchouli and lavender. While lemongrass tea is brewing, a couple of the other sisters come in to greet Kessie, and join her and Anna at the kitchen table, where they all talk quietly about 'Sister Elmina' and what she meant to them.

Kessie was given Elmi's old bedroom to sleep in – it had become a guest room when she spent more and more time in Nepal, but it still has some of her things in a chest of drawers. It is just as Kessie remembered it: neat, clean, and minimal. There's a sink in one corner, no doubt put in to avoid un-Zen queues for the bathroom when teeth need brushing. At the end of the bed, a blown-up photo of the convent in Nepal hangs on the wall, and on a shelf is a tiny framed shot of ten smiling orphan girls from the foundation in their starched white school shirts, with Elmi beaming proudly behind them.

After looking at these for a while, Kessie gazes out of the window, across the little garden and to the fields beyond, which are shrouded in thick cloud. A crow hops grandly along the path outside. She lies on her back on the bed and stares at the light – a bare bulb dangling on a wire.

The quiet is intense. She's forgotten what it's like to only hear birdsong out of a bedroom window. And it feels very peculiar to be able to lie down with no risk of being roused by an urgently crying child. Liberating, but discombobulating.

She gets up again and takes her clarinet out of its case – she'd promised to play it at the funeral, and she's out of practice. After warming up with a few scales, she has a go at the iconic glissando that begins Gershwin's 'Rhapsody in Blue'. She'd heard the piece live at her first-ever orchestra concert which her parents took her to when she was just six, and that glissando felt electric – it was the thing that convinced her that she wanted to play the clarinet, and that no other instrument would do. She had assured her mum not long after that she would play it in a proper orchestra one day. Of course it turned out that Auntie Elmi was the one who got to see that happen – not the Gershwin solo, which Kessie's never yet had the chance to play with an orchestra, but Elmi was sitting in the front row for her first professional concert. Is this really an appropriate tune to play at a monastic Buddhist funeral, though? She should probably double-check with Anna . . . but Anna didn't specify anything, and she doesn't see why she shouldn't. Auntie Elmi loved the piece and would have liked to hear Kessie play it. And her dad will definitely like it. She thinks of him unpacking his shabby case in the nearby budget hotel – of how comforting it is to have him there for her again, just him and just her, just for a few days. Cara is probably resentful that she wasn't invited, even though she'd only met Auntie Elmi a handful of times.

Anna told her she was welcome to look through Elmi's things, if she'd like to, and choose anything she'd like to keep. She puts the clarinet down, and pushes slowly through the wardrobe, along the monastic robes, then opens each of the drawers, feeling increasingly despondent, until she spots a rust-coloured wool jumper she recognizes and pulls it out. It has several moth holes in it, but she remembers Elmi wearing it several times, and decides to stitch up the holes and keep it. She pulls it on to continue her practice, and it feels like an embrace.

In the morning, she has breakfast with the sisters: a thin porridge, more like gruel, with chopped apple but no honey and certainly no sugar, and camomile tea to drink with it. As she's wondering whether it would be rude to ask if there's any honey, she remembers Auntie Elmi once fessing up to keeping a secret stash of sweets in her underwear drawer for the times she couldn't hack the minimal monastic diet.

Back in the bedroom, after brushing her teeth, she opens the underwear drawer, feels around the neatly rolled row of knickers, and lo and behold, finds a cylindrical object that feels familiar. Yes, it's an unopened packet of Polos! She checks the best before date: two years ago. But how bad can they be? They're only sugar. She opens one end and pops a sweet in her mouth. It's a bit chalky, for a Polo, but fine.

Outside the window, the cloud is lifting, and it's looking like it might turn into an inappropriately bright day, just like her mother's funeral day had been. She remembers walking to the church with her dad and Auntie Elmi, and greeting various family members and people she'd never met at the door of the church without smiling, feeling like she must be in a dark sort of play, and that it was surely meant to be grey and misty, like funerals she'd seen in films. How she'd clung to her dad's hand as she stared down at the coffin, unable to process the fact that her mother's body was actually inside that narrow box, about to be incinerated.

*

The temple's entrance is framed with gold lambs and dark red panelling – so much cheerier than most churches, Kessie reflects, but decides not to offer this insight to her dad just as things are easing between them. Inside it's just as she remembers from her last visit. A simple square room laid out with grey chairs, three large, yellow-gold smiling Buddha statues cross-legged before a sky-blue mural at the front, a row of pots bursting with flowers lining one edge of a patterned rug.

The chanting soothes her. She is just thinking about how grateful she is to be able to experience this without Zora in tow, when the thought makes her breasts hurt, and a sensation of damp spreads in her bra. For God's sake, why didn't she think to bring bloody breast pads? She'd assumed she'd just dry up by this point; she has only been doing one short feed in the morning and evening for the last two months. Her eyes start to ooze at the thought of the last feed before she left London, of Zora's happy disinterest as she stopped suckling. Kessie had decided that this funeral trip was maybe the excuse she needed to stop breastfeeding for good – and ever since the awful early days of breastfeeding hell, she expected to be jubilant at her eventual liberation from its shackles. Instead, it feels like her daughter is slipping away from her, just after their bond had been properly forged – that time is a twisted concertina, and that any day now Zora will be going off to school, then leaving home, then moving away, then having a child of her own . . .

Closing her eyes, she imagines Auntie Elmi hovering in the second bardo, like one of the BFG's dreams in a jar, waiting for her next incarnation. It does help to imagine her returning in a new form, as her Buddhist sisters believe. Perhaps she could return with Kessie's mum – reincarnated and reunited – as two trees, perhaps, growing side by side in a bluebell wood.

A prod in the ribs – her dad – reminds her it's time for her clarinet solo. She fumbles to pull her case from her bag and put the instrument together, then walks to the front, and stands still for a moment, waiting. Closes her eyes, collecting herself. When she finally begins the glissando, and somehow doesn't squeak, it seems like the sound is raising her soul up to meet theirs. Until she runs out of breath a bar too early.

They walk back to the cottage for a gathering with the sisters and other invited guests. The small kitchen and living room are packed. Kessie chats to Anna in the kitchen while filling bowls with grapes and nuts, and jugs with water, and boiling enough for all three teapots.

She finds herself opening up to Anna about everything that's been happening with Zora and Robin, and how reassuring it had been to have daily messages from Auntie Elmi, even at the worst times, when she often didn't reply, and now wishes she had. By the time they are sitting in the living room with the others, she has started to tell Anna the whole crazy story about Acorn, The Facilitator, the birth, losing her mind, Robin stepping in, adoption, Darsha, her dad . . . until she stops short, and bites her knuckles. 'Oh dear, I'm so sorry – I've just been rattling on and on about myself, and this whole gathering is meant to be about Auntie Elmi . . .'

'Not at all,' Anna reassures her kindly. 'Elmina would have wanted to hear all of it, and we do too. I'm just sorry that things have been so difficult for you.'

'Aunti Elmi endured much worse difficulties,' Kessie says, miserably. 'And she dealt with everything way better.'

'She was a marvellous person. But nobody is perfect. We each have our own challenges. It sounds like you've made yourself a wonderful little family now, and that you're finding peace together,' Anna says, eminently reassuring.

Sister Janice leans forward. 'Kessie, dear, I couldn't help overhearing your conversation – and I knew a little already from what Sister Elmina had told me – but my brother, who's a family law professor in Canada, was just telling me on the phone about a case he advised on that's *just* like yours,' she says. 'I expect you've heard about it already? I'm pretty sure he said it was the first *ever* case when two women friends were granted the right to be, what was it – co-mothers? I could be wrong . . .'

Kessie tips her head to one side. 'Really?' She's pretty sure she would already have turned that case up in her research for the application – or that Robin would, or the lawyer would.

'I could have got it wrong, of course! I could check with him, and ask him to email you . . .'

'Thanks so much, Sister Janice – it does sound really interesting. I'll look into it,' Kessie says, then tells them that she needs to pop to the bathroom. Once she gets inside, she sits on the lid and googles it, just in case.

Sure enough, several new news articles pop up about these two Canadian co-mothers. Apparently, both were friends because they were law professors in the same department. When one of them decided to have a baby on her own, using a donor, her friend acted as her birth partner – but then, when the little boy was born, he was severely disabled, and partly because of that, the friend carried on being involved, taking him to doctors' appointments and helping with his care at home. She moved into the condo above them, and came to love the little boy like he was her own – and after a while they thought, well, why shouldn't he be? Kessie skims through a few other articles. This only happened a few weeks ago. It seems incredibly fortuitous timing! But then their solicitor has already made it abundantly clear that the only precedents that British courts will take into account in any material way are cases decided in British courts. Still – it's something. It feels like a cusp, a turning point, a recognition. She's about to fire a message to Robin with a link, but then someone knocks on the door. 'Just coming out!'

She decides to surprise Robin with it when she gets home. Right now, she had better get back out there and be social.

'Kessie, there you are!' her dad says, as she re-emerges, vigorously beckoning her over. 'I'd love to reintroduce you to Jax and Daniel. You remember Jax from my jazz playing days? He was just telling me how impressed he was by your Gershwin.'

Kessie turns to see a wiry man with greying dreadlocks whom she'd spotted sitting at the back at the funeral, and had vaguely recognized – and, standing next to them, a tall bald man with beige skin and John Lennon glasses who's wearing a sharp suit and has bare feet. She exchanges polite air kisses with them both. 'It's been a long time,' Jax says. 'I remember you as a babe in arms. We used to spend a lot of time together, back in the day, Elmi and I, and your parents. Jazz gigs, open mics, disastrous road trips . . .'

'Jax is an excellent drummer,' her dad chips in.

'Well, that's mighty kind of you, sir.' Jax grins. 'We used to be in a band for a while, your dad and me – did you know that?' He gives her dad a hearty pat on the back, then looks at Kessie, a sad expression descending on his face. 'Ahh, but what a loss. Elmi was a remarkable human being. I know how close you two were. She and I were close once too. We were actually a couple at one point – not sure if she ever told you that.'

'No!' Kessie says. Elmi had only ever told her about Mick. But maybe she'd never really asked about her relationships before that.

'She called it off,' Jax says. 'My fault. I was all over the shop in those days. Addiction problems. Which I'm over now, thankfully – as much as you can ever be. But she looked after me for a long time when I didn't deserve it. I have many memories of her and Ehani together. Those two – they were always laughing, right?' He looks at her dad for confirmation, and he nods. 'Hard to believe they've both passed so young.' He reaches out his arms to Kessie, and she hugs him obligingly. He smells leathery and a little of coffee. 'Fabulous playing,' he says, pulling away. 'You reminded me of the great Benny Goodman.' He looks side to side at her dad and the other man.

'Sure,' her dad smiles. 'That's my girl. We both love Benny. Daniel here is a jazz fan too, aren't you, Daniel?'

The man smiles gently. 'Certainly am.'

'He doesn't play much these days,' Jax adds, 'but he's a big supporter of the jazz community – and live music – he's even starting up a whole new arts centre! He's the best person to tell you about that of course, not me. But, you know, he's also supported this new album project I wanted to tell you about. It's a jazz album for kids. Little ones. Not my idea, but I'm part of the band – it's the brainchild of another guy I often gig with, a younger guy. He's had kids of his own, and was sick of all the plinky-plonk fake electronic music out there for babies, so he decided to make an album of jazz versions of nursery rhymes and other classic kids' songs with real session musicians. We're recording in a couple of weeks. He already has a clarinettist lined up, otherwise I'd have suggested you after today.'

'Oh, thanks.' She tries not to sound disappointed. 'It sounds . . . amazing! I'll have to buy it when it's out.' It's one of those ideas that she wishes she'd thought of herself. She wonders how such an album might actually sound, and just how jazzy a nursery rhyme can get before it loses its nursery rhyme identity. Still, it is a genius idea. She's endured more than enough plinky-plonk music for Zora's sake this past year. The only album in that genre that she genuinely likes is called *Beatles for Babies* – though its particular plinky-plonkiness often prompts her to doze off too when she's meant to be getting on with chores.

'Excellent,' Jax says. 'You play much jazz?'

'Sure – well, I used to,' she says.

'Well, you should come along to an open mic night at Daniel's bar,' Jax says. 'I'll send you the details. Congratulations, by the way, on being a mother! Zora, your dad was telling me? How old . . . ?'

'Coming up to one! Hard to believe,' Kessie says.

'Lovely, lovely,' Jax says. 'So Daniel here chipped in quite a bit of funding to make this jazz for kids album happen. You don't mind me revealing that, do you, Daniel? Daniel is our most successful friend, you know. Bit of a dark horse – doesn't rattle on as much as I do, at least. He runs a big ethical investment fund – contributed to the Ehani foundation too, when it was set up. Not sure if you knew that.' Kessie didn't know that, and looks over to her dad, who nods. She wonders if that's the fund in which she's just inherited shares.

Daniel has a glimmer of a smile on his face, but is clearly content to let Jax carry on doing all the rattling on.

'Will the foundation be continuing without Elmi, do you think?' Jax asks Daniel. 'I hope so. It's just so awful – so sudden – impossible to get your head around, isn't it?' He turns to Kessie's dad. 'You're the one most in touch with God these days, Koji – and you've experienced enough loss in your life – do you believe it's all meant to be?'

'Well . . . there's a question.' Her dad launches into an answer, and Kessie turns to Daniel, keen to ask him more about his connection with her mum and with Elmi.

Daniel doesn't come across as a shy man, just slow to talk, and he has a quiet but steady voice. He tells her a bit about how he'd met both her mother and Elmi at university, and how, a few years later, when he'd been working as a banker for a couple of years and was beginning to have an existential crisis, they'd encouraged him to come to volunteer in Nepal one summer. He had been interested to explore his Buddhist roots – he has Chinese Buddhist ancestry – and the experience prompted him to eventually quit the City and set up his own ethical investment fund. The skin on his face is still fairly smooth for someone her parents' age, Kessie thinks. He's certainly got more Zen about him that most finance people she's met in Robin's work circle.

He asks more about her background as a musician, and about Zora. She shows him a picture of the baby on her phone, and he tells her fondly about his nieces and their kids, and how he loved to play with them when they were Zora's age.

He asks how she's found motherhood so far, and looks so penetratingly into her eyes as he speaks that she feels oddly seen.

She finds herself admitting that it was hellish for a while – and he tells her that one of his nieces really suffered too for the first few years. 'How did you get through it?' he asks, like he really wants to know.

So she talks about Robin, and how hard they both had to work for so many months to enable her recovery. 'It feels so wonderful to be back to myself again!' she tells him. 'And I'm suddenly hungry to be back out there, making music, connecting with people again, you know? I'm trying to figure out a career shift that could bring in a more sustainable income than freelancing, and could allow me to get my teeth into something creative and inspiring. I'll probably end up stacking shelves at the supermarket . . . But I'm so ready to engage my brain again. And work on something meaningful, you know? Maybe it took having a baby and a break from what I was doing to realize that I can do something a bit different.'

'Well, how very interesting,' he says. 'It's almost like you're pitching for a job.'

'Sorry?' she asks, flushing. How humiliating – and how rude of him!

'A job I'm about to advertise,' he adds. 'As Jax mentioned, I'm just setting up a new arts centre. I'll be looking for a programmer for music and community arts.'

'Seriously?' Her face smarts with embarrassment at how quickly she'd judged him.

'Absolutely,' he says. 'I'd been feeling dismal about the state of arts and culture funding in this country – to the point that I decided I'd better do something about it. It's going to be in Walthamstow, in an old factory space. It'll be Buddhist-inspired

– a centre for arts, culture and community. There'll be a small gallery, cinema and theatre space, with some studios for artists to record.'

She realizes she's gawping, and asks more about it – question after question, until eventually he says: 'Okay – how about we turn this interview around again. What might you do if you had the chance to devise a new community-focused programme at an arts centre?'

The question makes her chest effervesce like a vitamin. He's actually asking her this question – asking *her* – asking because he's genuinely interested in what she can achieve beyond busking her way through motherhood – asking because he might even allow her to act upon it! Ideas somehow start popping out of her mouth.

*

On the way back to the cottage she has a long chat with Robin. All has been fine with Zora, who's just gone down to sleep. Kessie recounts the events of the day – the service, the gathering afterwards, and the bizarre coincidence that she ended up having what felt like an informal job interview at a *funeral*. 'That's amazing!' Robin enthuses. 'Elmi would have been delighted. And you would be great at that role if it does come off.'

It's on the tip of Kessie's tongue to tell her about the Canada case, too, but she holds off.

The next morning, she meets up with her dad for a breakfast around the corner from his hotel before he heads home. She's decided to stay one extra day with the sisters. He assures her that he'll be back in London soon to see her and Zora – that he'll come once a month, or more, if she'd like him to, and will definitely do better at keeping in touch, if she wants to. He even offers to message her daily, like Elmi did – a sweet gesture, though she tells him that might be overdoing it. 'Just before I go – I've had an idea,' he says. 'A fun one, I think. What do you reckon about going back to WOMAD again next summer, like we used to with Elmi and your mother, but with Robin and Zora? My treat.'

'A festival again? Really?!' Part of her wants to cheer. Another part is annoyed with herself at not being strong enough to hold a bit more of a grudge after how crap he's been for so long. Does he really deserve such an easy ride back into her life? Is he really going to change? But he has listened these past few days, and tried hard, and made promises that seem sincere. And it has been a bone-deep relief to spend time with him again over the past week – with a more relaxed version of him than she's seen in two decades. And taking Zora to her very first festival, with Robin, too . . . She allows a grin to unfold. 'That could be awesome,' she says. 'The question is: do you still have those orange flares?'

He chews the side of his lip. 'Well, we both know that there's been some clearing out going on . . . but if they are tucked away somewhere, and if by some miracle I still fit into them, I'll bring them along. If not, I'll buy something equally outrageous from a charity shop.'

Kessie nods approvingly. 'In that case, I'll see what Robin thinks. Not sure how I'd cope with having a baby at a festival but I bet she'd handle it.' She hesitates. 'Cara . . . She wouldn't like WOMAD, right?'

'Doubt it,' he says, with a wink. 'I have got her into jazz though.

In any case, if you and Robin do decide you want to do it, I'll tell her it's our thing.'

The sisters refresh Kessie's memory of a walking route she did with Auntie Elmi last time she visited. She packs some oatcakes, cheese and an apple, plus the remaining Polos, and sets out.

Walking out on her own in the clear winter sun, with no bag of nappy supplies or spare baby clothes or formula or finger foods or purees, no sling, no buggy, no blanket, no muslins, no toys – just herself and a rucksack – she feels weirdly light, as if her bone matter were goose down. She tries to replay fragments of the conversation she had with Auntie Elmi the last time she walked this route with her. They had definitely talked about the foundation, about her mother and the kung fu nuns, about Kessie's love life and her donor plans . . . It can't have been long before she met The Facilitator. And now here she is, almost a year into motherhood.

She's still not sure of the extent to which Auntie Elmi, deep inside herself, ever got over not becoming a biological mother. But she definitely found fulfilment in her various caring roles. What might her final thoughts have been as she flew off that motorbike? Hopefully the kaleidoscope lens shone briefly on her, and her parents, and Elmi felt assured of their love.

She pauses briefly to look back at her footprints, and thinks of Elmi's, layered into this same path. *Skeleton leaves, memory chains.* A robin lands by her and hops along. *Robin.* She wheels around suddenly, with an uncanny feeling that her own Robin is about to pop out from behind a large beech tree, holding Zora. A childhood picture book comes back to her – one her mother used to read: a story about a winter bear, discovered abandoned by a family of children on a snowy walk, stuck up in some sparse branches, just waiting to be found and treasured.

Striding on, she can't resist thinking how incredible it would be if this job at Daniel's new arts centre were to materialize. And if more recording gigs were to come with it – more opportunities to perform. She needs to check in with the local nursery and see where Zora is on the waiting list. Could it be conceivable that she might even be able to take over as the family breadwinner for a while, so that Robin can finally quit her job, finish her master's, and do that PhD? She shouldn't get ahead of herself. And yet, and yet . . .

*

She almost power walks home from the Tube, excited to see Robin and to pick up Zora again.

'I'm back!' she calls – then realizes that it's the baby's nap time. How quickly the routine can be forgotten. She leaves her bag by the front door and goes through to her bedroom – and there she is, her baby, sleeping soundly, just as she should be, little face turned to the side, that perfect, soft profile with its raspberry nose.

Robin calls out a soft hello and Kessie walks up to her . . . then stops short, registering her distraught face. 'Oh Robs – what's the matter?'

'It's . . . welcome back! I'm glad the funeral went well.' Robin's body feels rigid as they hug. In the living room, she hands Kessie a letter.

Kessie takes it and reads, slowly and carefully.

They'd suspected it, after the awful social worker visit, but even so. The legal language is flint sharp. 'Application . . . Assessment . . . Evidence . . . Balance of probabilities . . . Best interests . . . Decision.'

It might just as well say REJECT in all caps.

As if you two women friends could be a real family.

They sit down on the sofa. Kessie rereads the letter, and they both look at each other, then at the fish, pootling about as usual, colours glinting in the light. The two baby swordtails are almost as big as their mother now. Kessie puts her arm round Robin's shoulders. So bony; she really needs to eat more. Her cheekbones look almost artificial, and her neck as long as a Modigliani. 'Well, I'll tell you a *good* news thing I was saving up,' Kessie says. 'There's a brand-new legal case, where two platonic female friends *have* been legally allowed to be co-mothers! It's Canadian, so might not count here, but I feel like it really should be relevant to our appeal. Look, here's the article.' She pulls it up on her phone and hands it to Robin.

Robin looks at her searchingly, then reads.

Kessie waits. 'I saved it to show you when I got back. You do want to appeal, right?'

Robin looks up at her quizzically. 'Do *you* want to?' Her face is blotchy, and mascara is smudged under both eyes. It suddenly occurs to Kessie that Robin might have been anticipating her taking Zora and walking away from this whole process if the initial application failed. Or even if it all got any more difficult than it already had. Especially since their argument over Darsha, and the lawyer's warning. It's not that she hasn't had flashes of thinking that – but never seriously.

But of course, it strikes her now: the news about her inheritance from Auntie Elmi might have made Robin think that, if Kessie finally had the money to up and leave with Zora, maybe she would.

'I do,' Kessie says softly. 'We're a family, right? You're Mawo to Zora. Also, do you realize you look like a cartoon panda right now?'

Robin scrubs at her eye sockets, extending the smears further, and smiles a little.

'Also, I've had an idea,' Kessie says. 'I want to use some of Auntie Elmi's money to take us on a holiday. Somewhere warm. Or just *different*. It felt so good to go away, even though it was for Elmi's funeral – I mean, I totally get why you needed that Californian trip . . .' She halts, knowing they're both picturing Darsha.

'A holiday would be really nice,' Robin says.

'Would you fancy going back to the Pyrenees? Your mum could meet Zora. And I'm dying to finally see her in action as a shepherdess, and to meet Chou-fleur and Brigitte Baardot.'

A cascading wail erupts from the next room, and Kessie bounds in to see the baby. She returns with her tucked under one arm, cooing, 'Maki, Maki!' Robin has put on Ella's *Gold* album and is crouching to haul laundry out of the machine. Kessie puts Zora down on her play tiles, rolls her the jingly ball to play with, before helping Robin hang the clothes up.

Smoothing out the not-so-little baby clothes on each rail, Kessie tunes into the lyrics that Ella is delivering as impeccably as ever – the song about 'A Fine Romance', with no kisses. She notices the arc of Robin's knobbly spine under her T-shirt as she bends to hang their bras on a lower rail. *Friendship – romance; romance – friendship.* Whoever wrote the lyrics – Dorothy Fields, was it? – probably intended it as a sarky riposte to a lover in an affair that was going stale, but still, if you think about it: does a romance need kisses?

She gets a bottle ready to feed Zora, who's already grabbing at her breasts in expectation. A brief pang, but no: that phase is done now. Fortunately, the baby accepts the bottle instead, and starts guzzling.

As Robin reads into the case further on her phone, Kessie types 'romance definition' into the search bar on her own with her free hand. Of course, romance can be a noun and a verb. There are multiple definitions, from medieval tales to a type of novel to a form of love. On which, Collins dictionary offers: 'a close relationship between two people who are in love with each other but who are not married to each other.' That innocuous two-letter 'in' – what does it signify? *Of love, in love; eether, either, let's call the whole thing off.* The OED list of definitions includes: 'a feeling of excitement and mystery associated with love', but also 'ardour or warmth of feeling in a love affair; love, esp. of an idealized or sentimental kind.' *Potato, po-tah-to. Tomayto, tomato.*

Chapter 33

Robin

That weekend they decide to head out of the city for a walk in the woods. Benjy and Dom recommended Northaw Great Wood, out in Hertfordshire, which seems a manageable distance. They book a Zipcar, and Robin drives north with *1989* blazing from the stereo, both of them singing along at the tops of their voices. Zora waves her arms around delightedly, without the need for any plinky-plonk nursery rhymes. 'She's clearly a Swiftie already,' Kessie observes. 'Ella, Joni, Taylor, Johann Sebastian, or *Beatles for Babies*. I'd say she's getting pretty good taste.'

After a while, Kessie looks up more about the place they're going and reads bits aloud. It's an ancient woodland, dating back to Norman times, and apparently features a huge variety of trees – oak and hornbeam, silver birch and hazel, hawthorn and blackthorn, crab apple and rowan, elm and elder, yew and goat willow. 'I don't think I could identify most of those, apart from oak and silver birch,' she says. 'Could you?'

'Never even heard of a goat willow. Do they have horns?'

'Presumably they bleat. And maybe ring bells. Anyway, there's a plethora of wildlife to look out for – badgers, pygmy shrews, pipistrelle bats, owls, green woodpeckers . . .'

'Pygmy shrews! How cute do they sound? But aren't shrews tiny anyway?' Robin sighs. 'I never spot any interesting wildlife on walks. Maybe I just need to look more closely. Or go on more walks. Both.'

'You need more time to go on walks,' Kessie says. 'Promise me you'll reduce your hours and finish the master's this year? We can manage financially now, and I'm determined to do my best for the arts centre job interview. It's such a relief to feel motivated again! And it shouldn't be all on you any more.'

'Thanks, hon. I actually just let the uni know I wanted to start the masters again. And I gave the nursery another call – they said they should have a place for Zora in the new year, if we want it, I've been meaning to tell you. Anyway, I'm so happy you feel like you've got your mojo back! I have good vibes about this job.'

Once they've parked up, Kessie helps wedge Zora into the baby carrier on Robin's back. She's getting so hefty these days, this kid. Kessie carries the backpack, which is jammed with snacks, drinks and baby gear, even for this short walk. Always so much baby gear. It's good to be able to share the load.

As they tramp into the wood, the trees begin to shelter them from the wind. Amazingly, for a non-rainy Saturday, they seem to have the whole place to themselves. At one point they hear laughter in the distance, echoing, but still don't see anyone.

It's a gorgeous path, even though most of the trees are leafless, saving up energy for the spring. Trunks and branches ripple with moss and lacy lichen, and with ivy and other epiphytes climbing their way towards the light.

Kessie asks if Robin's heard of 'forest bathing' – she hasn't. One of the sisters was talking to her about it at the funeral, apparently. It's an ancient Japanese practice which entails going into a forest and hanging out there, appreciating the sensory immersion of being deep amidst the trees, and it's fast becoming a global wellness trend.

'Seems kind of common sense,' Robin reflects. 'Does sound nice though. Just to appreciate being among trees, rather than always thinking about walking through them to get somewhere. Either way, I reckon the experience of being in a place like this is even more meaningful now that everyone's constantly on screens. I already feel miles better for it, don't you?'

'Definitely. The smells, the textures . . .' Kessie pauses to inhale. 'It's also just super nice to be out of town on a walk with both of you.'

Trying to tune into the birdsong, Robin picks out a song thrush duetting with a crow. Just like her and Max, she thinks: a total mismatch. He had messaged her out of the blue while Kessie was away and asked if she wanted to meet up for a drink. Said he missed her. Added a large X at the end. She'd already heard, from Benjy, that he'd just broken up with his new girlfriend – a white-blonde data scientist in her mid-twenties – and she'd felt absolutely nothing. She'd waited until the following day, then sent him a brief reply saying that it was a nice surprise to hear from him, but she was busy.

'Let's come back here again in the early summer,' Kessie's saying. 'When the leaves are lush and green. There are meant to be cuckoos here then. Horrible birds in a way, poaching other birds' nests, but still, I've never heard one.'

A patch of sun glints through the trees to one side as the path tracks along the bank of a stream that's cut into a small gorge. The path narrows through some thickets, then opens into a wide clearing, framed by bracken, with a picnic bench at one side. Kessie suggests they take a break, and peers into the baby carrier. 'Hey Zozo – you sleepy?'

Seems not: Zora screeches with excitement at being released, and crawls off over the grass in her waterproof onesie.

Robin pulls out a thermos and pours out two cups of tea. Her eyes meet Kessie's over the steam. 'This was such a great idea.'

They're both quiet for a while as the wind moves through the branches, and birds take turns to riff. 'Hey, listen to that wood pigeon,' Kessie says – 'it's jazzing. Hear that blues note? Ooh-ooooh-ooooh – ooh-ooooh . . .'

Robin frowns in concentration, then mimics it. 'You're right! Benny Goodman eat your heart out.' She looks around. 'This is such a magical glade. Especially now the sun's out and the wind's died down. Can't believe there aren't more people here.' She closes her eyes to focus on the woodland sounds, their echoey quality. When she opens them again, Kessie's face is tense.

'Robs – I wanted to ask you something.' She puts her cup down and clasps her hands. 'It's . . . on the subject of unconventional families. It's kind of a major thing. Or not, depending on how you look at it.'

'Right . . .?' Robin frowns. It must be the appeal: Kessie had decided against it after all. Which she'd be totally entitled to . . . She's getting off the bench, and rummaging in her bag for something . . . now dropping to her knees on the mulch. 'Kess, what are you . . .?'

Kessie slides a little box out of her sleeve and opens it. In it are two thin silver chains, each with a leaf pendant. 'Robin Suarez: will you marry me? I don't have a ring, but I do have these for each of us.'

Robin emits a spurt of laughter – but Kessie's face is searching, with only a glimmer of a laugh at the edge of her lips.

'I had a lot of time to think while I was away,' Kessie continues. 'And the more I thought about it, the more it struck me that, crazy though it sounds to marry your best mate, it also could make a lot of sense for us – emotionally, not just practically. It's like you're always saying: when you think about how people in other cultures arrange their lives – other species even – you realize there so many different ways of doing family, right? And so maybe this could be our way. I know we *both* thought it was ridiculous at first, but actually, it *could* be a really positive way to celebrate what we have! What we are to each other. But you might well still think it's an absurd idea, which maybe it is, in which case this necklace can just be a thank you gift. It only just occurred to me it's a bit like those bestie necklaces we used to have when we were little – one broken half of a heart each – do you remember?'

Robin's face feels like it's morphed into a weird shape. Her mouth is gummy and dry. Another crow caws directly above them as if it's mocking her.

'Ummm, please just say something so I can get off my knees?' Kessie says, wince-smiling. 'I'm too old for this . . .' But Zora has just spotted her, down on the same level, and starts crawling back towards them fast.

'Wait!' Robin says, and drops down too. The ground is soggier

399

than it looks. She looks into Kessie's eyes, then down at the necklaces. 'Kess, I'm so touched. These are beautiful, thank you. I . . . I'm just trying to get my head around it.'

'Putting it around your *neck* might be easier.' Kessie grins. Zora, who has reached them, makes a lunge for the box. 'Uh-uh, little one!' she tells her, pulling it away. 'Not for you!' She kisses Zora's forehead and gets up, stands behind Robin, and fastens one of the necklaces while Zora stares, intrigued.

Robin stands up too, and fastens the other necklace around Kessie's neck, and then they face each other. She feels oddly shy.

Kessie reaches out her fingertips, and they link. 'You really can just say no,' she says. 'I won't be offended.'

'No, no,' Robin begins. 'I mean, not *no* no . . . I'm just still processing . . .'

'I know we couldn't stop cracking up at the idea when the lawyer first mentioned it,' Kessie says. 'But on the other hand, I was thinking we could just look at marriage as a label that could help us to be recognized as the family we already are. And it could be a positive excuse to celebrate that, with our friends and relatives – by participating in one of these rituals that matter so much, as the anthropology research you read always seems to say. Or at least it might stop everyone just whispering behind our backs about what an eccentric pair of spinsters we are! But seriously, I just thought it could help us to form a stronger network. Like the understorey in this wood.'

'That's a lovely way to think about it.' Robin smiles.

'I'm not asking because I *need* you,' Kessie presses on. 'Like, in a practical way, any more, or financially. Or because I'm scared of doing the parenting thing on my own. I mean, I am a bit – but

I'm asking because it just feels like we're a trio, right? And because I'll always love you. Platonically.'

Robin bites her lip. 'You know, I ended up researching different species of love while you were away.'

'You did?'

'Turns out that's the kind of thing I do when I'm missing you. So I hadn't realized before, but the Ancient Greeks had lots of different words for love – did you know that? A bit like Inuit words for snow. So there's *eros* – that one's obvious. Then there's *agape* which is a purer, devotional type – like love of God – so maybe like how I feel about Joni's *Blue* album, and Ella's *Gold* . . . But then there's *philia* – so that's like a loyal type of love that you have for really good friends or family members, but it's kind of dispassionate compared to *eros*. And *then* – then there's *storge*. So that's a more intimate and familial type of love, like the love between parents and children, but also between other people in a family. It's deeper and more unquestioning than *philia*. Which also makes it more enduring. It's been described as an empathy bond, which I like. Apparently the English word love comes from the Sanskrit word for 'desire' which seems a bit narrowly *eros-y* in comparison, right?'

Kessie nods, slowly. 'It does. That's so interesting.' She tips her head to one side. 'So – do you *storge* me?'

Robin laughs. 'I totally *storge* you. Oh my gosh . . .' She sways, sinks down onto the picnic bench and covers her face with her hands – until something hits her thigh.

'Peepo!' Zora again – on her feet now, grasping the side of the bench with one hand, and brandishing a handful of wet leaves in the other, which she dumps in Robin's lap.

'Why, thank you, sweetie pie,' she laughs. 'Hey, do you like this pretty necklace Maki bought me?' Zora squints at it, tugs at it, then turns around, sticks one leg out, takes a step, then another, then falls to her knees. Robin gasps. 'Hey did you see that? Did she just walk?'

'No way, that's wild!' Kessie claps. 'Well done little one!' Zora turns around to look at them, full of glee, then attempts to get to her feet again. The look of astonishment on her face when she manages it, for a few more seconds, is priceless.

'Talented child,' Robin says. 'Check her out – just before her first birthday. I reckon you knew this was a big moment for us and you wanted the limelight, didn't you?'

Zora tries to haul herself up again, without success.

Kessie sits opposite Robin again, her forehead creasing.

'Sorry Kess, I . . . Oh gosh, it's like one of those those excruciating rom com moments when someone says 'I love you' and the other person doesn't say it back, except obviously I *do* love you, I mean, *storge* and *philia* and . . .'

'Don't worry. You know, it's funny – I found myself researching some love etymology too.'

'You did?'

'Inspired by Ella, actually, when we were listening to her singing 'A Fine Romance', and I was like: huh, what does 'romantic' actually mean anyway? So I looked it up, and it basically just means something that expresses love. None of the definitions of romance involve sex. One of them described it as a kind of excitement and mystery linked with love. And I was like: oh, okay then, so why can't platonic romance be a thing? And romantic close friendship. I feel like that's what we have, in a way. Is that the same thing as *storge*?'

'Great question. Eether, either, Potato, po-tah-to . . .? But your proposal just now – that's *easily* the most romantic thing anyone's ever done for me.'

'Really?' Kessie looks sceptical. 'I remember Max being pretty romantic in the early days.'

'Well, he made some grand gestures at first, sure. But he never proposed. And he would never have thought to do it in a beautiful glade like this. He never even bought me jewellery. And you asking me here like this reminds me – how brave and big-hearted you are! And maybe also a genius. I mean, how have you actually just managed to make something we both agreed was batshit sound like it's an awesome and totally plausible idea?'

'Baba – bababa!' Zora calls out from a few metres away, back on her feet, teetering like a drunkard on a boat. Robin applauds her, holds out her hands for Zora to walk towards, then returns her gaze to Kessie, whose face is unreadable again. Yet the shape of her features is so familiar that she feels like she could draw them with her eyes shut, if she were any good at drawing.

Another wood pigeon lands nearby, not the jazzy one, and coos determinedly, as if it were saying: *come oooon now – say yes;* come *oooon now – say no.*

'Soooo . . .?' Kessie asks, scrunching up her nose.

'I mean . . . *yes!*' Robin laughs, gets up and runs around to her. 'Come here. I really do *storge* you to the moon and back. And Zora too. And I'm all for our friendship being platonically romantic.' After they've hugged for a bit, Robin takes Kessie's face in her hands. 'But – I'm still – just a bit scared of this going wrong, you know? Like that awful argument we had on the bus . . . That was so awful. I *hate* fighting with you. I know all couples, friends, bicker argue occasionally but . . . are we both sure we're happy with our draft agreement around the whole sexual – romantic – partners thing?' She pictures Darsha splayed on the bed, the supple enfolding of skin, of breath.

'I am if you are,' Kessie says. 'Despite the fact that my libido's back.'

'Oh yeah?'

'Hell yeah. The other day at the swings I met this hot dad whose kid was really sweet with Zora, and I didn't mean to flirt, but he *definitely* flirted back. And afterwards I was thinking: even if he were single, and we were to have a fling, I'd still feel exactly the same about you – about us.'

'Brilliant. Me too. Well then, that settles it – let's get married!'

*

The light is beginning to fade as they climb the hill towards the car. A large ash tree has fallen across the path, and they both have to clamber over it, which is especially awkward with Zora on her back. 'So, I guess this is an excuse for another joint party,' she says. 'Promise I won't get wasted and wreck it this time.'

'Get as tipsy as you like! But no vomiting. Or I might have to call the whole thing off.'

'That's fair,' Robin says. 'I'll share a bottle of fizz with you and then stick to tonic. Any thoughts on a venue?' Her old fantasy about an urban wedding comes to mind.

'Mmm,' Kessie says. 'Hey – imagine if we could have our *storge* wedding here, in this wood? In the summer? If that's allowed. Or another wood.'

'I love that . . . maybe with a treehouse and some hammocks . . .'

'. . . we could wear jumpsuits instead of dresses so we can climb trees, bring picnic blankets, have all the muso friends play . . .'

'. . . Benjy could do a quiz . . .'

'. . . we could dance as the sun sets – stay up for the dawn chorus . . .' As she says this, Robin thinks about Darsha – about dancing on the beach, and staying up all night in the bedroom, and listening to the dawn chorus up in the hills in that house of Riley.

Would Darsha come? It's possible. It would be awkward. At least they're in contact again. They had a video chat while Kessie was away for the first time since she left, and both agreed it felt harder to cut off contact than to continue as they were – and the chemistry, well, it wasn't gone. Darsha even suggested a new novel for them to read for micro book club. What if she wanted to come, and asked to bring Vi over as her plus one? But Vi would be very unlikely to fancy that. Even if she did – well, that would probably be all right. Hopefully her mum will find a sheep- and dog-sitter for a couple of days and travel over too.

'. . . Zora can be a small and hilarious bridesmaid,' Kessie adds, 'especially if she keeps on scoffing leaves. She'll be good enough at walking by then to carry flowers up the aisle, right? If we have an aisle.'

'. . . we could ask everyone to bring a cake to fuel all-night revels . . .'

Once they've concocted an increasingly elaborate series of plans, extending to a rope swing, a zip line and a treasure hunt, they concentrate on climbing the hill for a bit. Zora is getting heavier by the minute. Robin pauses for breath and spots a particularly gnarly old oak off the path. She walks over to it and lays her palm on a whorled lump bulging out of its trunk. 'Hey, check out this tree. Couple of hundred years old, would you say? It's seen so much. Trees like this always remind me of that night in the woods.'

Kessie comes over and lays her hand on the bark too. Robin suspects she's thinking about her mum. If only she, and Robin's dad, could be at their wedding. Kessie pouts. 'Another crazy idea on my part, that escapade.'

'Worked out, though.'

They walk on. A drizzle percolates through the skeleton canopy. Neither of them had thought to pack waterproofs. Zora begins to whinge, a tired, low-key grumble, and Robin sings her the French lullaby about the little sailor who goes out to sea for the first time, gets lost, and nearly drowns, until thousands of little fish leap out of the water to save him. Ahead of them, in the deepening shadow, Kessie whistles a high harmony. A small creature scuttles away from the side of the path, and for a second Robin thinks it could be a pygmy shrew – but it's only a grey squirrel. In the distance, a dog barks and a motorbike revs up on the main road, as the three of them wend their way up into the open.

Author's Note

I used to work as a barrister, and my imagination is often sparked by legal cases – so much so that I ended up leaving law to focus on writing. In 2016, the year I gave birth to my second child, the first ever judicial decision was made granting two platonic female friends the right to be co-mothers. Natasha Bakht and Lynda Collins, both Canadian law professors, co-wrote an academic article about their experience and its legal implications. This got me thinking about the structural problems facing many women and queer-identifying people who want to become parents, and how they are rooted in longstanding cultural assumptions. As an anthropologist, I began exploring ways in which other human and animal cultures go about family and childcare differently. My discoveries were illuminating, and sometimes jaw-dropping, and many wove their way into this book. Some elements of the story were inspired by my own experiences of early motherhood, and the experiences of women I know; but all the characters and situations described are fictional.

You can find out more about my work at http:
//www.ellenwiles.com

Acknowledgements

Writing this book reminded me how absurdly lucky I am to have a partner who is also a devoted co-parent, who compensates for my many domestic deficiencies, and who makes us all laugh when laughter is required (often). Syd, you are a wonder.

It also made me think afresh about what my artist mother's experience must have been like when I was tiny and money was tight, and to re-value the immense amount of time, care, and labour that she devoted to nurturing me at home when she would (at least sometimes) rather have been making beautiful work. It brought home to me how fortunate we both were (and still are) to have my kind, wise, and adventurous father in our lives.

It led me to dwell on how much I appreciate my friendships – particularly the closest ones who have become mothers too, or who have wished to, or have been allomothers – and to be even more grateful for those friendships that have thrived and deepened despite the many challenges that parenthood + the rest of life brings. You know who you are. Thank you! Special thanks to Katharine, Helena, Rowan, Rosie, Rachel, Richard, and Deirdre, who made time to read and give me feedback on early drafts; and to Sarah, for being my brilliant co-reading companion through thick and thin.

As for my children, Noah and Juno: this book wouldn't have been conceived without you, though I hold you responsible for multiplying the number of years it took to finish. You astonish and delight me daily, and my world is now unimaginable without you in it.

After researching for a book project, it is always such a pleasure when you get in touch with an expert and they respond with openness and generosity. Natasha Bakht was kind enough to meet me and to talk about her experiences of fighting for recognition as a platonic family. Anthropologist Sarah Blaffer Hrdy was warm and enthusiastic about the book and happy for me to quote from her work in an epigraph. The same is true of Penny Boxall: a talented poet who gifted me the use of one of her gems.

I am hugely fortunate to have Laura Macdougall as my agent – someone who is not only a literary powerhouse, but is also a sole mother to a happy and book-loving toddler, and yet somehow always finds the time to write prompt, clever, and clear-sighted emails. Olivia Davies is another super-talented agent who I am grateful to have in my corner, and who gave me generous and insightful comments on an early draft while Laura was on maternity leave.

A good editor is a blessing for any writer, and Cat Camacho has been wonderfully supportive of this book, thoughtful and careful in all her manifold efforts to transform it from rough draft to published object, and always lovely to work with.

Copyediting might seem to some like a technical exercise, but I was delighted to work through Cari Rosen's intelligent suggestions, all of which were on point, and many of which went above and beyond – even extending to a suggested recipe for pancakes, the results of which were wolfed ecstatically by my family.

Thank you, finally, to my students and colleagues at the University of Exeter, who regularly remind me that good creative writing involves both hard graft and play, and that its rewards can be transformative. A good number of you crowded into a bar for an event when I read aloud from this manuscript for the first time, swelled the air with laughter, and gave me heart.

ONE PLACE. MANY STORIES

Bold, innovative and
empowering publishing.

FOLLOW US ON:

@HQStories